STEALING HEAVEN

MADELINE HUNTER

RANDOM HOUSE
LARGE PRINT

All rights reserved under International and
Pan-American Copyright Conventions.
Published in the United States of America
by Random House Large Print in association
with Bantam Books, New York, and
simultaneously in Canada by Random House
of Canada Limited, Toronto. Distributed
by Random House, Inc., New York.

*The Library of Congress has established a
Cataloging-in-Publication record for this title*

0-375-43267-1

www.randomlargeprint.com

FIRST LARGE PRINT EDITION

10   9   8   7   6   5   4   3   2   1

This Large Print edition published in
accord with the standards of the N.A.V.H.

THIS BOOK IS DEDICATED
TO THE MEMORY OF MY FATHER,
JOSEPH CIRILLO,
WHO SHOWED ME THE MAGIC
OF WORDS WHEN HE READ TO ME
WHEN I WAS A CHILD.

STEALING HEAVEN

CHAPTER 1

London ✦ 1340

MARCUS SMOOTHED HIS palms over the stone wall's surface. It was cleanly worked and neatly mortared, and its facing and joints offered no toeholds for intruders who might seek to scale it. That didn't surprise him, since this thick curtain of rock protected one of the crown's properties.

However, it also served as a barrier to some of Marcus's property, and scale it he would. It had been many years since he had played the thief, not since the hell of his youth, but one never forgets such skills. This wall would not keep him out.

He moved through the night, over to where

the wall curved around a corner of the garden it enclosed. Here the flat stones could not be laid in straight courses and their corners would protrude. The best masons would finish the surface to be as smooth as on the straight sections of wall, but most builders were not that fastidious. That was something else that he knew a thing or two about from the dark years of his youth.

His fingers swept the joints, and he found what he needed. The jutting edges were shallow, but deep enough for a body practiced in such things. Groping his way in the silence, he climbed until he sat straddling the wall. A convenient fruit tree grew near the corner, its branches like silhouettes in the full moon's light. He jumped over to it, his soft boots barely making a sound. With the stealth of a cat, he lowered himself into the early autumn smells that filled the garden.

He studied the bulk of the house, guessing how its chambers were arranged. Would she be in the large one on the second level, the one on the left indicated by two windows rather than one?

The vaguest sound interrupted his inspection of the building. He slid toward it along the wall until he could see a section of the garden not shadowed by trees. The bright moon displayed a little pool, its glittering surface dotted with fallen leaves. A woman strolled down the path surrounding it, pausing every now and then at bushes to touch one of the late-blooming roses.

Her unbound hair, darker than the night, fell around her body, swaying with her step. She wore a straight, pale flowing robe with long broad sleeves. It was the sort of thing a woman might put on when she first rose from bed. He could barely see patterns on it indicating rich embroidery. The night was cool, but she did not seem to notice that the thin fabric offered little warmth.

She moved toward him, close enough that he could see her moonlit face. Pale of skin, and large in eyes and mouth, it appeared mysterious, and matched the descriptions he had been given. One of the knights who had brought her from Wales had called her a moon goddess, and the praise had been apt. Her subtle glow cast a spell on the garden. And on him.

She paused in her stroll, not more than ten paces from where he lurked in the shadows. "I know you are there. Go back the way you came, and no one need know that you dared such a thing."

Her voice was quiet and melodic, steady and

unfrightened. But then the princely blood that flowed in her veins would neither quicken nor slow easily, for any man or any danger.

"I know that you are there," she said again. "I can smell that more than plants are in this garden."

He could smell her, too. Something freshly earthy, a memory of spring, floated on the small breeze along with the scents of dying leaves and flowers.

He stepped away from the wall. She heard him, and turned.

"Who are you? Not a thief, despite your furtive arrival, if you make yourself known."

"Nay, not a thief."

"Whoever you are, it will go badly for you if you are discovered here."

"For any man but me, maybe so. But something that is mine is here. I am Marcus of Anglesmore."

She reacted. Barely, but it was there, a vague stiffening. She gave him an encompassing glance, from head to toes. "What is here is not yours."

"Not yet. Soon, however, since the illness that has confined you these last weeks is clearly over." There had been no illness, of course. Only a long lie. He had always suspected as much, and her barely clothed presence in this chilled garden proved it.

She cocked her head, and regarded him as if she could see him very clearly in the dim light. "It took you long enough to decide to find out how serious this illness was. Perhaps you do not welcome this either, and prayed the malady was fatal."

Her perception surprised him, although he had never prayed for her death. He simply had allowed the ruse to continue until the insult it implied had conquered his reticence.

He did not know why he had reacted so strongly against the offer of this girl. After all, the marriage promised power, and the favor of the King, and a chance to prove Anglesmore's loyalty beyond any doubt. His response had come from deep inside his soul, perhaps a rebellion by the part of him that knew how to scale garden walls in the night. It had made no sense, but still an inexplicable resentment had seethed in him ever since hearing King Edward's plan.

Until now.

He had hoped that seeing her would soothe that rebellion, and it did. She was not childish, as he had feared. She possessed a poise and confidence far beyond her young years. She had not screamed for guards or her women on discovering his intrusion.

She was not running away now, even knowing who he was. That was a good sign.

Perhaps a very good sign.

He walked over to her. She took one step back, but no more. He lifted a strand of her silky hair, and then pushed all the tresses back over her shoulders so he could see her face better. The moon's light did not illuminate her much, and the subtle details were invisible, but he could tell that his first impression, that she was beautiful, had been correct.

"I find myself thinking that I should thank my king," he said.

"You can barely see me."

"I can see enough to know you are lovely."

"And that alone reassures you? You are a man easily appeased, if a woman's beauty is enough to satisfy you."

"I see more than beauty, and I find myself pleased, not appeased, that is all."

"Aye, the true prize is the land and wealth that go with this marriage. A bride's beauty is merely a sweetmeat added to a full meal. It is the way with such things, I know. But the favor of a king always has its cost. Do you understand the price of this banquet?"

He understood. But, oddly enough, that was not the part that he had resented. "The duty that Edward gives me is a small cost, and his to demand of me even without the prize."

"With that duty goes danger."

"That is also the way with such things." He stepped closer, and deeply inhaled her spring scent. Rich. Full of sensual fertility and the delicate odors of flowers. It reminded him of carefree days as a child, when the warmth of May promised freedom and play and joy. "It is very sweet of you to warn me, though." He touched her face, and slowly skimmed his fingertips down the curving line of her heart-shaped face.

Very little space separated them. He could decipher the patterns on her robe now, and their intertwining Celtic lines. She did not retreat from his touch, but merely looked into his eyes. Hers were dark pools glimmering like the pond at their feet. He felt a subtle tremor beneath his fingers, but still she did not pull away.

Something invisible and wordless passed between them. A mutual sharpening of awareness. A recognition, and acceptance, of what was to come. Images of that possession entered his head, and the garden shrank to a very small space fully occupied by a stark intimacy.

"I remind you of the danger for your own sake," she said. Her words came low and halting, as if she knew that what filled the air made everything else irrelevant. "It would be a pity if the knight standing in front of me died soon."

He smiled at her warning. Then again, perhaps it was meant as a threat. Right now he

didn't care which it had been. His thoughts
were on other things. He rested his entire hand
against the warmth of her face. She did not pull
away, and a heavy silence beat between them.

His thumb wandered to her lips, and brushed
their full, velvet swells. "Why do you dislike
that notion? Does the knight please you just as
you please him?"

"You appear handsome enough, and not as
brutish as I expected."

"Not brutish at all with you, I promise. Here,
I will show you." He bent and kissed her alluring mouth.

She did not react with shock or surprise, but
a small hesitation stiffened her. Then a subtle
yielding seemed to sneak out before she could
catch it. She might have lost a debate before arguing very far.

He had intended it to be a small kiss, a gentle
first step to reassure her. Her acceptance served
to fuel his simmering blood, however, and the
small kiss became a long one. He took her face
in both his hands and gently tasted and nipped
until a barely audible sigh breathed out of her
and into him.

He gazed at the face he held. Her expression,
heavy lidded and bright eyed, appeared unbearably sensual in the moonlight. Desire began a
fierce pounding through his head and body and

the same primitive excitement pulsed in her. He felt it. He almost *heard* it. It flowed around them and between them and in them, luxurious, tantalizing, and seductive.

He should leave. He should woo her slowly the way a good man does his intended. He should not take advantage of her ignorance, and her vulnerability after her first kiss.

He knew full well how a chivalrous knight should behave. Instead he pulled her into his arms.

Shock this time. Confusion. "I do not think . . ."

He silenced her with another kiss, and caressed down her back. She was naked beneath the thin gown, and the feel of her feminine softness and warmth, of her full, invisible curves, inflamed him. Her body moved in reaction to his touch, both retreating and encouraging all at once. He pressed her closer, enclosing her in his arms, and turned his kisses to her neck. She gasped quick breaths, a series of tiny, astonished announcements of delight.

And then, with a pliant stretch, she surrendered and impulsively embraced him back.

She intoxicated him. Her scent, her body, the kiss she returned, maddened him. In his mind he was already on the ground with her, sliding the robe off, warming her with his hands and mouth, covering her with his body. Kissing her still, he lifted her in his arms and carried her to a bench near the wall.

He settled her on his lap, swearing he would only dally a bit more and then take his leave. But the feel of her on his thighs and the new closeness of her body, so available beneath the thin robe, defeated that moment of good sense. Nor did she resist. The kisses turned mutual and hot and savage. Passion made her wild and her abandon became audible. For an instant, no more, she hesitated one last time when he slid his tongue into the moist warmth of her mouth.

He wanted more. Everything. Now. He caressed her stomach, then higher to the swell of her full breast.

A startled, muffled cry escaped her. She broke the kiss, gasping for breath, and leaned away as she shook her head. It looked less like a denial than that she sought to clear her thoughts.

"This is wrong. A mistake," she whispered.

He eased her closer again while he smoothed his fingers over her breast's tip. Its erotic peak hardened more at his touch. "It is permitted. We will marry soon."

"Nay, we will not."

She disentangled from his embrace, jumped from his lap, and began to run away. He grabbed for her, but caught only a thick strand of trailing hair. Still, it stopped her. She froze, her back to him, her shoulders still trembling from the passion they had shared.

"Come back to me. You know that you want to."

"What I want is a small thing in this. In *all* of this."

"Not to me. Making you want me, and then fulfilling your desire, will give me great pleasure when we are wed."

"You and I will never wed."

"We will. Very soon. I will not permit more delay now that I know what is waiting."

She glanced over her shoulder. "It must have been the full moon. It makes some women mad."

"Nay, it was the pleasure. That too makes some women mad, and you are one of them. If Edward had not given you to me, I would fight to claim you now anyway."

She walked away. It made her hair yank in his hand, and he released it.

She gave him one last look. "Now the moon is making *you* mad. The King's man should not be swayed so easily by a few kisses in a garden."

Nesta rose from her bed, sleepless again. Naked, she walked to the window and peered down at the spot where she had recently behaved very stupidly.

She should stay away from moonlit gardens. They kept getting her into trouble.

Marcus would return in the morning. She did not doubt that. He would come, and demand entry, and no tale of illness would work this time. He would come to speak of the betrothal, or just to woo his lady, but he would be here all the same.

That was going to complicate things.

A muffled sound distracted her, and she turned to the bed. A dark head rose and darker eyes blinked away sleep. "Are you awake still?"

"Aye. Go back to sleep," Nesta said.

"You should put on a robe, or wrap yourself in a blanket."

"I do not feel the cold as most others do. You know that."

"Still, you might take ill. That would be a fine thing, and hard to explain a real illness after this long false one. And it might keep us here."

"Nothing will keep us here."

The head sank back into its pillow. "I have been told that he is very handsome."

"Not handsome enough. No English knight would be."

A deep yawn filled the chamber. Nesta turned back to the window. In her mind's eye she saw a man standing near the pool, tall and strong and young, with a stimulating vitality in his aura. Aye, very handsome, and exciting enough to take her breath away and turn her knees to water. But still, not handsome enough.

It had been her own fault, what had happened down there. She should have screamed when she heard the stranger in the garden. But the punishment for such a trespass would be severe, and she did not like the thought of bringing it on some poor soul who might only seek to steal a few apples to ease his hunger.

Only it had been no poor soul, and a very different hunger that she had confronted.

Her fingers drifted to her mouth, and the memory of those kisses filled her mind and body. Titillating sensations crawled deeply in her again. A mistake to permit that, but who ever expected him to be so bold? Or so compelling as he approached her with command and confidence, the moon finding lights in his dark blond hair and the depths of his dark eyes captivating her.

Nay, it had been the moon's fault, too, not just hers. And the garden, and the night. There was danger in the beauty of such places. They seemed removed from the world, and full of a magic that made people do unthinkable things.

He would come in the morning, eager to see

her in the light of day. And he *would* see her, because she did not have time to escape by then.

She imagined that meeting.

Perhaps she had not been so stupid after all. He had said that he would not delay any longer with this marriage, but tomorrow would change his mind. After he saw her, *really* saw her, it would take a few days at least for him to accommodate himself to this marriage again.

And before he had done so, she would be gone.

CHAPTER 2

NOT LONG AFTER dawn, Marcus returned to the house near the Guildhall in London. He rode into its courtyard as the Lord of Anglesmore rather than stealing into its garden like a thief. The guards at the gate wore the King's livery, but the elderly woman who opened the door a crack was Welsh.

She peered up at him solemnly from under her low-dipping kerchief and repeated the words with which she had met each of his earlier visits. "She is not well, Sir Marcus. We will send word when her strength returns."

It surprised him that his bride still thought to play that childish game, even after last night. Then again, perhaps she now persisted *because* of last night. She was an innocent, no matter how much passion slept inside her, and he may have frightened her.

Well, he would behave better today, and woo her gently. That should reassure her.

He pushed the door open wider and stepped across the threshold into the house's great hall. "I will see her today, be she ill or well."

"I will tell her you are here and see if she can receive you."

"I will see her now and I will announce myself."

"Sir Marcus, you mustn't intrude. She be abed."

"Then I will see her in bed." The notion stirred him, but then this morning it wouldn't take much to do so. He had spent most of the night restless and aroused.

He headed across the hall. The old servant scampered along and nipped in front of him. She blocked his way, glaring with indignation. He feinted to one side, and when she jumped to cut him off he slipped around her the other way. Laughing, he strode to the stairs. He took them two at a time, lighthearted and eager. The old woman hustled up behind him, alternately yelling warnings to the women above and threatening to report him to the archbishop.

He paused on the landing. Excited voices came from behind one door. He heard footsteps scurry toward him, and the unmistakable sound of a bar starting to slide. Half charmed and half annoyed, he firmly pushed the door open.

He expected a chorus of feminine shrieks to greet his abrupt intrusion. Instead the chamber instantly filled with silence. A servant stood near the door, wide-eyed at his boldness. Another glanced over from where she folded some garments near the hearth. Yet a third sat on the bed, her back to him, and this one did not even acknowledge his presence. Instead she tended her mistress, who indeed was abed, propped up on pillows and with a sheet tucked to her chin.

He saw long black tresses spreading out over pillow and linens, and glimpsed her lovely face, glowing pale in the shadows formed by the shuttered windows.

"My lady is ill," the servant near him whispered anxiously.

"Not too ill to stroll almost naked in the garden last night."

He walked over to the bed and filled his eyes with his future bride. The light was not much stronger here than it had been under the full moon, but it was less ethereal and diffuse, and it permitted more details to be clear. She appeared very young now, no more than a girl, and he regretted a bit how aggressive he had been.

He *had* frightened her. It was obvious from

the way she refused to raise her gaze and in the way her hands clutched the bedclothes up to her neck. Her head was bowed submissively, as if she expected him to castigate her for permitting those kisses.

"You do not have to be afraid," he said. "I am pleased and flattered, and do not question your virtue. I am glad that it will not just be duty that we share in our marriage bed."

She raised her head. Large dark eyes took him in as if she had never seen him before.

He suddenly realized that she hadn't.

It dawned on him in a rush of perceptions, all of them lasting no longer than a blink. Dark hair, but straighter than the waves he had grasped. Large eyes, but too vacant for a woman who had shared those kisses with him. Pale skin, but without the curving line of a heart forming the jaw and chin. Beautiful, exquisitely so, but lacking something he could not name but which had held him spellbound just hours ago.

The servant moved off the bed. With her gone he could make out the shape of the body beneath the blanket, much thinner than the curves he had caressed.

"Sir Marcus," the servant said. "I would like to introduce you to Genith verch Llygad."

The voice penetrated his confusion. It was

quiet and melodic, and lacked fear or deference. He swung his gaze to the woman standing beside the bed.

And saw a face much like the one he had just been studying, only older and less beautiful, but also more interesting. There was nothing at all confused or submissive in its expression. His blood instantly reacted, and he knew the truth.

"Hell." He barely breathed the word.

He had been commanded to marry Genith, a sweet, innocent virgin. But he had almost made love last night to her older sister, Nesta.

A whore.

And not just any whore.

The *King's* whore.

Nesta nipped away before Sir Marcus could react with more than that one low curse. He appeared sufficiently stunned that she doubted he would attempt anything improper with Genith. In fact, it looked as if he would not even be able to speak for a good long while.

All the same, she gestured for the servants to stay. As she swept out the door, she glanced back at her sister meaningfully. Genith barely nodded, but the reminder had been received. *Keep him dangling. Two days at most, and you are free.*

Her glance also took in Marcus, watching her departure. His handsome, angular face was set severely and his mouth formed a straight hard line. His expressive, deep-set eyes flamed, and the wayward, dark gold locks skimming his temples seemed to point to his glare. He no longer appeared stunned, but furious.

His examination made her pause in her stride, as if those fiery eyes locked her in place. If he had been compelling in the garden, he was twice so here, where she could see him more clearly. His livid, revealing gaze made the chamber disappear for an instant, and she half expected him to walk over and grasp her in a furious embrace. Caution rose in her, but so did a disgraceful excitement.

Shaking off his spell, she hurried down to the hall, and grabbed a basket waiting for her. Perhaps two days would not be soon enough. She had better arrange things very quickly.

One of the King's guards moved to stop her as she approached the gate of Genith's comfortable prison. She held up her basket to indicate her purpose and cast him a look so quelling that he faltered and stood aside.

She hurried to the markets on the Cheap and quickly bargained for provisions to be delivered to the house. She eyed the vendors and their wagons as well as their wares, and stopped a bit longer with a few. She did not waste any time doing so, however, for she had much to accomplish and this might be her only chance.

Soon, probably today, her presence in London would become known to Archbishop Stratford and the other councillors who governed the realm in the King's absence. Once that happened she doubted that the guards at the gate would let her leave again. She would be confined there, a guest of the crown, just as Genith had been.

Finally, most everything was bought. Now it was time to sell. Her own wares could not be hawked in a market, however. A side lane showed merchant shops, and she strolled along it, entering one to make some small purchases while she chatted with the owner.

Her questions procured the information that she needed, and she aimed down the lane toward a fine, tall house and entered the mercer's shop on its first level.

Walls full of luxuries surrounded her, creating a square cave of visual delight. Silks and fine wools, some in colors she had never seen before, formed stacks higher than her head. One could tell without a touch that even the basic linens were better than most. The other merchant had said this shop was one of the best, but the abundance of riches astonished her.

An apprentice assessed her, then hustled into a back room. Soon the master emerged. He did not appear much older than an apprentice himself, no more than in his mid-twenties. He was handsome, with golden brown hair and deep blue eyes.

"How can we serve you, my lady?"

She set down her basket on a shelf's edge in front of a stack of delicious velvets. "I am told that you trade in Flanders, and visit there often."

"Not often, but I go there sometimes."

She plucked out some parchments from the basket. "I have some tapestry designs to sell. I have sold them before to merchants who take them to Flanders and get a good price from the weavers there."

He took the parchments and unfolded them. "They are very handsome, but tapestry drawings are normally full size."

"Enlarging these will be easy for their workers. They will have men who know how to do it."

He smiled vaguely. "I can see that you know this trade better than I do."

"I have sold them before, as I said. There is a merchant in Edinburgh who buys from me."

"Then why not sell these to him?"

"Because I am in London, not Edinburgh."

She suddenly understood the suspicion behind the question. "You fear that I have already sold the same images to him, and seek to duplicate my good fortune by duplicating the images themselves, don't you? I assure you that each one is different. You will not find when you get to Flanders that the pattern is already in use. These are unique."

He looked them over once more, than began folding them. "One pound."

"You will get three in Flanders."

"I may get nothing in Flanders, and it will be many months before I find out. By then I could have turned the one pound into three without the trouble of leaving London."

For a handsome man with a gracious manner, he drew a hard bargain. "One pound then." It would be enough, and she had a bit more coin stashed away. The provisions today had not depleted that little hoard. She had bought them on King Edward's tally. Edward's orders had hauled Genith here and, by the saints, he could pay the cost of getting her out, too.

"Would you prefer coin or goods?"

She eyed the velvets bulging on the shelves above her basket. Reaching up, she fingered the sensual nap of a green bolt. It had been years since she had indulged in such pleasures. "Coin. I cannot afford your mercery now."

While he went to the back chamber to get the coin, she stroked the velvet again. Her mind's eye saw it cut into a slim surcotte, with a cotehardie of deep rose wool underneath.

"If you have more tapestry designs, bring them. If I carry three to Flanders, I may as well carry six," he said when he returned.

She took the coin and picked up her basket. "I thank you, but I leave the city soon and there will be no time to bring you more. Good day to you."

Her duties completed, Nesta walked down the street more slowly than she had come, admiring the colorful signs swinging overhead, enjoying the talk and laughter leaking into the lane from the open doors and windows. That was what she had missed most the last few years—joyful noise. She dawdled at some windows, watching the craftsmen work or feasting her eyes on the expensive wares. These were very fine shops, the kind that made a person itch to buy and buy and gorge the senses on colors and textures and glittering surfaces.

She was admiring the weavings in a draper's window when the air around her changed. A thundering storm had appeared out of nowhere to spoil her morning.

"When did you arrive in London? I was told that Genith's sister was in a convent in

Scotland." The voice by her shoulder was very annoyed.

She glanced up at Sir Marcus. His dark eyes glinted and his face appeared incredibly handsome but extremely stern.

"I arrived at sunset yesterday. And I have not been in that convent for some months now." She returned her attention to the weavings. "Shouldn't you be attending my sister? Composing poetry to her beauty or speaking other sweet words?"

"I will have a lifetime to attend on her, damn it. Right now I want to speak to *you*."

"I cannot prevent you from doing so, although your mood does not bode well for any courteous conversation. I trust that you will not create a spectacle."

"I will make a spectacle fit for hell if I want to."

"Then let us leave this lane of polite shops and return to the market, where other ill-mannered people and animals gather. Then if you start bellowing it will not be noticed."

She began walking up the lane. Long booted legs fell into step beside her.

"You should have made yourself known to me last night."

"I did not have much chance with your impatient assault."

"It was not assault, lady, and we both know it."

"You hardly asked permission."

"I did not need to ask permission. I thought I was with my future bride. You *knew* my error, and you allowed me—"

"I allowed very little, and would have permitted far less if you had not overwhelmed me with your boldness. I am flattered that you found me so beautiful that you could not control yourself, but look at the mess you have made."

He grabbed her arm and swung her around to face him. He pierced her with a gaze too knowing, too male, and far too full of memories of the garden. "It was not my boldness that overwhelmed you, Nesta. Nor merely your beauty that lured me. And it was your deception, not my actions, that has created this hell of a mess."

"If you expect me to blush with shame, think again. A woman as notorious as I am is spared such nonsense."

"I am not looking for shame but for some common sense. How am I supposed to live with both her and you in my household after what happened?"

She pulled her arm free and continued walking. "You were not yet betrothed to her, and you did not make love to me. Even a priest could not find any great fault. Also, I have no intention of imposing on your household. After the wedding, I will be gone."

"Nay, you will not. I have been commanded to let you stay with your sister."

"Thank you, but that will not be necessary."

"It is the King's pleasure, so the choice is not yours."

That shocked her so much that she almost stumbled. It was a problematic discovery. The awkwardness of living with him and Genith after those kisses last night was the least of her concerns.

She ambled around the market stalls, bending to sniff foods and examine objects so Marcus would not see her dismay. She purchased a little flask of mead and several candles. Marcus seethed alongside her the whole time. She chose a variety of dried stalks from a woman who sold herbs. One was hanging very high, and Marcus helped cut it down, then absently plucked a coin from his own purse to pay for it.

"Tell me, Sir Marcus, are you saying that the King has commanded that I am to live with my sister?"

"Since your husband is dead, you need a place. It disturbed him to learn you had retired to that Scottish convent for lack of a home. And that is his goal in all of this—to restore your family's honor, and return Llygad ap Madoc's home to his daughters."

"Except in marrying my sister, the home will become yours."

"It will also be hers again. And yours. Your nobility will be restored. Someday our son will gain it all, so your father's bloodline will sit in the lord's chair again one day."

Not only her father's bloodline. Not just the blood of a family that could trace its lineage back to King Hywel Dda centuries earlier. It would be diluted by that of this Englishman, and her nephew would be more English than Welsh, and sworn to do England's bidding.

"Does he expect this to appease the men who followed my father's banner? They will not lay down their arms, but only be angered."

"I do not know what Edward expects, except from me. And that is to wed the daughter of Llygad, and be lord of those lands until our son succeeds me."

"And crush the rebellion that her father started, so that it does not grow into something other than a small mountain band raiding English-held lands."

"Aye, that too."

She stopped and faced him. "Do you know why Edward disseized my father?"

"Your father raised his standard against the crown."

"Do you know *why*?"

He looked past her, avoiding her eyes, exasperated by the question. "Everyone knows why, Nesta. The songs about it are still very popular."

"Ah, the songs. Which one have you heard? That which describes how I was forced, or that which credits me with virtue and the King with restraint."

His gaze swung back, sharply. "Both of those, and also the one that says you were willing."

"There is a fourth song, of course. The one where the fault was all mine, where the Welsh temptress bewitched him. It is the favorite one in Wales among the common people. They laugh so hard when they hear of the great king made weak by lust that they split their sides."

"*That* one I can most easily believe, having been a victim of your spell."

"Well, for all of the songs, it is the endings that should matter to you, the parts that describe how my father was so insulted that he broke with the King, and with England. That is the verse that gives you our home, and my sister's hand."

The mention of her sister darkened his expression again.

"If you find that too unpleasant, do not do it. If bedding her after kissing me distresses you, refuse this marriage," she said.

He looked down in a way that seemed to see right through her. "Ah, so that was your plan. Beguile the dim-witted knight so he lusts after the wrong woman, and spurns the one he has been given. Very clever. Nay, lady, this marriage will go forward. As you said, the King's man should not be easily swayed by a few kisses in a garden."

He appeared too determined, and not at all inclined to delay as long as she needed. In fact, he didn't appear very distressed at all anymore.

That wouldn't do.

She lowered her head and looked up at him through her lashes. She tried to summon a blush. "My lord, you give me far too much credit, and yourself far too little. It was not I casting the spell in the garden, nor I doing the beguiling. Last night . . . I could not help myself. You were very good."

She had intended to be coy and audacious, and to confuse him again. But his eyes had locked on hers, and what passed between them made her voice falter on the last words. She felt her face truly burn.

The man gazing down at her did not appear at all shocked or perplexed. His expression did not soften, but its harshness transformed into a different sternness. The intimacy from the garden instantly appeared again, like a brisk, enlivening wind nipping at her, making her shiver from her scalp to her toes.

She turned away from his hot eyes and strode out of the market, toward the house.

In attempting to be clever she had spoken the truth.

She *hadn't* been able to stop herself. It *had* been good. Too good.

And he knew it.

"I hate him."

"You cannot hate what you do not know." Nesta sat beside her sister in the garden where she had found Genith upon returning from the market. Genith was still sniffing back tears, so Nesta did not insist that they go inside, much as she wanted to. She would prefer to discuss Marcus of Anglesmore anywhere but here, on the very same bench where she had embraced him last night.

"I know enough," Genith said. "He does not care for me, either. He sat in the hall pretending to attend on me but thinking about other things. Doing his duty, that is all. He barely looked at me, and asked me questions about my

life with our kinswoman in Wales in a tone that
you would use with a little child. I half expected
him to give me a doll. As it is, he brought no
gift, and scowled the whole time. He is the kind
of man who is always angry, I think, and I am
very glad that I will not have to marry him."

Nay, she would not. It had nothing to do
with Genith's preferences, however. It never
did for women, especially women of their birth.

Genith was destined for a different marriage,
to a different lord, in order to secure a vital alliance for the rebels who flew Llygad ap
Madoc's banner.

Nesta took Genith in her arms to give comfort and reassurance. The body that she held felt
very small and frail. She herself had been just as
slight and not much older than Genith when
she met King Edward. She had thought herself
very mature and worldly then, but the world
she knew was privileged and small and based
upon songs and tapestries, and the maturity
merely an illusion.

"That you do not care for this man is of no
consequence. But what of the next one,
Genith? It is a mistake to form your judgments
so quickly." She knew even as she spoke that she
could make no difference. There were certain
things a woman only learns through experi-

ence, no matter how often older voices might try to warn and prepare.

"I doubt he will be so angry and cruel in appearance and manner. No man could be."

She was terribly wrong there, but Nesta did not say so. Marcus might have a harsh quality to him, but she could tell that he was not cruel. Genith had never had to deal with a truly violent man, and Nesta prayed she never would. "There are ways to handle men like Sir Marcus, little sister. My own husband had a temper to match his fiery hair, but with me he learned to be courteous. If the man you marry seems hard, you must soften him."

Genith pulled away, and gave the sharp look of a girl who knows very little but thinks she is quite wise. "Soften him with my favors, you mean." The tone was disapproving. For an instant Nesta saw the pinched face of the pious kinswoman with whom Genith had lived since their father had been disseized.

"Not with your favors. With your virtue and grace," Nesta said.

Her own tone must have conveyed her annoyance, because her sister suddenly looked chagrined. Impulsively, Genith snuggled closer, like a child seeking comfort. The clutching embrace touched Nesta, and nostalgia squeezed her heart. They might have been back in their father's home again, ten years earlier, when Genith had truly been a child and Nesta had filled the role of mother. She laid her head against the silken hair tucked to her neck.

"I do not want to talk of husbands," Genith muttered. "Since this marriage to Sir Marcus will not happen, it does not matter that I did not find him agreeable. It will not be the same when I meet the man I am expected to marry instead, I promise. I will find something to favor in him, as you did when you went to Scotland."

Nesta heard resignation mixed with the acceptance. Aye, faced with the inevitable, a woman either finds something to favor or lives in hell. This conversation made her melancholy, and evoked memories of being where her sister was now, dealing with the realities of duty being forced on her.

She *had* decided to make the best of her marriage, but the best could be a far cry from the dreams of youth, spun while the world is still fresh and new and full of sparkling light. Sometimes she mourned the smiling innocence of those uncomplicated days, and their bright, vivid emotions. Already Genith's world was dimming too, and that saddened her so much that her throat burned.

She gently rocked with her sister in her arms, soothing the fading child. "It will be all right," she whispered, pressing a kiss to Genith's head. It was a motherly gesture and tone, but she admitted that she had really been speaking to herself.

She was letting maudlin emotions overwhelm her, and she forced them under control. It *would* be all right, but mainly because Genith understood her duty. That superseded everything, most of all the wistful dreams in a girl's heart.

Nesta guiltily acknowledged that a part of her was relieved that Genith was growing up, and accepting the ways of the world. Because if a dream should reach out its hand to Genith, Nesta herself would have to prevent her sister from grabbing it.

CHAPTER 3

So the King's whore has come to London."
Archbishop Stratford received the news with a
resigned shake of the head. His deep sigh exhaled enough breath that a curled parchment
began a sleepy roll to his writing table's edge.

"Aye, the elder daughter is here," Marcus
confirmed. It annoyed him to hear Stratford call
Nesta a whore. After all, there were several stories about that encounter between Nesta and
Edward eight years ago. If Llygad ap Madoc had
broken with the King over it, rape was more
likely, although Marcus did not want to believe
that of the King he knew as a friend. Still,
Edward had been very young at the time, little
more than twenty years old, and very full of
himself and his newly acquired power. . . .

He caught himself, and cut off the heated argument his head was making. Hadn't he himself referred to her as the King's whore? What did he care how it had actually been? No matter what the truth, the violation of his hospitality had been enough to send Llygad into the hills.

Stratford shook his head again. Despite his large-framed, powerful build, he had appeared shrunken and weary when Marcus entered his chamber at Westminster. His thinning grey hair was mussed, as if a hand had scratched at the scalp many times today. Governing the realm in Edward's absence was not an easy task, Marcus guessed, no matter what skills a man brought to it.

"Thank the saints that the Queen is in Flanders with her husband," Stratford said. "We had heard that Nesta was contented to go to the convent after her Scottish husband's death. We received no word she had left it to journey here."

"Actually, she said that she had not been there for some months now."

Stratford's veil of distraction instantly lifted. He pierced Marcus with the shrewd stare of a man who had played many dangerous political games in his life, and survived each time. "So much for the loyalty of a Scottish abbess. Some months, you say? Where has she been?"

Marcus shrugged.

Stratford muttered a curse hardly befitting a bishop.

"She does not appear accepting of this marriage between me and her sister, which is why I have come today," Marcus said.

"There is naught she can do about it. Genith will not have the courage to stand against me, once I have her alone."

The old resentment about this marriage twisted in the pit of Marcus's stomach. He had always known that the match was not Genith's choice, but he could do without it being so baldly stated. He reacted viscerally against the notion of having a woman coerced to his bed. He had seen far too much of that as a boy.

He suppressed the youthful memories that wanted to emerge, and the reaction itself. This was the way of such things for a man with his position. He had always known that whatever marriage he made would contain the shadow of it.

"I gave word to the men at the house to allow neither sister to leave the property until we are done with this," Marcus said.

"Your caution speaks well for your judgment, but I doubt it was necessary. I do not know how Nesta journeyed from Scotland to London, but

I doubt she has the coin to journey back. Nor is there anywhere to take the girl."

"She could sell a jewel and get the coin. She could take Genith to her father's rebels."

"She has no jewels or property of value. They were taken by her husband's son by the first marriage, and the little remaining was required by the convent for her place there. And ladies do not live in the forest with wild men."

Stratford said it confidently, but something in the reference to the rebels obviously provoked his mind. He began absently handling the parchments lying in front of him, fingering their edges with a distant expression in his eyes.

"You brought word when you arrived from the marches that their raids had ceased since midsummer," he said.

"There has been little trouble. So little that some of the border lords think they have disbanded." It was one reason why the expectation that he crush those rebels had not concerned him overmuch. Despite Llygad's attempts to rouse Wales to his banner, this rebellion had always been more a nuisance than a threat, the most recent in a long line of minor insurgencies in a land well conquered by the King's grandfather.

Shrewd lights entered Stratford's eyes. "We

do not think it likely that they will disband. If they did not last year after Llygad's death, they will not now. It has become a way of life for them, and an excuse to act like thieves. However, things have been too quiet in the west. The Welsh chieftains have been too accommodating. No complaints. No demands. A very odd silence has descended."

Marcus knew of the peace and silence. Like the other marcher lords, he had been enjoying the respite from petty jealousies and switching loyalties among the Welsh chieftains who still held status and lands, albeit with England's permission.

Stratford continued, thinking aloud. "With the King out of the country, and so many of his barons with him, if anyone thought to join with these thieves and make a move, it would be now."

"They would never follow Carwyn Hir. He took Llygad's place upon his death, but he is not of princely blood, not *uchelwyr*. If he approaches Welsh leaders for an alliance, I cannot see that he would be welcome."

"What if someone of Llygad's blood spoke in his name? Or Carwyn spoke in hers?"

Marcus saw where Stratford was going. He suddenly remembered the warning of danger in the garden.

"I wonder where Nesta has been these last months," Stratford mused, tapping his fingers on his table. "I should follow my instincts and keep her in close confinement here, but that will never do. Edward would have my head if he learned I had imprisoned her without any evidence."

So, the King still lusted for Nesta, or at least Stratford thought so. Marcus did not like the implications of that.

The archbishop became the image of a man who had made a decision. "We will make this marriage tomorrow, then you will take both sisters with you back to Anglesmore. That way you can keep an eye on Nesta, and see that she causes no mischief. Better to have her there, than wandering around God knows where. If any of her father's men seek to use her, you will know of it. If she is in league with them, you might even learn their movements and plans if she is in your household."

Stratford's strategy paralleled the King's, which Marcus had learned about in the private letter from Edward that came with the official one regarding the marriage. The King also wanted Nesta at Anglesmore. The King had written friend to friend, and spoken of making amends and finding her a place. Now Marcus suspected the King had other intentions as well if, as Stratford indicated, he still held affection for Nesta.

The notion of that made his distaste for this marriage twist again. Bad enough to be bound to a woman coerced. Worse yet to have the sister he really wanted ever present. A living hell waited if the King visited and expected to tryst with his old lover.

If she was willing, he would have no choice except to permit it. If she was not . . .

And all the while he would be expected to discover if Nesta plotted against the realm.

If he learned that she did, he would be the man who had to bring her to judgment.

"The ceremony will be tomorrow," Marcus explained. "I hope you will both come."

"Of course. I have had a new surcotte made," Joan said. "You are contented with this marriage, Mark?"

She persisted in calling him by his boyhood name, even though he never used it anymore. He had repudiated it, just as he had turned his back on the powerless youth who had been called that. Since taking his place as Lord of Anglesmore he had been Marcus, just as his father had been.

"Well contented. I have finally met her. She

is beautiful and modest and obedient, and rich lands and the King's favor come with her. What more could I want?"

The day had turned warm, and they sat in the garden of Joan's London house while the evening light waned. The table between them held three small clay statues. Joan had made them, and now they dried so that she could take them to a kiln. Down by the far wall of the garden, Joan's husband Rhys played with their two youngest children.

Marcus glanced to the house. It was of good size, as befitted a man who was a principal builder to the crown. Marcus himself had lived in this house for a few months as a youth, before Anglesmore had been restored to him and Joan had married the man who had given them shelter. A house too wide for one person, Joan had called it back then. She and Rhys had filled it to the point where it bulged with family and love.

He looked across at his sister. She was watching her husband and children. Tenderness veiled her expression. Marcus instantly experienced the jumble of reactions that he felt whenever he saw that look on her. His heart filled with happiness for her, but also resentment and even jealousy.

The latter emotions were not worthy of him,

but he could not deny they were there. They had been in his soul since he had learned which life Joan had chosen. As a youth they had ruled him, and kept him from visiting her when he came to London. The estrangement had lasted years.

In part he had avoided coming because this house and neighborhood reminded him of the bad years after his father died, when Anglesmore had been lost and he and Joan had been reduced to poverty. Mostly, however, it had been anger at Joan that had kept him away.

Finally, he had been forced to come. Addis de Valence, the lord who served as Anglesmore's warden after Marcus got his place back, had shown no inclination to relinquish his hold when Marcus came of age. Resentment at that had led him to confront Addis.

"You should have stood aside months ago. Why do you delay, and keep one hand on my shoulder?"

"I am waiting for you to show that you are a man."

The insult had been infuriating. "Meet me with swords and I'll damn well prove that I am a man if you have any question about it."

"I do not speak of skill at arms. There is a woman in London who waits for you to visit her. Whenever you journey there, she spends

her days listening for your bootstep. A man will
set aside whatever anger keeps him from that
house. It is the boy in you who cannot reconcile what happened, and what she sacrificed,
and how she then rejected all that she had
fought to regain."

And so he had come to this house, and was
glad that he did. But the anger still lived in his
gut. He was only alive because of Joan. He only
had Anglesmore because of her. She had slaved
for three years to get their place back after they
lost it. And then, at the moment of victory, she
had walked away from it, from *him,* because of
a man.

"I am glad that you have met her, and that
you are pleased. I pray that you find love with
her, Mark. It is worth far more than all the lands
in Wales." Joan no longer watched her husband.
Warmth still suffused her expression, only now
it was for him, her brother.

He did not respond. For one night, after
some kisses in a garden, he had dared to wonder if he might know what Joan hoped him to
find. It had been an exhilarating, but childish,
fantasy. The Lord of Anglesmore was born for
other things. Duty called.

Joan caught Rhys's eye and gave a little signal
with her hand. Rhys nodded, and rose from the
ground where he wrestled with his two little

boys. The children clung to his tall body as he stood, hanging from his shoulders and strong arms. With laughs and gentle hands, he pried them loose and lowered them to the ground.

"Come with me, brother," Joan said. "We have something to show you."

Marcus accompanied Joan over to a mason's workbench. A tall form stood on it, shrouded in canvas. It had been there every time that Marcus had visited since he resumed coming here four years ago. Since Rhys never seemed to be working on it, Marcus assumed it was an abandoned project, such as happens when a man moves on to other things. Rhys Mason no longer carved stone but designed great buildings for the King.

Rhys joined them and pulled off the canvas. A gleaming statue of Saint George was unveiled, its face bearing the likeness of the last Lord of Anglesmore. The marble had a slightly yellow hue, giving the face even more realism.

"It took many years, since I have other duties now," Rhys explained as he glossed his fingertips over a section of carved armor, his blue eyes and sensitive touch checking the surface. "Joan helped me rough it out, since my hand by itself does not have the strength for that. She also did some of the work on the face, since she knew your father's countenance."

Marcus gazed at that face, so real in the dimming light, so similar to the one of his boyhood memories. His last sight of it had been when it wore the mask of death, but Joan had shown their father years younger, and alert and alive.

His throat thickened. He had requested this of Joan years ago, but thought it had been forgotten. He pictured his sister and her husband working on it all this time, bit by bit.

"It is perfect," he said. "Weak hand or not, you have not lost your skill, Rhys."

"Our skill. It is not just my craft here."

"Now we have to find a way to get it to Anglesmore," Joan said.

"I can help there," a new voice answered.

Marcus turned to the voice, and the young man carrying a sack who came toward them from the garden's back portal. "Welcome, David. Come and see it."

David de Abyndon examined the statue with keen interest. His expression was much as Rhys's had been, and he even touched the surface the same way. "So, it is finally done. A great achievement. Too bad it will stand in an obscure chapel on the Welsh marches where no one will see it."

"I will see it," Marcus said.

"Well, if that is to be its lonely fate, so be it. I will be taking a wagon in that direction soon, and can haul it to Anglesmore. I doubt that you will want to be delayed by such a burden when you bring your bride home."

"My messenger found you then?"

"Tomorrow, he said. I will be there. You do not waste any time, since a day ago you had not even seen this girl. I assume that now you have, and found her very appealing if you are so impatient. Her recovery from that illness was sudden."

David was prying in the subtle way he had. As youths they had become friends while Marcus lived here with Rhys, and had found each other again once Marcus began returning to the ward. Eventually Marcus would satisfy his friend's curiosity, but not now with Joan listening.

David raised the sack he carried. "I thought you might be here with your sister. I have brought some things so that you can choose a wedding gift. I trust you were not so stupid as to deal with some other merchant."

Marcus had not even thought about his immediate need for a wedding gift. David's expression said he had expected as much.

"Come, have some wine and we will all drool over the luxuries," Joan said, leading them back to the table.

The sack contained a little illuminated book of prayers, a small jeweled cross, some folded parchments, a silver necklace, and a headdress of fine netted gold. Marcus lifted the book and carefully flipped its pages.

"She will prefer any of the other things to that," David said.

"How would you know?"

"Because she is a girl, which means that she has not yet learned that there is more to beauty than that which glitters."

David spoke like a young man who knew women well. Marcus suspected that he did. As a handsome, unmarried merchant, he caught the eye of ladies looking to satisfy more than their taste for silks. Marcus did not envy his friend his experiences, but he would not play the apprentice learning from the master of love. "A devotional book is most practical."

"Don't be boring. For the same cost you can have both the cross and the necklace."

Marcus conceded this was not the time to be practical, but he would not give David an easy victory. He lifted the headdress instead. Its woven pattern had an exotic look. He pictured it on the crown of a black-haired beauty.

The face in his imagination did not belong to Genith.

He asked the price and David named one far too low. He gave his friend a sharp look, and David increased it.

"That was my cost, I swear. It is no insult if I do not skin you alive, Mark. I merely choose not to take a profit from a friend on his wedding day. We merchants have very few scruples, but permit me the ones I can claim."

Joan was admiring the other items. "What are these?" she asked, reaching for the parchments.

"Designs that I brought to show you and Rhys. A lady sold them to me this morning."

Joan unfolded them. Marcus examined the drawings spread on the table. One showed a hunt scene, and another a May pageant. The third had no people, just birds and animals in a rich, verdant field.

"They are very good," Rhys said. He ran his thumb over a corner. "Colored with inks, like a manuscript. The parchment has been scraped, though, and reused after writing was removed."

"They are tapestry designs. I paid much more than I had to, but she was such a Welsh beauty that I could not bargain with any heart."

Marcus's attention sharpened to a sword's edge. "A Welsh beauty?"

"Raven haired, with an interesting face. Blind to my charm, I am sorry to say. I tried to lure her into returning by offering to buy more, but she said she would not be in London long enough."

Marcus touched one of the parchments. Colored inks, such as used in manuscripts. The women in convents often copied manuscripts. David's shop was on the lane where he had found Nesta this morning.

"How much did you give her?"

"Too much."

"*How* much?"

David raised an eyebrow at the sharp tone. "One pound."

Marcus muttered a curse. Nesta and Genith could journey to Scotland or Wales easily on that.

He stood abruptly. "I must leave now. I will see all of you tomorrow at Westminster."

Joan touched his arm. "What is it?"

"Nothing. I merely remember something that I must do this night."

He turned away from the curious looks the others gave him and strode toward the garden portal. The suspicion nagging him was ridiculous. Coin in hand or not, Nesta and Genith could not leave. The King's guards stood at the gate of that house.

Still, he felt compelled to go check. David

had said that Nesta had indicated she would leave London soon.

It would be just like that Welsh witch to find a way to do so.

The gate was closed but not barred. Worse, no guards stood behind it.

Marcus pushed it open and stepped into absolute silence. No glow came through the windows to indicate that hearths or candles burned.

It was possible that Stratford had called them all to Westminster, to prepare for the wedding there. Marcus doubted it, however, and his blood began a dangerous boil.

He strode to the house. More silence. No servants responded to his call. Head splitting with a furious certainty of what he would find, he climbed the stairs and barged into the bedchamber where his future bride should be.

Empty. Of course it was. No Genith, no trunks, no servants, and, it went without saying, *no Nesta.*

Returning to the stair landing, he began making plans. Stratford would have to be informed. Then he would rouse the men he had brought from Anglesmore and they would go after the bitch.

Only he didn't have any idea of where she had gone.

A sound broke into his heated calculations. A muffled groan came from somewhere behind him. He followed the sound through a tiny chamber containing two mussed beds, and into a garderobe at the corner of the house.

There, in the dark, he made out the shapes of two men seated on privies, doubled over in misery.

"What in hell is going on?" he demanded.

"My lord, tell the lady that we will be needing more of the potion. This malady has us purging our guts out," one of them muttered.

"When did this malady come on?"

"Late today. The potion, my lord. The lady said it was sure to help."

He could imagine how the potion "helped," and had no doubt who the lady was. "I'll have the archbishop send a physician to you. Take no more potions, or any food or drink from this house. I doubt that this malady will kill you, although *I* might once you are well again."

He left them to their pain, and examined the dark chamber. A little leather flask stood on the floor between the two beds. He smelled its contents. It was redolent with the scent of herbs and mead, but also something else, something oily like tallow or grease.

Nesta had made this. She had probably fed the guards a purgative in their midday food, then provided more in this potion to keep them incapacitated. While the two men moaned on these beds and sat on those privies, she had packed up Genith and the Welsh servants and ridden out the gate.

The scent from the flask wafted to him. Something in it plucked at his memory. A familiar, strong odor seemed to ride atop the others.

He smelled a dried stalk hanging from a vendor's stall, and saw himself reaching up to cut it down.

Hell's teeth. He had helped her procure the ingredients. He had even *paid* for one of them.

He threw the flask against the far wall. The skin split and the remnants dripped in dark streaks on the plaster.

He needed to know in which direction Nesta was headed, and he doubted that Stratford's men would glean much from their inquiries. The city's gate guards would feign ignorance, lest they be accused of some negligence.

But they would talk to their own kind, especially if a coin was offered. So would any travelers who had arrived in the city late today who might have passed a retinue of Welsh women on the road.

He needed information fast, and he knew two men who could get it if anyone could. Striding from the house, he headed back to his sister's garden.

CHAPTER 4

THE FIRE'S WARMTH enlivened her damp skin. Nesta luxuriated in the sensation as she knelt naked in front of the hearth in the rude cottage near the Welsh border. Sitting back on her heels, she washed with cool water that dripped down her body. The heat licked at each cold rivulet, creating a wonderful streak of contrast before the meandering drop disappeared.

It was done. Genith was away. In a day she would be safely hidden. In a few weeks she would be headed to the marriage awaiting her.

Not a marriage with the King's man. Not Marcus of Anglesmore. Genith would wed the man their father had chosen, and help to fulfill the dream of Llygad ap Madoc.

She looked to the tiny window, and judged

from its light the time that had passed since she handed Genith to her guardians. The swift escape from London had caused them to arrive in this village a day earlier than planned. She had spent many hours watching out that window, waiting for the horses, fearing that the wrong men would ride up first.

It had unfolded as it should, however. Tomorrow she and the servants would take a different route with the wagoner she had hired at the London market, misleading anyone who might search for her little sister.

She stared into the fire, mesmerized by its jumping flames. She imagined her father's face amidst them, and her chest tightened for that warrior with the heart of a poet. *Soon,* she whispered to him. The dream would be fulfilled soon. She would see to it. She owed it to him.

She dipped her cloth in the water bowl by her knees. Raising the sodden rag to her shoulder, she squeezed. Water ran down her back and snaked over her hips. Some slithered into the cleft of her bottom tucked above her feet. She moved her hand and squeezed again. Tiny liquid paths played over her breast.

There should be elation in this victory, but she could not shake a melancholy that ruined her contentment. It had been much harder than she had expected to take this step. When the Welsh escort rode up, she had even experienced a moment of panic. Suddenly, desperately, she had wanted to keep Genith nearby a little longer, safely tucked in her arms. They had been parted for so many years, and this brief time together had been bittersweet and heavy with memories.

Now they were parted again. If something went wrong, it might be forever this time.

She tried to shake off her sadness by thinking of Edward's plan, and the importance of foiling it. He wanted to make amends, it was said. A long time coming, those amends, and calculated to cost him nothing. Such was the way with powerful men. Even in penance they gained more than lost.

Well, she also had amends to make. The world would say she did it for revenge, but then the world, and the King, had always misunderstood most of it.

Rising out of her reverie, she completed her washing more methodically. It felt good to finally be clean again. Too many days on the road had left her soiled and sticky and feeling old.

She bent at her hips and splashed her face with water. Hands planted in front of her knees, she raised her face to the heat to dry.

And froze.

There had been a sound behind her. No louder than a breeze, it had accompanied her movement. The servants returning from market, no doubt. She sat back on her heels and listened for their steps and talk.

She heard nothing more, but her pulse began pounding. Her soul knew what her senses denied.

She slowly turned her head and looked over her shoulder.

Marcus of Anglesmore's tall, strong body leaned confidently against the chamber's doorjamb. His dark golden hair fell carelessly around his head and jaw, and the dim light in the chamber sculpted his face into stony planes in which dark eyes blazed as he watched her.

His hard expression made the back of her neck prickle. She calculated the danger he might present, and the time since Genith had departed.

She turned back to the fire, forcing composure on herself. "How long have you been there?"

He did not answer.

"The women?"

"They are safe and unharmed, but silenced."

"How did you know where to find us?"

"You were seen leaving London and heading west, and travelers passed you on the road. Still, this took longer than it should have, and I am most displeased. Clever of you to pay some of those travelers to lie about the roads you would take on this journey."

She waited for more. They stayed in silence for a long stretch.

Finally he spoke. "You have a beautiful body, Nesta, and it has given me pleasure to watch you bathe, but put something on now. Cover yourself." A note of exasperation sounded in the command.

Duty bound or not, angry or not, he had been distracted by her nakedness.

It was all she needed to know.

She rose to her feet. A robe waited on a stool by the hearth, but she did not reach for it. Instead she turned and walked to the chest near the door. His gaze took in the full view of her.

She plucked a sleeveless, sideless surcotte from the chest and slipped it on. Its panels dipped low on her chest and back, and fluttered along her sides, exposing glimpses of her hips and legs. Turning, she raised her gaze. Marcus's lowered lids and tight jaw revealed what she already knew. The hint of nakedness was even more enticing than all of it.

Good. The longer he was distracted by lust, the farther away Genith would get.

He speared her with a glare. "You like it, don't you? Making men want you."

"I suspect it is much like the feeling you get when you unhorse a man in a joust."

"What did your husband think of your tournaments?"

"He was not young, but lusty enough. It was he who taught me how to use my weapons."

He took dark amusement in that. "Where did you send Genith, Nesta?"

"I sent her nowhere."

"She left here."

"Perhaps she went for a walk. This cottage has been too crowded." She spoke lazily while she turned a bit and raised her arms to release the knot into which she had bound her hair while she washed. She noted with satisfaction that Marcus did not miss how the gesture revealed the side of her breast.

She strolled back to the hearth, kicking at the panels of the surcotte, giving him more to see. Each step bought Genith more time. She struggled to suppress the undeniable stirring in her breasts and stomach that his attention was causing.

Gazing into the fire, she waited for more interrogation. It did not come. That worried her. He should be furious with impatience. He should be bellowing demands for information. A good argument would delay him a long while, and she could keep him dangling until night with ambiguous tidbits and flashes of skin. Instead he just stood there, burning her back with his gaze, causing unwelcome thrills to tremble through her.

"Nesta." His soft, quiet voice was right behind her. She had not heard him move, and she started with surprise. The word sounded soothing and gentle, like the uttering of a man making love.

She glanced back at him. He didn't *look* gentle. His eyes held wicked lights.

She almost jumped in alarm when his hands circled her waist. "I am not a man easily distracted, Nesta. A glimpse of thigh or breast will never put me off my duty. Nor will clever lies." His breath warmed her neck, and then his lips skimmed the edge of her ear. "If you think to unhorse *me,* woman, you will need to use better weapons than that."

The bluntness of the offer dismayed her, as did the delicious chills shivering down her skin. So much for keeping this man dangling.

She squirmed out of his hold and turned, backing away. "Such a trade would be unwise for you. Would you have the King's wrath on you?"

He came toward her. "You expected me to look and desire but not to touch because you are Edward's woman? That is the armor you use in this joust of yours? It is very old and rusty, to my mind. I do not think the King will care too much. He has not seen you in eight years, and he let you marry another."

She kept inching away and he kept following. Her back hit the hearth wall. He blocked her. Dominated her. He gazed deeply into her eyes and they were suddenly back in the garden again, under a magical full moon.

A traitorous excitement trembled through her, and she knew that she had made a dangerous miscalculation. He appeared to take amusement in her predicament.

Her heart beat desperately. "You must leave this chamber at once."

"Coming now, that command has little weight. You should have said that on first seeing me."

He touched her lips with his fingertips. A jolt of exhilaration jumped inside her.

"You taunted me, Nesta." His touch drifted lower, down her neck to the low dip of the surcotte's edge. He watched his fingers trace a line across her skin. Back and forth, his light touch played at the top of her surcotte, and the swell of her breasts peeking above its edge. His vague smile suggested that he guessed what other lines were coming alive inside her. Tantalizing ones. Delicious strings of thrilling pleasure spun through her and began knotting deep in her belly.

"You tempted me shamelessly, lady. A man can hardly stand down from such a challenge."

"It was no challenge. I was washing and you intruded—"

"Hush."

His gaze and hand lowered more, to her breasts. His skimming touch made them swell. She struggled to keep her breath even, but when he brushed the tips her sharp inhale was audible.

He dipped his head to kiss her. Before touching her mouth he stopped, and pulled back to look in her eyes, as if checking her reaction.

She just stared like a witless fool.

Passion crackled between them like invisible lightning. No more stopping then. He pulled her into a dominating embrace and a rough, devouring kiss. Her body had already betrayed her, and she instantly found herself in a storm of pleasure and building desire. He asked for no reciprocation, but only took and took and she permitted it, gasping for breath, turning her neck to his hot bites, opening her lips to the next forceful demand.

She lost herself, forgetting she should not, forgetting everything, even who she was and what was at stake, just as she had forgotten in the garden. She joined the little battle, knowing she had already been defeated, not caring about anything but the voracious desire making them both wild.

The world had receded but somewhere, far away, cries were being raised. On the edge of her awareness a confusion rumbled lowly.

His fingers snaked through her hair, imprisoning her head in his grasp while his arm confined her body. He broke the kiss and gave her a deep look. Then he pulled her toward the small window, his hand still on her head, forcing her forward as he embraced her.

None too gently he turned her face to the window, making the world spin, confusing her. The sudden light shocked her and the crisp air nipped her flushed skin.

She blinked hard, and the blurred scene outside sharpened.

Sickening despair hit her stomach like a fist.

Four men wearing Anglesmore's livery were dismounting from their horses. Genith sat on the rump of one steed, with tears running down her face. Behind the saddle of another, his hands bound and his long dark hair falling halfway down his back, was one of the young men who had come to take Genith to safety.

"We had her before I came here. My men delayed to try and catch the other thieves," Marcus said lowly in her ear.

The hand at her head pulled her back from the window. Still hot-eyed with anger and passion, he released his hold on her body but took her face in a grip.

"Do not try to make me into your fool again, Nesta. And *never* taunt me as you did today. The craving between us goes both ways, woman, and it is my weapon to use as surely as it is yours."

He pressed another furious kiss on her, then thrust her away, toward the chest of garments. "When I give a command, obey it. Put something on and cover yourself."

The men of Anglesmore carried out the chests and set them in the wagon. The wagoner Nesta had hired in London kept up an argument with Marcus, explaining that he had not bargained for a journey to Wales, and how he expected an escort out of that bandit-filled land if he was forced to go there. The whole village had come to watch the spectacle and dawdled in groups on the dirt lane.

Nesta stood with her arm around Genith's shoulders. It had taken a long while to get her sister to stop crying, and Marcus's icy manner as he ordered the preparations had not helped matters any. Whenever he glanced their way, Genith had resumed weeping like a woman doomed.

Nesta touched Genith's arm and gestured to the young man who had been captured along with her sister. His hands were still bound, and a rope now tethered him to the wagon's side. Of middle height and slight of build, he appeared no match for the powerful warrior who had captured him. He wore a sack tied to his back that was too flat and long to only be holding food and garments.

"What is his name?"

"Dylan," Genith whispered. "The others ran when they saw all was lost, but he did not."

"Brave of him," Nesta said. Brave but rash. He should have run too, if capture was inevitable.

Dylan watched Marcus with lidded, sparkling blue eyes. He showed no fear. Nesta looked back to her sister in time to see admiration flicker as Genith regarded the prisoner.

"Do you know him? Is that why he stood by you?"

Genith blushed. "He served last winter at our kinswoman's household. I was surprised to see him with the others here. I did not know that he had joined them."

"Do not let Marcus know this. He may think that Dylan pursued you, and accuse him of abduction." It would be a very neat explanation for Genith's escape, Nesta admitted to herself, and she would need a good one soon. She could not risk the young man's life in that way, however.

It turned out that Dylan was in danger with no help from her. After the chests had been moved and the horses prepared, one of Marcus's men pointed to the prisoner and addressed his lord. "Might as well hang him now. Easier that way, and he's either a thief or a traitor."

Marcus stood at the cottage door, dwarfing the threshold behind him. He examined the young man tied to the wagon, and Dylan gazed back fearlessly. Two pairs of fiery eyes locked on each other. Dylan's challenge could not have been more clear if he had voiced it. Nesta could almost hear Marcus weighing the trouble awaiting if he did not hang Dylan immediately.

"Would you punish him for foolishly following his elders?" she called to Marcus. "His greatest treason was to his own safety, in not fleeing like the others. Besides, the sack on his back clearly carries a harp, and he can entertain us on the evenings of this journey."

That brought Marcus's gaze on her instead. His expression suggested she had been very stupid to remind him that she existed. "You would have me spare him, Nesta?"

"Aye." She hoped that Marcus would not hang Dylan merely to spite her.

"And my bride. What would she prefer?"

Genith lowered her gaze modestly. "The decision is yours, my lord, but if he can sing for us and ease this journey, I would have him spared."

"Then it will be so, for now." He gestured for the women to get into the wagon. "We will delay all punishments until we get to Anglesmore, where the rights of judgment are legally mine."

Nesta helped Genith into the wagon, and climbed in to settle beside her. She could have done without Marcus's reference to *all* punishments.

They crossed Offa's Dyke, the ancient border of Wales, before nightfall. Marcus decided they would camp rather than seek shelter at some manor house. They were in Clun now, a marcher estate held by Fitzalen, the Earl of Arundal, and Marcus did not want to be explaining the situation to Arundal if he was in residence here.

The women created a little camp adjacent to the men's. After a meal had been cooked and served, one of his soldiers eagerly brought the prisoner forward. He put Dylan near the main fire and cut his bindings. Dylan removed the sack from his back, and withdrew his harp.

As soon as the fingers touched the strings, Marcus knew that Dylan was a bard. His voice and skill announced it as surely as the old legends he sang. The harp itself, inlaid with silver knotted lines, possessed an ancient look. Marcus guessed it had been given to Dylan by an older bard, who had in turn received it from one, and on and on back through time.

Aye, he should have hung the young man. Dylan would not have to raise a weapon or attempt escape to be trouble. He need only sing the right song at the right time to speak sedition to the Welsh people.

Bodies gravitated to the pure sound of the music, and soon a hushed audience circled the fire. Genith's soulful eyes appeared glazed, as if the songs entranced her. Or perhaps the bard did. Marcus knew that should concern him more than it did. Still, he would have to find out the truth behind Genith's attempt to flee.

Seated on a log at the edge of the group, Nesta attended to the entertainment more impassively than the others, occasionally ducking her head as if Dylan could not even hold her attention.

Marcus circled through the trees surrounding the clearing, drawn to that bobbing head. The music trickled over and around him as he approached her, and the breeze and forest sounds seemed a part of the melody.

She wore an old flowing robe of a deep rose hue. Of the simplest cut, it hung from her shoulders and obscured her body. It barely revealed the shape that it skimmed, but he had no trouble seeing what was beneath. The image of her naked, tapering back and nipped waist, of the lovely curve of her hips flaring above the feet on which they rested, kept flicking in his head all day, like a banner snapping in the breeze.

He stepped toward her, but she did not notice him behind her. Instead her head ducked again as she bent toward her knees, reminding him of the suggestive pose she had assumed in the cottage when she leaned forward and rested her weight on her hands. In his mind's eye she completed the movement, rising on her knees so her pretty, round bottom lifted. . . .

Blinking the fantasy away, he looked to the ground and saw what occupied her more than the music.

She had smoothed the dirt at her feet, and now drew on it with a stick. The scene in front of her, of men and women surrounding a fire, filled the middle of the dirt. Animals of the hunt and birds of the forest watched from the edges. All of the figures, human and beast, directed their attention to a man atop the fire holding a harp. He was drawn larger than all the others, and in more detail.

It was another tapestry design, such as she had sold to David. He noted with some annoyance that she had not included him.

"It is clever," he said. "A pity you cannot save it."

"It is in my head. When I have time to use ink and parchment, I will remember most of it." She spoke as if she had known he was behind her after all.

"You were taught this in the convent?"

"I sought to learn it. There was not much else to do there except pray and learn Latin. And it proved useful. I sell the images to earn some coin for cloth and such, since I was left with little when I was widowed."

"You will not need to clothe yourself in the future."

She straightened, and tilted her head to examine her work. "Well, one never knows. Even so, I might continue. I have grown fond of doing it."

"Then we will make sure that you have inks and parchments."

He stood by her shoulder. Only the barest space separated them. He was very conscious of how close he was to her. He could feel her warmth on his thigh. He could imagine the skin beneath the rose cloth. He tasted her again, as if his mouth pressed and bit her neck as it had hours ago.

That embrace had been a livid response to the anger and hunger that had gripped him while he watched her bathe. It had been a furious impulse born of insult and desire, and he had succumbed too greedily. He could not regret it, however, no matter how the memory would torture him. He was glad he had forced her to acknowledge that a taste of hell waited for *both* of them.

He touched her shoulder with his fingertips. She flexed as if she had been waiting for it, and the vaguest tremble shook out of her and into him through the tiny contact.

Aye, hell awaited.

"I would speak with you, Nesta. Come with me."

She hesitated, but rose and faced him. Her expression remained composed, but for an instant he saw resentment in her eyes, and an unspoken rebuke for what he had done in the cottage.

He dared not take her into the trees because he didn't trust himself to have her alone. Instead he led her to the women's camp, where they could talk but still be seen.

A smaller fire burned here, and she sat on another log near its low flames. "Sit," she said. "I'll not have you looming over me like some threat out of hell. I am not easily intimidated, so you might as well rest yourself."

It was the only log, so he settled beside her—and knew at once that he had lost an advantage in doing so. They were too close. She had intended that. He was sure of it.

"Dylan sings beautifully," he said. "Your sister appears enchanted by him. Does Genith know him? Or has she fallen in love in one day?"

"You see more than is there. She is just a girl touched by a jongleur's love song."

He had to smile. "Nesta, have you spent your life around unusually stupid men? I ask because you act as if you assume I am denser than stone. Dylan is no mere jongleur, and he has not been singing about love. I know the Welsh language, my lady, and I recognize the old bardic songs."

She shrugged, and picked up a stick and began absently drawing in the dirt again. "Most of the English lords do not know Welsh."

"My family has been on the marches for hundreds of years. My grandmother was Welsh."

"Still, most of you do not know the language. I did not think you dense, just typical of the English families who hold Wales but rarely visit their lands here. Their English manors are more to their taste, and we are glad for that." She glanced toward Dylan. "He is no danger to you. Not in his songs, nor with my sister."

"He is if she fled to be with him. Did this man and his friends take her from you?"

"I handed her to them. I arranged it all." She said it blandly, utterly indifferent to what his reaction would be.

"Where were you sending her?"

"To my father's men. She does not want this marriage, and when I saw her distress I could not deny her. It was foolhardy, I know, but her pleas touched me, and your behavior when you met with her only made it worse."

He did not miss that she had turned it around so this was his fault. "So you sent your sister to the mountains to live out her life among bandits in order to save her from me."

She pursed her lips at the sarcasm in his tone. "I sent her from a marriage she did not want.

As to where she would live, I would have arranged something else later. But with you insisting on a quick wedding, I had to get her away at once."

It vexed him that she assumed he would swallow the swill she was offering. "There is a capricious logic to your tale, Nesta. The only problem is that I do not think you are capricious. You are lying."

"Why would I bother to do that?"

"Maybe to protect your sister, who sought to run off with her lover. Or maybe to hide the fact that you only want to thwart this marriage in order to spite the King."

Her attention sharpened on him. Color rose to her cheeks. "You insult me. Better to accept that I am capricious than accuse me of such childishness."

"A woman used and spurned can be very childish. I do not insult you. I only assume that you are *typical,* as you assumed about me. If I am wrong, your opposition to this marriage makes little sense. This union will benefit your family's honor. You should have been explaining that to your sister, to allay her girlish fears, not plotting to help her run away. Aye, to me this looks like the scheme of a smart woman made stupid by wounded pride, whose vision has turned shortsighted because of an old insult."

She was up on her feet before he finished, glaring at him. The low fire reflected off marvelous sparks of anger in her eyes. They reminded him of other sparks he had seen in them, of passion and desire.

Challenge silently crackled out of her, but as they gazed at each other it changed. The argument and its reason became submerged in the spiritual push and tug of their other battle.

Too much passed between them in that gaze. That she lied and that he suspected why. That each would find the other a formidable foe. That they wanted each other with a fiery desire that kept threatening to consume good sense. It was all there, instantly, harshly, and undeniably.

A glint of confusion joined the other lights in her eyes. She quickly dropped her gaze, but he saw it just the same. In his dazed absorption, it seemed a yielding and submission. He came close to pulling her onto his lap.

She stepped away, as if she sensed his impulse. "Think of me what you will, Marcus. Actually, I believe you may be right. Perhaps in my heart I did take Genith away in order to spite the King."

The rose drapery swayed around her as she

strolled to where Dylan still made lyrical sounds on his harp. Marcus watched her every step, and imagined the way the fire glow would play over her invisible body if the robe were removed.

She had not done this to spite the King. Her admission itself convinced him of that. She had merely retreated to another lie in order to feed him a story he would find palatable.

He suspected that the explanation was more complicated than the simple ones they had traded. When they got to Anglesmore, he would have to learn the truth.

CHAPTER 5

DYLAN REMAINED TETHERED to the wagon throughout the journey, a prisoner who walked while others rode. On the second day, as the way grew increasingly rough, Nesta could tell that he wearied. He finally fell, and the rolling wagon dragged him while he struggled vainly to scramble back on his feet.

Nesta smacked the shoulder of the wagoner and ordered him to stop. She climbed out and helped Dylan up, then told him to take her place in the wagon.

She soon had cause to regret her generosity. Her thin shoes offered little protection and she felt every rut and rock in the road. Marcus, riding at the lead of the entourage, glanced back and noticed her walking. He turned his horse aside and waited for the wagon to catch up.

As they passed, he fell into place behind her. She could feel the horse's breath on her shoulder, and its rider's attention on her progress.

Suddenly the horse moved beside her. A looming body leaned, and a vise of an arm imprisoned her waist. The world shook, spun, and blurred, and the next moment she was sitting sideways on the horse, in front of Marcus.

She frowned up at him. "What are you doing?" His face was very close. Too close. All of him was.

"Keeping a prideful woman from becoming a cripple before the day is out."

He retook his place in the lead. She twisted and stretched to see the wagon, but his body blocked her view of the women and other riders. And theirs of her.

They rode in a heavy silence, and the stomp of the horse's hooves beat out the rhythm of time that had slowed. She silently cursed the stupid flutters beating their way up from her stomach to her throat. She grew too conscious of the chest pressing her shoulder, and of the breath titillating her cheek, and of the fingers firmly resting on her waist, steadying her so she did not fall from her perch. She worried that his hand would move but also admitted dismally that a part of her was urging it to do so.

She groped for an excuse to get off the horse. "We should stop to eat soon, shouldn't we?"

"I did not intend to for some time. Are you hungry?"

"Aye."

His hand left her, and pulled at a leather string around his neck. A little sack emerged from under his tunic. "Open it."

Inside the sack were small pieces of dried venison. She wasn't really hungry, but she plucked one out anyway since she had claimed she was. "Despite a wagon and a mule packed with provisions, you wear your meal?"

"I am accustomed to wearing it."

"You hunger easily?"

"It is a habit, that is all." He tucked the sack away, and gestured to the terrain that they passed. "You must be glad to finally return to Wales. It has been a long time since you left."

"Too long." Not very long at all, actually. Did he suspect as much? He did not appear to be probing for information, but she had learned not to underestimate this man.

"It is much as you remember it, is it not?"

"Little has changed."

Very little. The Welsh travelers they passed

were a people always at a disadvantage under English law. The small towns were the domains of English merchants. The lands produced wealth that flowed to English coffers.

Her father had taught her to see all of this when, after her brother died and Llygad ap Madoc resigned himself to having no male heir, he had begun to open his elder daughter's eyes to the realities of their world.

The view was not all bleak, however. The English, both the marcher lords of old and the new lords established after the defeat of Prince Llywelyn fifty years ago, might claim this land as theirs, but the Welsh knew differently.

The mountains and ridgeways belonged to them alone. The bards kept the history and legends alive. The chieftains still dealt with their people in ways no English overlord could ever replace. At the *cymanfaoedd,* the hilltop assemblies, the people renewed their true allegiances.

These western lands might be thought a part of England now, but *Cymru* lived on as a shadow nation, waiting to be reborn to the light.

"We should arrive at Anglesmore in two days," Marcus said. "Your sister and I will marry soon after we get there."

"I cannot condone such a hasty marriage. She will need some time to accommodate herself to this."

"She had weeks in London for that."

"As her mind is now, it will be little more than rape if you do not wait. Or are you one of those men who assume that women can be given pleasure even as they are forced?"

The body pressing her side stiffened. She looked up and saw a tightness in his expression.

"I am not a man who believes that, Nesta. Which is why I want you to change her thinking."

"It is not for me to change her thinking, but you. If you became familiar to her, she might soften her opinions."

"I do not think she will soften any opinion until you give her permission. Since your plan to spirit her away has failed, it is time for you to do so. For the sake of your family, and her."

He raised his hand to signal a stop to the men behind him, and guided his horse into the moor. "Now, we will rest, and then the bard can walk again and you will return to the wagon. Since we speak of my marriage to your sister, the pleasure I have taken in holding you here should not continue."

"He watches you. They all do. When you came back to the main fire that first night, all the men watched, but especially him."

Genith's low words whispered into Nesta's ear as they lay beneath the stars, wrapped together in their blankets. All around them other bundles slept, the women on one side of the fire and the men on the other.

Nesta knew which man Genith meant. She had walked away from Marcus that night to break the magic of his eyes, but her heart had pounded so loud and long that Dylan's music barely penetrated her awareness. It had pounded the same way most of this afternoon after his hands lifted her down from the horse.

"It was not unkind, the way he looked at you, but a little frightening and dangerous," Genith added in a thoughtful tone. "I don't think a man has ever looked at me like that."

"That is because you are virtuous. I am a whore, so men feel free to look. It doesn't mean anything except that all men are lustful, and will look thus at any woman if the world says they can."

"You are not a whore. I know that."

"It does not matter what you believe, or even what is true. The world has decided, and so men do not hide their thoughts. But they are well aware of you, Genith, in a more respectful way. You are very beautiful, far more beautiful than me, and all who see you notice."

Genith did not disagree. Nesta guessed that by now Genith found it commonplace that everyone thought her entrancing. On seeing her sister after eight years, Nesta herself had been astonished. They shared similar features, but it was as if God had used the older face for practice and then, on forming Genith, had corrected His errors and achieved perfection.

Genith rose on her arm and looked to where Marcus slept near the horses. "He guards them as if he thinks someone will steal them during the night."

Not someone, Nesta thought. *Me.* The idea had crossed her mind, and she did not care for the evidence that Marcus had guessed that.

Normally she could disarm such suspicions with a few smiles and a bit of teasing. The thing about having men look at her with lust was that it made them vulnerable, and she was not above using that. Marcus, unfortunately, seemed to see through the ploy every time. Worse, as he had shown in the cottage, he also had the weapon this time.

She heaped silent curses on Edward and his chancellor Stratford. Why couldn't they have chosen a stupid man for Genith? Saints knew the English included enough of them. Or at least chosen one whose looking could be used, rather than shamefully savored? This man was making everything much more difficult than it should be.

"Have you decided what we are going to do?" Genith sounded fretful and confused.

She wrapped her arms around Genith, and relished the sisterly bond so much that her heart whispered a traitorous cheer that the escape had failed. "I know what to do. Sleep now, and do not worry."

She was lying. She had no idea what to do. Her conversation with Marcus on the horse had revealed more than he intended, however, so she at least knew how to thwart his plans until she figured out the rest.

Marcus pushed them along at a good pace, but once they crossed from Clun into his own lands that changed. Their approach to his home slowed as he paused to greet farmers along the road. In two villages he made the retinue wait while he dismounted and spoke at length with the reeves. Nesta overheard talk of wives and kinsmen, and not only discussions about duties and sheep and such.

Anglesmore proved an impressive castle that showed signs of recent expansion. The folk greeted their lord's return with good cheer. By

the time she climbed out of the wagon in the
inner yard, Nesta knew that Marcus's return
was welcomed and not dreaded.

She found that disheartening. Dissatisfaction
would have been more useful to her. She wasn't
surprised by the contentment, however. She
knew something of the recent history of this
place. For a horrible few years the people of
Anglesmore had suffered under the worst of
men. Even if Marcus had proven less than fair,
they would have been grateful to have him instead.

During the confusion of unloading the
wagon, Nesta saw Marcus approach Genith.
Before she could get to them, Marcus had
guided her sister through the manor house's
doorway.

Annoyed by the distractions that had permitted his quick move, she attached herself to the
steward and nagged along the settlement of herself and the other women into a chamber.

She prayed that her sister would have the
sense to neither agree nor disagree to whatever
Marcus commanded. In fact, she counted on
Genith knowing not to say anything at all.

"Three days hence."

Genith did not even flinch when Marcus informed her of the quick wedding. For a girl who had shed a lot of tears on the first day of their journey, she remained remarkably calm. She sat on a stool not more than an arm's span away from his chair, like a lovely form carved out of serenity.

She was one of the most beautiful females he had ever seen. As a boy he had dreamt of such ladies, and of possessing one when he reclaimed his place. From the shadows of the fetid alleys, he had watched them in the London markets, imagining himself dressed as richly as they were and not in rags, buying them small luxuries and receiving warm smiles in return.

He had been a smooth courtier in those fantasies, a champion of jousts and a hero of battles, and not a London gutter rat. In the pageant of his mind, his bed had been shared by many ladies of noble breeding before he finally took the hand of a sweet, innocent, perfectly beautiful girl in marriage.

Now the end of the boyhood dream sat within reach, but she moved him not at all. His lack of desire irritated him. So did her total absence of reaction.

"Have you nothing to say, my lady?"

Her face lifted, and her dark, vacant eyes regarded him. "We have not been betrothed."

"We will do it this evening."

"That will be a very short betrothal."

"If you had not taken ill in London, it would have been much longer."

For an instant she reminded him of Nesta. Not in her features, which were always similar, but in a fleeting spark of expression that indicated the mind was not quite as vacant as the eyes.

"I was not ill in London. I lied, in the hopes Nesta would hear of the marriage and come."

Her honesty about the ploy surprised him. "You sought delay so that your sister would be with you when you wed?"

"I sought delay so she might come and save me before I wed."

"Why did you want to be saved? Were you afraid?"

"I was not born for this marriage. You are beneath me. My father was *uchelwyr,* and the blood of kings and princes flows in me. I am meant to marry into another family of royalty." She insulted him calmly, as if explaining something so accepted that it needed no apology.

Marcus experienced irritation that she had been fed such ancient, useless ideas. There was no nobility left in Wales, and the lineages Llygad and others like him claimed were little more than creative concoctions. Genith had no doubt been taught them as great truths, however, and he had just spent two weeks riding all over England tracking her down because of it.

"Your sister has the same blood, but she married other than royalty."

"That marriage was arranged by Archbishop Stratford, as a way to make my sister invisible. The stories about her embarrassed the Queen, and the Archbishop convinced the King to do it. They also hoped that with her gone the stories would die, and that my father might be less angry. But he did not approve of the marriage, and it only made things worse."

So, Stratford had been dabbling in this affair from the start. Marcus was learning more from this girl in one conversation than he probably ever would from Nesta. "Was your sister forced into the marriage?"

She shook her head. "She agreed. I think she also hoped that it would lessen my father's anger, and have him make peace with the King. And so she left me."

Her last words came less calmly, and her eyes turned sad. Marcus pictured that leave-taking, with Nesta preparing to do her penance in Scotland and Genith, a child still, losing the only family left to her.

"Genith, you may think this marriage beneath you, but it is a necessary one. With it, you and your sister will be together again. Without it, the men who followed your father will die as traitors and thieves. We will be betrothed tonight and wed three days hence."

Again, no reaction came from her. She looked at him so blandly that it entered his mind that she did not know what marriage meant. *That* was the last thing he wanted to deal with.

"Come with me now, Genith. I will present you to the people."

He took her hand and led her down to the hall. She did not deny him the touch, but there was not true acceptance. Her fingers did not move, and remained limp and lifeless in his.

A chaos of activity waited in the hall. Squires removed armor from knights, and servants bustled around preparing for the evening meal. It took three calls for Marcus to command everyone's attention. The noise dimmed until silence reigned.

"I bring you your new lady, whom our good king has given to me to wife. Lady Genith is the younger daughter of Llygad ap Madoc. By this union, the King absolves Llygad of his treason. Our son will carry the noble blood of both England and *Cymru,* and will be a new lord for a new age of harmony in these lands."

He had chosen his words carefully, and practiced them during the journey. His pride in his newfound eloquence was ruined, however. Halfway through his little speech he completely lost the rapt attention of his people.

He saw it happening. First one glance away, then another. One head turning slightly, then a whole group of them. Finally the gazes shifted as one until everyone in the hall looked not to him, but to a spot behind him, just left of his shoulder.

When he finished, no one reacted because no one had noticed.

He turned his head to see the cause of the rudeness.

Nesta stood at the bottom of the stairway. She stayed in the shadow while Genith glowed in the light, but she might have been emitting rays of fire, so totally did she fascinate the people.

Marcus could almost hear the reaction to her. *So, that is she. The elder daughter. The King's whore. The wronged woman. The Welsh temptress. The heir to Llygad.*

She stood like a queen, self-possessed and shameless. Marcus half expected the Welsh in the hall to drop to their knees.

It occurred to him that Stratford may have made a serious mistake in sending her here.

He turned to Genith. "Go to your sister. Tell her about the betrothal and wedding, so that she can prepare you."

✦ ✦ ✦

"What did you speak of?" Nesta demanded as soon as she and Genith entered their chamber.

"The marriage." Genith strolled about, checking the room's measure. Her wandering glance took in the one bed, and the pallets waiting for the servants. Stepping around the one stool, she ended up by the window, and peered down into the yard below.

"Nothing else?"

"Nothing else."

"He did not question you about why you left me, and where you were going? He did not seek information from you?"

"We spoke only of the marriage he plans to make with me. It will be in three days. We will be betrothed tonight."

"Saints. He said soon, but I did not expect *this* soon. A betrothal binds you as surely as a wedding."

"I know." Genith rested her elbows on the window niche's edge and gazed out the thick slit in the wall. "Where did they take Dylan?"

"He is in a cellar chamber, beneath the north tower."

"Will Marcus hang him?"

"There is no proof that Dylan is with Father's men. Nothing has been sworn against him. I do

not think that Marcus will condemn a man
without just cause."

"What if he is very angry?"

"If anyone pays, it will be me." Nesta slid her
arm around Genith's waist. "You know what
to do?"

"Aye."

"Can you do it?"

Genith nodded. "I can do it."

CHAPTER 6

ANGLESMORE WAS A man's world. Nesta had absorbed that impression on riding through the gate, but it became abundantly obvious as the household gathered for the evening meal.

There were many more males than females. Furthermore, although some of the women showed aging faces, almost all the men's were youthful. Boys crammed the lower tables and created a raucous noise that thundered through the great hall. Marcus had an abundance of squires, and even his knights appeared new to their spurs.

Nesta knew why. There were no older men because they all had been killed. After the siege in which Marcus's father had lost this castle, there had been a massacre.

The noise diminished to a gentle roar when she and Genith entered. Many of those male eyes were momentarily distracted by her sister's beauty.

Marcus waited in front of the high table. He had donned a courtly sapphire pourpoint that emphasized his broad shoulders and lean muscularity. His dark blond hair had been neatly groomed, although errant short locks insisted on carelessly skimming his temples. His face, which could form harsh planes in anger, appeared calm and beautiful in the hall's glow of candles and torches.

Nesta's heart rose at the sight of him, and she glanced anxiously at her sister. Arguments and browbeating could be thwarted, but what if Genith became mesmerized by the man himself?

He pointedly did not look at her, but only Genith. Nesta felt herself melting all the same, and once more checked for Genith's reaction. She needn't have worried. Genith seemed not to notice Marcus's appeal, but only his danger.

As they approached the high table, Genith's hand suddenly gripped hers. "Look," she whispered desperately.

Nesta tore her attention from Marcus. Another man was easing over to stand beside his lord. Nesta took in the man's priestly vestments.

Marcus intended to perform the betrothal
now, prior to the meal, with the whole household as witnesses.

Genith's grip got tighter. "Not here, in front
of hundreds. I cannot."

"Request the chapel. It is a small thing, and
he will not deny you."

They found themselves at the table, facing
Marcus and the priest. Marcus did not appear
eager, but neither did he appear unkind.

"I regret that you do not have a kinsman
here, Genith, but although it is customary for
one to give me your hand, it is not necessary,"
he said.

"Nay, not necessary." She still clenched
Nesta's hand, and her trembling traveled
through that connection.

Nesta squeezed back in reassurance, and tried
to transfer some will to her.

It seemed to work. Genith's shoulders
squared. Her grip relaxed. "My sister is here, so
I am content that my family witnesses this. I
would prefer the chapel to this hall filled with
drink and ill-mannered boys, however. Such an
occasion deserves more dignity, and the presence of God, to my mind."

Nesta almost swatted her sister's shoulder.
They needed Marcus moved by a shy girl's fears,
not challenged by a proud one's demands.

Marcus's gaze sharpened. "We will do it as you prefer, Genith."

The priest led the way out to a chorus of objections from people who didn't want to miss the spectacle. Into the yard they filed, and on to the chapel, with a few knights following to bear witness. They entered the ancient structure built in the Norman style with a high stone ceiling and thick walls that kept it cold and dark.

The priest lit some candles and then beckoned Genith to stand beside Marcus. The lord's closest retainers gathered around. With heavy solemnity, the priest began rambling a benediction.

"I am not willing." Genith spoke so lowly that Nesta doubted that anyone had heard but herself. Even she would have missed it if she had not been straining her ears.

Nay, one other heard. Marcus's head snapped around.

The prayer droned on.

"I am not willing." Clearer this time, like a melodic response to the priest's Latin.

The priest glanced at her, but continued. The barest stirring flexed through the knights.

"I am not willing." A shout this time. A desperate yell. "I am *not willing*."

The last words bounced off the stones.

Genith backed away from Marcus, and shouted her denial again.

The priest halted his benediction, and stared aghast at Genith. The knights exchanged stunned looks. As the last of Genith's shouts died away into a brittle silence, Nesta grabbed her sister and pushed her toward the doorway before anyone could gather their wits.

One person in the chapel did not appear astonished. The lord of the manor silently watched their retreat. Nesta could not ignore that the dark anger in his eyes was not aimed at Genith.

"I am not sure what to do, my lord. One hears of such things, of course, but in my experience I have never been faced with it."

Father Robert wrung his hands with distress. He was a portly young man, recently ordained, and Marcus did not doubt that he had no experience with such things, since he possessed little experience at all.

"Normally such a problem is dealt with earlier, and the woman listens to reason. But this . . . so public . . ."

Not *so* public, Marcus thought. Not in front of the whole household. He had at least been spared that, although soon everyone would hear of it. Still, he should probably thank Nesta. Maybe he would, after he finished warming her rump with his indignation.

"What would you require to go forward?" he asked.

The priest looked miserable. "She will have to tell me freely that she has changed her mind."

"How freely?"

A shocked expression flitted over Father Robert's round face, but he swallowed it. "I suppose she need only say the words to me."

"Then I must see that she agrees to say them, mustn't I?"

Father Robert cast Marcus a horrified glance. He sighed hopelessly, and aimed for the doorway like a man who didn't want to know what would happen.

Marcus gestured for his knights to leave as well. They headed back to the hall, but one stayed behind. Paul, his closest friend, allowed his outrage to show once they were alone. He paced around, spitting curses that desecrated the chapel.

Paul finally squared off and gave the matter a sharp contemplation while he scratched his head through his curly dark locks. His full lips pursed in annoyance. "That girl is too proud, Marcus, and stupid as well if she dares such an insult."

Immersed in his own dark anger, Marcus only

knew one thing for sure. The woman who had dared this insult was not stupid.

"We will keep her from food until she comes around. Once we get her mark on the contract, this priest will not ask questions, I'll see to that," Paul said.

"I will not starve her."

"It is that or beating her. Otherwise she will pretend to agree, and the next time in front of a priest she will deny you again."

"I will not beat her, either."

Paul's gaze caught Marcus's, and understanding flickered. With a resigned sigh, he looked away. "Pity to lose the lands. Llygad's are no great prize, but the other property promised to you would bring a good income."

"I do not intend to lose anything, but I cannot force the girl. You know that."

Paul's expression said he did know that. Someone else had surmised as much, too. Like an opponent in a joust, she had ridden a few passes and immediately spotted his weakness.

Nay, not stupid. Brilliant.

He left Paul to go find the woman who had expertly foiled him today.

The chamber door did not crash open. It swung slowly, gently pressed by a strong, masculine hand. The quiet entry put Nesta on her guard more than if a battering ram had pounded the door to pieces.

Marcus stood at the threshold, his stance as casual as if he visited merely to pass some time. He filled the doorway with his strength, but no bluster or threat puffed him up. With his golden hair and skin and blue courtly dress, he appeared quite magnificent and disarming.

Nesta wasn't fooled in the least. Marcus was dangerously angry. It could be seen in the wicked humor of his eyes and the line of his crooked smile. It oozed out of him and affected the air like an approaching storm.

Genith did not see or feel it. Her tense body relaxed with relief.

"I must insist on staying with my sister," Nesta announced.

"That is not necessary. She is in no danger from me." He put a silken emphasis on the "she."

"You have no reason to be afraid, Genith. I blame myself, for not getting assurance of your willingness when we spoke today." He addressed her sister, but he looked only at her and Nesta knew that he did not blame himself at all.

In her relief, Genith broke into a bedazzling smile that would soothe any man in the world. Unfortunately its effect was wasted on Marcus, who had begun a predatory circling of the spot where Nesta stood.

"Go to the hall now, Genith, and take the women with you. I would speak with Nesta alone."

Happy and ignorant, Genith gathered the servants and left. As soon as the door closed, a new fire entered Marcus's eyes that more obviously revealed his mood.

The silence became suffocating. Nesta could almost hear the battle for control taking place in the man pacing around her. She closed her eyes and braced herself for a blow.

"Nay, lady, if I decide to do that, it will not be here. I will make your humiliation at least as public as mine was."

She opened her eyes and sneaked a glance at him, and decided that keeping silent would be the wisest choice.

"By now the hall is full of talk of it. But if I drag you down there by the hair and bend you over my knee, it will give everyone a better spectacle to laugh about."

"Since I am not the woman who denied you in the chapel, they will conclude that you try to coerce my sister by unjustly hurting me. Would you have your people think you are such a man?"

"If I seek to compel your sister, there are better ways to do it."

"Is that a threat?"

"It is the contemplation of a man who will not be manipulated by a troublesome sister. I warned you not to play me for your fool again."

"What do you contemplate? Beating her?"

"It has been suggested."

"I do not believe you will do that."

"You are so sure? Do not be." He snapped it as an angry warning.

But she *was* sure. There was much she did not know about this man, but she knew this.

Her certainty must have shown, because he stopped his pacing right in front of her and speared her with a steely gaze. "You are well contented that you have bent me to your will, aren't you?"

"This is not about you and me, but my sister."

"Nay, woman, it is all about you and me. Your sister is merely the prize."

He crossed his arms over his chest and inspected her. A glint, no more, of the other way it was about him and her entered his eyes, but his annoyance burned it away.

"I can make quick work of this in other ways, Nesta. I could threaten to hang the bard. If the price of his life was her hand, do you think Genith would continue to withhold it?"

The suggestion horrified her. Not just because Genith might submit, but also because she might not.

She resented his using such a bluff. She stuck her face up at him. "If this is between you and me, leave innocents out of it. Besides, you will not do that either. In fact, I do not think that you will coerce her in any way."

"Do not goad me by counting on my being weak, lady."

"I do not accuse you of weakness, but of honor. If you were a man who forced women, you would have already forced *me*."

It was a mistake to say that. She knew it as soon as the words blurted out. His expression darkened more, but a new danger slid through him. A sensual power flowed, shading and sharpening his anger with her, giving it a new edge.

Their mutual craving was suddenly, starkly there, absorbing her, trying to pull her across the narrow space separating them. Its intensity frightened her. It also excited her.

She could see him grabbing her, pulling her to him, kissing her with the confident possession he had in the cottage, obliterating her control and dragging her into abandon.

He did not reach for her. Her relief was tinged with a disappointment that horrified her.

He did not touch her, but neither did he retreat. He made no effort to quell what had risen between them and it remained thick in the air, an enlivening, threatening lure.

"As you can see, there would be no forcing to it, Nesta," he said quietly, cruelly naming her weakness to him. "To imply there would be is dishonest of you. Nor is it goodness or honor that restrains me. You are my king's woman and my future wife's sister. To take you would be both stupid and contemptible."

That certainly laid it out baldly. Not only the desire but also her expected compliance, and the impossibility, and impracticality, of ever acting on what wanted to happen between them.

A wistful sadness welled inside her chest. He had said nothing that she did not already know. A foolish corner of her heart ached at hearing it put into words, however. That uncontrollable part of her was shameful, and potentially very perilous. Unfortunately, it appeared to be growing, and making her more stupid with each day.

"It occurs to me that the easiest course is to lock you away, so that Genith does not have you whispering in her ear. With a little time away from your influence, I think that she will come around."

"A little time was all I asked to begin with. If you agree to that, there is no need to lock me away. I will say nothing to dissuade her."

He smiled. "So you think that a week of wooing is all it will take?"

"Well, two weeks perhaps."

He thought about that, and nodded vaguely. She was sure that her exhale of relief sounded as loud as a gale of wind.

Marcus appeared accepting of the delay. She assumed he would leave.

Instead, he finally did touch her. Not with a grab for passion, however. His hand went to her face, and his warm palm pressed her cheek. He looked down at her with a thoughtful, absorbing gaze.

"What mischief are you up to, Nesta?"

None. I only do my duty to my sister. The words did not come out, because her stupid heart had risen to her throat, blocking the sounds.

His palm stayed for a delicious moment, tantalizing her. She wanted to push it away, but she could not. She could barely breathe.

Suddenly, his touch was gone. With purposeful strides, he left the chamber.

She continued feeling that brief touch as if he had branded her. Free of his absorbing presence, however, she began to worry about the implications of his last question.

Aye, why couldn't the King have chosen a stupid man?

Marcus would not threaten to hang Dylan to coerce Genith, but he might have to hang the bard all the same. It was time to decide about that.

He did not return to the hall, but instead took the stone stairs down to the cellar chambers. As he descended, the glimmer of a candle turned a corner and moved up toward him. It illuminated a happy girlish smile and dark eyes not nearly so vacant as normal. Whatever private thoughts amused Genith, they, and the smile, disappeared in a blink when she noticed him standing on the step where he had paused.

She started, and almost dropped the large sack that she carried under one arm. Dylan's sack, containing his harp. Marcus looked at it pointedly and Genith hoisted it a bit higher, as if she feared his taking it away.

"You have been visiting the prisoner, Genith?"

"It is a charity to visit the imprisoned, I was always taught. I trust it does not displease you, my lord."

The girl was quick, he had to give her that. Not as quick as Nesta, nor as smooth, but then Genith was much younger and had less practice.

"He asked me to take the harp, since his chamber is so damp that he fears it will be damaged there if he is kept long."

"Bring it to the hall, and I will remove it to my chamber later. No harm will come to it there."

She appeared a bit disappointed by that. Balancing her candle and hugging her precious burden, she climbed the stairs until she had passed him.

He started down, but her call stopped him. "My lord, perhaps during some meals you might let him come up to sing. The people would like that, I think."

He was supposed to woo and placate this girl, and that included giving in to her little requests unless he had a good reason not to. His only one right now was that he might execute Dylan, and a dead man cannot sing. "If he stays with us, I will consider what you ask."

She favored him with a dazzling smile. It made her look more like her sister.

No guard stood outside the prisoner's chamber since none was really needed. The key hung on the wall, and as Marcus took it down he realized that Genith must have let herself in as well if she was given the harp.

He unlocked the door and pushed it open. An amazing sight awaited him.

Dylan did not lie on the floor in the darkness. Rather, two candles burned on a makeshift table, and a rough bed had been constructed against one wall. Someone had thoughtfully provided a crockery chamber pot. The remains of a good meal, the same food being enjoyed in the hall, sat on a plate beside a small jug.

The young man jumped to his feet from where he lounged on the bed. He raked his long hair back from his face so that his brave indifference could be seen.

Marcus looked at the straw and blankets, and thought of the girl who had just left, and decided that henceforth there would be a guard after all.

He walked over to the table and lifted the jug. Wine, not ale.

"You are comfortable, Dylan?"

The youth regarded him with the fiery defiance he had shown from the start. "Comfortable enough."

More than enough, to Marcus's mind. It was a wonder the chamber had not been decorated with carpets and tapestries.

He knew how these comforts had come here. Not through Genith and Nesta, although they may have seen to some. Others, servants and squires and even knights, had brought them. As lord he was sworn to the English crown, but many within these walls had a lot of Welsh blood flowing in them. Bards were revered among the Welsh, and word had spread that one now lived in the cellar.

"How old are you?"

"Nineteen."

"Are you one of Llygad's men?"

He only got a hot stare in response to that question.

"Nesta said that Genith was headed to her father's men when we caught up with you."

"Doesn't mean I'm with them. The woman paid me a coin to help escort her sister. Like most, I can use it."

"If you intended to escort Genith to Llygad's men, you would have to know where those men are."

A touch of fear flickered in Dylan's eyes, barely visible among the rasher, belligerent lights. "The others knew, not me."

"I think that you are lying."

"Can't prove it."

Of course he could. It would not take much

to break this one. He would not even have to raise a hand. Dylan's thinness spoke of a life that had known hunger, and he would fear knowing that gnawing pain again.

"Do you know who I am, Dylan? Where you are?"

"Aye."

"Then you know that I am one of the lords who need not wait on the King's courts. I hold ancient rights of judgment on these lands. If I say that you hang, you hang. If I say that you are beaten, the lash will fall. You helped to steal what was mine, and I think that you knew it was mine as you did so. Tomorrow I will ask again if you know where Llygad's men are. Think about your answer tonight, because if you lie again I will not be inclined to mercy."

The youth did not so much as flinch through all of it. He just stood there, braver than a man twice his size would be, hearing the ultimatum that might mean his death. As Marcus left, he was treated to that bold glare once more.

He climbed the stairs. Tomorrow he would decide whether to carry out his threat, but he already knew what the decision would be. He should hang the bard because, as Paul had said in the village, Dylan was either a thief or a traitor, and most likely the latter.

He wouldn't, however, and not because it would distress the girl whose favor he needed. He wouldn't because Dylan's rebellious insolence reminded him too much of someone else. Himself, not so long ago.

CHAPTER 7

HE BURNED.

Nesta's presence fueled the hellfire that tortured him.

Flames licked at him during meals. Her sister sat between them, but even the barrier of Genith's ice could not cool the heat.

During the day, Nesta had only to walk nearby or look at him to make his blood crackle. At night a blaze roared. As he gazed out at the stars or lay restless in a bed damp with sweat, his imagination knew no constraints. He mentally made love to her a hundred times, often in ways he had never taken the time to try with other women.

For a few days he tried avoiding her, but that did not help much. He would enter a chamber and know at once she had been there from the lingering spring scent, and her ghost would invade his head to fan the embers. And so, since it made no difference, he stopped avoiding her at all.

Which only meant that he burned all the more.

Paul noticed. A week after returning to Anglesmore they were walking across the yard when Nesta passed them going in the other direction. Marcus was so distracted in watching her that he stepped on a chicken.

Amidst the flying feathers and squawks, Paul pointed a finger right at his face. "I speak as your friend and not your sworn man now. *Don't.* If you want the sister to have cause to deny you, that is the best. If you want the King to reduce you to the smallest of men, that will do it. Nothing but trouble there, and you know it."

Marcus laughed. "Hell, but that's the truth. Still, I find myself not sleeping well these days."

"Then take a servant or call a woman to come from the town. Or better yet, get on with wooing the one you are intended to bed."

Marcus abruptly turned their talk to other things. The last thing he wanted to discuss was the wooing. Paul had helped him plan his gentle assault on Genith as thoroughly as a military campaign, since Paul had a natural talent for such things.

Unfortunately, Paul did not have to execute the strategy, Marcus did.

It wasn't going so well.

He himself had no talent with such things. The kind of pursuit learned by poor boys in London was very different from what noble-women expected. Later, during his visits to court, he saw how the game was played but felt stupid when he attempted it himself.

Fortunately there had been enough ladies who made it easy, and did not require much wooing at all. Some actually seemed to find his lack of courtly skills charming. His lovers at Anglesmore had been much the same way, women who let him know they were willing and who did not expect him to plead and cajole.

He preferred it that way. He liked bold women. Experienced ones. Women who did not expect to be talked out of their virtue with poetry and lies. The kind of women who ac-cepted sensual pleasure as a joy, and who did not think it shameful. He had little interest in the ones who denied their desires. He had no pa-tience at all with the ones who yielded but later fretted about having sinned.

"It is time to take her to the town and show

her off. The people are curious anyway, and you can buy her gifts," Paul said, forcing the conversation back to the grand plan and reminding him of the next step.

"Tomorrow, if the weather is fair, I intend to do that."

Marcus wasn't sure that he actually said the response that ran in his mind. Just then Nesta walked by again, heading to the garden, and for that brief span of time she was the only thing that existed.

He found himself strolling after her.

Paul hurried to catch up. "What *in hell* are you *doing*?"

"I am just going to tell her that I will take Genith to the town tomorrow."

Paul threw up his hands. "You are mad. I am sworn to a madman."

Marcus shook off the voice of doom at his ear. He wasn't a madman. He was being very practical. The wooing wasn't going well, but one word from Nesta and Genith would thaw.

Nesta lined up little covered pots that looked to contain ointments. Then she plucked a rolled parchment from her basket, and unfurled it on the two boards pushed together to form a crude table. A tiny brush emerged next, and she settled herself on the sun-bathed bench, opened the tiny pots, and bent over her work.

Marcus watched from under a tree near the portal. Absorbed in her preparations, she had not heard him enter.

He smiled ruefully at his predicament while he walked toward her. He had never wanted a woman in this relentless way before. Actually, he had never much wanted any particular woman at all before. Now he was suffering this hell because of the only woman for miles around whom he dared not touch.

Nesta heard his approach, and glanced her acknowledgment before returning to her parchment.

He stood over her and watched the tiny brush make precise little strokes of color. He peered into the pots of inks. "You have no blue."

"It is hard to come by."

"The monks at the Cistercian abbey probably have some, and also more parchment if you need it. Tomorrow I will take Genith to the town, and while there I will send to the abbey for both."

"I could use the parchment, but the blue is too expensive. I am accustomed to working without it."

She was finishing a design based on the one she had carved into the dirt that night on their journey. It still did not include him, but he would buy her the blue anyway and to hell with the cost.

"Are you succeeding with my sister? As I promised, I have not whispered in her ear," she said, as if guessing the excuse he had devised in order to stand beside her a while.

"I am knocking on a barred door. One made of ice, not wood. She is polite, but distant. I think that I bore her."

"I doubt that you bore her. More likely you frighten her."

"I can't imagine why. I am very mild with her. Besides, I don't frighten you, even when I want to."

She looked up, and an arrow of flame shot through his blood when her gaze met his. "That is not true, but you and I are speaking of two different kinds of fear, I think." She dipped her brush and returned her attention to the parchment. "As to my sister, why not allow Dylan to sing tonight? It will soften her much. She told me you had promised to consider it, but you have not done so and now she thinks that you do not care about her pleasure."

She was correct there. He didn't really give a damn about Genith's pleasure. Furthermore, the fact that the bard was still unpunished was no credit to either his strength as a lord or his duty to his king. He did not want songs in the hall reminding him of his weakness.

"It would also please *me* to have Dylan sing." Nesta looked up again, and favored him with a mesmerizing smile.

A brushfire of desire swept him in reaction to that smile. The corner of his sense that did not succumb, however, sharpened with suspicion. She was toying with him, despite surely knowing that he barely resisted grabbing her. Considering their isolation in this garden, she must have a good reason to dare it.

"If it will please both you and Genith, I can hardly refuse." He made a retreat before she had him forgetting his duty entirely and behaving like a fool. Or a madman.

Two days later, Nesta broke her fast quickly and hurried outside. Carts and wagons filled the yard. Every morning farmers brought in provisions to feed the large household and to trade among themselves, and she had formed a habit of frequently joining them.

She circled around, stopping to chat with the Welsh men and women who were regular participants of these morning markets. It had not taken her long to determine who might be an ally. In ten days she had learned much about the sentiments of the people, and who was complacent with England's yoke, and who was not. Those who disapproved of Genith's marriage had let it be known in subtle ways.

One of them, a burly, swarthy farmer named Iolo with whom she had become very friendly, was here today. She worked her way to the wall where he waited with his wagon. When she finally reached him she made a display of inspecting his chickens while she spoke.

"The designs are on their way?"

"Aye, my brother will seek out the man in Bala as you instructed, to sell his. The other went north with a wine merchant." He pressed two coins into her hand. "A pity you should see the least profit of anyone."

"With so many sales between me and the tapestry weavers, it is always thus."

Nesta stepped closer while she poked a fowl. "You will come again tomorrow morning, as promised?"

"I'll be here, my lady. Over by the keep, with meat and hides from my brother's farm."

Nesta returned to the hall, and sought out Marcus. He was sitting with his man, Paul. She stood by the table until he turned his attention to her.

"My sister says that although the town is small, one can find wares from all over there, even from Flanders and Castile."

"Many merchants who come to Wales travel north through these parts and stop there."

"I should like to go see it for myself tomorrow. I have been too long within these walls. It would please Genith to come again too, to show me the better shops. May we have your permission on this?"

He contemplated her with an enigmatic expression. "I will be visiting the farms tomorrow, so I cannot accompany you."

She already knew that. "Surely another can escort us. It is for our own pleasure, so we can admire the goods as women do. We will not stay long."

"I suppose that a knight will be protection enough, since you do not go far."

She turned to go, but paused and looked back at him. She began to express her gratitude for his allowing Dylan to sing the last two nights, but her voice died on her lips.

Her glance had caught his gaze scrutinizing her from head to toe, then lazily traveling back up again. She suddenly felt naked.

His gaze met hers. Except for their confrontation the first night here, he had done well in hiding his interest these last ten days. It was always there, however, shimmering through the air like the heat from a hearth, alerting her to his presence and to the looks she did not see. The hidden attention had left her unsettled enough, but now the mutual temptation silently roared between them.

She felt her color rise, and hurried away. She had been experiencing an inexplicable hesitation over her course of action. Marcus had just reminded her that there really wasn't any choice for many reasons, including the unholy passion that kept pulling them toward each other.

"Are you writing it as I told you?" Nesta peered over Genith's shoulder while her sister scratched her quill on the parchment.

"Aye, aye. This is stupid, though, and I don't know why I bother."

"I do not want him blamed."

Genith scratched out a mistake, and continued. "I do not much care if he is."

But I do, Nesta thought. Genith's letter to Marcus, explaining that her decision was not because of him, who had behaved most courteously, might not help very much. Hopefully, however, it would keep Stratford and the King from directing too much anger at him.

Still, he would be in the thick of it. That concerned her more than she wanted it to. None of this was really his fault. He only did the King's bidding. It did not seem fair that he should answer for things he could not affect.

Well, it wasn't her fault that he would. Still, she wanted to protect him as much as possible, in the small ways available to her.

"Be sure you include that you feel compelled to fulfill our father's wishes. Make that very plain."

"It is plain enough, three times over." Genith straightened and put down the quill. "Read it yourself, while I help with the packing."

Nesta snatched up the parchment. It was a new sheet, one of several that had arrived this morning from the abbey along with some inks. When Marcus took Genith to the town, he had not forgotten to send for it as he had promised.

Satisfied with Genith's letter, Nesta knelt beside her chest to finish her own packing. Garments had already been tucked in the sack, but now there were harder choices to make.

She examined the few personal items that she had brought from Scotland. The box of inks and brushes and quills would have to come, but that left little room for anything else. She should stuff in a few veils and one decent headdress, so she would not look too much a peasant when she met people of good blood.

The ancient gold armlet and her father's ring, all that remained of her family's status, would both be necessary.

She tucked the items into the sack, and it bulged like a sausage. Regretfully, she reached among the objects that would not fit, and lifted a stack of parchments. The notion of leaving them behind pained her.

Sitting cross-legged on the floor, she plucked at the yarn that bound them and read the top one. It was the first she had received from her father after going to Scotland. How excited she had been when it came, tucked in the bag of a jongleur headed for Argyle. She had gladly paid the coin her father had promised as a reward, and savored the words over and over until she knew them by heart.

That first letter had been gentle and endearing, but also critical of her decision to accept her marriage. She hadn't cared about that, but only that contact with her father had not been lost forever.

She had found a way to write back, and so other letters had come, full of his lyrical sentences full of grand dreams. She could tell from his references that not all of his missives completed their journeys, but several scrolls had found their way to her every year.

She pulled the final one from the bottom of

the stack. After she went to the convent the tone of the letters had changed, and the dreams had become plans. She had understood what lay within the cryptic messages, but this last one had been quite explicit.

No merchant or jongleur had been entrusted with this letter. One of her father's men had journeyed from Wales to place it in her hands. Her father had been ill when he sent it, and died before it reached her.

His last words. His dying command. That he had never seen her response with her promises did not make any difference.

She read it over several times, hearing her father's voice saying the words. She branded her mind with the marks his hand had made. Her gaze lingered on the last lines that expressed his love for her and Genith.

It was too explicit. A smart man would comprehend what it contained. She did not need to take it, but she dared not leave it.

She rose to her feet and carried it to the hearth. She lifted the roll to her lips and kissed this last physical vestige of Llygad ap Madoc. Blinking back tears, she threw it into the flames.

Swallowing her sadness, she tucked the sack under the bed and closed the chest. Eventually she would get its contents back. The day would come when Marcus would permit that.

Genith was instructing the servants on her packing. A veil of green silk, a little carved box, and a mirror of polished metal were lined up on the bed. At Genith's gesture, a servant reached for them.

"You cannot take the luxuries he bought you yesterday," Nesta said.

"You said one sack only, but these are small and will not take up much space."

"It is dishonest to keep his gifts even as you repudiate him."

Genith stroked the veil and pouted. "*You* are taking the parchment."

"Only so I can write to you, and I will leave a coin for it." Nesta pointed to several garments that had been discarded. "Take these, not the silk. Choose for practicality and warmth. Be sure to hide the sack under the bed when you are done." She strode to the door. "Get to bed as soon as possible. I will return shortly."

She hurried down to the hall where most of the household still gathered. The adults sat in groups, talking and listening to the music flowing from Dylan's harp. Children ran wild, playing games and tumbling about. Nesta settled herself among three ladies married to some of Marcus's knights.

Marcus sat at the high table with their husbands. The oldest man there, he still appeared very young tonight as he joined a boisterous conversation that had the men laughing and grinning.

The happy chaos filling the hall kept lapping over him, and he tolerated the interruptions as few lords would. When some boys' flying bean sack hit him in the head, he merely tossed it back and watched their play with an expression that suggested he would not mind joining them. When a small child climbed onto the table and crawled down its length, Marcus simply plucked the boy into his arms and kept talking until the apologetic mother fetched him.

Dylan's lyrical harp added more merriment to the chamber, but his performance this night was subdued. He only sang a few songs and mostly just played his instrument. On evenings past he had chatted with those around him, and Nesta had exchanged a few words with him each night. Now, however, he appeared disinterested in the household activity.

As the ladies engaged Nesta in spirited conversation, she watched Dylan carefully. The bard's expression looked very sour. On occasion his deft fingers grew clumsy on the strings. Finally he paused right in the middle of a melody and wiped his brow with his sleeve.

Some servants noticed. An old woman hobbled over and peered curiously at his face. The woman gestured for the guard who had brought the bard up from his chamber.

Dylan rose unsteadily, grasping his harp to his chest. The guard moved to help him, but suddenly another man was standing there. Marcus had noticed Dylan's condition too, and had come to investigate.

Nesta ran over. "He appears ill."

"Very ill, since it is the first time he has not scowled at me since we met." Marcus motioned to the guard. "Take him down, and get him another blanket and some ale."

Dylan barely reacted. Accepting the support of the guard, he began shuffling away.

Marcus's hand reached out to stop them. He gently relieved Dylan of the burden of the harp. "You will drop it on the stairs in your condition. It will be waiting for you where it always is."

The guard led Dylan away.

"Perhaps he is too ill for that cellar," Marcus said. "If I spared him from the noose, I don't want him to die from the damp."

"I think that he will be fine in his chamber, since you are sending a blanket."

"You think moving him up here too great a charity, Nesta?"

"Having gone below, I doubt he wants to move at all. Also, if he is really ill, it might be best not to have him near others who might catch the malady."

Marcus considered that. "I will have a fire pot brought down all the same. The weather is turning cold."

He walked back to his men, and Nesta narrowed her eyes on the harp that he carried.

Her plan had worked perfectly, except for that one detail.

CHAPTER 8

VERY FEW SOUNDS broke the stillness. Several fowl heralded the first light with clucks and squawks, and a dog barked in the outer yard, but no human noise came from the long shadows emerging in the dull grey world outside Nesta's window.

Nesta watched and waited. Behind her Genith breathed gently on the bed, and the servants were dead to the world. She guessed that they did not toss fretfully because they knew that she did the worrying for them.

She herself had not slept much. She had remained in the hall longer than she had planned, relishing the joyful noise. How much she envied those people, with their simple lives and pleasures. It reminded her of her girlhood, and the security of having a place in the world, of being one stone in a wall built over generations.

It had not only been the merriment that kept her in the hall. She had also stayed to watch Marcus. Pinned in place by a bittersweet melancholy, she had not been able to tear herself away from his presence. Her wistful mood had led her to see more of him than she ever had before.

Despite how his very person proclaimed his status as lord, there had been something about him that reminded her of the squires who gathered around him. Those boys sensed that they had an ally in him, and that he understood their explosive emotions. He was a god to them, and they found excuses to stay near him and curbed their worst excesses to please him.

She had seen more than that, however. Watching him with his people, she had known that he would not back down from the duty laid on his shoulders. He would indeed be in the thick of it. He would do it for his king and his family honor. He would do it for the lands and the power. He would do it because of the years when Anglesmore was lost to him.

He would do it for the same reason she would, because he had been born for it.

The grey outside turned silver, and then the first rays of gold peeked over the wall. Suddenly the silence was pierced by intrusive sounds that echoed unnaturally loud, of servants moving and horses snorting and people talking. Marcus and several other men came into view, dressed for riding, and grooms brought their horses to them.

She had not needed to watch for their departure. She admitted with some chagrin that she had stood by this window so that she could catch a final glimpse of him.

He mounted his horse and sat there, all golds and bronzes and tall strength. These last few weeks he had been an inconvenience. Before the day was out, he would be an enemy.

Suddenly his preparations halted and his body stilled. His gaze swept up the stones of the building until he was looking right at her window. She stepped back quickly, but not before she saw the thoughtful expression on his face.

Horses moved. A gate opened. The small retinue trotted from the yard.

Nesta stayed near the window, seeing that handsome face in her mind, picturing Marcus galloping toward the road. She let him disappear on the horizon of her imagination, then took a deep breath, swallowed the thickness in her throat, and spurred herself to action.

Shaking Genith and the women awake, she issued orders. "Rise and dress quickly and go down to the hall to break your fast. I will join you soon, but must do something first."

She left them and made her way to the stairs. Trusting that she would not meet any servants already beginning morning chores, she descended to the second level.

She had never been in Marcus's bedchamber, but she knew it was here, along with another that he used as a solar.

His chamber door was open, making it easy for her. She slipped inside and glanced around. The bed was luxurious enough, with its rich red draperies and feather mattress, but there was something spare about the rest of the furnishings. Nipping around the bed, she discovered a straw pallet on the floor under the window, as if a servant slept here and not outside the door.

She could not find what she sought, and cursed under her breath. It must be in the solar.

She hurried into the other chamber, and halted in her tracks. It was not deserted as she had assumed it would be. The steward sat at a table near the window, perusing accounts.

He looked up at her entrance. "My lady?"

She scrambled for an excuse for being here, and grabbed the only one that might make sense. "I hoped to find Sir Marcus and he was not in the hall. I have good news for him about my sister."

"He has already left. No doubt he will regret having done so if the news is that which he awaits."

"No doubt." She subtly examined the chamber. Her eyes lit on a familiar sack propped against the wall. Dylan's harp.

She desperately sought a reason to take it with her, but there wasn't any. The bard was ill, and would hardly be playing for entertainment in the early morning anyway. The steward appeared elbow deep in accounts, and she doubted he would leave this chamber soon.

Biting back her irritation, she retreated and headed down to the hall.

Her failure to get the harp created a terrible complication.

Noise wafted through the window from the yard. People shouted greetings and curses. The farmers were arriving with their provisions.

Nesta set a veil over Winnifred's head, draping it so it fluttered low on her brow and over her cheeks. She secured it in place with a rolled circlet of cloth, and examined the results. Winnifred was the youngest and tallest of Genith's servants, and the eyes peering back at her held wary fear.

Nesta flipped a long cloak around Winnifred,

pulling the edge high on her face. "You will be in no danger, I promise you. Everyone will understand that you only do my bidding."

Winnifred nodded. Nesta gave her one last inspection, grabbed a basket, and led the way down.

Through the hall they filed, and down to the yard. Nesta pulled open a door that led to the north tower's cellar and they aimed toward Dylan's chamber.

"How is the bard?" Nesta asked the guard.

"I brought him some bread and ale at dawn, and he appeared weak."

"Sir Marcus instructed that my woman is to tend to him. She is a healer and has brought some potions and herbs." She lifted the basket meaningfully.

The guard unlocked the door for them. After they entered, Nesta managed to ease it mostly closed. She greeted Dylan loudly, then stepped very near and whispered. "I could not get the harp. I am so sorry."

Dylan's bright eyes dulled. Winnifred began making noises with the basket and clucking about the prisoner's condition.

"Will you still do it? If you refuse, I cannot blame you, but—"

"I will do it." Dylan's expression appeared

bleak, but his voice carried resolve. "For my lady, I will do it."

Nesta didn't turn a hair at that. She was in no position to question the motives behind Dylan's choice. Besides, more than one just cause had been won because of a man's chivalrous love.

She gestured for Winnifred. "Good. Then let us tend to you."

A short while later, Nesta and the cloaked servant left the chamber. The prisoner was lying on the bed, huddled in blankets and face turned to the wall.

"We gave him a sleeping potion, and some herbs for the fever," Nesta told the guard as she closed the door. "He should sleep most of the day."

She caught up with the servant, and together they mounted the stairs and entered the yard. Iolo's wagon stood a few feet away from the cellar portal. When Nesta hailed him, he walked to the end of the wagon to greet her.

While their bodies blocked the view, a veiled and cloaked figure climbed into the wagon and crawled under the hides.

Sir Leonard's eyes glazed over long before they reached the town. Nesta and Genith continued to dull his wits with relentless chatter about women's things.

They gossiped about ladies he did not know. They debated at length the beauty of certain new fashions. Genith launched a chamber-by-chamber description of how she intended to turn Anglesmore inside out with new furnishings when she was mistress.

Once in the town, they dawdled in each shop, commenting in detail on the wares. By the time they had finished with the third one Sir Leonard looked like a man performing a penance he considered too great for even his worst sins.

"You must find this very dull, Sir Leonard," Nesta said as the trio headed toward a grocer's shop.

"Nay, nay, you and Lady Genith are delightful company."

"How courteous of you to say so. Still, if you would prefer to wait at the tavern, we will fetch you when we are done."

A bit of hope flickered in his filmy eyes. "My lord said—"

"Sir Marcus required your escort on the road for our safety. I doubt he expects you to follow us around here in the town. What could possibly happen to us now? Besides, I will confess that this is much less enjoyable when there is a restless man pacing around."

He debated it. "How many more shops do you think to visit?"

"No more than three or four."

She might better have said he was due for a flogging. "I suppose that I could wait in the tavern. . . ."

"We will be sure to meet you there when we are finished." She moved a little closer and smiled at him until he blushed. "I would consider this a great favor, and so would Marcus if he knew. I intend to speak with Genith about her future duties as a wife while we dally over these wares, but with you attending us . . ." She gave him a look that made clear just what duties she referred to.

He flushed deeper, and without another word aimed his steps toward the sanctuary of the tavern.

They visited the grocer, but did not stay long. Taking Genith's arm, Nesta strolled along the town's main road until they were out of sight of the tavern. Ever so calmly, they turned between two buildings. Much less calmly, they quickly walked back along the alley until they reached their horses.

Nesta slipped a coin to the boy who held the

horses, and he asked no questions. He helped them both to mount, and then they were trotting through lanes, aiming for the open fields. Once there they rode as if the devil followed.

Nesta did not catch her breath until they pulled up at the designated crossroads. With that deep inhale came the full realization that there was no turning back now.

Iolo and his wagon waited for them. Another man stood beside the big burly farmer. Dylan had shed the veil and cloak, and paced expectantly.

His expression of worry cleared as soon as they approached. He reached in the wagon for the two sacks Winnifred and he had hung on their bodies under the cloak, and tied them to the saddles.

Nesta caught Dylan's arm. "You can still change your mind. The danger here is greatest for you. If you are caught this time, there will be no reprieve, because we steal horses now and the blame for it will fall on you."

"My lady, Carwyn Hir needs the horses more than Marcus of Anglesmore." He swung up on a mule that Nesta had bought from Iolo. "If I could have found a way to steal ten, I would have done it."

Put that way, she didn't feel so much a criminal. With thanks to the good Iolo, they headed northwest across the countryside, toward higher land.

Marcus entered his solar where the steward still fussed over accounts. As he removed his cloak, he noticed the bard's sack propped against the wall.

Its presence surprised him. After visiting the closest farms, he had sent Paul and the others on while he turned back, but perhaps his precautions had been for naught.

He looked at the sack again. He had just assumed . . .

"Lady Nesta was looking for you," the steward said as he rolled up a parchment. "Soon after you left, she came here with good tidings for you about her sister."

Suspicion turned to certainty in that instant. If Nesta had something to report, she could have told him last night. He doubted that Genith had woken at dawn with a sudden change of heart.

He strode out of the chamber and down to the cellar. The guard quickly unlocked the door while explaining how the woman Marcus had sent had given Dylan a sleeping potion.

There was no bard in the chamber. Marcus threw back the blanket only to find a very frightened Welsh woman cowering against the wall.

The guard mumbled a litany of excuses and apologies. Marcus did not stay to hear it. Back in the yard he paused, and watched the last of the farmers and merchants straggle out the gate. No doubt one of the first wagons to leave had carried a young bard among its wares.

He had known this was coming. He had been waiting for it ever since Nesta had cajoled him into letting Dylan join the household at night. He had seen her talk to him, and surmised that some plot for his escape was being hatched.

He had even guessed that it would be today. Nesta's argument for leaving Dylan in the cellar had struck him as odd, coming from a woman who had suffered on the road to spare the young man discomfort. Her request to visit the town, and his profound sense that she was watching his departure today, had supported his suspicions.

She was clever and subtle, but he had begun to comprehend how her mind worked.

This time she had succeeded because he wanted her to.

He returned to the steward. "The bard has escaped. Have a horse prepared for me, with provisions for a journey in the hills."

The steward rose in alarm. "How many will go with you?"

"None. One man can track him better than a whole troop. If Dylan guesses he is being followed, he will disappear instead of leading me to Llygad's men as I want."

"The preparations will be made at once."

"There is no need for special haste. I want to be sure he is enough ahead before I follow. While I wait, give Genith's servants some duties to perform. Keep them away from the ladies' chamber."

He headed down to that chamber, to see if he was correct about the rest of it. He already knew what he would find, however. If Nesta had planned Dylan's escape, she had also arranged to have Genith leave with him.

The only question was whether Nesta herself was also fleeing to the hidden stronghold of Llygad ap Madoc's rebels.

Nesta's mind worked hard.

She thought about the events of the last days, and how accommodating Marcus had been about Dylan. She considered the good luck of having Sir Leonard as an escort. He was not the most clever man, which had been very convenient. Mostly, however, she kept seeing the expression on Marcus's face this morning as he gazed up at her window.

By the time afternoon brought a light, wet snow, she concluded that her plan had worked far too smoothly. She suspected that Marcus had let it unfold. There could only be one reason why.

He planned to follow them and find her father's men.

She studied the ground beneath their horses' hooves. The late fall rains had left it soft. Glancing back, she had no trouble detecting the impressions that would lead Marcus right to them. Worse, if the ground froze their tracks would be preserved for days.

She told Dylan to head toward the side of the valley in which they rode. Once they reached the first rise of the land, she stopped her horse.

"I think that we need to separate. Dylan, you will take Genith to my father's men. Go over the hills. It will be slower, but safer. I will continue along this vale, and make it appear as if all our horses did so."

She pulled a large fur provided by Iolo off her saddle and handed it to them. "You will need this more than me, as I do not feel the cold much. Dylan, tie it so it falls behind your mule and sweeps the ground. Maybe it will smooth the snow enough to obscure your tracks. Genith, reach in your sack and give me your blue veil, the one you wore the first night at Anglesmore."

Dylan tied the fur to his saddle. "And you, my lady? How will you find us?"

"I will eventually go to Bala. Tell Carwyn Hir to wait seven days, and then send a man there to guide me the rest of the way. You, however, must bring Genith immediately to Carwyn."

The sudden change in plans distressed Genith. "You said we would stay together."

"I had hoped to, but I think Marcus will follow sooner than I expected. I cannot risk that."

She reached for Genith's hand, and wished that she could take the time to reassure her. She had pictured their next leave-taking in many ways, and secretly dreaded it, but she had never intended it to be like this, hurried and precipitous, with the bulk of two horses separating them.

She yanked a small purse from her neck. "Take this, for food and shelter, and give the rest to Carwyn. Dylan will see to your safety, and I will join you soon." Leaning toward Genith, she managed a clumsy embrace. "Go now. Dylan, my sister's future and honor are in your hands. I want your oath to protect her with your life."

Dylan swore as she asked. He turned toward the hill, and gently called for Genith to ride ahead of him.

Genith hesitated, and turned soulful eyes on Nesta. "I know that this is no different from leaving you at the village, but it saddens me more. If something happens, and we do not see each other again—"

"We will be together again soon."

"It could be many years—"

"Nonsense, sister—"

Genith placed her fingers on Nesta's mouth, silencing her. Eyes tearing, she had her say. "It could be many years. Do not deny me these words to you. I love you very much, Nesta, and I will always cherish this time we have had together. For a short while it was like the old days, and I would have gladly kept Sir Marcus dangling for another month to preserve it a bit longer."

Nesta smiled ruefully. "It was our misfortune that Sir Marcus does not dangle so well, eh?"

Despite her tears, Genith had to laugh at that.

Dylan waited twenty paces away, looking to the hills and not them. Nesta swallowed her emotion and patted Genith's hand. "Go now, before he has two wailing women to deal with."

Reluctantly, and with many long looks over her shoulder, Genith rode over to Dylan. They filed up the hill, the long fur cape sweeping like a train behind the mule's tail, smoothing the snow behind them.

Nesta watched as their forms grew small and hazy through her filming eyes. Her mind's eye saw her sister as an infant and a little girl, and she felt again the small arms hugging her during the night.

At the crest of the hill, Genith stopped and once more looked back.

Nesta had to be the one to break that poignant connection. Turning, she headed back into the vale, making sure that she rode over their tracks to confuse the evidence.

At the point where they had turned to the hill, she removed her cloak and tied it to her horse just as Dylan had tied the fur to his mule, only she draped it so that some of her horse's prints would show. Hopefully, if Marcus followed today, he would assume that a faulty attempt had been made to cover the tracks of three horses, and that a few still survived.

Kicking her horse, she trotted down the vale.

Two hundred paces along, she pulled up and added one final touch. She took Genith's veil, and snagged it low in a bush.

She peered once more to the crest of the hill, half hoping to see Genith still there. Her sister was gone.

Misgivings and sorrow suddenly filled her. She had never anticipated how the cost of her promises would become such a burden, and how doing the right thing would bare her heart to lacerations and regrets. For months the excitement of laying her plans had stimulated her, but now, gazing at the spot where Genith had last been seen, a terrible heaviness filled her chest.

She battled the sorrow by reminding herself that this was all bigger than Genith or herself, or Marcus, or even the King. The happiness of one person meant very little in this world. Did a knight think about such things as he donned his armor to fight for his lord or his God? Had her father weighed his own comfort and life before raising his banner?

Nay. Nor would she be diverted by the womanish emotions overwhelming her now.

Dreams had their sacrifices, and quests had their dangers.

✦ ✦ ✦

It was easy for Marcus to follow them. Within a few days he would know where Llygad's men were. Once he did, those men would have no choice but to disband.

He looked to the high hills rising beyond the vale. If Dylan led them up there, it would become more difficult to follow, but he did not doubt his ability to do so.

He had learned to track men the only way it could be learned, by doing it. When he was eighteen a band of thieves had holed up on his lands, raiding villages and travelers. With his guardian Addis de Valence teaching him to see the small evidence left behind by men on horse or foot, he had led the small troop that caught them.

Dealing with those men had been the first judgment that he took completely on his own authority. A villager had been killed and his wife raped, and hanging those thieves had been just. Still, saying the words had been hard, as Addis had warned it would be.

That one of the thieves was his own age had made it harder. It had been like watching himself die. He might have ended that way if he had remained in the gutters of London. He knew too well how poverty could make a man fearless, and how one did not debate consequences when stealing bread or apples to ease the pain in one's stomach.

It had been his first judgment, and his first executions, but also his first mercy. There had been a younger boy among them, old enough to hang to most men's minds. That one he had spared.

It had been years since he had thought about that boy, but he did so as he followed the tracks. He wondered what had become of him, and if he had a family now or if he had perished on some other gallows. Perhaps he had joined Llygad's men. The notion made him laugh.

Suddenly the tracks changed. Marcus halted and dismounted to examine them more closely.

It appeared that someone had continued in the vale, but had tried to hide their tracks, probably by sweeping the ground. Still, a few marks had survived.

The hoofprints aiming to the mountain were more numerous and confused, however, as if other riders had joined them. Brushing aside some snow, he deciphered that wasn't the case. Horses had gone this way, but then turned back.

He swung back on his horse. It appeared that they had considered going to the hills, but thought better of it. He continued down the vale, noticing the occasional print still visible despite the swept snow.

Something up ahead caught his eye. A bit of

blue fluttered like a wounded bird amidst the white and grey landscape. He rode up to it, and recognized one of Genith's veils.

He narrowed his eyes on that veil, and knew at once that Nesta had deliberately left it. She would never be so careless as to permit this flag to hang here otherwise.

Pivoting his horse, he retraced his way and then followed the other tracks up to higher ground.

Marcus came upon them suddenly. With all of his attention on the ground, he almost rode right into them before he realized they were there.

They had stopped by a stream to rest. Dylan was filling a water bladder and Genith stood watching him. The bard said something and Genith laughed.

Marcus waited in the trees. There was at least a couple of hours of light left and they should move on. He doubted they planned to camp here.

Genith turned and strolled along the stream, on occasion stretching to relieve the stiffness of a day on a horse. As she did so, Dylan ceased his chore and watched her.

Marcus saw the bard's face. He read without

any trouble the thoughts reflected in those fiery eyes. It did not surprise him when Dylan strolled after Genith, and came up behind her and spoke words that Marcus could not hear.

He saw Genith's surprise at what she heard, and then her delight. Before she turned to the young man behind her, her eyes filled with pure lights that Marcus knew well. It was the loving expression his sister wore when she watched her husband, and the sweet beauty of it on young Genith speared his heart.

They joined in a hesitant embrace. Dylan ventured a tentative kiss. Things grew less careful, and a drama of newly discovered rapture unfolded beside the stream fifty paces from where Marcus watched from the trees.

The sight of their young passion touched him, and left him feeling old and empty. He could not have intruded and stopped it if he had wanted to. He could not have moved.

Dylan wrapped his arms around Genith and tucked her head under his chin. As he pressed a kiss to her hair, his gaze swept the trees, and stopped at the spot where Marcus sat on his horse.

It was not clear to Marcus that he had been seen. Dylan made no move to release Genith, or to run for their mounts. Those young rebellious eyes filled with expression, however. They were not the eyes of a man who intended to release what he held.

Marcus read the resolve in them, and guessed that if he followed these two he would not be led to Llygad's men. He wondered what oaths Dylan had sworn about Genith. As a bard, Dylan would know how to choose the words carefully.

Marcus looked upstream to where a horse and mule rested. Leonard had said that the ladies had stolen two horses, so one was missing. Nor had Nesta interrupted this little idyll. If she were here she would have. Whatever Nesta's plans for Genith, they did not include permitting liberties with a bard. It must have been her horse that he started following in the valley.

Marcus looked at Dylan again, and at the happy girl nestled in his embrace. He sent his own message with his eyes, in the event Dylan could see him.

Then he turned his horse, and went back the way he had come.

CHAPTER 9

NESTA CURSED. She did not mutter the profanities, but yelled them with the full force of her diminishing strength.

She cursed the snow, and the skittish horse, and the hare whose sudden appearance had gotten her thrown. She damned the King and the archbishop and the empty, silent valley quickly being obscured by darkness. She heaped the worst blasphemies on the ankle spearing her with excruciating pain as she limped along. The yelling helped clear her head from the dizziness that wanted to blot out her sight.

She fell again, and this time did not try to get up. Her ankle would not let her, and there was no advantage in doing so anyway. It would be completely dark soon, and already she was not sure in which direction she headed. Sitting in the wet snow, she wrapped her arms around herself and cursed some more.

The shout died on her lips as she caught sight of a moving shadow. Low and dark, it slinked across the glow of the snow a few hundred paces from where she sat. She squinted in that direction, and two tiny lights peered back at her. The nape of her neck prickled.

A wolf. She cursed again, a quiet whimper this time, and glanced around in panic. If there was one, there were others.

She groped for the eating knife hanging from her girdle. Her hand was so cold she could barely grasp the hilt, and her stiff fingers had trouble removing it from its cord. It would not help much, but she felt better just holding it.

Battling a fear that wanted to become madness, she strained her ears to hear the animals' movements. Nothing but silence assaulted her, but they were there. She sensed them watching and pacing and deciding what she was. She would have sold her soul for a torch and a sword.

She sensed the wolves move closer, and let the profanities out with force again so they would know she was not helpless. Maybe these beasts would understand that she intended to die fighting and furious, and conclude she wasn't worth the trouble.

She felt one very near. Rising to her knees, she shouted and jabbed the air around her with the knife. A feral scent wafted to her, then moved away.

Suddenly she could see them. Four dark, long forms flew across the pale light of the snow. They streaked away from her, getting swallowed by the night.

She soon understood their retreat. A horse galloped toward her. Her heart rose in relief at the muffled beat of its hooves and she called out to the rider. The sound was barely out of her lips when he was upon her.

It was Marcus, and he had her traitorous mount in tow.

He just sat there a while, looking down at where she knelt in the snow.

"Swearing profanities right before you are eaten by wolves is not wise, Nesta," he finally said. "Praying for eternal salvation would make more sense."

"I have not been in a prayerful mood of late."

He dismounted and came over to her. "Just as well. If it had been prayers I heard echoing through this valley, I might not have known it was you." Hands on hips, he struck a lordly, severe pose. "Separating from the others and riding alone was dangerous and stupid."

"I had expected to reach a village in the north valley by now."

"It seems you did not."

"Aye. Now, please help me up."

"Not yet. You have given me nothing but trouble for weeks, and I find that I like seeing you thus. Kneeling."

She was so relieved and exhausted that she wanted to weep. She had no strength for a battle of wills now. "I am kneeling because I hurt myself when the horse threw me," she said miserably. "I am very weak and I am cold. I know that you are angry with me, but if you could just help me now, I promise to kneel another time so that you can take pleasure in humbling me at your leisure."

He quickly reached for her and lifted her up. "Where are you hurt?"

She balanced on her good leg while she held his shoulder. "My ankle."

"Jesus, woman, you have no cloak and your gown is soaked. Small wonder you are shivering." He lifted her in his arms and carried her to the horses.

"My cloak is tied to my horse."

"Not anymore."

He did not put her on the extra horse, but

helped her onto his. He swung up behind her, tucked the edges of his cloak around her, and aimed toward a wooded hillside.

The sudden warmth only made the chill at her core awaken. She began shaking uncontrollably, and he pulled her close to him in response. "This is so stupid," she said with chattering teeth. "I never feel cold, and now I cannot get warm."

"I will get you to a fire soon. There is a small lodge that my men and I use for hunting the next hill over. There will be dry fuel and flints there."

"Are you saying that after all of this, I never even made it off your lands?"

"You would have to ride more than one day in this direction to do so, if you stay in the valleys."

She burst out laughing. "The enormity of my failure is astonishing."

"Genith and Dylan got away, and that was your goal. Crossing the hills as they are, they are well away from my lands now."

The news revived her spirits immediately. "They are gone?"

"I followed but I lost them. So, you did not fail. You merely sacrificed yourself to succeed. It is fortunate that I found you before you paid

with your life. That would be a high price indeed to save your sister from the comfort and
luxury that she would have known as my wife."

Nesta decided not to provoke him with more
talk. She relaxed against him and into the gait of
the horse. Marcus's warmth began to leach the
terrible chill out of her.

She had not eaten since morning, and now
with deliverance came a raving hunger. Very
gently, she touched her fingers to his chest and
lightly pressed, hoping he would not notice.

He did. "What are you doing?"

"Checking whether you still wear your
meal."

He pulled the little sack from beneath his
tunic.

She greedily opened it and plucked out a thin
chunk of dried venison. She sighed with contentment as she chewed to get it soft. It tasted
better than the most luxurious savory.

"You seem well pleased, Nesta."

"Well, I won't be wolf food now. I am less
cold and hungry, and, as you said, Genith is
away. So you are right, I did not fail. I expect
that I am feeling much as you do when you
plan a battle strategy that succeeds."

He tilted his head and looked at her as if he
could see clearly despite the dark. "There is one

important difference. I have known my share of victories, Nesta, but, unlike you, I was never captured by the enemy afterward."

"You are not exactly the enemy." Nesta waited until they arrived at the lodge to point that out. It seemed an important clarification to make.

"We will see." He dismounted, pulled her down and carried her into the lodge.

She waited in the dark, balancing on her good foot while she leaned against a rough-hewn log wall. He moved invisibly through the space. A tiny spark flared, and a flame quickly grew. Soon firelight revealed the lodge.

It was of good size to hold a hunting party, but low roofed and rude in construction. Built for shelter and not comfort, it provided little more than a dry place for men to camp.

Marcus found some furs in a corner, and spread them in front of the stone hearth.

She took in those furs, and the man looking too handsome for safety in the light of the fire.

"Actually, Marcus, I am not cold at all anymore. I think we can ride back to Anglesmore tonight."

He crouched to build the fire with more fuel. The smallest smile softened his mouth. "Your garments are wet, the horses are tired, and the ground is slippery. It will be wiser if we stay here."

Not wise at all. That little smile had said as much. "You appeared well provisioned for your journey in the mountains. No doubt you intend to sleep under the stars."

"If the only shelter available was the stars, I would have settled for that. Since my journey has ended, however, I am glad for the warmth of this lodge." He rose and faced her. "Does the notion of sharing this space with me unsettle you, Nesta?"

"Of course not." That was a bald lie. "Unsettled" did not begin to describe it.

He came toward her and her good leg wobbled. She made a little hop to regain her balance.

Not bothering to lift her into both his arms, he merely circled her waist with one and swung her to the fire. "Get yourself warm. I don't want to be explaining how you perished from a chill, so you should remove the wet gown. You can wrap yourself in that large fur until your garments dry. It will be modest enough. Now, I must see to the horses."

He started to go, but she stopped him. "You said that you followed them. Did you catch a glimpse of Genith? Did she appear well?"

"If Dylan could lose me in those hills, he

knows them better than I do. Bards are accustomed to long journeys, and know how to survive the rough lands. Do not fear for your sister."

He left, and she heard him moving the horses behind the lodge. There would be some shelter there for them, she guessed, and maybe more furs to warm them, too.

She clumsily dropped to her rump on the furs, and shook out the largest one. Pieced together from the skins of many hares, it was a motley of browns but big enough to serve as a mantle.

Getting off the gown was not easy, but she eventually shimmied out of it and her shift. The fur wrapped her completely, and its nap provided a luxurious sensation against her skin. Soon, however, along with the heat of the fire it made her overwarm. The light wool of her gown did not look likely to dry very quickly. She would have to swelter most of the night.

She let the fur fall open. The soft pile beneath her beckoned to her exhausted body. Fixing her ears on the sounds coming from behind the lodge, she cast the mantle off and lay down on her stomach.

It would be tempting to sleep thus, but of course she could not. Still, a deliciously languid relaxation crept all through her. Vigilant to the warning signs of Marcus's return, ready to swaddle herself again when she heard them, she gave herself over to the wondrous sensation playing on her cool body like so many warm, pattering fingers.

The wattle and daub sealing the cracks between the timbers had dislodged over the years in dozens of places, and little streams of golden light penetrated the night through the gaps. Even as he continued his work with the horses, Marcus had no trouble seeing Nesta in front of the hearth.

The glimpses of her body as she undressed entranced him. The image of her wrapped in the fur, her hair in disarray, and the white of her throat hinting at the nakedness beneath the bundle, set his imagination romping. In his mind's eye the fur fell open, and those large dark eyes watched him as he slid it away.

Then it did slide away, as if she knew he watched and issued a challenge. She stretched and rolled onto her stomach and laid her head on her crossed hands.

Bedding down the horses went very slowly after that.

His chore finally done, he carried his blankets and provisions around to the front of the lodge.

Nesta did not stir when he entered. She still lay there, glorious in the light of the fire.

He paused by the door, half expecting and half hoping that she would turn her head to him and smile a seductive invitation. When she did not move, he paced around until he could see her face.

She was asleep. He looked down on her beauty, and realized that he had seen her naked a lot, considering he had never taken her. Images of doing so, fantasies constructed on too many restless nights, flew through his head.

He bent and pulled the edge of the fur over her bottom so she would not be too embarrassed when she woke.

Taking some food and a wine bladder from one of his bags, he walked to the far wall of the lodge and sat on a bench. He could see her from here, her pale skin gleaming among the furs. The long, sinuous lines of her body made gentle white hills within the mounds. Her dark hair tumbled around her shoulders, and one enticing long lock snaked over her back, its curling end brushing the swell of her breast.

Eventually she would wake. Before morning, he was sure. Fate had not brought them to this firelit lodge so that she would sleep through the night.

He enjoyed watching her. He was glad that

she had not deliberately let him see her
stretched out like this. He could not have refused a blatant offer, but that was not really how
he wanted it to be.

Court ladies granted men their favors, but he
wanted no favors from Nesta. It was not a
courtier's desire that fired in him whenever she
was near. His reactions were too raw for that,
too vital and too violent. The warrior she battled wanted her, as did the lord whom she
thwarted with impunity. So did the starving
youth who watched with resentment from the
alleys.

He made himself comfortable on the bench.
He waited for her to wake up, so that what had
begun in that garden could be finished.

The pain in her ankle poked into her dream,
nudging her toward wakefulness. She shifted
her foot and the pain subsided. Sleep lured her
again. Enough consciousness intruded, however, for her foggy mind to grope for the reason she should not succumb to the blissful rest.
A very good reason, as she vaguely recalled.

She suddenly remembered where she was.

She jerked alert and felt her hands beneath
her cheek and the furs beneath her stomach and
breasts. The sensation of various warmths on

the back of her body told her that the fur covered her hips, but little else.

"I found a cup and mixed some water and wine in it if you are thirsty. It is right beside you, near the fire," Marcus said.

His voice came from her left. She turned her head and peered into the shadows obscuring the far end of the lodge. The highlights of his hair and the fires of his eyes were all she could see distinctly. He seemed to be sitting on a bench against the wall.

She thrust her arm back and pulled the fur so that she was covered a bit more. She contemplated how to sit up in such a way that she could cloak herself completely without first exposing herself more. Something in the way Marcus sat there said that if she asked him to turn away while she arranged herself, he would refuse.

"You should not have let me lie here like this. You should have woken me," she said while she twisted her head to examine the furs.

"After your ordeal, you needed the rest. You should not have risked me finding you naked, however. Perhaps your soul secretly wanted me to."

"It certainly did not."

"I wonder. All the same, I covered you some. That was generous of me."

Covered her some, but not much. Generous, but not too generous. The implications of what he had done made her heart beat faster.

He had not only left her like this so that he could look at her. He had also done it so that she would feel vulnerable when she woke. Vulnerable, and alert to their isolation, and sensitive to the sensuality already thickening the air.

She found the mantle and tugged it around her as she sat up. In the process she revealed more than she wanted, but there was nothing else to do. He did not move, but he watched. That alone made her skin prickle, and the nap of the fur felt even more luxurious on her enlivened skin.

She reached for the water with a nonchalance she hardly felt. From her neck to her thighs, her body was in turmoil. "How long have you been back from tending the horses?"

"A good while."

I have been watching you lying there naked a long time.

She noticed a pile of blankets and saddlebags that he had dumped near the door. "Did you bring in my sack? There are garments in it, and I can wear one while this gown dries."

"There was no sack. It must have fallen from your horse before I came upon him, as your cloak did."

She was almost sure she had noticed the hump of her sack on her horse when he rode up in the snow.

She cast him a suspicious glance. What she saw made her heart jump. Her gaze locked on his warily for a moment, but in that instant a mutual acknowledgment of the craving was nakedly there, just as it had been too often since they had met.

He was going to be trouble. Any man would be in this situation, but this was different, and the ways in which it was different had just been silently spoken. She would be fighting a power that a big part of her did not want to defeat, and he knew that. He counted on it.

She quickly looked to the fire and fussed with the fur, managing to pull it high behind her neck so that it completely swaddled her. She felt outmaneuvered, and he hadn't even moved. He calmly sat in the shadows, as distant from her as the lodge permitted, but his masculine aura dominated the space. To her annoyance, her whole body sparkled with anticipation in response.

"You are unsettling me," she admitted with irritation.

"Good. I like you unsettled."

"I think perhaps you are the enemy, after all."

"Not tonight, my lady. Not yet. If I am, that

is for another time and place. What happens here is a thing apart from that."

His insinuation sent a thrilling chill up her back. "Nothing will happen here, except a good night's rest."

She spoke as firmly as she could.

He gave no response.

"You make me think that I would have been safer with the wolves in the valley."

He laughed. That should have reassured her, but it sounded as if he merely acknowledged that she was right.

He moved, and she immediately tensed. But he only stretched out his legs. "There is some food in that sack near you," he said.

She grabbed the sack desperately, in order to have something to do. The air between them was too full of the forbidden desire that they shared. The lodge swarmed with enchanting images that must never be made real. The memory of his fingers on her breasts produced a sensation almost as real as true touch would be, and a sly arousal began winding through her.

"There is a lot of food in this sack," she said, poking at it while she munched on some cheese. "Enough for a journey of many days. You planned to follow us then, and not just catch us to bring Genith back."

"I had hoped that you would lead me to your father's men."

"Edward would have been pleased if you had succeeded."

"I still intend to. However, since I lost the opportunity to follow Genith there, my only chance of learning the way now is from you."

"I do not know the way."

"You have never been there? Never met with Carwyn Hir?"

"I have never seen the man. There is nothing I can tell you that you want to know."

"I believe that you can tell me quite a lot that I would want to know. But as I said, all of that is for another time and place."

He rose to his feet. She almost jumped out of her skin.

"Is the fire warm enough?" He strolled toward her. "I can put on more fuel."

"Please do not. The chill has left me and now, with this fur and the fire, I am sweltering."

"Perhaps you have a fever."

He was being very considerate. Very thoughtful. She wasn't fooled in the least. Danger poured off him, hitting her in eddies that increased in force as he approached.

As the fire's light illuminated him, she noticed that he appeared very calm, almost indifferent.

Except his eyes. They burned with a seductive warmth. He wore the expression of a man peacefully contemplating what he shouldn't.

He bent to tend the fire anyway, then stood in front of it, his boots mere inches from her leg. He loomed too tall and too strong and too beautiful, and much too close.

"I have no fever. I merely do not feel the cold as much as most. Before today, I had only been chilled once in my life. My first year in Scotland, I could not get warm. I shivered for a whole winter, no matter how many garments I wore." The words came out in a rush, revealing how flustered she was. Confusion and expectation beat inside her, and her voice sounded frantic to her.

He stepped away. It didn't help much. He leaned against the hearthwall and cocked his head, as if she had said something interesting. "Maybe it was not the weather that chilled you, but the marriage that you were forced to make. Genith told me how it was arranged. How did the King convince that Scottish knight to agree to it? The man must have had little allegiance to Edward."

She shifted so that she could face him. The pain of moving her sore foot made her grimace, and she extended that leg to ease the discomfort. Her toes peeked out of her fur cocoon. His gaze fell on them, and suddenly they appeared scandalous.

Bending, she shifted the fur to cover them, but her movement made the fur slide down her back, so she had to fuss at pulling it up again.

Marcus just watched, vaguely amused by her predicament.

Not only amused. What had pulled between them from that first night was so alive and vivid in this lodge that she thought she would touch it if she waved her hand.

Her good sense, what was left of it, tried to dispel the mood with more talk. "My husband's brother was the laird and had been taken by an English knight in battle. The people could not afford the ransom, and Edward offered this marriage as a solution."

"Marrying you forgave the ransom?"

"Aye. Unfortunately, those people were not glad to have their old laird back. The brother was a stupid man, and my husband had proven himself a better leader. With that resentment hanging over me, I was never accepted. I was a stranger too, and along with the stories about me and Edward, well, I was considered a bad bargain all around."

"I doubt that any man would think that having you in his bed was a bad bargain, Nesta."

"We found common ground at night, but day always comes." She spoke pointedly, so he would know she referred to *this* night.

His eyes indicated he had gotten the message. However, she saw something else too. A spark of . . . what? Rebellion? Resentment? It was enigmatic in its source, but she knew that while he had understood her warning, he would ignore it.

"Since you said that your husband taught you to use your weapons, I doubt that he cared much about the days, and what people said about you. I think that he died a very contented man."

"Perhaps he decided there were a few advantages in Edward tying him to the King's whore."

A smile barely twitched on his mouth. "You feel compelled to remind me of Edward's interest in you?"

"It is well that I do. If you get Genith back, things are as they were with her and this plan of the King's. Even if you do not get her back, nothing has changed with who I am."

He pushed away from the wall and took the few steps to her. Her heart jumped. She almost dared not look up at him. When she did, his expression astonished her. The face looking down at her was severe and warm at the same time. Predatory and gentle all at once.

"With your beauty and your mind as your weapons, and Edward as your shield, you are an impressive adversary, Nesta. But at the moment Edward is in Flanders. The field belongs to me, and you are injured."

He lowered to his knees beside her outstretched leg. He was so close that she inhaled his maleness with each breath. His profile, heart-stopping in its beauty, waited within reach. She imagined her fingertips trailing along the square jaw and stroking the hard mouth, and instinctively angled away from him so she would not follow the impulse.

He reached beneath the fur. "We should tend to your wound, so you are not too much at a disadvantage tonight."

He lifted her leg out of the fur and set her foot across his knees. He gently pressed the ankle's red swell. His frowning concern charmed her, but his touch sent a tremor right to her loins.

"It will heal in a day or so," she said, trying to retrieve her pale leg and hide it again.

"It should be bound." He looked to where her garments lay drying. Grabbing the shift that was almost dry, he rent it in two and tore off a long swath.

The binding took too long. She suffered it, fighting the way the intimacy affected her, clutching the fur so that it would not open above her knee. Excitement plucked mercilessly, defeating her with an alluring anticipation of more.

He pressed against the bandage when he was done. "Does that hurt so much as before?"

He could tell that it did not, so there was no point in lying. He seemed pleased with the results. In alleviating her pain, he had removed her only advantage.

She made to pull her leg away. He grasped her shin firmly, not letting her go. The set of his mouth, the brittle lights in his eyes—they all told her that a decision had been made.

She tried to look away, tried to find something sharp to say that would stop what was going to happen, but words could not end the primitive thrumming soundlessly connecting them.

Too much of her reveled in what twisted taut between them. Delectable anticipation sent spirals of arousal through her body until her breasts tingled and vulva throbbed. She wanted to throw off the fur and stretch out and have him kiss all of her.

His hand smoothed slowly up her leg. The caress was warm, firm, and possessive. She closed her eyes and savored the luscious sensations it aroused.

Impossible, of course. Disastrous.

"You must not."

That hand went higher. Luring. Dangerous. Wonderful. "You know that you want me to."

"What I want is a small thing in this. In any of it. I told you so in the garden that night."

"Right now what you want is all that matters, to my mind."

"Your mind is not working well. Stupid and contemptible, you once called this, when you had your sense about you."

"Contemptible because of Genith, but she is gone, and I do not think she will be back."

His slow, purposeful fingers trailed to the back of her knee, sending shivers up her thigh to join the knot of excitement in her stomach and the itching pulsation growing between her legs. He stroked higher, brushing aside the fur's edges, making a gap so more of her showed, and watched his hand and her nakedness and the visible trembles he was causing.

With her last remnants of sense, she tried again. "If no longer contemptible, it is still stupid."

His gaze shifted to her face even as his fingers continued tracing their delicious, seductive paths. "Not stupid and contemptible, Nesta. Necessary and important. More than anything I can think of."

"That is because you are not thinking at all. Men never do at such times."

"Then you do the thinking for us, lady. Stop me, as you did in the cottage."

It was a blunt challenge that he knew she could not meet, just as she had not in the cottage. The part of her that said she should, that recognized too well the complications and betrayals waiting if they did this, had lost its voice. Only the woman in her lived now, woken by the sensual force that had been pulling them to each other every moment since they met.

"Lie down, Nesta."

The command frightened her. That was absurd. She was no innocent. Still, she could not deny this passion raised panic as well as pleasure.

"Nay."

He shifted so that he angled alongside her, propped on one arm, his masculinity dominating her. He eased the fur down her shoulder and pressed a soft kiss to her skin. It might have lasted an hour, so clearly did she feel every instant of that spot of warmth tingling into her blood. He began a gentle assault on her neck with slow, biting kisses that evoked pleasure so intense that her primitive self began a silent chant of exultant encouragement.

Mindlessly embracing what he offered, she angled her head, exposing her neck. Deliberately, he found pleasure spots that left her gasping.

Withdrawing his hand from her leg, he gently pressed his fingers down the length of her neck. They journeyed lower, along the edge of the fur where it met her skin. He found where the mantle overlapped, and moved his hand beneath the fur to her breasts.

He caressed the tips lightly. The pleasure rendered her helpless. Any hope of controlling the course of this, of controlling herself and him, died then. She lost herself in the overwhelming sensations, and in the masculine power taking command of her.

He stopped kissing her neck. She opened her eyes to find him watching her reaction to his touch. His dark gaze contained layers of lights that seemed to go on forever, deep into his soul and out into hers.

He teased at her breasts while he watched her face, and she tightened her jaw against the cries that wanted to flow out of her. They filled her head instead, a mad litany of demands and pleas and gratitude.

"It was wicked of you, Nesta. What you did in that garden. We might have never known this passion could exist between us. We could have been spared its power."

He took her mouth in a demanding, probing

kiss that sent her reeling. His hand returned to her naked leg, and boldly ventured higher in possessive strokes.

"Move your other leg, Nesta. Let me touch you."

She obeyed, and barely swallowed a moan of impatience as her muddled mind urged him on. Her breath caught when his hand reached the wetness on her inner thigh and then ruthlessly sought its source.

Incredible pleasure centered where he teased. The hunger that she had imprisoned for weeks surged free, and all she could see was the flickering fire highlighting vague forms in the lodge. Except for him. Marcus remained very clear and precise despite her filming eyes.

"Lie down."

She obeyed this time.

He swung his leg to kneel above her, his knees straddling hers. Sensuality made his face hard and beautiful. His eyes were those of a man who had been wanting something too long.

Not unkind, Genith had called that expression, but a little dangerous and frightening. Her sister had not understood the piquant appeal of both the danger and fear if the man was one you desired.

He gently tugged at the fur. The soft nap slid

across her breasts and stomach, teasing her skin as its heat slowly peeled away to expose her to the cool air. His gaze followed the moving edge as if he felt its titillating path as much as she did.

"You are beautiful, Nesta. The memory of your body has not left me since that day in the cottage. There has not been a moment, day or night, when you were not in my head."

His gaze and dominating pose made her tremble. Finally it became too much. She reached to pull him into her arms.

He ignored the gesture. Instead of coming to her, he unhitched his belt and cast it aside. He pulled off his surcotte and other garments until his naked body loomed above her, hard in the dancing light of the flames.

Firm fingers closed on her left leg. He bent it up from between his knees and angled it to his side. "Rest your foot here." He bunched the fur mantle into a mound. "I do not want to hurt your ankle."

She obeyed, but it left her spread and exposed. He moved the other leg, making the exciting vulnerability worse.

She reached for him again. This time he came to her, not fully against her, but braced on his arms so that a small span of air and space still separated their bodies.

"How do you like it, Nesta?" He spoke lowly

as his mouth and teeth did wonderful things to her ear.

"If I said slow and careful, and full of pretty words, would it make a difference?"

He turned his attention to her breast. "I think not." His tongue swirled on her nipple and her body stretched toward the titillating thrill. "I do not know many pretty words, and with the way that I have wanted you, I expect that it can only be hot and furious."

She caressed down his back to his hips. "Then let it be so." She slid her hands around his loins and closed her fingers on him.

He looked down between their bodies at what she was doing. When he turned his gaze back to her, his eyes blazed.

She took his head in her hands and brought his face to hers. She kissed him, taking control this time, using her tongue and teeth to let him know her own impatience.

The frayed cord snapped. She felt it in the body she caressed and knew it from the devouring kisses he pressed on her mouth and neck and breasts. He eased down on her, his hips nestled between her thighs. His body sealed itself to hers while their savage embrace and kisses both vented the desire and stoked it.

With her body she entreated him to come to her. She raised her hips as he entered her, and they impatiently slammed together in a desperate quest for union.

There was the briefest pause while she absorbed the delicious fullness, the permeating contentment, and the heady intimacy of his strength in her arms and body.

Rising up on his arms, he moved in her. Despite his warning, it was slow and careful and beautiful. She laid her hands on his chest as a blissful contentment soaked her. Every rejoining became a luxurious ecstasy to be savored. In the fire's light his face showed all of his hard beauty, but there was no harshness in the tight lines. His gaze took her as deliberately as his body did.

It was good. Too good. She had known pleasure before, but in Scotland love-play had been a game between friends that sated physical needs. This was different in ways that left her spirit and heart as naked as her body. Their connection was tinged with an invasive and poignant intimacy. He might have been claiming her soul as well as her body.

He stopped, joined to her, completing her in more ways than she could name. He came down, into her arms, so that his skin lined her deliciously and the connection grew closer.

He kissed her. It started gently and sweetly, but deepened quickly as their mutual desire swept in like a wind. Male power poured off him as if a dam had broken. His passion turned as hot and furious as he had warned it would be.

Her craving met his and then spun out of control. They fought a battle where they both strove for the same victory. A new delicious shivering began where he stretched her and she rocked into his hard thrusts, demanding more until the quivering filled all of her and grew unbearable. Relinquishing her hold on everything except him, she let him drive her to a crazed climax that had her clawing at his back and screaming into the silence.

Sanity returned just as his own end came. Holding her right leg over his hip he drove deeper with hard, claiming thrusts that prolonged the pleasure drenching her.

He spoke lowly in her ear, but not pretty words. He only said her name, once. But the way he said it, gently despite his violence, quietly despite the hot fury of his release, touched her so profoundly that it might have been the sweetest poetry.

CHAPTER 10

As she lay with him she felt bound by a peace and warmth as soulful as a nostalgic memory. She savored the mood, and the hard body in her arms, and the heart beating in rhythm to her own. She could not fight the saturating intimacy, did not want to, but she recognized that danger lurked within the bliss.

Pleasure had become a physical thing that she took or gave on her own terms. That she controlled. This had been very different. The power of what had happened, of just how weak it might make her, both intrigued and frightened her.

She should have been the one to run away, instead of Genith.

He rose on his forearms and looked down at her. Beneath the warm contentment in those dark, intense eyes she read the deeper reflections of his mind. He was contemplating the same thing as she was.

Two clever people were concluding that they had just done something most unwise.

He shifted to her side, breaking the physical bond. The other one would be harder to sever.

Lying beside him in front of the fire, stretched out to his thoughtful gaze, she felt more naked than she had ever been in her life. She subtly dragged the edge of the fur over her hips.

Smiling as if he knew what she was about, he brushed the covering away again as he caressed down her length. His hand paused on her stomach.

"You have never carried a child."

"Nay."

"The King hoped you would not, didn't he? I think Edward chose that old knight hoping that you would remain untouched."

"I suspect he was assured of it. That part of the bargain was quickly forgotten, however. As to a child, Duncan and I both did what we could to avoid that, but perhaps fortune just smiled on me. A child would bind me there forever, even after he died. It was not my home, and never would be, and I did not want such ties."

"That convent was not your home, either. Were you so unhappy that a nunnery was better?" His expression was too thoughtful as he watched his hand smooth over her body. She could see his mind working at something.

"It is no woman's first home. No one is a stranger if everyone is."

"But your father was still alive when your husband died. Why didn't you go to him, or join Genith?"

"The choice was not mine. I was sent to Scotland for a reason, and that did not change with my husband's death."

"An old husband, and then a convent." His fingers splayed over her hips and thighs, as if he drew his mental wanderings on her body.

She knew where his thoughts were going. "Aren't you going to ask me what happened with Edward? Don't you wonder if there were others besides him and my husband, and just how much a whore I have been?"

"Sleeping with your husband was not whoring."

"It is not my husband that distracts you now."

"You are so sure of what distracts me, Nesta?"

"You are a man. I expect that you are wondering how often I have surrendered my virtue as easily as I did this night."

"In this I am not like most men. I know that a woman's heart is rarely as simple as the words 'virtue' and 'whore' imply. When I was a youth I lived among real whores, and some of them were the most honest women I have ever known." His gaze turned inward, as if he no longer saw either her body or his caress. "Actually, I am only alive today because a good woman sold herself."

A stillness fell over him after he said it. His tone had been distracted, as if he gave voice to a truth he rarely put into words.

He glanced in her eyes, and then returned his attention to his wandering hand. "Do you know the history of Anglesmore? How Roger Mortimer, when he usurped the young King's power, sent a man to disseize my father?"

"I know what happened. It is still evident in your household, and the youth of the men."

"The knights have come from elsewhere, but the boys are the sons of men who died when the castle fell. With their fathers gone, their families have no way to provide for them. They petition me, and I take them for service or training, even though there are already too many."

"That is generous of you."

"I never have thought of it as generosity. I even tell myself no more, but then another one comes and I see there is no other way, so I take him too." He smiled charmingly, and appeared quite boyish himself. "There are complaints about their mischief and noise. The cooks swear that they steal food, and the priest is aghast at their sins." He seemed to find the priest's dismay the most amusing part.

The lightness left his mood as quickly as it had come. He looked in her eyes again, and this time did not turn his attention away. "Do you not find it curious that I did not die that day? I was only twelve, but others my age fell."

She would have liked to lie, but he watched with eyes that would see through that. "I have wondered about it."

"I was supposed to. The massacre was an act of blood lust, but the deaths of my father and me were ordained. However, the man who took the keep grew besotted with my sister on seeing her. The price of my life was that she go to him." His mouth formed a bitter, hard line. "I did not realize it at first. Like a fool I thought God had spared me. Then one morning I went to her chamber early to speak with her, and saw them together. I knew everything then. I should have fallen on a sword to spare her more of it. Instead I feigned ignorance and kept silent so the bargain could continue and I could live."

The revelation astonished her. Not that it had happened, but rather the flat, calm way he faced the cost both to his sister and his own conscience.

"Thus did my sister whore, Nesta. After she and I escaped, the women who slaved in the London tile yard where we lived also worked on their backs at night. They did it to feed their families, not for pleasure and certainly not for love." Again he gave her that direct look. His hand gently brushed strands of hair away from her face. Combing her locks out onto the fur occupied him for a spell.

"Is that how it was with you, Nesta?"

The sudden turn in the conversation stunned her. She was touched that he confided in her, but had not expected him to want the same of her.

"You want to know what happened with Edward, and if I was under some obligation?"

"You misunderstand. I have decided that I do not want to know which of the songs is true. I have not been thinking of your past. I find myself contemplating the present, and whether you did this with *me* for another reason. I can hardly damn you if you did, but I still wonder."

His frankness alarmed her. He insinuated that he could think of many reasons for her to have done this.

"It was only for my pleasure, I assure you."

His gaze snapped to her face, and she knew then that he had been contemplating more than her motivations. He too had felt the power of what had passed, and been surprised by it, and knew in his heart that they had shared more than pleasure.

She expected him to challenge her, so intensely did he examine her. He let it pass, however, as if he agreed it would be better not to speak of that when there was no future for it.

His gaze warmed, and his hand left her hair. He caressed her body more purposefully. "If it is only for your pleasure, I should be sure that you are well pleased. Besides, I always said, if a thief is going to hang, it might as well be for a horse and not an apple."

"When did you always say that?"

He smiled slyly. "When I was a thief."

"So now I am a horse?"

He shook his head. "You are the stairway to the stars. It is heaven that I am stealing here."

He cupped her breast and brushed the tip with his thumb. Her nipple immediately hardened and an arrow of intense sensation streaked down her body, reigniting the hot torture.

"What would be your pleasure, Nesta?"

She smiled. "If I said slow and careful, would it make a difference?"

"This time it would. I think that I will make it so slow and careful that you are begging for me."

"I do not beg."

"I think that you will."

He indeed made it slow and careful. So slow that the pleasure almost unhinged her. Flicks of his tongue aroused one breast and the slow grazing of his fingers teased the other.

It felt so good that she never wanted it to stop, but soon the torment grew so intense that her body begged even if her voice did not. He made no move to answer the pleas implied by her rocking hips, but continued teasing her, letting the delirium build. She wantonly arched so her breasts rose to the delicious torture.

It became too much. She throbbed where he had filled her, and she wanted that completion again. The pleasure he gave her both increased the ache and denied it. She grew frantic with a building hunger.

She reached to caress his phallus, to return the pleasure and also encourage him to need her too. To her shock he took her hand, and the other one, and pinned them in a gentle grip above her head.

"You will do nothing to hasten this. I want you as mad with desire as you will ever be, and more desperate for me inside you than you thought possible."

"I already am."

"Not enough."

He caressed down her body and she anxiously moved her leg. Just the anticipation of his touch excited her more. His first slow stroke left her moaning with relief, but soon she only craved more and more. Ecstasy beckoned, just out of reach, torturing her so exquisitely that she heard herself sighing her approval to every incredible touch. He insisted on bringing her to the edge slowly, and soon nothing existed but the pleasure spilling through her, body and soul, and the single-minded thought that they be joined.

Suddenly he was gone. His hand left her body and he slipped from her embrace. Confused and dazed, she opened her eyes just as he lifted her toward him.

He sat and settled her on his legs, facing him, taking care with her sore ankle as he wrapped her legs around his hips. He pressed the tip of his phallus to her passage and her essence cried with joy. He went no further, however, but stopped with them barely connected.

She could not believe that he was capable of such annoying restraint. Soon she also could not believe what that small connection was doing to her.

Draping her arms around his neck, she narrowed her eyes on him. "If my ankle was not sore, and I could move, I would make short work of this."

His fingers began a devastating arousal of her breasts. It made her come alive where they were partially joined. "You can still make short work of it."

Her mind began splitting. Awareness of the lodge retreated again, leaving her conscious of only the fire and him and the tremoring pleasure that itched to find fulfillment.

"You mean I can beg. That is unkind. You want me humbled."

He took her face in his hands, and held her head close to his as he looked in her eyes. "I want you to admit that you want me as much as I want you. And no matter what happens in the days ahead, I want you to remember this night, and *me*."

With ruthless determination he made sure that she did. He used his hands and mouth to bring her to delirium again. She could not move, and so her arousal just built and built.

Between her cries she showered kisses on him, tasting his skin, inhaling his scent, filling her memories.

Finally the last shred of control left her, and she whispered the desperate request he sought. She did not have to plead or beg, she merely asked for what she wanted. It seemed the most natural thing in the world to do.

He lifted her hips and brought her closer. As he filled her he claimed her with a kiss that smothered their mutual groans. Wrapping her in a binding embrace, he led her toward the heaven that waited.

Day came too soon. Its bright light poked through the tiny gaps between the timbers, heralding a clear day. Marcus woke and cursed the evidence of fair weather. No excuse to stay here, then. He had hoped to hold off the reckoning, and the decisions this woman in his arms would inevitably make.

Nesta slept on. The fire was down to embers, but they were cozy beneath the fur mantle, their entwined bodies making enough heat. Saturated with a contentment he had rarely known in his life, he watched her peaceful expression, so lovely in the leaking light of dawn, and counted the dark lashes brushing her skin.

With Genith gone, she would petition to leave Anglesmore. He already knew the arguments that she would make. She would even use this night, and the danger from the King, as a reason, even though the biggest danger in what had happened here had nothing to do with Edward. It was that other risk that would really compel her to leave. She would want to flee the bond discovered in this lodge.

He could not let her go, of course. Not only because of the pleasure, and the chance to know it again. Not just because of the intimacy.

She had indeed been captured by the enemy, and there was much she could tell him that he would want to know. She was up to some mischief, he was sure of it. It involved Genith and Carwyn and those rebels hiding in the hills, and his best chance to discover her plan before she destroyed herself was to keep her nearby.

She turned in her sleep and nestled closer until her face pressed his chest. She appeared so small and feminine that it was tempting to forget the sharp mind that worked inside that pretty head.

The movement stirred her and she slowly emerged from her dreams. Awareness came to her slowly, and she frowned a little before she remembered where she was. She favored him with a sleepy smile he would never forget.

Then full alertness hit her. She absorbed the new light of day streaking through the darkened lodge, and her face fell.

They lay in their embrace, closer in some ways than they had been in their passion. Marcus could almost hear the silent debate taking place inside her head.

"When I left Anglesmore, it was assumed I would be gone many days," he said.

She exhaled a deep breath that said more than any words. It was the sigh of a woman who understands the world too well. "Day always comes, Marcus. An hour in a moonlit garden or a night in a firelit lodge does not change what the sun illuminates."

"Very little sun enters these walls."

"Enough to show us both who we are."

He sought to win the argument the only way he could. He kissed her. She accepted it, and held his head to her as she made it long and sweet. When he moved to caress her, however, she turned her head away. "Do not. It will be too sad."

He could not disagree. Already a wistful melancholy drenched the air. Still, he resented the cool determination with which she announced the end. Sad or not, doomed or not, he would have gladly continued this passion a fortnight and allowed duty to wait for a while.

She cast aside the blanket and knelt, unmindful of how cold it was outside their makeshift bed. He filled his mind with her as she dressed, and regretted every part of her body as it disappeared beneath the torn shift and wrinkled gown.

She reached for the remains of the food. "Just as well that we are not staying. We did not pack this food last night. The bread is hard and the cheese is wet."

"I can hunt. The fear that has you ending this is not one of hunger."

She ignored that, and rummaged through his garments until she found the little sack of dried venison. "Fortunately, you never eat the meal that you wear."

She threw his clothes to him, and he dressed while she pried at the drawstring. His head emerged through the neck of his tunic to find her immobile, staring into the sack.

"It is not for eating, is it? Not really." The gaze she turned to him had all of the softness he had seen while they made love. It was as if she looked right into his soul and understood all that she surveyed. Memories from the night filled his head, clearer now than in the actual living of them, and longing filled his chest. He suddenly understood why he did not want to leave this lodge, and the loss that waited when he did.

She held the little sack as if it were stitched from cloth of gold and not rawhide. "Do you wear it to remind you of the starvation, or as a talisman against it happening again?"

The question astonished him. He busied himself with his belt. "As a youth, after I returned to Anglesmore, I grew accustomed to wearing it, that is all."

He reached for the sack and took a piece of venison, to prove it was a convenience and nothing more. The small strip of meat was very old and tough, but he chewed with determination.

She finished her own dressing. As if both of them wanted to delay opening the lodge door, they were fastidious in folding the furs and banking the fire. Neither of them spoke as they obliterated the evidence of the night.

Finally all was prepared. They stood by the dead fire in a space still full of the night's shadows but stabbed by dozens of arrows of bright sunlight.

Her hand sought his. "I should have asked about it. Last night I should have had you tell me more about your years in London, and your father's death, and your sister's sacrifice, and what you owe to Anglesmore and his memory and your own past."

"I did not want to speak of such things."

"Aye, but still I should have asked."

He pulled her into his arms. The embrace was too much like one shared by people parting, and the warmth of her, the spring scent now mixed with sensual odors, moved him. Very deliberately he caressed her, branding his memory so that her feel would never be lost.

As they walked to the door, he thought of nothing but the night. She pulled it open, not him. Beyond the threshold spread a dazzling day, and a bright sun melting the last of the night's snow.

As they walked to the horses, her last words repeated in his mind. He realized that if she had asked him about those things last night, he would have told her everything, just as he had told her about Joan buying his life. It would have been easy to speak of it, even though he never had before with anyone else.

The omission was not just hers. He should have asked about her own father, and more about her years in Scotland, and what she owed to Llygad's memory and to Wales and to her own past.

He had not asked because he did not need to. He already knew most of it. Not the most dangerous parts, he was sure, but the reasons.

He knew because, during the hour before he had followed her and Genith and Dylan, he had read her letters.

She had hoped that the daylight would burn away the intimacy, but it did not happen that way. They were as connected on the ride back to Anglesmore as they had been in each other's arms, and the sweetness refused to die throughout the miles they journeyed.

She rode her own horse, with her sack tied behind her saddle. As she had suspected, her belongings had not been lost. Marcus had left them outside so that she would have no garments. When he had retrieved the sack from the hay in which it was buried, it never entered her mind to scold him for the wicked deception.

They did not speak much as they rode through the valley. There was much that needed saying, but they both knew what it was and so it was unnecessary to voice the words. Her heart both relished the slow journey and dreaded its progress. She knew that she should be steeling herself for what was to come, but she found herself incapable of relinquishing the intimacy by contemplating its end.

Only as they faced the gate, side by side, and

looked up at the massive walls and towers of Anglesmore's power, only then did her rebellious heart accept the truth. They had shared a magical night in another world. Entering the gate would return them to the real one, and to their duties.

They stayed there a long time, immobile on their horses. Marcus looked at her, and she saw that he understood what the next steps would mean.

A different man and woman might have thrown caution to the wind. Others may have even turned from the gate, and sought other shelter and other lives. But she was Nesta verch Llygad, and he was Marcus of Anglesmore, and such as they were born for destinies bigger than happiness.

Separate destinies. Opposing ones.

Her heart filled with a searing pain. Her throat began burning, and she blinked a sudden film from her eyes. She dared not give a name to what she was feeling. She resisted admitting what the last day's joy and sadness revealed. If the emotion overwhelming her was recognized, she would be sliced in two, and one part of her would eventually have to betray the other.

Still, she found that she could not move her horse. The bravery with which she had thrown open the lodge door had deserted her.

She peered up at the remorseless, iron teeth of the hanging portcullis. "Do you dream much, Marcus? Vivid dreams that you remember on waking?"

"Not so much anymore. I did when I was young."

"I rarely do too. I am glad for it, I think. If they are bad dreams, I am terrified. If they are good dreams . . . if they are good ones, life seems so drab and ordinary the next day." She smiled at him, and wished they were not in view of the wall so that she could give him a kiss. "I have been in a dream for hours now, but the morning has truly come."

He vaguely nodded his acknowledgment of that. There was no need to express how completely the dream was about to end. He was a clever man, and he understood.

Neither one of them moved first. At the same instant their two horses stepped forward, and they rode through the gate.

CHAPTER 11

YOU SAY THAT you found her on the road?
She spent the night alone out there in the cold
with no horse, no weapon, and no cloak?"

Paul asked the question early the next morning as they broke their fast. He was not very
good at being subtle, and Marcus noticed the
overly deliberate nonchalance in his friend's
tone.

"She is a resourceful woman, and stronger
than most. I daresay she could survive more
than one night with the little she had with her."

Paul nodded solemnly. "To be sure. Still, she
was fortunate that you came upon her."

"The good fortune was mine. I might be
thought negligent if she perished."

Paul began responding but bit back the

words. Marcus had no trouble guessing what
had been sacrificed to better judgment. More
than a few eyebrows had shot up when he and
Nesta had ridden in the gate yesterday.

Without discussing it, they had both known
the story to give. No one had dared to question
it outright even though the possibilities had
been obvious to everyone. Now, as Marcus
watched Paul biting his tongue, he decided that
the household's curiosity about that night had a
benefit. It kept everyone from examining the
rest of the story, and the peculiar detail of how
Marcus had lost Genith and Dylan in hills that
he could journey through blinded.

Paul angled forward so he could speak confi-
dentially. It appeared he had decided that better
judgment could go to hell. "No one will be
bold enough to say it to your face, of course,
but you should know that there is a lot of talk.
Wondering, mostly. After all, she is not reputed
to be the most virtuous woman, now is she?"

Marcus had intended to take this in stride, but
now a sharp annoyance stabbed his head. "Talk
is inevitable, but are you saying that it is not my
possible lack of chivalry that is being bantered
about? That Nesta is being blamed for any sins
that may have happened?"

Paul shrugged. "To be expected, isn't it, with
a woman who has been the King's whore? It

should quiet down soon enough, now that she is preparing to leave. Her servant confided the plans to Jane, the groom's wife. I say it can't be soon enough."

Marcus broke off a hunk of bread and ate it. He drank his ale. Paul turned the conversation to other things and some time passed during which Marcus brought the livid fury that had blazed through him under control.

His meal done, he rose. "Paul, send men to the town and farms and speak with the people. Let it be known that I want to parlay with Carwyn Hir. Perhaps someone in these parts knows how to get word to him, and the message will travel."

Paul agreed that might work, and that an attempt at negotiations might bear fruit.

"I also ask that you do what you can to stop this talk, for the lady's sake."

Paul nodded, but did not appear very hopeful.

"There is one more thing, Paul. Let it be known that if anyone ever calls her a whore again, that person, man or woman, will be exiled from these lands forever."

Paul's gaze snapped up. He grimaced with exasperation and dismay. "Ah, hell, Marcus, you *didn't*. There's going to be hell to pay now, that's for sure."

Paul was right about that. There was going to be hell to pay, and some of it was waiting in a chamber up above. Marcus aimed there, to speak with the woman whose servant had conveniently been indiscreet with Jane, the groom's wife.

He found Nesta sitting near the window, her makeshift table arranged to catch the sun rays flowing through the thick window slit. Only one little pot was open, and she used her brush to fill green into the back of her design.

He strolled over and examined the parchment. It showed seven women holding various objects and seated on the backs of seven primitive men who crawled about in loincloths.

It was almost complete. She must have been laboring over it since their return yesterday. He had thought that her absence from the hall had been a way to avoid him, not the result of absorption in her designs. He did not care for the evidence that her head had not been filled with thoughts of their time together, as his had.

"It is the seven virtues triumphant over the seven vices," she explained with her head still bent.

He knew what it represented. The image of chastity caught his attention. The face of lust on whom she sat bore a striking resemblance to himself.

"You have been laboring hard at this, Nesta. You have had a sudden burst of artistry."

"It passes the time."

"It also provides you with coin, you once said. Do you need some now?"

"One can never have enough coin."

"True, especially if one is planning a journey. I have heard talk that you think of making one. Put that idea aside. You will be staying here."

She paused her delicate strokes. Straightening, she cleaned the little brush, set it down, and covered the ink. Finally she rose and faced him.

Nesta the adversary had returned.

"I had assumed that you would see the rightness of my leaving, but it appears that you are not nearly as clever as I had thought."

"Clever enough to know that I need to keep an eye on you."

"I think that it is not just an eye that you want to keep on me."

"Nay, it is my hands and my mouth and my whole body, but you will not be staying because of that. You have been determined to thwart the crown's plan for making peace with your father's men. I intend to make the peace without your interference."

She frowned with frustration. Her fretful expression touched him. He moved to embrace her, but she shrugged him away and his hands only came to rest on her shoulders. Since she seemed to accept that, he let them stay there.

"I know something about duty to a father's will, Nesta, and much about responsibility to a father's memory. In this you and I are the same. Whatever burden Llygad's life and death placed on you, however, I cannot allow you to encourage his men in their rebellion. Not just because of my duty to my king and not only because it will mean their deaths at my command. In the doing of it, you place yourself in danger. I will not allow you to engage in anything that might be seen as treason. Already Stratford is suspicious of you."

A belligerent glint entered her eyes. "Let Stratford be suspicious. I do not fear him."

"If he finds evidence to support those suspicions, at the least he will have cause to put you away."

"He has already done so once. I will survive it again."

Her reckless attitude both angered and worried him. He gripped her shoulders tighter. "Tell me what you are up to, Nesta. If it is truly treasonous, we can end it cleanly and no one will be the wiser. If we do not, even the King's favor may not protect you."

She looked in his eyes so long that he thought

she would confide in him. A sadness passed over her expression, however, and her gaze slid past him.

Gently, she stepped out of his hold and limped to the window. "If it were truly treasonous, it would be your duty to hand me over to the King's judgment. If you did not, you would be as guilty as I, and would risk everything with your silence."

"What I risk is my concern alone."

She did not respond. She merely gazed out the window. It meant he could not see her face. Her pose, perfectly balanced despite her sore ankle, held a serenity that was in stark contrast to his own churning emotions.

Her silence became a dismissal and her posture a repudiation. It amazed him that she could act so indifferently after what they had shared. Then again, perhaps he had misunderstood, and they had not shared much at all.

He reacted to that notion with a furious denial, but he quickly swallowed it. If that was how it had been, it was probably for the best. Hadn't he always sought out women just like the one being so cool now? Experienced ones, who could enjoy pleasure and then walk away?

He began to leave, annoyed by the hollow sensation growing in his heart. "Nesta, if you have the means to send messages to Carwyn

Hir, let him know that I would meet with him. It would be as in a truce, so that we can learn what became of Genith."

"And so you can also offer him absolution or death?"

"Aye, that too."

"You assume that I can contact him. You are convinced of my treason then, and have been for some time, I think. You do not have many scruples about the women you bed, do you? Or did you even seduce me out of duty? Perhaps you hoped to trap me into indiscreet confidences with the intimacy?"

If she had kept silent, if she had said anything else at all, he would have left the chamber. Instead his legs took him to the window in long strides.

He grabbed her and swung her around. "That night had nothing to do with what we speak of here. I said it would not for me, and later asked if it did for you. Neither of us was fettered by thoughts of duty or obligations or trades or traps. To say otherwise is unworthy of you, and an insult to us both."

She looked pointedly at his grip on her arm. "Forgive me. I seem to have forgotten what that night *did* have to do with."

Her flippant response infuriated him. "This. It had to do with *this*."

He pulled her to him. She squirmed to get away but he imprisoned her resistance in an embrace and silenced her objection with a kiss.

He had sworn to himself that he would not touch her again, but his passion soured in triumph at the taste and feel of her. He sensed her flex of yielding even before it rippled through her and he urged her to join him with his caress. She held back for an excruciating instant before responding in a burst of madness that made him burn so hotly he thought he would die. They might have been back in the lodge again, sealed together, breathing each other's air and sharing each other's essence.

Memories from that night filled his head. The low voice of reason chanted the cost, but he ignored its irritating caution. He wanted her with a ferocity that made the last weeks seem tame. He pushed her against the wall and took her breasts in his hands. A throaty groan sighed out of her as he caressed and teased and commanded her to totally capitulate to the delirium with him.

He thought she would. Thought she had. Her soothing hands stroked up his back to his shoulders, and slid down his arms to his hands. She held them to her breasts and returned a kiss of such poignant depth that he thought his body would split in two. Then her fingers closed tightly on his wrists and stilled his caress. She broke the kiss and stayed there, breathing deeply, her head resting against the wall, her eyes closed and her expression sad.

Her lids fluttered open. "Now I remember what that night was about. Lust."

He wanted to hit her for that. If not for the softness in her gaze that said more than any words, he might have. "Calling it base does not make it so, Nesta."

"Considering your duty, it would be unbearably reckless for either of us to call it anything else." She slipped away from him, and limped to her table. "You must not touch me again. If you have any affection for me at all, if you truly do not think me a whore, you must do what I have done, and make that night a magical memory from another world."

"Your ability to be practical impresses me, my lady."

"Well, I have had more experience at that than most. When the troubadours sing about me, they do not warble love songs."

She sat down calmly, but Marcus noticed that the hand that uncovered the ink pot was shaking. He watched the clumsy fumbling with the brush that belied her indifferent words. He felt the confusion and fear in her that could not hide behind her careful pose.

She began to continue her design, but a careless movement sent the ink pot's little top clattering to the floor. It rolled over to his feet. He picked it up, placed it beside the pot, and walked away.

He had made no promises, but he would not be touching her again soon. With the way things stood, if he was right about her complicity in the rebellion, to do so would be as contemptible and stupid as he had once said it would be.

A man should not bed a woman he might one day have to hand over to the executioner.

Nesta was careful to do nothing to fuel Marcus's suspicions during the next days. She had no doubt that he would lock her in her chamber if he had cause, and so she gave him none.

She avoided Marcus whenever possible, and soon the raised eyebrows regarding them lowered. They saw each other mostly at meals. Those long hours were hard, because she sat near him and saw the questions in his eyes when he looked at her.

Sometimes it was the gaze of the King's man that she saw, wondering what role she played in the rebellion. More often it was the smoldering regard of the young knight with whom she had shared an illicit passion. The intensity of those stolen glimpses would leave her flustered and dazed, and far too aware that passion denied could be more heady than passion fulfilled.

She had told him that she had made that night into a magical memory, but that had been a hopeless lie. The memories lived in her with a reality that she both resented and relished. They occupied her mind, as did the impossibility of ever reliving those moments with a man who opposed all that she lived for.

Marcus suspected just how much in opposition they would be. The confrontation in her chamber had made that clear, just as it had revealed that the passion was not dead. It could not be ignored and would stand between them as a lure to damnation. For certainly a person who forsakes who she is for any reason, even love, can only know hell afterward.

She continued visiting the little market that formed in the yard every morning. A week after her return, she was there soon after dawn to sell Iolo her latest tapestry design.

Iolo appeared excited. He tucked the parchment into his tunic and handed over the coins. "My lady, I've something to tell you . . ."

Nesta hushed him with a subtle slice of her hand. Marcus was in the yard, and had noticed their exchange. He strolled up behind Iolo and eyed the coin in Nesta's hand.

"Only a few pence, Nesta? You labor hard for very little."

"I am in Wales, not London or Edinburgh. Most likely five men will take their profit before my designs find their way to a weaver. This one may not go far at all. There are those who buy them to tack on their walls for decoration, but they will not pay a weaver's price then."

"I don't suppose that there is a letter for Carwyn Hir folded in with the design?"

"Of course not. I told you, I do not know the man."

Iolo's color rose when he heard Marcus's challenge.

Marcus noticed. He held out his hand. "May I see the design one more time? It was my favorite one. I especially admired the countenance of lust that your brush made."

"This is not the one with the virtues. I sold that to a passing merchant days ago."

Iolo groped in his tunic and produced the design anyway. Nesta crossed her arms and tapped her foot while Marcus unfolded the parchment.

No note fell out. No scrap fluttered to the ground. She enjoyed Marcus's surprise.

"Did you think I would pass a letter right under your nose?"

Marcus refolded the design and handed it

back to Iolo. "Pity that you did not. I asked you to contact him."

"Do not wait on me to do so, since I can't. I have told you many times that I am but a pawn in all of this, not a king or a knight."

He did not appear convinced, but with a shrug he walked away.

A heavy exhale blew out of Iolo. "My gratitude for warning me, my lady. It wouldn't have done for him to hear what I was about to say." He backed up against the wall so there would be no more surprises. "There is a man in the town. A stranger. Staying at the wainright's. He sought me out. Knew my name because of my brother's journeys to Bala. He wants to meet with you." Iolo lowered his voice to a whisper. "I think it is one of your father's people. He didn't say so, but that is what I think."

"He will not let you bring the message to me?"

"He must see you himself, he said. I was to tell you it was very important."

It must be, for such a risk to be taken. The danger was not only the messenger's, but also hers.

It must be about Genith. Perhaps Carwyn had sent word that she was on her way to her marriage. Another possibility occurred to her,

however, and her stomach turned. Maybe
Genith had taken ill, or been injured during her
journey. The image of her sister suffering in that
rough camp full of men, with no woman to attend her, invaded her mind.

"I will try to find a way to come, Iolo. Tell
this man to wait. He is not to leave unless I send
word through you that meeting him is impossible."

Marcus visited the yard again the next morning.
He watched Nesta move among the farmers
and merchants, and saw the way they greeted
her. She had been doing this since she came, he
guessed, since she chatted with some as if they
were old friends.

Most of them were Welsh. That these lands
had been a part of England for centuries did not
matter. That the blood flowing in their veins
was as mixed as his own was irrelevant. If asked,
those men and women below him in the yard
would call themselves Welsh. Nesta was not the
King's whore to them, but the daughter of
Llygad ap Madoc, and the closest thing they had
to royalty.

The farmer Iolo's wagon made its slow way
to the gate, passing Nesta on the way. She said

a few words to the big man, and it seemed to Marcus that an expression of concern flickered beneath her smile.

He thought about the tapestry design that Nesta had sold Iolo yesterday. Others had been sold that way, most likely. Slowly, methodically, for months and maybe years, Nesta had been procuring coin, and not just for her own use. No doubt purses had been sent to Carwyn Hir.

Was that all she was about? Sending money to the rebels, to help sustain them? He did not think so. If tapestry designs could travel, so could letters. He would have to keep a much closer eye on Nesta now, and make sure he intercepted any that did. He began contemplating how to arrange that.

A little commotion at the gate diverted his attention. The last of the market wagons had been stopped, and a few began backing up. The gateway cleared for a short while, and then another wagon appeared, coming in and not going out. On its bench sat a huge blond man, and beside him, looking small in comparison despite his own considerable height, lounged David de Abyndon.

Marcus raised an arm in greeting, and went down to meet them. A merchant's wagon was no novelty in the yard, but everyone paused to gape at the blond giant.

As he passed Nesta, Marcus gestured for her to join him. "Come and meet an old friend of mine."

David stopped the wagon near the wall and climbed down to accept Marcus's greeting. "I thought we'd never get here, Mark," he said. "We had trouble on the road with bandits. Good thing I brought Sieg here, or I'd be held for ransom with no one to pay it."

Marcus glanced at Nesta at the mention of bandits. She appeared much more interested in the two visitors and the canvas-shrouded wagon.

"This is Nesta verch Llygad, David. I think you met her once."

"A man does not forget meeting such beauty. Greetings, my lady."

Nesta obviously recognized him. Marcus almost heard her mind realize that David had something to do with Marcus discovering she had fled London.

"You sold your newest tapestry design too soon, Nesta. I'm sure that David would have given a better price."

"Perhaps there will be more before he leaves."

"I hope you are staying long enough to make that true, David."

"Several days, if you will have us. My rump

is sore from that board, and my back broken and bitten from bad beds." He paced around to the back of the wagon. "I brought it. I said I would, and I hope that you are grateful since it diverted me seven days from my journey's path to get it here."

He untied the canvas and flung it aside. There, amidst some rugs and chests, lay the statue of his father that Rhys and Joan had made.

Marcus had seen it in the dusk, but it appeared even more accurate a likeness now as sunlight flooded the face. A hundred memories crowded into his head and heart. Some of them were painful, but the oldest and strongest were beautiful.

"Thank you, David. I am most grateful."

"You must allow me to pay you for your journey," Marcus said. He and David were in his solar, and his friend was inspecting the furnishings and objects with curiosity.

David always viewed things with a merchant's eyes, and Marcus could see him weighing value and assessing quality. A few questions had already been asked about where some items had been procured. Marcus assumed those were the ones of which David approved.

"Do not insult me. Bringing the statue was a favor to a friend." David lifted Dylan's harp off the table where he had placed it to remove the sack. He plucked at the strings and cocked his head at the sound. "Where did you get this? It is old and rare."

"That is a story that must wait for a long evening and much wine. Right now I want you to tell me about these bandits you met on the road."

"It was early this morning. About five came at us. They lost heart once Sieg drew his sword, so it was of little account. Not your normal thieves, though. They had a banner."

"Describe it."

"A red dragon. That is an ancient symbol in Wales, is it not?" David spoke as if the conversation barely distracted him from his examination of the harp, but his vague smile said he knew the importance of what he was revealing.

"It is also the banner of Llygad's men," Marcus said. "I will need to send messengers and learn if others have been attacked, but it looks as though the odd pause in their activities has ended."

"They are far from home if they are here," David said.

"Sometimes they venture out of the mountains. Better pickings, for one thing." Other possible reasons for their arrival poked into Marcus's mind, however. He began mentally planning a little expedition to clear the rebels off his lands.

"Do not let Sieg know if you plan to go after them. He is restless for action, and will delay my journey if the chance for fighting presents itself."

David set the harp down, and lifted a leather bag he had brought in with him. "I have some gifts for you. Cloth. This red is for you, so you can have a decent court garment made. You can wear it at your wedding, or are you already married?"

Marcus shook his head. "Genith is gone."

"Gone? She has died?"

He pointed to the harp. "Gone. With the man who owned that."

"Hell, we do need a long evening and lot of wine, don't we. Well, you can give this blue silk to someone more deserving, then." He set the red and blue cloth out, and picked up the harp again.

Another fabric poked out of the sack. Marcus tugged the corner into better view while David tested the instrument's sounds. "This green velvet is very rich. Is that for me, too?"

David tucked the harp into his arms and tried

the strings again. A little melody managed to come together. "That is for the sister."

"Do you mean Nesta?"

"She admired it in my shop that day, and I thought she might like to have it. It would be rude to gift you and Genith and not her."

Marcus stroked the luxurious velvet. He glanced at the handsome merchant absorbed in the harp. He thought about how David had remembered Nesta's coveting this cloth, and how he now planned to bestow this gift privately.

"David, you are an old friend, but let me make something very clear to you."

"What is that?"

"If you give Nesta this velvet, I will kill you."

The fingers on the harp did not pause. David did not even look up, but a vague smile formed as he watched the strings. "It sounds as though we need a *very* long evening and at least a barrel of wine, Mark."

All afternoon Nesta watched the statue being moved. It became a major project, with many men involved, but they probably finished in half the time they should because the huge Swede named Sieg lent his strength to the task. Finally a long line of satisfied men filed out the chapel door and headed to the hall for some ale and supper.

Once the yard was quiet, Nesta nipped down from the wall walk from where she had observed the work. This statue made her curious. That it bore a likeness very similar to Marcus did not especially fascinate her, nor that it was the first marble statue she had ever seen. It had been the expression on Marcus's face when he saw it in the wagon that compelled her to go. She suspected that the statue embodied some of the things she had neglected to ask him about that night.

Total silence shrouded the chapel. Like the lodge in the morning, only narrow shafts of light entered the cold, dark stones through the little high windows.

She found the statue in an alcove tucked inside the shallow transept. The figure of the last lord of Anglesmore rose above the stone marking his crypt. It was so lifelike that it might have been an image of the resurrection after the final judgment, when the bones leave the grave to enter the body again.

The single candle's flickering light abstracted the form into mysterious planes. Still, she recognized the face, older than the one she knew so well, and felt the power of the presence. It awed her that something made of stone could possess so much life.

"It captures him too well. It is as if his spirit dwells in it."

The quiet voice startled her. She swung around to see Marcus leaning against the opposite wall of the transept, studying the statue from the dark.

He came over to her, and the light affected his face much as it did the statue's. It was as if the stone image over the crypt had come to life to walk among the living, rejuvenated.

"My sister made it, along with her husband. It took many years, and now I wonder if she delayed the completion, so that she could keep it with her. Perhaps she relinquished it now because she sensed that I needed it, so I would remember."

"Do you need a statue to remember?"

"I need nothing to remember him. But the rest . . ." He gestured to the stone floor. "His bones were not here when I got Anglesmore back. He had died a traitor, and only saw a decent burial because the castle priest helped my sister take the body to a village plot. His crime had been to stand by his king when all others forsook him, and to hold to his oath of fealty while others violated theirs."

Nesta knew he was speaking of the deposition of the current king's father. Everyone knew how Marcus's father had not joined the rebellion led by the Queen and Roger Mortimer, and how he had paid when it had been successful.

"An oath or a promise is not to be broken," she said. "Everyone understands that, and if Mortimer had not been so ambitious in these parts it would have been different for your father."

"Perhaps, but it was not." A thin smile lined his mouth. "My father left me a rich legacy, and his example through his death is part of it. A man sworn to a king does not forsake that king, even if he is not fit to rule."

His tone surprised her. It carried a note of resentment, and a hint of the rebelliousness that could show in him sometimes.

"Do you blame your father for the stand he took, Marcus?"

"Much pain and grief flowed from it, and not to the good. I cannot blame him, but I can see that he might have been wrong." He stepped into the alcove and gave the statue a closer inspection. "I am told the craftsmanship is superior. What do you think?"

"I think that it was carved not only with skill, but with heart."

"Perhaps that was what moved me as I stood

over there looking at it. I had hoped it was his ghost warning me not to allow notions of duty to destroy all that matters to me."

He returned to her side, and although his eyes still met that of the figure's, his gaze seemed more inward. "I did not even avenge him myself. Others took the risks and wielded the swords."

"You were too young."

"Still, I did not forge my own destiny. Others handed it to me, just as others had taken it away. And I received justice only because of Edward's generosity. He restored Anglesmore to me, even though my father had not supported the moves that put him on the throne. It was one of his first acts after Mortimer was put down. He did not have to do that."

So there it was. What he owed to the body in the crypt, and to the young King whose word had absolved the family. He lived with an intricate knot of duties and memories and obligations.

She did not know what to say in response. She had no statue to show him of her own father, nor oaths of fealty to honor. But more than ever before, more than the morning in the lodge or the moment they entered the gate, she understood with horrible clarity what they would both sacrifice, and why.

"Edward is a good king, Marcus, and not like the last one. There will be no compromise with honor in serving him and your oath. His favor is to be welcomed, and worth much. He has proven that already, with his generosity to you."

He turned away from the statue and faced her. The flickering light reminded her too much of how he had appeared that night by the hearth, and his expression bore similar lines to those his face had worn while he watched her passion join his. Regret squeezed her heart so tightly that her chest hurt.

"Aye, Nesta, he is very generous," he said. "Up to a point."

It was a subtle warning, but also a clear one. About Edward and about himself.

As she left him and sought the chapel portal, her heart was heavy with the realization that he did not just suspect her of treason. He was convinced of it.

CHAPTER 12

THE NEWS SPREAD through the manor that men carrying Llygad's banner had attacked David and Sieg. The exploits of the rebels made for good stories, and their ability to avoid capture had reached legendary status. Even those at Anglesmore who did not favor Llygad's cause found the tales of his men fascinating, and everyone was happy to have something to talk about.

The excitement paled when Marcus prepared to go after the thieves. Nesta could see how that confused the sentiments of even the Welsh farmers who came to the market the next morning. A bit of raiding and thievery was one thing, but if Marcus rode out there could be se-

rious fighting. No one liked having their allegiances divided that way.

But ride out he did, with Paul and four other
knights and a troop of men-at-arms. Nesta had
been waiting for him to do so. There was only
one reason for Carwyn Hir to send men onto
Marcus's lands. He was trying to give her a way
to get to the town to meet with his messenger,
and that would be easier if Marcus was drawn
away from Anglesmore.

No sooner had the gate closed on Marcus's
troop than she set about doing just that. It had
been three days since Iolo had told her of the
man waiting to speak with her, and her heart
harbored the dreadful fear that he brought bad
tidings about Genith. The worry had grown
until it made her nauseous as she lay in bed at
night.

Sieg had insisted on joining Marcus's action,
but David remained at Anglesmore. She sought
him out soon after Marcus's departure, and
found him in the garden playing with the harp.
In a very short time he had taught himself
enough that a simple but lyrical melody flowed.

"Thank you for the cloth," she said. "It was
kind of you to remember I had admired the
green velvet."

"I brought it for Marcus. If he gave it to you,

that was thoughtful. Your thanks should go to him."

"However I received it, I am grateful. Now that I have it, however, I am impatient to see it made into a garment. I have dreamed of a surcotte since I first saw the fabric in your shop. The women here are busy with other sewing, but there is a tailor in the town who I think could do it as I want. Have you been to the town?"

"Not yet." Most of his attention remained on his fingers and the strings.

"It is of good size for Wales, although none of our towns are very big. Still, it has a few merchants wealthy enough to buy even your foreign luxuries. Why don't we go to the town today? You can bring your wares, and I can visit the tailor."

"Why not, indeed?" He set the harp aside. "The day promises to be quiet and tedious with Mark gone. I will have the wagon prepared, and if we leave soon we should be back by nightfall."

Delighted that her suggestion had met with quick approval, Nesta ran up to her chamber. Digging in her chest, she grabbed her engraved, gold armlet and pushed it up her arm, under her sleeve. She stuffed the velvet and some

other items in a cloth sack. By the time she returned to the yard, David's wagon was waiting.

"What is in the chest?" she asked as she
climbed up to sit beside him on the board. No
one made any attempt to stop her. In his haste
to go after Carwyn, Marcus must have forgotten to give any orders about whether she could
leave the castle.

"Good cloth from Flanders, and small rugs
from Castile."

"That sounds very valuable. Don't you fear
the thieves taking it?"

"I count on Mark keeping them far from
here. Besides, if I thought thieves would attack
us, the objects of my trade are the least of it.
You would not be coming."

Nesta decided it was fortunate that David was
English, and ignorant of just how bold the
Welsh could be. Then she noticed a lethal long
dagger attached to his belt, and decided the
merchant was probably not wholly dependent
on Sieg for protection.

The road to the town was quiet, no doubt
due to rumors about the raiders. Nesta found
David pleasant company. He had traveled
widely, and explained how he had just returned
in the spring from a long journey to Saracen
lands.

"What brings you to these parts?" she asked.

"After your exotic travels, it seems odd for you to peddle your goods out here."

"The western lords are grateful for the luxuries, and are willing to pay a higher price than those in London. I often come to western shires, and then make my way north to Scotland."

"You intend to go north when you leave here? Perhaps I will have a tapestry design or two for you to take. You will not see the profit that you would if you brought them to Flanders, but what you do see will come more quickly. I know a merchant in Carlisle who will buy them from you."

"I am always interested in a quick profit. Pity I did not bring the others with me."

Chatting became more of a chore as they neared their destination. Excitement over meeting the messenger, and worry about the news he brought, distracted her. She kept up the conversation with effort. As they rolled into the town, she pointed out the shops that carried high-quality wares.

They parted at the wagon. Carrying the linen sack, Nesta strolled away as calmly as she could even though her blood thrummed with impatience and caution.

She visited the tailor, but did not stay long. Opening her sack she laid out the velvet, a scrap of parchment showing a drawing of the surcotte she wanted, and an old gown that could be used for her measure.

David was nowhere to be seen when she slipped out of the tailor's shop. She ducked around to the alley and made her way to the edge of town where the wainwright crafted his wheels.

Iolo had said that the messenger stayed in a storage shack behind the works. She picked her way across a ground littered with bits of wood, and scratched at the wide, crude door of a structure that looked like a little stable.

She heard movement, and sensed someone peering at her through the door's cracks. Since most of her father's men had never met her, she shoved up her sleeve and held her arm high, so that the armlet and its engraved dragon would be visible.

The door opened, but no one stood there. She stepped into a darkened space. Wheels of various sizes lined its two sides, but the center remained clear. Ahead of her she saw another large door. Wagons and carts could be pulled in, fitted with their wheel, and then rolled out the other end.

"Nesta verch Llygad?" The deep, quiet voice was to her left. She pivoted to see a tall man standing against the wall, as if he had positioned himself to fight several swords.

"You took your time getting here, my lady."

"I am being watched. If not for word of the raids, I might not have been able to come at all. You should have trusted Iolo to bring me a message. We both risk too much with this meeting."

"This is not for the farmer's ears, or anyone's but yours. It is about your sister."

"She is ill? Injured?"

"Nay."

"Oh, Jesus, do not tell me she is d—"

"The bard did not bring her to us. They sent a message from the coast. He has family in Eire, and we think they went there."

Good for you, Genith. The thought jumped into her head along with a flood of relief. An image of Genith, smiling and happy, secure in Dylan's embrace as they faced a distant shore, flashed through her, lifting her heart and making her smile.

The joyful reaction disappeared in a blink, however, as the full implications of Genith's rash act crowded it out.

"This could unravel everything," she muttered.

"Now you see why I could not speak of it to

Iolo, and why I had to come myself with this news."

He stepped closer, and the light from the entrance made his height and features clearer. Nesta suddenly realized who was with her, and just how big this risk had been.

"You are Carwyn Hir, aren't you."

He was not powerfully built, but his height held a lanky, wiry strength. The bones of his face gave him an attractive, if craggy, appearance. Intelligent blue eyes sparkled with amusement at her surprise, and the mouth above his dark beard smiled.

He was younger than she had thought. Probably younger than herself. She had always assumed that a man her father's age had taken his place.

"You should not have come," she said in a desperate whisper, even though no one was around. "If you are found—"

"If I am found, we will both hang. So let us speak quickly, for there is much to decide. Your sister's disloyalty means the strategy must change, and we must agree on new plans now, before word of this betrayal spreads to our allies."

A hundred thoughts crowded her mind all at once. She took a deep breath and tried to force some order on them. Genith had caused a disaster, and the alternatives racing through her head seemed poor substitutes for the straight road that her father had drawn and that she had spent two years clearing.

"Perhaps I can take her place." She said it without enthusiasm. The very notion had a sickening sensation spilling into her stomach.

Carwyn shook his head. "The great lord that your father arranged for Genith to marry will not accept you instead. You are reputed to have lain with Edward. Aside from his pride, he will know that your past with the English king will only give Edward a personal vendetta as well as a territorial concern. It was why it was Genith and not you from the start."

"We have no choice, then, but to explain what has occurred. Genith's marriage was supposed to seal an important alliance for us, and we must make that alliance happen anyway. I will send the message, in my father's name. I will find a way to bring the message myself if I have to. The marriage of my sister was only symbolic anyway. The goal still has appeal, and the plan remains sound."

"It is not the alliance to be secured by your sister that concerns me, but those with the Welsh chieftains. That marriage might have only been symbolic, but it would have created assurances in their minds. It is the support of our own people that needs to be buttressed. You are Llygad's daughter, and have spoken with our leaders, visited them and cajoled them in your father's name. It is time for you to come and join with us, and do so again."

Her mind accepted the logic of it, but something inside her, something spiritual and powerful and furious, rebelled with a tremendous onslaught of denial. Her role in this should be done now. She did not want to spend the next weeks journeying throughout Wales, exhorting men who should need no convincing that it was now or never for the dream sustained by generations to be realized.

Carwyn reached out and his finger traced the engraved dragon on her armlet, still visible below her scrunched-up sleeve. "A different marriage will make our cause strong and solid. One between you and me, so that when I lead these men, I do so for you and what you represent. All of Wales will know the meaning of it, and no man will hold back then, or lose heart."

His suggestion shocked her. Horrified her. She stared, paralyzed by a wordless repudiation so visceral that her blood pounded in her ears.

"That was not part of my father's plan, Carwyn."

"Your father never comprehended that your

legend here was not one of shame. He never understood your power to inspire."

"You are not of the blood."

"Your status is beyond that of blood. When you accept me, the people will too. I will become the sword that you wield. Even if Genith had completed the marriage alliance, I would have suggested this. Now, with her gone, it has become essential."

He walked to the back doors and opened them. He left and returned with a horse that he proceeded to prepare for a saddle.

He expected her to agree. Just assumed it. The cause was in danger, and the marriage he proposed might save it. She sought the argument to reject his logic, but the chaos in her head and heart did not permit clear thinking. The sense that she was trapped, that duty decreed she take this step, only raised her panic.

Time slowed as he saddled the horse, but then it seemed only a blink had passed before it was done. Carwyn brought the horse forward. "Come, Nesta. Our men are keeping Marcus well away from here. We will be far gone before he returns."

She could not move. She could not speak. Her imagination showed images of herself with this man, lying with him. The notion repulsed her, and not because of his person or birth. Her heart screamed a furious refusal and began wailing, mourning the loss of another man and the enlivening excitement that she knew whenever he looked at her.

A shadow fell over them. A presence her spirit recognized invaded the shed. Carwyn's head snapped around, but she did not need to look to know who was there.

Amidst the new panic that sent her blood racing, another emotion also gushed. Wonderful, delicious, utterly traitorous relief.

It all happened in a chaotic instant. Carwyn's gaze darted to her. "Go, save yourself," she ordered. He swung up on the horse as the shadows drew nearer.

Bootsteps rushed behind her while Carwyn turned the animal. She pivoted to face the enemy.

Marcus and David ran up next to her, their attention on the horse and its rider. David drew the dagger off his belt and balanced it in his hand. "Dead or alive, Mark?"

"Alive."

The expression on David's face was that of a man who knew he could make his aim. She could not permit that. The daughter of Llygad could not allow Carwyn to be captured.

Her eyes locked on the blade, and its rise, and

the tension and movements of the arm that aimed it. At the vital instant of release, she lunged and threw herself into David.

Hands grabbed her and threw her aside. She landed in a heap against a wheel.

Shaking her dazed perceptions clear, she looked up. Marcus loomed above her, his sword in his hand. The expression on his face was indescribable. She saw fury, but beneath it there flowed a sadness, as if he had always hoped his suspicions were wrong.

David ran to the misaimed dagger and snatched it up. He headed to the barn's far door as the tail of Carwyn's horse disappeared outside it.

"Let him go," Marcus called. Then his voice turned very quiet and calm, as if he spoke for her ears only. "Let him go."

He sheathed his sword and pulled her to her feet. That only brought her closer to his silent anger. She faced him as fearlessly as she could, but caution returned with her wits.

The full implications of his arrival in this shed suddenly struck her.

He had surmised that the reason for the raids had been to draw him away. He had expected her to make some move, and even guessed that a meeting would take place. He had ridden out and then turned back, just as he had the day she helped Dylan to escape, and had told David and others to cooperate with any plan she hatched.

He understood her too well. It was as if he read her mind. How much else had he guessed? How much danger did he present to her?

"I said that you would not be leaving, Nesta."

Relief split through her fear. He did not know why this meeting had really taken place. He thought it had only been a ploy to get away.

David joined them, and Marcus's relentless gaze finally broke away. He took her arm and pulled her out into the yard. The wainwright ambled out from his home, taking in the knight and merchant and her. Sieg was leading the wagon and Marcus's horse out of the alley.

Marcus released her. While he went for his mount, she walked over to the wainwright. The man was of middle years, short and spindly with thinning hair, and he smiled ruefully as she approached.

"I think I'll be going back home to Powys, looks like," he said. "Won't do to stay here now, with him knowing I let one of them live in my shed."

"This is your home, even if you have family in Powys. Your trade is here."

"Trade is where the craft is, my lady. I'll be all right all the same."

Her gaze skimmed the house and shed that he

would sacrifice. "You risked much to help me. I am sorry that you will lose everything."

"My grandfather died fighting with Llywelyn. My father had his livelihood taken away. When the time comes, we do what must be done and can't count the loss, can we. Whether we live in the marches or the west or north, whether we serve the English as clerks or priests, the chance to have *Cymru* back will not be forsaken because of some wooden wheels or a bit of bread. It was thus for my grandfather and me, and it will be thus for my grandchildren and theirs."

His words touched her in ways he could never know. Her eyes teared, and shame ripped at her. She turned away from him, embarrassed by his loyalty because her own had been so unreliable.

Marcus walked his horse toward her. David waited on his wagon, and Sieg on his horse.

The chance to have Cymru back will not be forsaken for some wheels or a bit of bread. She had been ready to forsake it for something less necessary to her life than those wheels and bread were to the wainwright's. Something as frivolous as pleasure, and the foolish, childish dreams that could sleep in a woman's heart.

Marcus lifted her onto his horse and swung up behind her. As if he guessed what had happened, he did not speak to her. He left her to her private humiliation.

She tried to ignore his tense body behind her, and the fury pouring off him. She spilled all of her attention onto her self-loathing and disgust. She made it a point to not notice how comforting it felt to have him there, even if he was angry.

She tried to block her mind to how his arms surrounded hers much like a gentle embrace, and how his breath on her hair soothed her turmoil in a reassuring way.

Marcus dropped Nesta inside the gate, and then turned his horse and rode toward the hills. He went to a spot he had often visited as a boy, where the ground dropped away precipitously into a valley. As a child it had seemed to him that he could see the whole world from here, and he still found the vast view soothing.

It did not soothe him this day. He paced along the ridge, daring the red stone to crumble beneath him.

He had always known that he would face the devil's choice about Nesta. He had hoped, however, that it would not be this soon, and this dangerous.

He was furious with her, and with himself.

Despite his warnings, she was pursuing whatever scheme she had become embroiled in. Today had proven that, just as it had proven that protecting her had become his first thought, his *only* thought, when she was in danger.

In his mind's eye he saw her in that shed, talking to that man, her face a mask of confusion and dismay before she realized she had been caught. But he also saw her expression as she hurled herself at David, unmindful of the dagger's point or edge. He did not doubt that she would have taken the blade into her own body rather than let it find its true mark.

In that instant he had accepted, finally, just what he had in her. Not only Llygad's daughter, but Llygad's heir. Not just an ally to a small rebellion, but the heart and soul of it. She had been its cause and its beginning, and now she was its lifeblood.

He picked up a handful of rocks and threw them with all his strength, one by one, into the void in front of him. With each thrust his mind shouted a curse. Nesta was involved in something bigger than Genith's marriage. He knew it in his soul. And she would never tell him what it was, would never betray her father's cause. Not if he tried to beat it out of her, not if Stratford tortured her. Certainly not for the pleasure and intimacy they had shared in that lodge. She had already made that very clear.

The realization of just how clear only added possessive fury to the black turmoil rolling in his head.

The snort of a horse interrupted his heated thoughts. David rode up, dismounted, and calmly lounged against a tree.

"I came here to be alone," Marcus said.

"Nay, you came here to make a decision. An ear that forgets what it hears can be useful at such times."

Marcus ignored him and resumed pacing along the ridge, debating whether he could only protect Nesta by locking her away.

A chunk of stone, dislodged by his boot, skittered over into the empty space. Moments later, the small thumps of it bouncing down the steep hill penetrated the silence.

"Mark, when we were boys you used to do that on rooftops when you were angry at the world. You would balance on the top edge and dare fate. I was awed by your stupid bravery then, but this edge is not made of tile and we are no longer youths. Step away from that ridge before you go over."

Marcus grudgingly moved a few paces onto more solid ground.

"Back there at the wainwright's, we could

have stopped him," David said, getting to the heart of the matter in his irritating, placid way.

Aye, they could have. Either David's dagger or a shout to Sieg would have done it. But the lord of Anglesmore had stopped them.

"Did you notice the bearing of the man, David? Not a farmer, but a soldier. Did you notice his height? He was almost as big as Sieg."

"Tall or not, soldier or not, we could have stopped him. If he was one of her father's men, all the better for your purposes."

"David, in Welsh the word for 'tall' is *hir*."

"You think that was Carwyn Hir himself?"

Marcus nodded.

"So, you permitted the leader of those bandits to escape your grasp."

Marcus resented him laying out the betrayal of his duty so bluntly.

"It is a good thing my ears do not remember what they hear. Still, I understand why you did not want him taken. Knights need their quests, and it would have ended the rebellion in one afternoon. That is no fun."

The little jest did not fool Marcus. David had guessed the real reason. "It would have also proven Nesta's complicity beyond all doubt," Marcus admitted.

"Ah. Well, it appears that you have made a choice, doesn't it. The woman over your king.

I think that you made it long ago. That was why you had Sieg and me assist you today, instead of your own men. Will you go join her father's bandits in the hills now? The alliance of a marcher lord would give them status and power beyond whatever numbers you bring with them."

A shock of instant comprehension made Marcus freeze.

David was right. The alliance of a Lord Marcher would immediately turn those bandits into an army. Word of it would make their numbers swell a hundredfold. It would change everything.

That was the marriage Llygad had arranged for Genith. Genith was intended to marry a marcher lord, but not Marcus of Anglesmore, the King's man. Llygad had planned on a different Lord Marcher, with different ambitions. One who chafed at his duty to the crown, and considered himself sovereign. One who would support an uprising that would cast off England's hold not only on the Welsh, but on himself. Who exactly, Marcus did not know, but there were many who would be tempted.

It was brilliant, and it could work. Small wonder that Nesta had been so tenacious in seeing her father's will done.

Exhilaration at his discovery mixed with a deadly pulse in his heart. It was one thing to suspect that Nesta was involved in a dangerous plot. It was another to know for certain.

"I have not made the choice you accuse me of, David. I merely chose to avoid having to hand her to Stratford as a traitor." And he never would, if he could help it. The question was, could he?

"It sounds as if she *is* a traitor."

"Not to *her* country. Not to *her* people."

"An interesting argument. I will have it carved on your grave after the ax falls."

His new certainty left him restless and furious again. A part of him wanted to smash his fist into David's face. Anyone's face. But David's ruthless probing had also cleared his head, and his options suddenly loomed very sharply.

"You think I am a fool, don't you. You do not care for her."

"You are wrong there. I admire her greatly. She would have made a great merchant." He smiled at the notion. "If you are not going to join her, and you are not going to expose her, what will you do?"

Marcus had come to this ridge to determine the answer to that, and he suddenly realized that he knew what it was.

He gazed down at the crumbling ground two feet from his boot. He would be walking a similar edge for the next few months.

"I am going to stop her."

Nesta followed the steward up the stairs to the manor's second level. The formal way that Marcus had summoned her to his solar did not bode well for her.

She instinctively touched her bodice near her heart, and felt the little bulge there. Upon arriving back from the disaster at the wainwright's, she had found her father's ring and hidden it in her clothing as a talisman against more weakness.

For hours she had been numb, living in a daze as she accepted what she had done, and had refused to do. Her delay in agreeing to join Carwyn had almost gotten him captured. In the light of that, other delays and betrayals had suddenly grown in significance.

She had let Marcus seduce her into complacency, and at the most crucial moment in her father's plans. Worse, she had let him get too close and know her too well, so that slowly, bit by bit, he was anticipating her every move and then blocking it.

She touched the ring again, and squared her

shoulders. She tried to swallow the alarm that had risen in her when the steward came for her. Marcus had not returned to the manor until late, and had been cool and indifferent at the evening meal. Perhaps he had captured Carwyn after all. Maybe, on reflection, he had realized just what he had seen in that shed, and surmised just whom she had met.

She half expected to find a manor court waiting for her in the solar. Instead only Marcus was there.

Nay, not Marcus. Not the young man who had held her in his arms. The person sitting in the large chair near the hearth wore little warmth in his expression. He was all nobility and power and sternness.

She had been summoned to face the King's man.

The steward departed. Marcus coolly examined her. He appeared calm enough. His arms rested on the sides of the chair in a relaxed pose. He did not speak, and seemed to be waiting for something.

It entered her mind that, considering the formality of this audience, perhaps he expected her to kneel. She would not. He was not *her* lord.

"Who was the man you met at the wainwright's?" His voice was quiet, but firm.

She had done much thinking in the last

hours, and already knew what she would reveal. "One of my father's men."

"I should not have let him go, then. It was careless of me. Did he come to take you away?"

"He came to give me information about Genith. Dylan betrayed me. He did not take my sister to them. They have received word that Dylan and Genith fled to Eire."

"That must be a great disappointment to you. I read the letter that Genith wrote to me before she left. In it she told me that your father had arranged a different marriage for her and that she felt obliged to fulfill his wishes."

"Aye."

"Who was this other man?"

"Since it will not happen, it no longer matters."

"I suppose it does not. Genith surprises me. I think there was more to her than I saw. I would not have said she had it in her to defy you so boldly."

His words touched a quiet anguish that existed below the bleak shame she had faced these last hours. Genith had surprised her, too. She had not fully known her sister. With Genith gone for good, now she would never have the chance to.

She had been hiding from the sadness of that, but now it deluged her. She remembered their parting on that snowy hillside, and Genith's tears and Dylan's patience. Dylan had known what he intended to do, and Genith's soul had suspected. Only she herself had been ignorant. She had been so distracted by the grand design that she could not see what was right in front of her.

She would never see her sister again. Genith's betrayal of duty suddenly seemed insignificant compared to that.

She dropped her gaze so that Marcus would not see the trembling she felt in her lips. At least this conversation had taken the path that she wanted. She forced composure on herself, and walked through the door he had opened.

"She is truly gone for good this time, Marcus. Even Carwyn Hir cannot hand her back to you. The marriage the King offered to you will not happen. Cannot happen."

"So it would appear."

He sounded far too calm. That chilled her more than harsh anger. "Any responsibilities you had regarding my father's men are also ended, since they were attached to this marriage."

"You make a good point."

"Needless to say, there is also no reason for me to stay here. Edward's request about that was also tied to the marriage."

"The clarity of your reasoning is impressive, Nesta. It would seem that Edward and Stratford's simple strategy for appeasing your father's men and returning Llygad's home to his family has completely fallen apart."

"I am sure they will find some other plan. However, as you say, this one has fallen apart. Therefore, I think it would be best all around if I returned to the convent in Scotland as soon as—"

"Of course, if one looks at it another way, the strategy can still work."

"It cannot. My sister has all but died. The prize has slipped both your grasp and mine."

"I was told to marry the daughter of Llygad ap Madoc. That is still possible. There is another daughter available."

She looked up at him in confusion. It took a five count for her to realize that he meant *her*.

"You are *mad*."

"I think I am very clever." His sly, triumphant smile showed just how clever.

That smile piqued her annoyance, and her worry. It was far too confident.

She strode toward him. "Think, Marcus. There were reasons why it was Genith you were to marry and not me."

"You refer to the King. Once it is done, he will accept it. Stratford will reason with him when he returns from Flanders. Even if Edward still wants you, he will see that this is the best solution. It will also please his queen to have you married, and to a man who has no fondness for dallying at court."

"You are wrong. There are some things that kings do not accept with grace, or subject to political convenience. You may pay for this with everything."

"I think the risk is small. Edward is very practical."

A little panic began beating inside her. She could feel the bulge of her father's ring next to her heart, weighing heavily with all of her renewed resolve. She could not permit Marcus to pursue this.

"That was not the only reason," Marcus said. "You were not given to me as a bride because your reputation would make the gift an insult."

She already knew that. As Carwyn had said, that was the same reason why her father had planned his great marriage alliance around Genith and not her.

"You should heed that reason, Marcus. It will besmirch your honor if you marry the King's whore."

"I told you that I do not think of these things as most men do. Fulfilling my duty is worth a little talk. *You* are certainly worth it."

"The King's man should not be swayed by a night's pleasure."

"The King's man sees a simple solution to many problems, that is all. That I will enjoy having you in my bed is, as you once said, merely a savory added to a full banquet."

"When Edward returns, all will assume that the King cuckolds you, with your permission."

"So long as he does not try it, I do not care what is assumed."

"And if he does try it?"

"You will deny him."

"Do not be so certain of that." She snapped it in frustration and anger.

"I am sure of it, Nesta."

She should have been flattered, but his cool certainty only infuriated her.

She was the daughter of Llygad ap Madoc, and this English lord must be made to accept that this plan of his was unacceptable.

"This will not happen." She put all of her will and strength into her tone, and enunciated each word clearly, one by one.

He rose, unimpressed. "If I decide on this solution, it will happen, Nesta. You can be sure of that."

He strolled toward her. She found herself backing up, as she had that day in the cottage. "I will deny you, just as Genith did."

That seemed to impress him even less. He came toward her too confidently, too deliberately. Her caution rose to a chaotic pitch. She did not want him near her. She wanted him back in that chair, being the lord, not approaching her like this.

Her reaction raised her ire again. The real danger came not from him, but from the corner of her heart that had been weak to him too often. She stopped moving and dug in her heels. She would let him see what the daughter of Llygad was made of. Not silly, womanish stuff.

He came too close. So close that she had to look up at him. She did so, and let him see that she was not impressed either.

He touched her cheek. It was an enemy's touch. The Marcher Lord's examination of his future property. "It will happen, Nesta," he repeated.

She pushed his hand away. "You would force this marriage on me? You did not with Genith."

"It was never forcing the vows that stayed my hand with your sister, but forcing her to my bed. I do not think that will be necessary with you."

He spoke with that cool certainty again. Her head almost split with fury. How dare he be so confident in his power to subvert her?

"I will not be willing. If you do this, you will have a cold, childless marriage."

"You are so sure of your resolve? I am not. After all, I am the man you begged for."

He touched her face again. He laid his palm on it, possessively. The rough warmth of that touch made her heart rise in a distressing, frightening way. His deep gaze summoned too many memories, dangerous in their allure. The armor of her anger began cracking. With one touch he had proven just how weak he could make her.

"If you force this, it will not be a true marriage. My heart will not be willing."

"I will have a lifetime to win your heart, Nesta."

The daughter of Llygad itched to scratch his face and pummel his chest. But another woman, the one who had looked in his eyes during the heights of passion, was incapable of ignoring what he was saying. Her heart lurched hungrily, hopelessly, at the notion that this man welcomed a lifetime with the King's whore.

Her furious denial died, and a desperate plea took its place. "Do not do this. I will be torn in two, and forced into betrayal no matter which half wins."

"If I have my way, there will be no need for betrayal. No chance for it. If I do not have my way—I have no illusions, Nesta. I know what I have in you." His head dipped, and his lips brushed hers.

Too late it occurred to her distraught mind to refuse the kiss, and the brief connection flushed her whole body, increasing her dismay.

Horrified, she ran for the door, anxious to be away from him so that she could once more rebuild her resolve.

CHAPTER 13

NESTA ROSE the next morning and girded herself for battle. Armed with several new arguments against Marcus's ridiculous idea of marriage, she sallied forth to challenge him.

When she did not find him in the hall or the yard, she concluded he must be in his chambers. She asked a servant to see if he would meet with her.

A while later, Paul sought her out. "I am sorry, but my lord has secluded himself in his chamber and will not be available today. He has given word that no one is to enter, not even the servants."

"Is he ill?"

"I do not think so. He said that he has an important decision to make and needs time alone.

I believe—I could be wrong, of course—but I believe that he is praying for divine guidance."

"Praying? All day?"

"You do not approve?"

"Nay . . . I mean, aye . . . it is just he never seemed overly devout to me."

"He is a great lord, with many burdens. If he seeks God's counsel, we should all be grateful," Paul said solemnly.

Nesta decided that was true. If Marcus was conversing with God, and the decision he pondered was marrying Nesta verch Llygad, she would not need the arguments she had spent half the night constructing. God would never approve of abusing a sacrament by forcing a woman into marriage.

She retreated to her chamber to work on her parchments. As she passed the second level of the castle, she noticed the silence coming from Marcus's chamber. A monastery's cell could not be more quiet.

She paused and cocked her head, searching to hear the low mumble of prayer through the stones. Her ears finally caught the vague buzz, but it came in fits and starts, as if Marcus provided two sides of a conversation.

As she continued up the stairs, another sound broke the silence. A laugh, long and hearty, penetrated the heavy door of Marcus's chamber.

She raised her eyebrows and continued on her way. God must have said something very humorous.

In her chamber, she set up her makeshift table and unrolled a parchment. It would be nice to use a sheet to write to Genith. She wondered if she would ever hear from her sister, or if they were dead to each other.

Thinking about Genith only made her sad, so she turned her thoughts to the next few days. If Marcus was rethinking this marriage, he might rethink everything, and allow her to leave. Of course, whether he permitted it or not, she would have to find a way to do so. The ring nestled between her breasts would not let her forget how essential that was.

A deep melancholy pierced her right below the ring's weight. She bit her lower lip and picked up her brush, and told herself it was sorrow about Genith that caused the pain.

Marcus did not rejoin the household until dinner the next day. He appeared rested and very calm, as if his retreat had soothed his body as much as his soul.

At the end of the meal, he called the steward over. "David is leaving in two days. I have decided to make a small feast for him tonight, since his travels will keep him eating tavern food for months. Help me plan it with the steward, Nesta. Such things can use a woman's touch."

Nesta thought of the wily merchant whose face never revealed his thoughts. The way she saw it, he had all but lured her to damnation in the wainwright's shed. She thought he deserved a fist, not a feast, but she offered some suggestions on the meal just the same. She would have to hide her resentment about the role David had played that day. He was willing to pay too much for her designs, and she had one to sell him.

That night they enjoyed a wonderful feast. It was noisy and crowded and raucous. Nesta sat beside Marcus. He was in such good cheer that the animosity between them disappeared with the flowing wine.

Unfortunately, that meant that the other emotion that bound them had its way, and a nostalgic intimacy settled over her as the evening progressed.

Marcus must have felt it too, because he grew less careful in his behavior with her. When they spoke the affectionate warmth in his dark eyes acknowledged what they had known together. He took to feeding her wine and bits of food with a charming, teasing delight.

"I am glad to see that your religious retreat has returned your good humor," she said after swallowing one tidbit. "I trust it has also returned your good judgment."

"My judgment has never been so sound, Nesta. Completely so."

"Not completely so. You should not be so obvious with me in front of all these people."

"You look so lovely tonight that I could not help myself."

She laughed. "It is the wine. All women look lovely after a man has drunk several cups."

"I have not noticed any other woman. Nor have I seen you notice any other man."

She felt herself flush. "Did you spend your last day practicing pretty words, Marcus? Do you think to sweet-talk me into a marriage that you cannot force?"

"Would that pretty words could sway you, Nesta. Nay, I have accepted the steel of your resolve. But do not deny me my pleasure in having you here beside me. If I am too familiar, talk of that will disappear when you do."

That surprised her. "You agree that I can leave?"

He shrugged. "I have spoken with David. You said that you want to go back to Scotland, and the convent. He has agreed to escort you there."

"I did not expect to leave so soon." She tried to ignore the way his words had emptied her out. She told herself that her dismay was with the proposed destination. When she left here she did not want to go to Scotland at all.

"You will be safe with David. He and Sieg are worth ten men-at-arms." He lowered his voice. "Word has come that your father's men have been raiding again for some time now, in the marches and the midlands. I must see to that, as I am bound to, and it is better if you are well away from the strife. I cannot bring you to Scotland myself, or spare the men to escort you, so David's offer is welcome."

She did not know what to say. He had capitulated on all points, so she could hardly argue now that she should remain at Anglesmore until she hatched her own plan for escaping and joining Carwyn.

The steward came down the table, placing silver cups filled with new wine in front of them. Servants carried in a tray of cakes to finish the meal.

Nesta stared numbly at the preparations for the final course as the din in the hall flowed into a distant, seamless noise. Suddenly she felt totally separated from the happy household spread in front of her. She became isolated from everything and everyone.

Except Marcus. She felt him beside her as if their bodies touched. The deep knowing of him that had emerged in the lodge wove its spell, heightening her awareness of him to a poignant sensitivity.

Two mornings hence, he would give her what she wanted and send her away. Then he would be all but dead to her, like Genith. His generosity moved her, exposing profound regrets that she dared not examine.

He leaned toward her. Touching her chin, he turned her face to him. He lifted his wine cup to her lips. "You will like this. It is a special wine, sweet to flatter the taste of the cakes."

It seemed to her that he knew what she was feeling, and that his expression held its own regrets. She sipped the wine absently while they watched each other, their heads so close that his breath warmed her cheek.

The wine became an invisible kiss.

He slid his arm around her shoulders, and held the cup more purposefully. While she drank, his head dipped behind hers, and he whispered in her ear. "Come to me in the garden tonight."

Two days and she would be gone. She would leave with David, but she would not go to Scotland with him. Marcus must know that. He was not stupid.

Two days and he would take up his duty, and she hers. They would be adversaries again. Enemies. And something hopeful and glorious would truly be no more than a magical memory.

"Say you will come," he whispered.

She drank more wine. She nodded.

laughter . . . bright colors and giggling women . . . hands turning her as she smiled and smiled . . . heady, wonderful happiness.

A sea of faces, moving to and fro like waves . . . torches, and talk she could not make out . . . Marcus, incredibly handsome and gentle. His warm hand in hers, and distant voices, and his wonderful eyes looking in hers until the world fell away.

A kiss . . .

A kiss, warm and sweet like the last wine of the feast. Nesta felt it and tasted it again, and opened her eyes to embrace the man who had given it to her.

The kiss and the dream disappeared. She found herself on her bed, alone in her chamber. Squinting, she looked to the light coming through the window slit.

It was midday. She had slept through the morning.

She sat up. Her head felt thick, and lopsided

with an inner weight. Remnants of the dream
fluttered through her mind, growing vague
even as they fell.

She had drunk too much wine at the feast. So
much that she did not remember returning to
this chamber and this bed. She tried to shake
the fuzz from her head. Her last clear recollec-
tion was agreeing to meet Marcus in the
garden.

Had she gone? A fine thing if she had, and
now couldn't remember it.

A kiss . . . She remembered that very clearly.
His hands holding her face and his mouth
touching hers and a hungry response overwhelming her so badly that she would not let
him go.

A very wonderful kiss. She rose and began
dressing. If that was all she remembered from
their last shared passion, it was a beautiful memory at least.

She descended to the hall where the servants
already prepared for the midday meal.
Everyone moved in the lazy, subdued way typical of people after a night of revelry.

The steward noticed her. He bowed.

That was odd. Just how odd worked on her
mind as she walked through the hall. Heads
turned. Faces grinned. Sidelong glances slid her
way. She grew increasingly uncomfortable.

She felt her face burn as she comprehended the implications. In her drunken state last night she must have done something indiscreet. The whole household appeared to know she had met Marcus in the garden.

Her women entered the hall from the sewing room. Winnifred ran over, wearing a smile so broad that her ears moved.

"Oh, my lady, it was so beautiful. Like a tapestry come to life, it was. To see you so happy—to witness such pure emotion—I like it here, and am glad to stay. Now Philip says maybe he and I will marry too—"

Nesta held up her hand to halt the onslaught. Parts of Winnifred's rambling had gotten through her stuffy head. A horrible suspicion began ruthlessly clearing her mind. "What do you mean, Philip and you might marry *too*?"

"With your and my lord's permission, of course. I know Philip drinks a bit, but he is a good man, and, well, we all of us drink a tad too much now and then, don't we?"

Nesta ignored the allusion to her recent behavior, and forced the only point she cared about. "What do you mean, *too*? Who else is getting married?"

Winnifred's broad smile wavered. "Why, you, of course."

"I certainly am not." Even as she said it, she

realized what had happened. Lightning replaced the cloud in her head.

The knave! He had lied to her last night at the feast. He had fed her wine and tidbits so everyone would see them acting like lovers and thus accept his announcement of their marriage this morning. He had gotten her besotted deliberately so that *she* would be abed and unable to refute his scurrilous lie.

"If Marcus announced that he and I will marry, he did so without my acceptance or permission," she said. "You are to go to every person within these walls and explain that. I will treat with Sir Marcus myself."

"My lady, all heard—"

"I am sure that all have heard. Now, let them hear the truth." She turned on her heel to go and heap hellfire on Marcus. "Where is the deceitful churl?"

"Churl! My lady, it is not wise—"

"Where is he?"

Silenced by her yell, Winnifred pointed to the threshold.

Nesta strode out to the yard. Marcus was nowhere to be seen, but she spied Paul near the stable. She aimed for him, her eyes narrowing and her body tight with outrage.

No doubt the farmers this morning had heard this lie too. She pictured the story spreading like a fire through dried fields, over the farms, into the hills, throughout the land. That was Marcus's plan—to have the Welsh, especially Carwyn and her father's men, believe she was tying herself to the King's man. It could change everything. It could make her useless to her father's cause.

She quickened her pace. More silly smiles greeted her as she passed. A knight's wife, who had considered herself the leading lady of the manor, made it a point to move out of her way and make a deep curtsy of deference.

Nesta bore down on Paul. "Grin or bow and I will scratch your eyes out. Where is Marcus?"

Paul backed up a step. His thumb jerked toward the stable.

She pushed past him and entered the stable full of shadows and horse smells.

Marcus was just taking the reins of his horse from a groom. He noticed her intrusion. "Good morrow, Nesta."

"A devil's fart on this morrow. Marcus, I am going to *kill you*."

The groom's shocked eyes peeked over the horse's rump. Marcus turned to him with a man-to-man grin. "Women. They are so changeable. Happy one moment, distraught the next."

"I am not distraught, you scheming bastard. I

am so angry that I would cut you down if I were a man."

He walked his horse to her. She straightened to her full height and glared at him.

"You must not speak to me like this, Nesta," he said quietly. "A lord cannot permit such disrespect."

"You have not begun to hear the depths of the disrespect waiting for your ears."

"Then let us go where it is for my ears alone." He grabbed her and threw her onto the horse and quickly swung up behind her. "I am taking my bride for a ride," he called back to the groom. "Tell the others our departure will be delayed."

"I am not his bride," Nesta insisted furiously, glaring back at the groom so he would know she meant it.

"A maiden's misgivings. You know how that goes," Marcus said to the thoroughly stunned groom.

"I am not a maiden, and the whole world knows it," Nesta hissed.

Marcus moved the horse to a trot and they shot out the stable door. As they passed Paul, Nesta saw him shake his head and make the sign of the cross.

✦　✦　✦

She refused to touch him. Despite their speed, she would not hold on to him. She bounced along, grasping the horse's mane and the front of the saddle. Marcus tried once to steady her with his arm, but she smacked it off and gave him a glare that warned not to try it again.

He finally reined in at the foot of a hill. She slid down as soon as the horse stilled. She did not want him helping and touching her.

She strode away from him, and fought to contain her trembling rage. She found just enough composure to speak coherently, and turned to face him.

"I will speak to everyone. I will tell them that you lied."

"Nesta—"

"Listen to what I say and believe I can make it so. I will be sure all the Welsh in the region know what you did. The fire of your lie will be followed by the blaze of truth and my words will overtake and consume yours."

"Nesta, hear what I am trying to say—"

"If you attempt to pursue this, I will not submit and say the pledge or vows. Starve me if you want. Beat me. I will deny you with my last breath. I will—"

"Nesta, we were betrothed last night. The whole household saw you accept me. They all heard you make the pledge."

Shock took her breath away. For an instant her whole body went cold. Then, as full comprehension pierced her astonishment, the heat of fury trickled through her again.

"You plied me with wine and then took advantage of my condition. I will explain that—"

"No one will believe you. You were very happy, Nesta. Delighted. You refused to break the betrothal kiss, and hung on me long after it was over."

A kiss . . .

"All of the witnesses will say that you pledged your troth willingly. Eagerly."

Bright colors and laughter. Words that she could not hear.

Marcus strolled toward her. His dark eyes regarded her warmly as he gently brushed an errant strand of hair from her temple. "You also pledged your love. The women were in tears, you were so eloquent."

Dear saints. She felt her face burn, with anger and embarrassment. "I was out of my head."

"You did not appear to be. Perhaps for once you were in your right head, free of the burdens you carry."

"If I spoke words of love, I assure you I was not myself."

Her mind veered from memory to memory. She tried to pull the ones that mattered out of the fog, but only little snips would come. Instead she saw herself at the table, and Marcus being so solicitous. Flattering her. Feeding her tidbits.

Agreeing to send her to Scotland. Lies, that. But why bother with such deceptions?

The answer broke through her confusion. He had done it so she would drop her guard, and act softly toward him. If they appeared affectionate, what followed would not appear odd and abrupt.

She saw him again, mesmerizing her with his attention, raising a wine cup to her lips . . .

"You *churl*. I was not in my cups at all. You fed me a potion!"

He did not turn a hair. "An excellent one. Paul knows this wisewoman—"

"You spent a day in prayer and God told you to *drug* me?"

"I prayed very little that day. I retreated to my chamber to test the potion on myself first, to be sure it would not harm you. David held the vigil with me, to let me know later how I had been affected."

"Then you know that your actions and words were not of your own will. Just as mine were not. I will petition to have this annulled."

"You must do so to the archbishop. Let me think . . . ah, that would be Stratford." His eyes sparked with wicked amusement. "I have sent a messenger to him already, to let him know what has transpired. If he objects to this marriage, you will not need to petition at all, and the wedding will never take place. If he finds it convenient to his plans . . ."

"If he does, it will make no difference. There will be no wedding, and this betrothal is not legitimate."

"In the eyes of the world, it was most legitimate."

"You have managed to deceive the world, but you know the truth. This was despicable. I thought you a better man."

That provoked him. Jaw tight and eyes burning, he strode to her and grasped her shoulders. "I will not let you endanger yourself through complicity with Carwyn and his plans. Nor will I let you put me in the position of having to hand you over for judgment as a traitor. Deceiving you last night was an easy choice, Nesta, once I weighed my options."

She stuck her face up at him. "Very neat to your mind, no doubt, but despicable all the same. Now, hear my resolve, Marcus. I will not let you make me into a war prize that you subdue through marriage. I will not allow nonsense like passion divert me from what I must do.

Bride or not, defying you will also be an easy choice."

She shook off his hold but did not move away. She would not give him the satisfaction of thinking she feared him. She met his fiery gaze with her own glare while their wills silently battled each other.

One piece was missing, and she needed to know just how much of a knave he had been. "I have no memories of the night. Was there anything more than that one betrothal kiss?"

"You offered but I refused."

"How chivalrous."

The firm line of his mouth did not soften. "It was not chivalry, but pride. When I take you again, I want you to remember it."

"That memory will never be made. That kiss is all the warmth you will get from me in this false alliance."

She put all of her outrage into the repudiation. He didn't even blink. If anything, a hint of amusement softened the stern set of his face. The eyes gazing at her became those of a man who assumed he could have her if he wanted to.

She resented those possessive lights, and the confidence they implied, and his assumption that he could make her weak. She resented even more, however, how the connection began casting a little spell that made her heart sparkle.

Still furious enough to kill, she strode away. "I will walk back to the castle. If you insist on staying with me, keep well away. I do not want to know you are there. I do not even want to hear your horse's hooves on the ground."

CHAPTER 14

ALL IS ARRANGED. Sixty men will ride with us. I called the feudal summons from some of the farms, so the defenses here will not be depleted."

Paul sank onto a bench as he gave his report. He had not washed or changed, and his garments and curly black hair showed the sweat and dust of an afternoon of hard riding. The recent visits to the farms had not caused his condition, but rather the earlier hours in the saddle beside Marcus's.

Marcus understood why his friend's eyes appeared dull, and his manner tired and subdued. Making the summons, even part of it, meant that they were going on war footing. The order had been a tacit acknowledgment on Marcus's part that Carwyn and his bandits would not be easily suppressed.

He had taken the step after seeing the results of their raiding on the western edge of his estate, and after receiving a messenger from a midland lord saying they had grown bolder in the southern valleys as well.

Marcus gestured for the attending servant to give Paul some ale. Paul downed the whole cup and wiped his beard on his sleeve. "Been a while. Since an army was formed here, that is."

A long while, Marcus thought. Not since his father had gathered one in anticipation of Mortimer's siege. The young men receiving the call to service during the next few days would remember coming as boys to claim the bodies of their menfolk from that bloody yard. The images of that massacre would be in everyone's head.

The last summons had resulted in disaster. Marcus decided it was a good thing that he was not superstitious.

"Do you think word of the betrothal will change things?" Paul asked. "I can't see them disbanding because of it, myself, no matter what Stratford thought. He doesn't know the Welsh, does he?"

Not as well as Paul did. Although Paul could trace his lineage back to a Norman archer who had come with the Conqueror, most of the men in his family had married Welsh women. Paul probably had as much Welsh blood in him as Nesta.

"His plan sounds good. Sounds right," Paul continued. "But it leaves out too much that he doesn't comprehend, seems to me."

It certainly did. First and foremost, it left out the tenacity and intelligence of Nesta verch Llygad. "I do not think they will disband."

"Ah, well, maybe it will at least delay things a bit. Confuse them. It feels as if winter will come early, so—"

"I do not think this will delay things. I think it will hasten them. I am counting on it. I have a feeling that time is my enemy in this. I will force their hand, and see what happens."

"Force it as you did the other night?"

Only Paul and David knew about the potion. And Nesta, of course.

She had neither spoken to him nor looked at him for two days now.

"She'll try to get word to them about how that really was," Paul said.

"I hope that she tries. I need to know how she communicates with them."

He had allowed her to go into the yard in the mornings, to continue meeting with her farmers. Only now there was always someone watching her, to see if she slipped a message to one of them. So far, none had been passed.

Paul heaved himself to his feet and gave a groaning stretch. "Bed for me. Those men will start coming tomorrow, and I've my work set getting them ready." He hesitated, and gazed into the hearth fire while his lips pursed. "Won't be like the last time."

Marcus knew that he was not referring to the defeat.

"Was an English army then, and our people fought like lions, I'm told. This time we go into our hills. Most of the men coming with us are at least partly Welsh, Marcus. What good will they be against their own?"

"I will not be relying only on them. I fear that before this is over, there will be English enough swelling our ranks. In the meantime, these men will not let us down. They will do their duty." He caught Paul's eye. "As we will, my friend."

Chagrin flickered in Paul's expression. He was embarrassed to have his own ambivalence seen for what it was.

As Paul left the chamber another man, not at all soiled and sweaty, entered.

"You appear to be a man with much on his mind, Mark. Lordly things, no doubt. I will leave tomorrow and let you have your fun."

"You are welcome to stay."

"There is war in the air, and I always stay away from that. Sieg is displeased with my decision, however. He thinks if we stay he will get at least one good battle in."

"At most one, if I am fortunate."

David took some ale from the servant, and then sent the man away. Marcus had learned not to mind the way the merchant would do things like that, as if he normally only pretended to know his place, and felt no need for the lie when among friends.

David settled himself on the bench where Paul had been. "Your bride spoke with me a while ago. Very courteous and sweet, she was."

"Did she try to bribe you to sneak her away?"

"She offered no money."

"If you dare to insinuate that she offered better than money—"

David raised a calming hand. "Whoa, friend. I would not risk my neck by taunting you thus. She offered no money because she was seeking *my* money." He slipped his hand into his pourpoint and withdrew a parchment.

It was another tapestry design. Marcus unfolded it. It showed a river flowing from top to bottom, with a lady on one side and a knight on the other.

"The quality is far inferior to the others she sold me. Less care in the coloring and design," David explained, assuming Marcus couldn't tell the difference. He could, however. Anyone could see that this design was not one of Nesta's best.

"She told me of a merchant in Carlisle who would buy it. That intrigued me, since when she sold me the others she mentioned a merchant in Edinburgh. The woman established an entire trading network from her convent. I told you she would make a great merchant."

Marcus fingered the parchment spread on his lap. Perhaps . . . nay, that would make no sense. But Carlisle was not far by sea from Wales . . .

"Perhaps not a trading network, David. Perhaps an information network." He rose and carried the parchment to his table and moved three candles around it. David joined him and they examined the design.

"I see no letters or symbols. It would have to be the image itself," David said.

Marcus studied the lady and knight, separated by the river. Genith and her intended husband? Was this message alerting someone to the failure of that alliance?

If so, who? Carwyn Hir already knew about it, so it could not be meant for him. Surely the marcher lord who was to have taken Genith's hand had been told by now.

He examined the design again. This image might have an interpretation that fit what he knew, but the others had not. What message could be read in the seven virtues and vices, or in that image of Dylan playing his harp in the forest?

None that he could think of.

In all likelihood these designs were only what they seemed, a way for Nesta to earn coin.

He folded the parchment and handed it back. "Bring it to the merchant in Carlisle."

"You are sure?"

He wasn't sure, but even if it bore a message he would allow it to go. He had decided he wanted this to unfold now, while he might still control its size and direction, and interfering with a message might only cause delay.

"Bring it to the merchant. As quickly as your travels permit."

David tucked the parchment away. "I will leave before the household rises, so I will make my farewell now. Will you visit London before spring?"

"If Edward returns, I am sure that I will." The King would undoubtedly summon the man who had dared to betrothe the King's lover without permission.

David smiled in the enigmatic way he had. "I could stay here longer if you like. You are not well practiced in deceit. I could counsel you in that."

"My deceits are over, I hope. Now I only have to fathom hers."

They clasped arms, and Marcus walked with David to the door. His friend stepped through the threshold, but paused and turned.

"She will not give it up, you know. Not even for you. The words of love she spoke at the betrothal might be in her heart, but her head does not accept them."

It was as clear a warning as David would ever give.

"Have a safe journey, old friend, and do not spend all your profits on beautiful women."

A glint entered David's deep blue eyes. "Guard your own profits from beautiful women, too."

She will not give it up. Not even for you.

Marcus knew that. He had not needed David to warn him.

He crossed his arms on the top of the wall as he looked out into the night. In the darkness below he could barely make out the forms of cottages, and the gristmill by its stream, and in the distance the black mounds of the hills that announced the rising of the land to the west.

The cold was sharp enough that he regretted not bringing a cloak. Paul had been right. The swings from warm to cold that marked the autumn in these parts were already ending. It looked to be an early winter, and a bitter one.

He thought about Nesta, sleeping in her chamber. She was probably naked, and uncovered because she did not feel the chill. He considered going there, just to see her. Not her body. Images of that were in his head so clearly, so persistently, that he did not need the reality. It would be nice to see her resting, however. To see her face without the veil of anger and resentment that she wore when they met now.

She will not give it up. He did not expect her to. He knew something about the constancy of women. His own sister had taken up a quest and held to it, clung to it, when most men would have been discouraged. Even her love of a man had not dissuaded her. It was only at the end, when she had won, that Joan rejected the life that had demanded the quest and joined Rhys in another.

And Joan *had* won. His presence on this wall was proof of that. What if she had not? And what if the man himself had thwarted her?

My love has made me a girl again, so that the

world appears fresh and new. It fills my heart with sparkling light. The grace of heaven could not be more powerful.

Beautiful words. Nesta's words. Spoken at the betrothal with the earnest honesty of someone seeing the depths of her own soul. Stunning words, that he already knew would be the last ones that his mind would hear at the moment of his death.

Forgotten words. An admission of the heart, but not the head. After the vigil in his bedchamber, David had warned that the potion made one as if drunk beyond awareness. It removed a person's normal restraints.

Marcus wondered what words he had spoken while he tested the potion on himself. The ear that forgets what it hears had not said, but considering David's last words, Marcus could imagine.

The castle had fallen quiet and the moon had risen high in the sky. Marcus left the wall's vast embrace of the night, and sought the more intimate one in the garden.

As he descended he passed the level where Nesta slept, and the urge to go to her almost overwhelmed him. It was not only lust that spurred the impulse. His passion for her was bigger than that. So much bigger that it frightened him.

The image that he had examined on the parchment this evening floated behind his inner eye. A knight and a lady, separated by a river.

The farmers looked at her differently. Spoke to her differently. They still greeted her in the mornings with smiles and gossip, but she could tell the betrothal had changed things.

They were no longer sure of her. Marcus had confused them with that public ceremony, and her willing compliance had been well reported. She could not slice through the lie even though she denied its legitimacy to them over and over again.

She tried to buy back their faith. She slipped a few pence to children, and gave one of her veils to a girl who was marrying. She made a small design for a woman whose husband was very ill. It showed a cross and two angels, and the woman gratefully took it home to tack up on the wall beside her ailing man's bed.

The morning after she handed it over, the woman pulled her aside in the yard.

"They took it from me. The image. When I left, outside the gate, Sir Paul was waiting and he took the parchment."

Nesta had seen Paul in the yard yesterday

morning, but had not realized he had been watching her. "Did he give it back?"

The woman nodded. "Had me wait while he brought it inside, but he was back with it quickly. My husband was grateful for it, my lady, and for the prayers that you said you would say for him."

Nesta moved on, and glanced around the yard and wall while she did. Paul was not present today, but she noticed another knight lounging on the steps to the hall. He had been there a long time, now that she thought about it. He seemed to make it a point to look everywhere except at her.

So, Marcus expected her to send out a message, probably to Carwyn. Did he plan to follow its meandering path as it was handed from one person to another, and discover the rebels' camp? Intercept it and read it, and have all revealed?

As she finished visiting with the farmers, she kept one eye on the knight, who kept one eye on her.

"We got it." Paul barged into the solar with his triumphant announcement.

"Got what?" Marcus looked up from some accounts that the steward had left for him.

"Her message. She was clever, I'll give you that, but I was watching today, and I saw what she was up to." He crooked his finger as he backed out the door. "Come see."

Marcus followed Paul out to the yard and up to a section of wall that overlooked the gate. Down below a thick group of farmers had been hemmed in by his men. Sir Leonard had pulled a man aside and now methodically probed fingers beneath his tunic and into his sleeve despite the farmer's howls of indignation.

"What is he doing?" Marcus asked.

"Searching for the message. Or rather, parts of it. She is incredible, Marcus. She does not send out one piece of parchment with her words, but many little bits. Look here."

He opened his purse and plucked out a tiny scrap. Written on it was only the word "think."

Down below, Leonard had let his victim leave, and had called the next farmer forward.

"I noticed her passing something to one of the men," Paul said. "Then a bit later, she did it again. Very sneaky, she was, slipping the pieces into sleeves and cowls and such. One could barely tell it was happening, and even the farmers appeared unaware. When they passed through the gate, I stopped them and found these bits. So now we are looking for the rest."

Leonard was searching slower than the market was emptying. The crowd now backed up through the gates. The mumble of complaints about the delay grew from a low rumble to a loud roar.

A woman was next in line. Stout and furious, she stepped forward, planted her hands on her hips, and glared a dare at Leonard.

He paced around her, debating how to proceed. He stopped behind her and cocked his head. Reaching out, he plucked at the folds of her veil where it bunched on her shoulder. He lifted his hand triumphantly to display a speck of parchment.

The woman's indignation dissolved into astonishment.

"Go down and help him," Marcus said. "Try and get those wagons out of here before nightfall."

"I'll put several men on it, now that we know her game." Delighted by his own cleverness, Paul headed for the stairs. "Once we have all the bits, I'll bring them to you. Won't be long before we have that message in hand."

Late that afternoon Marcus sat in his solar with twenty-six small parchment squares spread out on the table in front of him.

Each bore one word. He and Paul had been arranging the bits this way and that for hours, trying to see how they should line up.

It appeared hopeless. He had kept at it because some of those words indicated the message was one that he needed to read. Some scraps contained the words "treason," "plots," "Carwyn," and "plan." The rest, however, made no particular sense.

"This is much harder than I expected," Paul admitted. His smug glee had left him long ago.

Of course it was. Nesta had devised this. "There must be hundreds of possibilities."

"I still say that if we can determine the first word, it will go easier," Paul ventured. "Hell, but she is clever."

"Too clever. What if one of these pieces was lost, or blown away? Who waited to pluck them from their hiding places?"

"Could have been anyone, right? If the wainwright helped her, others might too. Or maybe all these farmers knew what she was about, and she pretended they did not to protect them. If so, they would know to remove their bits once they were down the road, and then deliver them to someone."

Marcus returned his gaze to the damn words. His humor was not helped much by two of them. For hours now, he had been forced to see "stupid" and "Marcus" in close proximity.

Paul frowned, and his attention appeared to focus on just those scraps. He picked up "stupid" and, cocking his head with much internal debate, began moving it toward his lord's name.

As if he felt Marcus's stare, he glanced up. Flushing with chagrin, he put "stupid" back down. "Nay, that would make no sense."

Giving up, Marcus rose and walked to the window. In the yard below, Nesta and her servant Winnifred were playing with a leather ball. A group of the castle's girls had joined them, and feminine squeals rang on the stone walls as veils and garments blew around slender bodies. A lot of men and boys had gathered to watch and cheer, and also catch a glimpse of ankles and legs.

It was a joyous spectacle, and he wouldn't mind being down there too. Instead he was holed up in this chamber trying to decipher the witch's plans.

Sighing with resignation, he walked back to the table. He peered over Paul's hunched shoulders.

Paul had done some aimless rearranging, and Marcus blandly observed the results. Something in the new combination plucked at him. Reaching over, he moved several bits. Then several more.

They began falling into place. His hand moved rapidly, filling in the gaps, just knowing where the words should go. His eyes narrowed on the emerging message.

Damn the woman. She was going to drive him mad.

Paul went very still. He snuck a glance over his shoulder and made a weak, apologetic smile.

Marcus stared at the message that they had just spent the whole day discovering and deciphering.

Marcus I send no messages full of plots to Carwyn. Do you think I would be so stupid as to plan treason by such dangerous means.

CHAPTER 15

NESTA DARED NOT send a written message to Carwyn, but she needed to explain the betrothal just the same. She asked some farmers to pass a verbal message west, but she could not count on it arriving as she said it, or even completing the journey. She was stuck, forced to hope that Carwyn would see the truth and know what to do.

News trickled in about Carwyn's continuing raids, indicating that he did. More revealing was the evidence of Marcus's response. Young men began arriving from the farms. The yard and nearby field rang with the practice of arms.

Nesta watched it all, and read the implications. Perhaps being confined to this castle did not render her impotent to the cause, after all.

She would know exactly what Marcus intended to do. She would know the size of his force, and whether and when he called up the neighboring lords. It would all play out in front of her, and even if Marcus locked her in the cellar, he could not hide any of it.

She was not sure that she wanted to know, however. She did not want to have the chance to betray him so directly.

She admitted that as she strolled along the wall walk late one morning as the last of the farmers left the yard.

She realized with dismay that time was dulling her anger. She had to think about his deceit very specifically in order to work up her outrage now. She no longer carried it with her all day and fretted about it all night.

That worried her. She needed that anger. She needed it when they passed each other in the hall. She desperately needed it when they sat beside each other at meals. She never looked at him, but she felt him there as they ate. Eventually, when the food was finished, she felt him physically, as he firmly covered her hand with his on the table so that everyone could see that, despite her distant behavior, she belonged to him.

Slowly, appallingly, that touch was bridging more than the space between them. Last night, to her shock, she realized that she spent the whole meal waiting for him to reach for her.

She circled the wall two times, examining her response to him, fighting the truth of her weakness, and eventually admitting the shame of it. Her inner argument left her disgusted with herself.

She stopped and looked down into the yard. Marcus stood at the top of the keep stairs, his body encased in armor. The sun glinted off the metal and made his hair glow, turning him into an image of chivalrous beauty and strength much like the ones she put in her designs.

He was watching her. Despite their distance, she felt the intensity of his attention. Stripped of its defenses by her self-examination, her heart flipped foolishly and then sank painfully.

Once more he would ride out, as he had so often since their false betrothal. He was finding evidence of more than small raiding parties.

Some of the men he had called to arms had not come here, but had headed into the hills instead. There had also been reports of *cymanfaoedd*, meetings being held throughout the region.

If that was true, she should rejoice. She felt no triumph or elation at the notion, however. Marcus looked glorious in armor, but she did not like seeing him in it.

A spike of anger pierced her. A new wrath, unlike the one she had clung to these last days, stabbed hotly. There was nothing righteous in this blade of rage. It was unholy and unforgivable. In that instant of seething rebellion, she hated her father, and his dream, and Wales itself.

Marcus rode out the gate. She ran to a section of the wall overlooking the western fields, and watched him join his men and ride away. Waves of yearning and anger and head-splitting confusion hit her, and she gritted her teeth with frustration.

Beneath the chaos there flowed a heartbreaking helplessness. They were trapped on a fast current that would take them where it chose now, and steering clear of rocks would be nigh impossible.

Nesta woke in the middle of the night. Her sleep had been fitful, and alive with vivid dreams of swords and death.

She sat on the edge of the bed, suddenly alert. Her women dozed under blankets, but the chamber seemed sticky and hot to her. She rose and stepped over to the window, and lifted a corner of the oiled parchment that had been placed over the thick slit to keep out the night's chill. The flow of cold air felt delicious.

The sky looked clear and beautiful and full of stars. Its vastness offered a soothing balm. She reached for her gown and drew it on and hastily tied the lacing.

She felt her way through blackness, down the stairs. Utter stillness met her every step, even as she passed the second level. In a chamber there Marcus slept, at peace no doubt. There was no reason for him to toss with bad dreams. The path of his duty lay straight and cleanly marked. She was the one getting lost in a maze of conflicting loyalties.

She stepped outside and breathed in the crisp air. She lifted her hair so it could dry the dampness that her restless night had left on her nape.

The yard seemed much larger now with the absence of people and activity. The walls loomed high and ominous in comparison to its stretching void. The hollow silence of the castle intensified, unsettling her. She aimed for the garden, seeking a place less remindful of a tomb.

The familiar shapes of low boxwood and bushes, of fruit trees and ivy beds, lightened her spirits. A garden did not need people in order to be alive and natural. The flowers might have died, and the last leaves might be falling, but the space was still redolent with the odors of life. It contained a thousand reassurances that no mat-

ter what one person's strife, the seasons continued their cycle.

She strolled along a side path littered with
fallen apples. She did not think about her father
or Carwyn Hir or even Marcus. She let the
quiet beauty of the night garden create a spot of
solace for a while.

Halfway along the path, the mood suddenly
changed. A streak of lightning might have
flashed in the sky, so abruptly was she pulled out
of her reverie. With one step she passed from
peace to turmoil.

She recognized the reason, and halted. She
was not alone in this garden. Someone else was
here, and she knew who it was.

She peered into the deep shadows beneath
the trees. She found him the last place that she
looked, on a bench against the garden wall, not
twenty paces from where she stood.

"It is odd for you to be here, Marcus. After a
day in the saddle, you should be sleeping like
the dead."

He rose. "I often visit here at night, Nesta."

"Do not come near me."

He ignored her command. The way he
walked had her on the alert. Her inner voice
warned that she should leave immediately.

She pictured herself fleeing like a mouse,

confirming her weakness. She stood her ground, but her blood quickened with something too much like fear. "I am not surprised that you seek this place out at night. It is so peaceful, and perfect for contemplation. Better than a church."

"I do not come here for prayer or contemplation, Nesta. I have been waiting for you. I have come almost every night since we first arrived here."

"You assumed that I had a habit of visiting gardens at night?"

"You did so once. I thought you eventually might do so again." He came up beside her and looked down. "It appears I was correct."

"I came here tonight looking for solitude."

His fingertips brushed at the hair framing her face. "I think that you came here looking for me."

"That is not true. I—"

His fingers touched her mouth, silencing her. He left them there, and she felt the quick pulse of her lips beating against his warm, firm touch. The same trembling beat took possession of her body.

He took her hand, and gently tugged her toward the bench. Her heart broke with the desire to follow. Heaven waited in the shadows.

She halted after a few steps.

He felt her resistance. "Do not give me excuses, and denials, and arguments. I know how divided your heart is. But that is for tomorrow, and for the world outside these low walls. I ask for nothing more than to have you beside me in this garden, free of our burdens."

His words undid her. She followed, despite knowing this was madness. The worldly woman in her sighed with exasperation at the silly girl whose heart pounded because a handsome knight spoke of needing her.

He sat and drew her toward him. She found herself on his lap, and not on the bench by his side. She tried to move off him.

His arm held her firmly. "There is no danger with me. You are at least my match in this, as everything else. You have never done one thing with me that you did not want. Resting in my arms is hardly a defeat."

She should not listen to him. She should break his hold on her, and run from this place. The daughter of Llygad should not be enticed to any intimacy with this man, let alone one of the spirit.

But the closeness, the warmth, the support of his strength, spoke to her heart more seductively than his words. Just the sound of his voice lured and excited her. She should run away, but she could not.

Her body gave up and relaxed like a physical sigh, and she laid her head on his shoulder. She touched the hand resting on her hip, and relished the small connection of skin on skin. She might have found an unexpected lull in a relentless battle, so comforting did she find their embrace.

"I hate you," she muttered. "You have put me in an impossible place. I asked you not to. Begged you."

"I did not have a choice, Nesta."

"And I have no choice. So here we are, and our lack of choices makes this embrace a mockery. A prelude to each of us betraying the other."

"There is no mockery in the contentment that I have holding you."

More than contentment passed between them. Desire covered them like a cloak. The fierce wanting had been given new life with this embrace, and it pulled and twisted and made every part of her tingle.

"I do not think that you only want to hold me like this, Marcus. I think that you have been waiting in this garden for more than that."

He kissed her cheek, and she felt his smile form against her skin. "That is true."

"Do you hope to befuddle me with passion? Should I trade everything for this ecstasy?"

"I am not asking for what you cannot give. I do not expect you to abandon who you are. I only want what is already mine."

"That was one night of pleasure."

"I am not speaking of the pleasure, or of one night."

His quiet statement moved her heart, and did befuddle her, as no physical passion could. She dared not respond to his allusion. Speaking of that would acknowledge emotions that must be ignored. It pained her to deny them, but she had to unless she wanted her heart to be shredded one day.

"There is confusion and deceit in what you propose. We meet as lovers during the night, and battle each other by day."

"There is already confusion in it, Nesta. Staying apart has not resolved that. I do not see much deceit in this embrace. Each of us knows where the other stands. I do not see what has transpired since we returned from the lodge as a repudiation of what happened that night. Do you?"

Nay, she did not. She had tried to make that repudiation, though. God knew how hard she had tried, and how miserably she had failed.

"You speak of exploring a passion that is doomed, and that we ourselves will destroy."

"I speak of having what I want while I can, before the world forces me to give it up."

He made it sound so possible. Almost sensible. The warmth of his embrace reminded her of how real their special intimacy could be.

Her body wanted to accept his strange logic and reckless offer, and her heart did too. The voice in her head that warned of unimaginable pain quieted to a dull whisper. It would not be silenced, however.

His hand turned her chin. He moved, so that his arm cradled her shoulders. His gaze absorbed her so completely that his eyes became a star-filled sky in which her soul floated.

He kissed her, and the cautious whisper spoke no more.

It was a sweet kiss, as gentle and luxurious and soulful as the one from her drugged memory. Its poignant mood touched her heart like a magician's wand, and a glorious, sparkling sensation that spoke of dawn and spring and endless joy broke all through her.

She slid her hand behind his neck and held him to her so it would not end. She waited for him to touch her. She wanted him to. Needed him to. Her breasts itched for his caress with an anxious craving that already made her body move and left her breathless.

She took his hand, and laid it on her breast.

He broke the kiss and looked into her eyes.

His touch left her body and he gently slid her

to the bench beside him. Taking her face in both his hands, he kissed her again, then stood.

"Not here. I do not want you excusing it later as madness in a moonlit garden, or a magical dream in a firelit lodge. Nor will it be a seduction where pleasure buries your good sense. I am not looking to subvert you with passion. Consider whether you believe I am telling the truth about that, and make your decision."

To her astonishment, he walked away.

"You know where to find me, Nesta."

CHAPTER 16

He waited for her to come to him.

He waited so hard that time slowed.

As the night slid past, he moved from the chair to the window and finally to the bed. His mind shifted too, from expectation to resignation and finally to fury.

He cursed himself for not just taking what she offered in the garden. Saints knew he would never do anything *that* stupidly chivalrous again.

He imagined her sleeping peacefully, relieved that his demand for clearheaded surrender had saved her. His mind's eye saw himself entering that chamber and throwing out the servants and using his hands and mouth to defeat the misgivings that kept her from him.

That they were sensible misgivings ceased to matter as his thoughts churned and boiled.

Finally, he admitted she would not come. He swung off the bed smothering him with its soft warmth, suddenly understanding Nesta's immunity to the cold. The fire had shrunk to mere embers in the hearth, but he was hot. It was not just anger and arousal making him burn. An agitation of the spirit warmed him, and kept his body alert and alive and unable to rest.

As he stripped off his clothes, he tried to tell himself that her resolve was probably for the best, but his attempt at acceptance was futile. He wanted her, and nothing else really mattered. Wanted her with the kind of reckless persistence that caused a man to risk everything to obtain the object of his desire.

He stretched out on the pallet that lay on the floor between his bed and the wall. His body found some comfort there, but not his mind. She filled his head, as she had every night since he first saw her. Memories flowed and merged as he embraced her phantom presence.

A vague sound broke the silence. He snapped alert.

He rose. Nesta stood near the door, barely illuminated by the dim fire. The faint glow made little golden lines and lights on her shadowed form. She still wore the gown from the garden. Perhaps she had not been sleeping either.

They looked at each other, and the twenty paces separating them instantly filled with the sensuality that her arrival promised. The air grew thick with it, and each breath he took made his desire sharpen.

She did not move for a long while, and then she turned her head to look around, as if she was surprised to find herself in this strange place.

He waited for her to decide if she had made a mistake in coming. Not that it would make a difference now.

She strolled to the fire, and the light made her beauty more distinct with each step. "The chamber appeared empty when I came in."

"I was lying over here."

From her new position, she could see the pallet at his feet. "You prefer the floor to a feather bed?"

"Sometimes. I can see the sky out the window from the pallet."

"Why not move the bed so that you can see the sky in comfort?"

Because when I was a youth, it was not a window but a hole in a thatched roof that I looked through, and it was not a feather bed, but a pallet on a dirt floor that I lay on. "That puts one too high. I prefer to look up to the sky, not over to it."

She cocked her head, as if thinking about that. Her gaze took in his nakedness, slowly and completely.

"You are undressed. I disturbed your sleep."

"I was not sleeping."

She turned to pace slowly in front of the fire while she examined its dying light. "You are magnificent, standing there with the moonlight flowing over your face and chest, and your dark eyes lit with tiny fires. I have told myself that it is your beauty that makes me weak with you, so I must look away now, since there are things we must agree upon if I am to stay much longer."

"You have terms?"

"I do not negotiate a surrender, Marcus, only a brief truce. That is the first thing that must be understood."

"I told you in the garden that I understood that."

"I know what you said, but I think that you really believe it will be otherwise."

Maybe he did. Eventually. Ultimately. In the least he counted on her not minding as much when he defeated her. "I do not believe that."

"I wonder." She kept her gaze to the fire even though her sight appeared inward. "I also do not want any love talk. If we do this, it is for our simple pleasure. If we pretend it is more than that, being true to both our duties and each other will become impos—difficult and painful."

Impossible, she had almost said. He did not respond to this demand, but let his silence speak his agreement. If she did not want to speak of love, he could accept that. He would accept anything right now. He knew, however, that the pretense they would live was not the one she avoided, but the one she insisted upon.

Her expression hardened a bit. "I also do not want anyone to know about this. I will come to you here, after my women are asleep. I do not want your men laughing about the Welsh whore. I am notorious because other English knights did not show chivalric concern for a lady's reputation because she was Welsh, and I will not be made a fool again."

Someday he would ask her to explain that part of the episode with Edward, but not tonight. He did not doubt that her being Welsh had made a difference. Edward was no saint, but there were no songs about his English ladies. "As you wish, although it is not unusual for betrothed couples to sleep together."

"We are not betrothed. I do not come to you as a bride, nor will I ever."

He decided that was also a topic for another day. "Then we will be discreet."

"There is one more thing. You must withdraw before you finish, so that I do not get with child."

"I cannot do that. It was my intention in the lodge, but . . . With another woman, it would be possible, but not with you."

Her expression fell with . . . what? Disappointment? Relief? "Then it cannot be any way at all. I will not risk that."

He couldn't believe his ears. He had waited all night, days, *weeks,* and when she finally came to him she dangled paradise in front of him only to snatch it away.

She turned away without looking at him, and aimed for the door. She actually was leaving.

The hell she was.

He reached the door at the same moment she began opening it. Pressing his hand flat against it, he forced it closed again.

She stayed with her back to him, her body almost filling the small space between his skin and the door. The closeness of her spring scent, of her soft warmth, made his blood flow hot and fast.

"I think that you could do what I ask," she said, resentfully. "In Scotland—"

"I am not an old Scot. And I cannot do it because in truth I do not want to do it, and that is all that will matter when the moment comes. If I only experienced the simple pleasure that you demand, I'm sure I could. But when I am inside you, careful thoughts disappear from my head. I will not make a promise that I already know I will not keep."

"Then, as I said, this cannot happen at all." She began to yank the door open again.

He slammed it closed once more, and kept his hand on it while his other arm circled her waist.

"I cannot let you leave, Nesta. You must know that." He kissed her shoulder, tasting the skin along the gown's edge. "We will leave it in heaven's hands. If you are not meant to bear my child, you will not."

She twisted in his hold, her eyes flashing with anger. "An easy bargain for a man to make."

Very easy, because he wanted her to bear his son, but he was not allowed to speak of that, or of the other things he wanted.

He pulled her closer until his body pressed her back and bottom. His demanding embrace startled her. She braced her hands against the door to keep from being imprisoned against him.

He swept her hair aside so his mouth could reach her neck. The rapid pulse under his lips beat its hot rhythm into his blood, and it quick-

ened more when he closed his mouth on it
more aggressively. Resistance left on her gasps
until her neck grew pliant to his assault. "You
say that we will only know brief truces and simple pleasures, Nesta. So be it. But during these
truces expect no quarter. My possession of you
will be whole until the finish. I will not withdraw."

"You are mad. You speak of daring fate." Her
voice sounded wonderfully breathless.

"We have been daring fate since the night we
met." He pulled her hips closer yet, so that his
arousal nestled against the small of her back.
Her bottom rose slightly in response. "Now,
stop speaking of terms and conditions, and give
yourself to me, Nesta. It is why you came here."

She looked over her shoulder with eyes
sparkling with passion. A few fires of rebellion
still flickered, but as she looked at him a soft
yielding washed away those tiny flames. She
started to turn toward him.

"Nay, stay there."

She arched an eyebrow. He could tell that she
expected him to take her at once. His body
yelled for him to. "Not yet. You bargain for
simple, brief pleasure for a reason, but I'll be
damned if there will be anything simple and
quick about tonight."

Still holding her hips to him, he reached

around and plucked loose the tie of her gown's lacing. He pulled the crossing threads out row by row, and her breath quickened as each level slid free. She was naked beneath the gown, and her hips began a subtle, erotic flexing that showed how anticipation was affecting her.

She looked down between her braced arms at what he was doing. "You are making long work of that, Marcus."

Her impatience pleased him, and he only went slower in response. The sides of the gown began separating, releasing her breasts. He felt their swells half peeking through the gap above his hand. His movements brushed against them as he pulled the lacing out, and each time Nesta tensed. Her hands pressed the door harder.

He stopped with the lacings at her waist. He pulled the two sides of the gown aside so her breasts were completely naked. He angled his head so he could see the sides of their pale, full shapes rising erotically out of the garment. Nesta's eyes were closed and her face flushed. Deep breaths escaped through her parted lips.

Reaching around her, he slowly skimmed his fingers along the bottom of one breast. A low sigh of affirmation breathed out of her, and her hips pressed against him more deliberately.

He continued circling her breast with his slow caress, and her sighs grew anxious. Finally, he barely brushed the tip with his fingers. A deep tremor accompanied her sharp intake of breath.

"Is that how you want it, Nesta? Or harder?"

"Like that," she whispered dazedly. "Just like that."

He gently rubbed again, and the tip swelled harder against his fingers. She arched into it, so that her hold on the door became more for balance than bracing.

He teased at her, and his own arousal turned hotter and harder with every sound and movement he drew from her. As the simple pleasure pushed her toward abandon, her begging and astonished cries flowed quietly into his head.

Keeping his hand to her, he began raising her skirt with the other.

She realized what he was doing. "Aye," she whispered.

He stepped back, easing her legs with him until her upper body angled more severely toward the door. Pulling the skirt high, he draped it over her lower back so that her bottom and legs were exposed.

She appeared unbearably erotic like that, braced against the planks with her naked bottom waiting for him. He caressed down her buttock to her inner thigh, and felt the thick moisture that revealed just how ready she was.

"Part your legs."

She did so. He slid his phallus between her thighs, but did not enter her. "Close them now. And turn your head sideways. I want to see your face."

She obeyed the latter command first, so he saw her expression when her thighs closed on his hardness and when he altered his stance until he pressed up against her hot, moist folds. The sensation of velvet softness, and the way he could feel the vague throbbing of her need, almost undid him.

He reached around to caress both her breasts. A low throaty cry purred out of her and her face became an image of beautiful sensual rapture.

He played at her breasts lightly, and she reacted to each touch. Her hips moved in stronger rhythms as she sought relief from the pleasurable torture, and each flex of her body created an erotic caress where she held him. Soon his senses absorbed nothing but the sight and sounds and feel of her. Her lovely, low exclamations of pleasure sang around them, luring him to bliss.

His body ached with an insistent demand that he make the small move that would join them. He almost succumbed, but a part of him wanted this tantalizing pleasure to continue forever.

Instead he separated from her and turned her to face him.

She sank against the wall and looked at him with confusion as she blinked to clear her head. Only their heavy breaths broke the utter silence. She appeared so beautifully sensual with her naked breasts visible through the open gown and her hair disheveled and her eyes glazed by the delirium of desire.

Her gaze lowered from his face to his chest. Pushing away from the wall, she placed both hands near his neck and felt her way across his shoulders.

"When I was a young girl, I dreamed of a knight like you." Her caress descended deliciously as she lined his chest with her warm, soft palms. "Tall, with broad shoulders and a lean strength. Carved hard and confident. He even had golden hair, although his mouth was sweet and bowed, and not harsh like yours."

She trailed a finger down his chest to his stomach. "He would play the lute for me, and sing poems to my beauty, and be pure in heart and body. He dared great deeds to impress me, and won every time." She smiled at the memory as she watched her fingers slide lower and then move teasingly up his phallus. "Such are the foolish ideas on which girls are raised."

He gritted his teeth as her fingertips stroked

him. Hooking his finger through the lacings of her gown, he pulled out the next level. "Boys too. I dreamed of being such a knight. Only I did not sing poems, and I was not so pure."

"Did you win the hand of a lady?"

The lacing snaked down another level. "Of course."

"Someone like me?"

"Actually, she was mild and biddable."

She laughed. It sounded so lovely, and made her look so fresh and beautiful. She might have suddenly become once again the girl she spoke of.

He slid the gown off her shoulders, and it dropped to hang around her hips. He took her breasts in his hands. "Of course, I was just a boy then and knew nothing of passion. I had not yet learned how dull a mild and biddable woman could be."

Dipping his head, he flicked his tongue on the tips of her breasts while he pushed the gown down her hips. It dropped to her feet, leaving her naked. The pleasure from his tongue hampered her balance, and she staggered and grasped his shoulders.

He straightened and pulled her into his support, embracing her tightly and completely, holding her hips and shoulders so that all of her adhered to him and her breasts pressed his chest and the moisture of her arousal wet his thighs.

She met him in a furious kiss, the first kiss of the night. He lost himself in the tumultuous joining. He claimed her mouth with hard possession while he embraced her tremors and listened to her gasps. He caressed her nakedness firmly, finding the little dip at the small of her back and then the soft swells of her bottom.

Her muffled moan entered their kiss and she arched her bottom, asking for more. Her grasping hold tightened on his back when he traced down her cleft. Her kiss turned biting and demanding as he explored the depths where her thighs joined. She broke the kiss completely when he slid his touch higher to stroke the hidden, soft valley where his phallus had recently nestled. Hanging on him, she pressed her face to his shoulder as the pleasure trembled through her.

He lifted her in his arms and carried her to the bed. She stretched out and pulled him down on her and the broken kiss resumed, only hotter and deeper. She spread her legs and bent her knees to accept him.

Body shredding from hunger and mind splitting with pleasure, he pushed up and knelt so he could see her. Her dark tresses fanned out over the bed. Her breasts rose and fell gently from her frantic breathing. Closer to his knees, her shapely thighs angled and rose to reveal dark shadows.

She watched him look at her, with the subtle movements of her body speaking her impatience. While he looked she took her breasts in her own hands and gently squeezed their nipples.

It was unbelievably carnal, and gave his arousal a new edge. He touched the inviting softness spread open to him and watched her delirium build until every sound she made, every movement, was that of a woman unhinged by pleasure and begging for completion.

Her primal sensuality completely unleashed his own. He slid down so he could kiss her inner thighs, then turned his mouth to the flesh that his fingers caressed.

Her breath caught and her movements stilled, and in that instant he knew she had never done this before. His discovery gave him just enough control to make it slow and careful as he tantalized her into acceptance.

The pleasure peeled her apprehension away. He used his tongue to intensify the pleasure and she turned wild. Her cries filled the chamber and joined the pulse of his existence. He felt the pleasure make her tense as the intensity turned excruciating for them both. Her cries came faster and louder until her scream of release rang off the stones.

Barely controlling his own passion, he rose up and slid into her. She lifted her knees to absorb him until he penetrated as deeply as possible.

He withdrew and reentered slowly several times, luxuriating so much in the sensation of feeling her again that his consciousness began shattering. Then it was his turn for madness and he succumbed gladly. He thrust again and again, hard and furious, as all the waiting and wanting of the last days found expression in this claiming of her.

Despite her recent climax, she joined him. Her body rocked in rhythm to his, and her lips at his ear whispered for him to make it harder, hotter, deeper. Her urgent pleas swam in his head and destroyed his last restraints. She groaned in contentment as he took her harder yet, and her joyful cries accompanied the rise of his passion to its violent, soul-splitting peak.

For a few moments he knew nothing but a saturating peace. It created a spaceless place in which there was no strife, no anger, no death. She was with him there. Not physically, but essentially and completely.

The alluring void began slowly filling. He became aware of her body beneath his and of her heaving breaths on his shoulder. Her arms still grasped his body in a desperate embrace. He rolled to her side and pulled her into the curve of his body and drifted into a daze still suffused with the perfection.

He did not know how long they lay there. It might have been a few moments or half the night.

Finally, Nesta eased out of his arms. "I must go. It will not do to fall asleep here."

He caught her arm. He was in no mood to consider what would and would not do. "I will wake you well before dawn."

"Mark—"

He pulled her down beside him. "When you come to me, you will not leave my bed so quickly. That is one of *my* terms."

Her sigh said he was impossible, but she did not argue. She relaxed back into their embrace.

"You called me Mark," he said.

"Did I? Perhaps hearing David use it so much made it slip out."

"I was called that as a boy, but not since becoming lord. My sister still uses it, as sisters will. David does too, but I think it is deliberate. I think that he likes to remind me that I was not always so important, and that he knew me when I was hotheaded and reckless."

"You dislike the name, then. I will be careful and try not to use it again." ·

She turned into him, snuggling closer, her eyes shut in sleepy contentment. He combed his fingers through her luxurious hair while her breath warmed his neck and shoulder.

"There is no need to be careful. You may call me Mark if you want."

She opened one eye and glanced at him, as if she found that interesting. He couldn't imagine why she would.

He nuzzled her ear. "The knight of your girlhood dreams had a bowed mouth?"

She nodded. "An angel's mouth."

"What were you thinking of? A mouth like that is stupid on a man. I saw such a face once, and the man who owned it walked around looking like a half-wit. A mouth like mine is much better, even if it is harsh."

"After tonight, I am bound to say that your mouth is perfect."

"If it gave you pleasure, I am glad. I also think you have not known that intimacy with anyone else."

"Does that make you glad, too?"

"Aye."

Her lids lowered, as if she contemplated how to respond. "In truth, I have known very few of tonight's intimacies with anyone else."

He almost asked if she meant the acts or the heights their passion had reached, but that would touch on the kind of talk she did not want.

He looked down at her breasts and kissed one, then the other. "Let us see how perfect my mouth is. I wonder if I can make you cry for me again if I do nothing but use my lips and tongue."

He could.

CHAPTER 17

HER DAYS WERE betrayals of her nights, and her nights of her days.

Every afternoon she swore she would not go to him, and every night after her women fell asleep she found herself slipping into his chamber.

It was reckless and dangerous and she knew that it did not speak well for her judgment. She was not a silly girl, and she should be able to resist the allure of a handsome man and the pleasure he offered.

Still she went, drawn by the sparkling emotions she experienced in that chamber, tempted by the sweet lightness her heart would know for a few hours. The days and their duties did not exist in his arms. For three glorious nights she explored forbidden passion with the man charged with destroying all she had lived for these last few years.

If they had just shared simple pleasure, as she had demanded, she might have stayed in her own bed. However, other joinings lived within the physical ones, and her heart could not contain them. Nor could she ignore the delight that she took in the friendship they shared before and after they made love, when he held her on that feather bed and they laughed and spoke of unimportant things.

On the fourth night, despite her longing to continue those truces, she forced herself to remain in her chamber, to prove to herself that he had not completely vanquished her will.

He did not take it well.

"Where were you last night?" Marcus asked the question as soon as he sat down at the high table. The evening meal had been delayed because he had ridden out before dawn and not returned until late.

"I knew that you needed to leave early this morning, and thought it best not to disturb your brief rest." It was a lie, devised in a blink when she saw his tight jaw. She wanted to kick herself for being such a coward.

She forced herself to summon something of the woman she had been before she met him.

"There will be other nights when I do not come. Nights when I am tired, or when I have my flux. Or when I do not choose to come."

His hand reached to cover hers on the table. It seemed a more possessive hold than normal. "If you are tired, you can sleep in my arms. If you have your flux, you can still give me your company. If you do not choose to come, I want to know why."

She sighed with exasperation. "You already know why."

"I think that I do, but it is not the reason you will throw at me. It is because you are afraid."

"I have nothing to fear from you, Marcus." Annoyance made the statement more a challenge than an admission of trust.

"You have everything to fear from me. I am the man who holds your life in my hands by day and your heart in my hands by night. The daughter of Llygad does not worry much about the former, but the woman in you is a coward about the latter."

She really resented his calling her a coward. That she had used it herself did not matter. She did not want evidence that he understood the war taking place inside her, or that he suspected the ground her duty was losing.

"But what you fear with me is something we are not allowed to speak of, isn't it, Nesta? My apologies." He raised her hand and kissed it. "Come to me tonight."

"I am not yours to command in this, Marcus. Even our mockery of a betrothal does not give you that right."

"*You* have given me the right. Come to my chamber. There are things I must tell you."

Of course, summoned like that, she could not go.

She lay in bed that night, glad he had made it easy for her. He might speak seductively of not subverting her, but that had been his intention all along. Now he was annoyed because she had proven that those brief truces would be on her terms, and that the pleasure would not make her clay in his hands.

She managed to feel very proud of herself for a while. The contented sleep of the virtuous did not come, however, and the night passed with her tossing on the bed, arguing the rightness of denying him, trying to ignore that her confusion only proved just how divided her heart had become.

She was awake when commotion broke out in the yard at dawn. Suddenly it sounded as if a hundred horses milled inside the walls.

She went to her window and lifted the oiled parchment. A small army had entered Anglesmore. She took in the armor and weapons and the tall knight in the lead. His handsome profile was so harsh as to make Marcus appear mild. Banners flapped around him. They bore no colors and marks that she knew.

As she watched he turned his head to reveal the other half of his face. A horrible scar sliced it from top to bottom, defiling the beauty he had been given. It was the kind of scar that made one wince and look away.

The implications of the scene outside sank in. A horrified sense of betrayal spilled through her.

She threw on a loose gown and stormed out of her chamber. She went down to Marcus, and not as a lover. She found him in his chamber, already armored.

He glanced at her, dismissed his squires, and coolly turned his attention to adjusting his knight's belt.

"There is a new knight in the yard, a fearsome man with two faces," she said.

"That is Addis de Valence, who was warden here after I got Anglesmore back. He was also one of the men who helped the King depose Mortimer. He is my good friend, and you will treat him with every courtesy."

"He brought a small army with him. At least fifty entered the yard, and it sounds as if there are many more outside the gate. They do not look to be stopping for a brief rest."

"The steward will see to their comfort while I am gone."

She didn't give a damn about their comfort. "You called for him, didn't you? You asked him to bring that army here."

He nodded, and went to a table holding some bread and ale and downed the contents of the cup. He appeared very calm. Her own blood was boiling.

"Your message must have been sent some time ago. You knew he was coming, and said nothing."

His gaze snapped to her, suddenly fiery and stern. "Is that what you expected? Is that why you came to this bed? You thought that I would confide in you before I made my moves? I promised not to try and subvert you, but did you just assume that *you* would subvert *me*?"

They were devastating questions, and they sliced to the center of the turmoil filling her. The truth behind her feeling of betrayal stared her in the face. She *had* expected him to warn her. She had thought that because of their intimacy he would give her a fighting chance.

He must have read her thoughts on her face, because his expression hardened. "For a woman with such famous experience, you do not know men well. A knight does not discard his duty so easily. This knight certainly doesn't. Not for the brief truces and simple pleasures you offered, especially when you have made it clear just how brief and simple they are to you."

Grabbing his sword and gauntlets, he strode past her. "Your father's men have begun killing. Word has come that some Welsh chieftains have joined them. So now we truly have a rebellion, as your father wanted and you planned. A little one still, and I will not permit it to become a big one. I will not see Wales flayed alive in the name of a doomed cause. Hopefully, Addis will be enough help." He paused at the door. "If you had come last night, I would have explained this to you, so that maybe you would understand."

After he left, she could barely move. She gazed numbly to where he had been standing, looking so handsome and perfect in his armor, so beautiful despite his severity.

She could see the bed from the corner of her eye. Memories of sharing it with him hurt her heart. She thought that she had truly left the days behind when she came here, but her disappointment proved that she had not.

Nor had he.

Had his mind been full of strategies even while he held her? In the sweet silence after they made love, had he been counting knights and archers, and deciding how to crush the dream?

She shook her head at the depths of her self-deception. It had been foolish to pretend that their passion could exist separately from their rivalry. She laughed at how absurd the notion had been, but as she did a sharp fullness in her chest rose to thicken her throat. Disillusionment flowed up until her eyes teared, leaving her laughing and crying at the same time.

She turned and fully looked at the bed, and grinned at her stupidity as the tears snaked down her cheeks.

Addis de Valence, Lord of Barrowburgh, gazed thoughtfully up at the hilltops. "The alliance that you suggest would lead to strife such as these parts have not seen in two generations. If Llygad's men join with a powerful marcher lord, these bandits will start a major war," he said. "It is well that you called me instead of the local barons, Marcus, if this is your suspicion. It would not do to have a viper in your camp."

"I called you for other reasons. I trust your restraint, and your control of your men. I do not want this to end in a bloodbath."

"You may have no say in that if this grows. Edward will not lose Wales, even if it means burning it to the ground to keep it. He cannot afford to. The solution in Scotland was hardly a victory. He cannot have ongoing trouble on two borders, nor have men whispering that he is weak like his father and is losing everything that his grandfather gained."

Marcus listened as he and Addis shared some ale during a brief pause on their ride. Around them his men also took their rest. They had ridden hard for hours to reach the northwestern edge of his lands, to investigate reports that some of Carwyn's men had ravaged an English manor and attacked a convoy of merchants.

The evidence of raids had been plentiful, but once again the thieves had disappeared. Addis had joined the troop even though his own arrival had occurred just before their departure. He still wore the armor that had clad him when he rode through Anglesmore's gate.

Marcus weighed his old warden's words, not surprised that they matched his own conclusions. Everything that Marcus knew about warfare and governance, and much that he had learned about men, he had learned from Addis. He could not have had a better teacher. Addis was a great warrior, and under his tutelage Marcus had quickly made up for the crucial years of missed training. Through Addis's example he had also learned to be a different kind of lord from what most men would have taught.

Addis downed more ale and frowned. He appeared fit and young, especially if one saw him as Marcus did now, from the good side. The other, the side with the scar, displayed the marks of experience that gave him the wisdom that Marcus respected.

"I can think of three border lords who might be tempted, but only if the prize was Wales itself, with himself as king," Addis said. "The autonomy of the Lords Marcher has always bred ambition for more. No English king has ever truly controlled them."

"You speak of me and my father."

"Your grandfather was given Anglesmore late. Your family has lived here for generations, but only recently has the power been yours. The fealty is stronger then, as your father proved. It is different for the families that have held their lands since the Conqueror set them up as little kings. They see themselves as sovereign in ways the new lords never will."

They remounted their steeds and moved forward. "Somewhere in the mountains an army is forming, Addis. I do not think it is very large yet, but there have been some deaths for which the English lords will want to extract a harsh revenge."

"If you called me and my men, you must be planning a campaign."

Marcus nodded. "I have been tracking the men who raid for days, and getting nowhere. They stay on the move, and are not rejoining Carwyn. He is keeping me occupied while he builds his strength. I will not give him more time to do so. It is my intention to go into those mountains, and use Llygad's own manor as a stronghold. I will bring this little war to him. I want to finish this before whatever alliance is at work is a fact."

"And the daughter? With her in your household, you may already have a viper in your camp. Since this betrothal has not stopped them, but only made them bolder, you should remove her to Stratford. He will learn quickly enough if she is involved."

"I cannot do that."

"It is the wisest—"

"I cannot." It came out harshly. He set his horse to a faster pace, and felt Addis's gaze on him as the horse beside him kept up.

"You have learned much about hiding your thoughts, Marcus, but your face will always be an open book to me," Addis said.

Marcus glanced over and saw a slight smile on Addis's mouth. "Just do not tell me that I am a fool. God knows I tell myself that ten times a day, and I do not need to hear it from you."

"I am the last man to tell another that wanting the wrong woman makes him a fool." The smile thinned to a hard line. "But I warn you now that if this woman's betrayal lures you to your destruction, I myself will hold the sword that takes her head."

Marcus rode on. The betrayal was probably inevitable, and all the small pleasures in the world would not stop it. His destruction, however, was not. Nor was hers.

They crested a hill and a little village came into view in the distance. Marcus's attention sharpened on a commotion swirling around the collection of huts and cottages.

The people were just dots, but they clustered and milled like so many ants on a piece of bread. He could see three horses at the edge of the crowd.

"Llygad's men?" Addis asked.

"We will see." Marcus spurred his horse to a gallop, and led his troop into the shallow valley.

He knew long before he rode into the village that he had not found any bandits. A different kind of violence had disrupted this tiny hamlet.

A tall tree grew in the clearing by the water

well. Three bodies hung from one of its thick branches. Several men and women sagged in heaps beneath the swinging feet, numbed from the horrible ordeal of sparing their kinsmen from suffering by speeding their deaths. An old woman still clung to the legs of a man, her weight stretching him.

Marcus and Addis reined their horses up thirty paces from the execution. Marcus surveyed the crowd of stunned villagers, and his gaze quickly lit on two men wearing the livery of Arundal, the powerful lord who held some marcher estates, including Clun to the northeast.

They sat on stools near a tree stump to the side of the well, calmly drinking ale and munching cheese. Not their ale and cheese, Marcus guessed.

A stormy darkness began seeping into his head. He dismounted and pushed through the crowd. He heard his voice speak with a calm he did not feel. "What has happened here?"

One of the soldiers, a burly red-haired man, brushed his mouth of cheese crumbs. "They attacked a merchant from one of our towns. We were sent after them, and we caught them here."

"You are no longer on Arundal's lands, but mine."

The man shrugged. "Saved you the trouble, then, didn't we?"

The madness in his head grew. He looked at the hanging bodies. "You are sure these were the thieves?"

"Followed them here, as I said."

The old woman released her grasp on the legs and spun around to Marcus. "My son had not left this village in weeks," she said defiantly. "These men are not bandits or thieves. Ask anyone here. We tried to tell them, but they listened to no one."

Addis led three members of their troop to the tree, and they began the task of cutting the bodies down.

Marcus watched the morbid ritual, and heard the wails of the women as they claimed their menfolk. The fury in his head turned ugly.

"It sounds as though you hanged the wrong men. I think that you wearied of tracking thieves you could not find, and decided to end the duty quickly. After all, one dead Welsh man is as good as another."

They protested, but the glint in their eyes showed they agreed with the last part.

Marcus walked over to them, and absently poked at the stolen cheese. "You have dared to usurp my rights of judgment on my own land, and then execute innocent men while you eat their families' food?"

The two ceased chewing and froze. Their nonchalant demeanor disappeared.

"Hard to say where one estate ends and another begins in these hills," the red-haired man offered. "If we have erred, my lord will compensate you."

"If you erred, it is not for your lord to pay, but for you."

Silence fell all around them. The two men rose, and with quick, nervous glances took in the wall of armor and horses. It grew so quiet and still that a low whimper to Marcus's left sounded like a scream of despair.

He turned, and saw a woman staggering from a tiny hut. Blood trickled from her lips where she had been struck, and other marks showed on her face and neck.

He strode forward and swept the woman into his arms. For a moment, as he examined her battered face, rage owned him so completely that he lost hold of his sense.

Another figure darkened the threshold of the hut. A man, also wearing the livery of Arundal, strolled out, smiling and contented. Fixing his garments distracted him, and he was well away from the door before he noticed the many stares aimed at him.

His glance shot to his comrades, and then to

Marcus. He tried a smile. "She was one of the thieves' woman," he said, assuming that explained it.

Marcus carried his burden over to some women and laid her among them. He returned to the tree, and gazed up at the thick limb. "We need three new nooses, I think."

The red-haired man straightened with indignation. "You cannot. We are sworn to—"

"If I err, I will compensate him."

His men prepared the tree. The condemned watched aghast as the ropes appeared and nooses were formed. A villager gladly braced his weight against the ladder set against the trunk.

Marcus waited, his head bursting.

Addis came to stand beside him. "You must not. You know that," he said quietly.

"Are you saying my judgment is not just?"

"It is just, and I share your outrage, but this is unwise."

"It is very wise. If I let them go, there will be no judgment at all. Arundal will not punish his own for killing a few Welsh villagers."

Three of his archers were binding the men's hands. The three soldiers reacted with horror at this evidence that Marcus was serious. The archers began pushing the first one toward the tree.

"Then do not let them go," Addis suggested. "Bring them back to Anglesmore, and keep them until you are satisfied that there will be justice. But if you do this, the other marcher lords will see it as evidence that you cannot be trusted to protect England's interests, and you will have a little war with Arundal even as you try to deal with Carwyn Hir."

"Do not preach politics to me. This is not about that."

"Nay, it is about powerless people made victims, and a woman raped by a man who expected no one who matters to object. It is their misfortune to have committed these crimes on the land of a man who has suffered such things himself. I understand that, but others will not." He placed his hand on Marcus's arm. "You must not do it this way."

The darkness in his head left little room for Addis's words, but they found a small place to settle all the same. He watched the first man get pushed and dragged up the ladder. He let the noose be fitted and tightened. All the while he felt that hand on his arm, beckoning him away from recklessness.

He waited until the last moment and then, although his essence yelled a rebellious denial of the decision, stopped it. Three men wept with relief, the terror finally showing itself.

The man from the hut wore a thin silver chain around his neck, and Marcus yanked it off. He brought it to the battered woman, and pressed it in her hands. "It is not compensation for your husband or your misuse," he said quietly. "I know that."

He strode to his horse. "Bring them. This reprieve will be a brief one. Relieve their garments of any coin or valuables, and give it to the families they offended. Leave one of their horses, too."

The villagers parted for him as he led his troop away. It sickened him to see their expressions of dull resignation. He knew what they thought. Marcus was English and they were Welsh, and they believed that no soldier sworn to a man as powerful as Arundal would ever be punished for a crime against such as them.

Addis left him to his scathing mood, and the long ride back to Anglesmore was a silent one. Marcus's anger grew, and it soon encompassed not just this day's events, but the followers of Llygad, whose increased violence had provoked the incident.

He knew that what had happened in that village was merely a taste of what might come. If he could not stop Carwyn Hir soon, if war broke out, the Welsh would be at the mercy of the armies called up to crush it, and the tenuous justice that they knew in this land would disappear.

CHAPTER 18

SOMETHING HAD HAPPENED. Something bad.

Nesta's worry built as the soldiers entered the hall. They were all subdued, and their mood rained silence over the whole household, especially the men of Addis's company who had increased the crowd and noise this evening.

She fixed her gaze on the entrance. As man after man passed the threshold, her heart beat harder and her breath grew shallow. She waited so hard to see Marcus's head that she thought her chest would burst.

The last of the troop straggled in, and the entrance cleared. Sickening fear slid through her in a cold chill. She knew that her concern was not rational. There would be more commotion if Marcus had been hurt, but dread numbed her all the same.

Two shadows darkened the threshold. Two bodies, encased in armor, stepped into the light. Marcus and Addis. Relief broke with a burst of joy, but the dark expression on Marcus's face instantly had her alarm prickling again.

Chaos claimed the hall as the servants arrived with food and ale for the men. Marcus stood in its midst, not appearing to notice the activity. His attention shot around, and came to rest on her sitting near the far wall. The world parted, creating a lane between the two of them in which nothing existed but their connected gazes. Danger flowed down that alley to her.

Marcus caught a passing servant and spoke to the man, who hurried off into the crowd. Soon, rows of servants began stringing through the crowd, carrying buckets of water and following their lord to his chambers.

The story of the day's events spread. Nesta heard the tale from the English wife of one of the knights. The words entering her ears created a different image than the lady intended to impart, and Nesta narrowed her eye on the stairs where she had last seen the lord of the manor.

It was a good thing Marcus had retired and was out of her sight and reach. In delaying justice for Arundal's men, he had only proven that he was just one more English lord preserving another one's right to treat the Welsh as a conquered people.

Seething resentment grew as she thought of those poor villagers. She remembered the freezing worry she had experienced while she waited for Marcus to appear. Not once during those horrible moments had she thought about her father's men, and who among them might have been wounded and killed. She hated the way her heart kept betraying her. It made her furious with herself, and with Marcus.

A servant approached her, carrying a tray of food and drink.

"My lord asked that you bring this to the solar."

"I am sure you are mistaken. You can bring it."

"His command was that you do it, my lady."

No doubt this food was for Addis. Marcus had surely told him about the betrothal, and now wanted his bride to attend on their guest in the appropriate fashion. She had no intention of maintaining the deception for this visiting baron.

She rose and took the tray. It was time to clarify the situation.

The solar door stood ajar. Putting her back to it, she pushed it open and entered with her burden.

Only the hearth provided light, but it was enough to beautifully display the back of a man sitting in the tub. The skin appeared golden in the fire's glow, and a thousand dots of water shimmered on it. She took in the broad shoulders and lean muscles. Wet hair hung to his neck, but it was too light to belong to their guest.

Aside from him the chamber was empty. No servants lurked in the shadows, waiting to assist.

She carried the tray to the large table near the window. Setting it down in his view, she pivoted and aimed back to the door with her eyes lowered.

"Stay."

The order caught her as she passed.

"I would prefer not to."

"I did not ask what you preferred. Close the door, then bring me some wine."

Gritting her teeth, she pushed the door shut and went to pour the wine. Delivering it meant that she had to face him.

She tried to avert her gaze, but she saw him all the same. Saw the shoulders she had held and the hard chest she had kissed. Saw the strong arms that had embraced her, and moved her body at his will. Saw the wonderful, masculine hand that now grasped a cloth and squeezed rivulets of water down a well-formed leg.

She held out the goblet of wine. His other hand closed over it, and imprisoned her fingers beneath his.

Startled, she looked up. His face appeared as harsh as she had ever seen it. His eyes held dangerous, vivid lights. Not only anger flamed in them. The fuel that fired them was more complex than that. And whatever else passed in that gaze, she could not deny that she also saw a bit of the way he had always looked at her, and she reacted a bit as she always had.

She pulled her hand free and walked over to the table to fuss with the rest of the food, slicing cheese and meat. "I expected Sir Addis to be here, not you."

"I gave him my chamber. He will use it while he is here."

"If you summoned me so I would know where you will sleep henceforth, there was no need. There was no danger that I would slip into that chamber looking for you and find him instead, I assure you."

No response came at first, but she could almost hear an unspoken one in the pause. "I summoned you so that we might speak," he finally said.

"It could have waited until you are done with this."

"In my present humor our talking could not wait. It has been in my head for hours."

"Then the bath could have waited, so I would not have been summoned like a servant to attend you thus."

"I found myself impatient for this too. I wanted to wash a day of riding off me. And also the stench of death."

"I thought perhaps you wanted to cleanse yourself of a bad judgment, much as Pilate did."

The sounds of washing instantly stopped. An ominous silence came from the tub.

She sliced more meat, and cursed the way her hand shook.

"A different judgment would not have brought those three men back, Nesta, and if I were you I would not be throwing accusations at anyone tonight. The way I see it, the death of those villagers is on your head."

She swung around. "How dare you say that. Arundal's men commit murder, and you blame *me*?"

He rose from the tub, revealing his nakedness, but neither of them cared. He grabbed a towel and dried himself with strong, deliberate wipes. "I blame your father and his followers and anyone who has aided or instigated the strife growing in these parts. When a baron pursues these criminals, he will not stop at his border and let them escape. It is the boldness of the recent raids that put those villagers in danger, and it will get worse in the weeks ahead. You think to strike a blow against England, but the people who will feel the most pain will be the Welsh themselves."

He threw the towel aside and grabbed a simple robe. "I wish you had been with us today. God, how I wish it. When I saw you in the hall I almost grabbed you by the hair to drag you back to that village, so you could see what your grand scheme had brought to pass."

She thought her head would burst from swelling anger and resentment. "No scheme of mine brought it to pass. The unchecked power of Arundal did, and the smug confidence of those men of his who assumed that if they erred no one would care. And they were right, damn you. And so it has been for hundreds of years on the marches, and now in the west and north as well. Today does not lay bare only the dangers of my father's dream. It also proves the necessity of it."

The robe slid over him. He stepped toward her, his eyes blazing, his damp hair falling around his face. He came close enough for her to *feel* the anger he barely kept in control. "Just what is your father's dream, Nesta? I have guessed, but it is time for me to know for certain. A free Wales, independent of English rule? Was Llygad up Madoc so bold as that? That is a high price to make Edward pay for casting his eye on a daughter."

"He did not raise his banner because of me. Eventually he would have anyway."

"But he chose that moment. He knew the stories about you and Edward would get the attention of the Welsh, and that his violated daughter would make a fine symbol of Wales itself. As with the woman, so with the country. Used by England, perhaps even raped. Exploited for England's pleasure and gain. Denied the dignity and courtesies reserved for the English themselves. It was perfect. Did Llygad plan it? Encourage the King's interest in you, and hope the story would spread?"

Her hand swung of its own accord, aiming for his face as she vented the burst of outrage that his accusation evoked.

He caught her wrist before she connected, and held it in an iron grip. "What else has been your role in this? You will tell me now."

"I will tell you nothing."

He stepped yet closer, still holding her wrist, using his strength to dominate her. "Whatever it is, it is over. You will do no more damage. If you can stop it, you will do so."

"You are a fool if you think it was ever in my power to stop it. You are doubly a fool if you believe it is in *your* power."

"It will be stopped, Nesta. If not by me now, by Edward later." His other hand took her face in a controlling hold. "In either case, you are out of it. Do you understand that?"

She narrowed her eyes on him. "I am the daughter of Llygad ap Madoc, and my nobility was already ancient when yours was first created. There are still some of us who do not cower in front of English power. Who do not submit to commands from such as you."

"I have been too indulgent with you. Too careful with your pride, because of what has passed between us. That was a mistake." His hand dropped from her face, but he did not move away. Nor did his anger retreat. "When I found you in the snow, you offered to kneel later at my pleasure. Now would be a very good time, lady."

"I'll be damned first."

"You will do it, because of your promise, and because you are my bride—"

"I am *not* your bride."

"—and because I command it. You will also do it because I will make you if I have to."

He meant it. She did not doubt that he was

angry enough to force her body to assume a position of submission, even if he could not bend her will.

She looked into the eyes watching her. Looked deeply enough to see not just the lord but also the man. There was more to this battle they fought than England and Wales. There always had been.

Because of that, she was not without weapons to match his.

She just gazed up at him, not at all cowed. The challenge in her expression only goaded his determination. This would end here, now. He would not live with this particular viper in his camp any longer.

The glint in her eyes turned knowing. She stepped back, but not in fear. "You are right, Mark. I did promise to kneel. I will do so now, to make good my word."

As she strolled away, her hands went to her head, and she began releasing her hair from its knotted style. "But you do not only seek the fulfillment of a promise, do you? You want me humbled, and at your feet like a petitioner. When a woman submits like that to a man, she normally does so without jewels or other vanities. That way she appears much more a beggar."

She kept her back to him as her hands did their work. Her long, waving tresses began falling in luxurious strands, down her back. She shook her head when they were all free, and the long sway floated back and forth in a sensual shimmer.

Marcus suppressed his reaction. He'd be damned if—

Her hands began releasing the lacing on the side of her gown. "Of course, if I am to be humbled, we should make it as complete as possible, so that your pleasure in your victory is all it can be."

His gaze fixed on the delicate plucking of her fingers on the lacing. He knew he should stop this, but the slow release of her gown's closure mesmerized him. An onslaught of furious desire buried the anger that had demanded she kneel. It remained alive beneath the hunger, however, giving his reaction a keen edge.

She shrugged the gown off her shoulders. It slid down her body in a slow, tantalizing path until it pooled at her feet. The firelight revealed the shadowy shape of her body beneath the shift.

She turned to face him, her eyes downcast.

The soft cloth of the thin shift fell over the swells of her breasts, and the hard nubs of her nipples pressed the fabric. The evidence that she too was aroused obliterated every thought except the desire to have her.

"Is this humble enough?" Her gaze rose, and the primal sensuality that had always bound them yelled its silent demands. There was no submission in her eyes. She was all challenge and daring and female power. "Perhaps not."

Her hands reached for the fabric on her shoulders. Not averting her gaze, connected to him as if by a chain, she slowly revealed her luminous skin. "You were correct that day in the cottage. I enjoy making you want me. No touch could be as tantalizing as the way you are looking at me now. It gives me more pleasure than a tongue licking all over my skin. It makes me shiver with delicious anticipation."

Her words and the slow slide of the shift revealing her nakedness, had his head storming.

Her hair draped around her, swaying as she stepped toward him, and glimpses of her body came and went as she moved. She approached until she stood right in front of him, her breasts peeking seductively through the tresses and the scent of her increasing the madness threatening to own him.

She reached for the closure on his robe and undid it, then brushed the garment down his body. "I had intended to leave by now, but the craving indeed goes both ways, and in unhorsing you with this weapon I find myself defeated too." She looked up at him, and he thought he would drown in her eyes. "You appear angry still. I think that I will kneel, after all. Because I choose to."

She lowered herself elegantly, fluidly. Her closeness made him burn. He gazed down on her dark crown while her fingers began an exquisite torture. She caressed his hips and thighs, and finally, luxuriantly, his phallus. His breath caught and a furious, relentless urging pounded through him.

Her breath warmed him, and then, when he was close to begging, her lips replaced her hands. With her first kiss, his mind split apart.

It thrilled her more than she had expected it to. All of it did. The plan had been to defeat him, and show him her strength, but her own yearnings betrayed her as they so often had before.

Even now, as she made love to him, the control was not all hers. Her body cried with anticipation, impatiently demanding its turn. The craving slyly subverted her. Heaven beckoned, a state of bliss where the two of them dwelled as one and the strife that had brought her here no longer existed.

Leaving him incomplete, she rocked back on her heels, and rose.

Control tightened his expression, making him so compelling in his passion that her heart almost couldn't take it. An angry question flashed in his eyes.

She shook her head in response. Nay, she was not leaving. Not now. That would be impossible.

She went near the hearth, and knelt again, facing it. Sitting back on her feet, she waited for him to join her, so they could finish this with a joining that made neither of them victorious or vanquished.

Time pulsed past, but she could feel him as surely as if they embraced. He was looking at her, and letting the expectation tantalize them both for a while.

"Move your hair off your back, Nesta."

She pulled it forward, so her back and bottom were bare.

"That is how I saw you in the cottage that day, while you bathed. Your lovely back curving in to your waist, and the roundness of your hips and bottom. You looked very erotic," he said. "I wanted to stride across that rude chamber and take you at once. It has always been that way between us. Finally having you did not change it, as I thought it might."

Hoped it might, was what he meant. She had hoped so too. But what wanted to happen between them had always been bigger than mere lust. It had even been bigger than duty, and Wales and England. Bigger and more compelling in ways that frightened her.

She heard him move, and then come up behind her. His leg warmed her shoulder.

A pillow dropped to the floor in front of her.

She looked at the pillow, then glanced up at him. "Only because I choose to, Marcus. Only in our passion do I submit, because it excites me to do so."

He eased down behind her, his thighs spreading to flank her hips. Arms circling her, he leaned her back into his warmth. "Then do so, Nesta, but first kiss me."

He turned her enough so their mouths could meet, and claimed her with a savage kiss that contained all of the night's emotions, both harsh and loving.

Releasing her, he moved her body. Rising on his knees, he eased her forward and pressed her head to the pillow so her back arched and her bottom rose. The vulnerability sent a shocking thrill of anticipation through her.

As if he sensed how the position tantalized her, he let her wait. She felt him there, right behind her, looking at her, and imagining what he saw only made it worse.

He touched her where she pulsed, and she thought she would faint. It was the first caress of the night, but her body was so anxious that it almost undid her. Intense pleasure streaked through her.

Another touch, more deliberate. A moaning sigh escaped her.

"That is right, Nesta. Let me hear your desire. Making you want me gives me great pleasure."

With slow, masterful touches, he forced madness on her. Delicious, mindless need consumed her. He made her want him until the sounds of her own cries floated in the fog of her mind.

Holding her hips, he joined them with a slow, deliberate penetration. The sensual chaos in her consciousness calmed with the welcome fullness. It felt so wonderful. Hard and complete and connecting.

He withdrew slowly, and the exquisite sensation made her throb. A hard reconnection turned the pleasure feral. She looked back to

where he rose behind her, strong and controlling, his body astonishing in its masculine
beauty. His gaze met hers in the instant comprehension they had always had of each other
when it came to passion and desire.

Welcoming this special submission, she let
him take her into ecstasy.

"Stealing these tastes of heaven with you has
also meant knowing a lot of hell."

His quiet voice broke the stillness as they lay
together on the pallet beneath the window, letting the brisk night air cool the heat of their
bodies. It was very late. She should have returned to her chamber long ago, but their lovemaking had not ended until long after the
household had retired.

She lay sprawled on him, her ear to his chest
and her thighs flanking his hips. This last joining had not been furious like the first, but so
soulful and sweet that her heart had wanted to
break. As his hold had guided the rise and fall of
her hips, she had been able to see his face in the
moonlight, and the way he looked at her, and
the times his gaze had slid to the sky behind her
head.

That was where he was looking now.

She did not break their embrace, but listened to his heartbeat and nestled in the surrounding strength of his arms. Escaping into the magic of their passion had been wonderful, and she wanted to pretend it would not end. She could not ignore, however, that the emotions that he had brought back to Anglesmore tonight still churned in him.

She did not need his quiet statement to tell her that. She felt it in him, as she had even in their pleasure. A dark current flowed in him, touching everything, even his desire and ecstasy.

"You were wrong, Nesta. What you said earlier. That no one would care about those villagers. I did not see the bodies of Welsh people hanging there. I saw the bodies of *my* people. If I had followed my blood not only would Arundal's men be dead, but I would have probably taken my men into Arundal's land, looking for him."

"I am glad you did not go that far, although a war between two marcher lords would be useful." She laughed after she said it, hoping to lighten his mood. Their profound connection meant that she sensed too well the turmoil in his head and heart.

He kissed her hair, as if acknowledging her small attempt to soothe him. They lay silently in

their embrace, and she tried to let their closeness bring some peace.

"How was it between you and Edward?"

The question jolted her out of her stupor of
contentment. "I thought you did not want to
know which of the songs was true."

"The man who holds you does not, but the
Lord of Anglesmore has decided he needs to
know."

"I do not think the King holds any affection
for me now, if that is your—"

"I am not concerned about his reaction to
our love. I need to know for other reasons."

Our love. They had slipped out, forbidden
words spoken while he concentrated on something else. The affirmation planted a spot of
startling, pristine happiness in her heart. Her reaction was instant and helpless.

She rose up a bit, so she could see his face. He
still gazed at the stars, and did not even appear
very thoughtful. His expression was too calm,
too firm.

His eyes burned with the lights of a man who
had made a decision and only waited for the
signal to ride. *I saw my people.*

His gaze shifted to meet hers. Suddenly it was
just the two of them in the world, bound by a
mutual knowing of each other that was deeper
than any words.

"Was it rape, Nesta?"

She knew what he was contemplating. Whether it was because of her or the villagers, or because of the centuries his family had lived in Wales, his loyalty was wavering. Only one thread had ever held it to England, and that was what he owed the King.

One word from her, and that thread would break. This man of all men would not feel bound to serve a rapist. Especially one who had violated the woman he loved.

Her heart started pounding. A victory she had never sought was waiting in the dark eyes gazing into hers. If one marcher lord joined her father's men, others might too. The new English lords to the north and west could never stand against the power of the borders. The odds of her father's plan working would increase tremendously, and the alliance Genith was supposed to have made would surely unfold as it should.

It was all there, a breath away. But the bigger temptation was a personal one. She saw Marcus and her united in all ways, joined by day as well as night, hand in hand in duty as well as passion. Her heart filled with a yearning so intense her eyes misted from wanting it so badly.

"Was it?" A demand this time, as the arms

surrounding her nakedness tightened possessively.

She wanted to say it. Hungered to. She felt
him beneath her, around her. Sensed what was
in him, and understood it even better than he
did. United, aye, but for the wrong reason.
Joined by a duty, but one that would cause the
destruction he wanted to stop. Hand in hand,
but perhaps in defeat and not victory.

They were his people, but this was not his
cause.

A horrible pain lodged in her heart. Sharp
and ragged, it stole her breath. In that instant
she realized how much she loved him. The regret ripping through her, the temptation to say
the words that would bridge what separated
them, was mellowed only by the complete certainty of that love.

"Nay," she whispered. "I was in no way coerced or forced."

A series of reactions flickered in his eyes.
Relief and surprise and even a bit of disappointment. Then, deeply, a flash of anger, as if
he resented her refusal to give him the excuse
he wanted.

He pressed her head back down on his chest,
and the peace lapped over them again. She
could feel whatever had provoked his crisis of
the soul receding on its tide.

"Then I want you out of it, Nesta. I want you done with it."

She did not respond. There was nothing she could say.

What he and she wanted was of little importance in this. In any of it.

CHAPTER 19

MARCUS, ADDIS, AND NESTA stood together near the rushing stream, drinking the crisp water with which they had filled their cups. Marcus surveyed the forest-covered hills flanking the small valley in which they traveled. They had crossed into Merionetshire, the crown lands known to the Welsh as Gwynedd. When they remounted, they would have to climb into the mountains in order to reach the old manor of Llygad ap Madoc.

"Two boys and three girls," Addis said to Nesta, in response to her question about his family. "Then there is a third boy, whom we fostered." He launched into a description of his children and their achievements while Nesta listened politely.

Marcus looked past them to the dense clus-
tering of men and horses that stretched along
the banks of the stream. From this domestic
conversation, one would never guess that Addis
and he led an army, or that Nesta accompanied
them as something of a prisoner.

He had brought her because he dared not
leave her to make mischief from Anglesmore,
and because her presence might be useful.

She also came, however, because he wanted
her with him. He had not voiced that reason to
Addis, but he suspected that Addis had guessed
it. Someone sleeping in the bedchamber would
have heard what occurred in the solar.

Nesta walked the twenty paces to the stream's
bank. She took out a cloth and dipped it in the
water and began dabbing her face and neck.

Addis sidled closer to Marcus, and glanced up
at the tree-covered hill to their left. "We are
being watched. Have been since we entered
this valley. I know it, you know it, she knows it,
and half the men know it."

Marcus nodded. There had been no evidence
of being followed, but one could feel the presence of others.

Addis gestured to a group of three men
standing to one side. They had also come as
prisoners, only more obviously than Nesta had.
"Good that you had them remove Arundal's

colors. It was wise of you to bring them, too. If Arundal had arrived at Anglesmore demanding their release, the men guarding the keep would be hard-pressed to refuse him."

"My bigger concern was the danger they faced from those guards, Addis. Many within my walls are Welsh, or have a lot of Welsh blood, and even my English knights think they deserve execution. If I did not hang them that day in the village, I do not want to return and find them dead through some accident or suspicious illness."

Addis peered to where the valley narrowed and rose. "We will be riding no more than two across up ahead. If there is going to be trouble, it will be there."

Marcus laughed, and clamped his hand on Addis's shoulder. "You broach the subject as a mother does with a grown son. The warden in you wants to give advice, but you hesitate lest you insult me."

Addis smiled with some chagrin. "It is habit, from when you needed advice."

"I still welcome it, so do not be so careful with my pride. As for the eyes in the forest and the narrow path ahead, we will tell the men to carry their shields."

Nesta strolled back toward them. Addis noticed her coming, muttered something about passing the order, and walked away. Nesta watched him go, then turned her gaze on Marcus conspiratorially.

She favored him with a private smile and tender look. He reacted as he always did, with an onslaught of desire and yearning that blotted out most of the world. For a moment nothing existed but the sight of her, and that smile, and the bright sun, and the sound of the rushing stream.

During that mesmerized instant, her face fell. Frowning, she quickly looked to the hills. Shock replaced the warmth in her eyes. With an expression of horror and determination, she ran toward him, her mouth open in a soundless yell.

He saw her come as if time had slowed. Whistles penetrated his awareness just as she slammed into him with all of her weight. She clutched him in a hurtling embrace that had him staggering back while the world swirled.

His balance and senses abruptly righted themselves. He found himself surrounded by her arms, her body pressed to his.

All along the stream activity erupted. Men yelled, swords flashed, and horses pranced. A line of archers marched forward and sent volleys of arrows into the forest.

Arundal's three men lay in heaps, each pierced by several arrows from longbows.

Marcus looked down, and saw another one sticking out of the ground where he had just been standing.

No one attacked. No more whistles sounded. The battle stance of his men slowly relaxed.

Marcus embraced the woman who still shielded him with her body. A turmoil of reactions overwhelmed him. Astonishment that she had sensed the danger before Addis or himself. Anger that she had risked herself so thoughtlessly. Joy that she cared enough to do so.

He set her aside firmly, and went over to Arundal's men. Colors or not, they had been identified.

Addis joined him. "There will be hell to pay with Arundal when he hears of this."

"He will probably hear of it very soon, too. Words travel faster than a horse in Wales."

Men lifted the bodies and slung them over saddles. Squires brought their horses, and he and Addis mounted.

"No need to pass the word about those shields now," Addis said. Behind them every man had steel facing the hill to their left. "I think that I will carry mine too."

Marcus took the hint, and lifted his own.

He was probably the only one who needed to, from the looks of things. Except for the one bolt still rising beside Nesta, no others had been aimed at other than Arundal's men.

"Perhaps they wanted to free her from this betrothal you made," Addis said.

"Perhaps."

Addis gave the woman waiting for them a thoughtful examination. "I suddenly favor her much more than I did a short while ago."

The first sight of her home made Nesta stop her horse. A flood of reactions poured through her, and shock tinged every one.

She had never realized how poor her father's manor was. Only the lowest of English lords lived like this.

Pushing her horse forward, she tried to reconcile what she saw with her memories. When she lived here as a girl, she had thought it very grand. Compared to everything else that she knew, it had been. In the eight years since she had left, however, she had learned what true power and position looked like. In comparison, this appeared very primitive.

Riding beside Marcus, she entered the gate in the wooden stockade wall. The low tower rising inside it was built of stone, but the rest of the house was timber. That was still typical in Wales. When Edward's grandfather had conquered the princes of the north, the mighty stone fortresses he strung throughout Wales had symbolized England's domination more surely than the men who held them.

The details flashing at her sapped her spirit. Outbuildings in the yard bore thatched roofs, and some had not seen new straw in years. Two children played in the dirt near the wall, wearing tunics so short that their bottoms showed. A woman watched them from where she had been feeding chickens, and her bare feet peeked out from beneath her ragged hem.

Nesta felt Marcus's attention on her, and looked to find him watching her reaction as they paced their mounts through the yard. She shrugged. "It is different from what I remember."

"It has not been maintained well these past years. That often happens when a knight holds property that is not his, and the King has put a castellan here."

It was not only the lack of care. Everything was smaller. Older. Sadder.

"The lands are not large either," she said. "Not much of a dowry for Genith to bring you."

"Well, a big swath of the forest to the south was included, as the King's contribution."

"If you married Genith, perhaps, but not me. You had better join me in praying that Stratford annuls this betrothal. A marcher lord should get more than this with his bride."

"When we marry, this marcher lord will get everything that he wants."

It was a sweet thing to say, and ambiguous enough not to broach the forbidden topic of love. His expression revealed more than any words, however.

The last two nights of abandoned lovemaking had further broken the boundaries in which they tried to keep their passion. As if they both sensed the end nearing, they had grabbed more of each other than was wise until her heart had ached even as she held him. The hunger they had brought each other had not just been physical, and she had let herself get lost in his eyes, his scent, his possession.

Word of their arrival spread, and the yard began filling with manor folk. A few recognized her, and the shouted welcomes increased in number and enthusiasm and drew yet more people from the buildings. Their calls got louder and louder, and rolled over the manor and across the wall and into the forest, turning into a joyous chant of her name.

The demonstration moved her. Throat thick and eyes brimming, she paced her mount through the crowd, picking out faces she knew and waving her acknowledgment. Dozens of hands rose to touch her body and garments, slowing her progress.

Marcus took it in placidly, as if this outpouring did not concern him. That surprised her. Surely the implications must be obvious to him. This would not be like Anglesmore. Any one of these people would do her bidding.

"Will you lock me in chains now?" she asked.

"If I had intended to, the chains at Anglesmore are stronger. This changes nothing. It is your home. It is not surprising that they are glad to see you again."

Her home. Her people. She surveyed the little sea of smiling, hopeful faces. Happiness welled up inside her, colored by profound emotions of pride.

He was wrong. It changed everything.

A woman lifted a child toward her, and shouted a petition for her blessing. Thus had mothers presented their babes to her father. Although she felt very awkward doing it, she placed her hand on the little head and mouthed the words. The warm softness of the skin and downy hair beneath her palm, the helplessness of the child, touched her so deeply that she could not move for a moment.

She suddenly understood Marcus's impassive reaction. Aye, it changed everything, in ways that contradicted and confused each other.

Coming home reminded her as nothing else could what she owed to the man who had last been lord here, and to his dream, and to Wales.

But if war came, the first ones to suffer would be the Welsh in this manor and that forest and the nearby hills.

Simple people. Poor people.

Her people.

"Thank the saints you are here."

Hubert uttered the statement after pouring more ale into Marcus's cup. They stood alone beside a table near the hall's hearth. After the castellan's welcome, Addis had returned to the army outside the walls to see to the placement of camps.

Hubert downed another cup, his third. He was a fair-haired young man, the third son of a powerful baron in Sussex, and had been given his position as a favor to his father. Evidence in the manor indicated that he had no talent for managing an estate, or for anything other than battle. From the worry masking his features, Marcus suspected that even when he wielded his sword, Hubert liked to know he was favored to win.

"Two days ago I sent some men out to see what was what in those hills. There had been rumors, although I'm always the last to hear such things. It is like living in a den of thieves who don't even speak your language. Hell of a thing. Anyway, one of my men was a long time gone, and comes back this morning with word of an army. An army! A half-day's ride into those damn mountains, and treacherous paths the whole way. They are scattered into many small camps. Hell of a thing."

"How large an army?"

"He did not introduce himself and take a count, now did he? At least a hundred, probably more. He saw some banners, but did not know the colors."

So, it was true that some chieftains had joined with Carwyn. And if some did, more might. One scent of potential victory and that army would swell tenfold.

"Where the hell did they come from, that's what I want to know. I doubt there are a hundred families for miles around."

From Powys and Gwynedd. From Glamorgan and Brecon. From the Welsh lands held by the English for centuries, and from those only held for fifty years.

And they had probably been packing their weapons and moving here for weeks, long before Nesta verch Llygad arrived at Anglesmore.

No wonder Nesta had been sanguine about this rebellion. No wonder there had been so little attempt on her part to contact Carwyn Hir. Her role was mostly done. This was where she had been during those months after leaving the convent. Traveling through Wales, visiting the old leaders, letting them know the time was now. Sealing that marriage alliance that would lend her father's men legitimacy and strength.

Marcus looked across the timber-roofed hall, to where Nesta sat surrounded by women and their children. Her dark eyes glinted with joy as they threw family news at her, filling in the big hole made by eight years' absence.

I am nothing in this. In any of it. That part was not true, and the evidence would be plentiful if Stratford and the King looked for it. Even now, she was the daughter of Llygad, and a symbol to the men camped in the distant mountains.

"How many did you bring?" Hubert asked.

"Over two hundred, with Addis de Valence's men included."

"There could be a thousand out there for all we know."

"I doubt that." *Not yet.* But maybe there

would be soon. Maybe bearing banners that Hubert would quickly recognize.

"Well, it is a good thing I sent messengers to the King's men in Danbigh, and to some of the marcher lords. Also to Warwick."

Marcus's attention snapped away from Nesta. "Warwick does not even hold lands here. You feared for your safety so much that you asked for help from an English baron?"

"I asked help from a baron not in Flanders with the King. Of course he is English. We all are. Hell, you brought Barrowburgh with you."

Marcus bit back his response. He began calculating. It would take two weeks for troops from England to make their way here, but the lords in Wales would arrive sooner. Once they did, he would be obligated to finish this with blood, not guile.

Peals of laughter drew his gaze back to Nesta and the domestic scene surrounding her. Her happiness sent light spilling through his heart.

He remembered the way she had thrown herself at him by the stream, and saved him from that bolt. It had been an instinctive betrayal of her father's cause, and he loved her for it.

He knew, however, that she had not completely forgotten her duty. He was counting on that. Counting on her making good her resolve to not be subverted.

He needed her to find the heart to commit another betrayal, this time of him.

He needed her to make her move, and very soon.

Mallets pounded to her right and left as Nesta stood on the wall walk. Within hours of arriving, Marcus had relieved Sir Hubert of his responsibilities, and set men to work reinforcing the shaky defenses. All around her were the signs of a manor being prepared for war.

The scene spread out on the hill below reinforced that impression. Most of the army Marcus had brought lived outside the wall, in camps carefully positioned and clustered. Some of the men had been sent into the forest, and as dusk now fell she could see the dots of distant fires, showing where sentries ringed them.

The pounding around her stopped. Boots lumbered away. That surprised her, until she felt the body along her back and the arms sliding around her waist.

"There is more light left," she said. "They could have worked longer."

"The food is ready, and they hardly mind the reprieve."

"I think they know the reason for it, despite your attempt at discretion."

"Probably so, after your bravery at the stream."

They had not spoken of that during the last hours of riding here. She did not regret her re-action, even though it had not been the result of bravery. It had not even been a decision. One moment she had sensed danger, and the next she was holding him.

"Do not scold me for being reckless, Mark." The horror of seeing that arrow in the ground returned, evoking a heart-numbing premoni-tion of grief. No matter what else happened now, she would not want to live if he died.

"It would be ungrateful to scold. But prom-ise me to never do such a thing again. Better an arrow finds me than you. I was born for such dangers, and accepted them long ago."

She leaned into him, and let him support her. His arms felt so good. Closing her eyes, she let them transport her back to memories of the night before last, when he held her whole body until dawn and its journey threatened. It had been a long taste of heaven, emersed in such poignant sharing that finally, when he slept, she had gazed out at those stars that he loved and silently wept.

She wanted to weep again now.

"Where were you put?" he asked.

"In my old chamber in the stone tower. I used to share it with Genith. Now I will share it with three other women who sleep there." She had not brought her servants, but many others had rushed to take their place. "It is a small manor."

"Not so small, but not big enough for three barons."

"When my father had important visitors, the men slept in his chamber. I assume that Hubert has done the same, and taken you and Addis in with him?"

She felt him nod. They were laying out the only reality that mattered right now. They would not be able to share a bed at night, even for a while.

"It is probably for the best." It pained her to say it. She expected to feel the tightening of his hold that said he disagreed. Instead he only kissed her neck, not in passion but in a comforting manner. She realized that he understood why it was for the best, and how lying with him would only make being home that much harder, and more confusing for her.

They knew each other well. Too well. Only in the bliss of their passion could they forget how well, for a while. Or at least she could.

Nothing existed for her then but a glory full of sparkling happiness.

He nestled her closer. "I do not need to make love to you, Nesta. Holding you like this, every now and then, will sustain me. But before we retire, bring me something of yours. A veil, perhaps."

She twisted and cocked an eyebrow at him. "For when you ride out? It would be most peculiar if you carried the favor of Llygad's daughter with you then."

"When I ride out, it will be as the King's man, and we both know that. The veil is for now. Do not laugh at me, but I would like to have it when I lie in bed. I would like to have something of you with me, if we cannot be together in fact."

For a man who claimed not to know pretty words, he managed to surprise her with lovely ones sometimes. Words like this, uncalculated, and so honest and open. An anguished joy, shaded by the pain waiting for them in the next days, stabbed her heart.

He kissed her, sweetly and gently, and then turned his gaze to the fires of war sparking in the gathering dusk.

CHAPTER 20

THE NEXT MORNING, Marcus watched from the wall as a commotion milled at the western edge of the camps. Soon a file of riders approached the manor house, escorted by Paul. Their banners bore colors that Marcus knew well.

Another baron had arrived, but not one of those whom Hubert had called. It was Arundal, hearty, fat, and balding, accompanied by ten men.

Marcus and Addis met them outside the gate. Arundal cast his heavy-lidded gaze upon the camps and scowled. "Your man here stopped us as if we were the enemy. What in the saints' names are you doing here, Marcus?"

"My duty, as our king charged me. What are you doing here?"

"Came to get my men. I was visiting my castle at Holt, and word came that you held them. I went to Anglesmore only to learn you had brought them here." He smirked as he dismounted. "You brought a very big shovel just to root out a few thieves."

"Roots grow long and deep in these mountains. Still, you are right. My men are young and eager, however, so I let them come."

"And you, Addis? Were your men so eager too?"

"I was at my manor in Wiltshire, and decided to visit an old friend. The chance for some action was a tempting lure to stay."

Arundal accepted without question that any man would welcome a chance fight. A less arrogant expression covered his face as he gestured Marcus aside.

"About that matter in the village. I will compensate you as is customary. When I heard you had taken my men, I was angry, I will admit it. Then learning they accompanied you here, well, I confess I was angrier yet. I realize, however, that you only sought to protect them from some revenge or whatnot in your absence."

"That was my intention."

"You can give them to me now. I will see that they are punished."

"Fate has done the job for you. We were attacked on the way here, and your men were killed."

Arundal's eyes narrowed to slits. "Bold of these wild men. Also rare for them to invite such a skirmish. Perhaps it is good that you brought a big shovel. How many did you lose?"

"Just three."

The implications sank in. Arundal's face turned red. "Someone from the village must have been there, pointing them out. I'll burn that place to the ground."

"I remind you that it is my village."

"Then *you* burn it."

"I have bigger matters to take care of now. When I am finished with them, we will discuss this small one. However, to my mind, justice has been done, and a mercy too. Better a few quick arrows than hanging, which is what I would have demanded of you for their crime."

Arundal puffed with outrage. He called gruffly to Addis. "You did not see to his education properly. Explain to this boy how it is."

Addis strolled toward them. "Murderers are now dead. I cannot see going to war over this. As to the man you insult by calling a boy, his sword arm is better than yours, so do not let your indignation lead to any rash challenges." He clapped a calming hand on Arundal's shoulder. "Come, and refresh yourself while we talk. It has been too long since we saw each other."

Not only Arundal spoke over the ale that they all shared in the hall. Before the first cup was finished, Hubert joined them and related the situation in the hills. The chance for a pitched battle got Arundal's thoughts off his dead men as nothing else could. He all but rubbed his hands together in anticipation.

Marcus caught Addis's eye in a mutual acknowledgment that they would never get this baron and his ten men to leave now.

Arundal plunged with enthusiasm into discussions of preparations. "Hubert says you don't know how many are out there."

"I am riding out today to assess that," Addis said. Arundal's eyes lit with anticipation of quick action, but Addis adroitly cut him off. "I am taking only a few men. Just a quiet scouting party, to learn how things lie."

"All the same, I'll be sending to Clun for fifty more. They can be here faster than anyone else, and we might need them."

Marcus had no good reason to object. He wanted to, however. He did not want an assortment of troops pledged to other than himself crowding the field outside. Keeping control of events would be nigh impossible. He had always suspected that time was his enemy, and now it truly was.

"Send for them if you want, but we are only facing a small band here. If my shovel is already too large, there is no need for a bigger one, and the countryside cannot support too many for a long spell."

Arundal's lowered lids showed he did not care for this disagreement with his judgment.

"There is one other thing. Your men are yours to command, but I received the King's charge on this, and I will decide if and when we move," Marcus added.

Their guest liked that even less. His smirk made it clear that he considered Marcus the least of the three barons sitting around the table. He glanced to Addis, as if seeking an ally in the view that Marcus should step aside.

Addis returned a cool gaze. "He had Edward's letter on this."

Arundal rose. "I'll send my messenger back now, and call for those fifty." He threw Marcus a sarcastic smile. "If the King gave you such a heavy duty, you must be his new favorite, Marcus. You get to lead men against thieves instead of the French, and guard these hills instead of the realm. He gives you a traitor's daughter as a bride, and all of this"—his gaze and arm mockingly swept the crude hall—"as a dowry. Then a girl escapes your hold and you are left with the King's own whore in her place. The enhancement of Anglesmore's honor is impressive. I envy you your place in Edward's heart."

Dinner was delayed that day.

Addis rode out as he intended, so Marcus sat at the high table with Hubert and Arundal. Some knights filled a few tables, but the manor folk had not come.

Time slid past. Hubert kept glancing to the doorway expectantly, waiting for signs of the meal.

"Does a man have to hunt and cook his own boar in order to eat in this hellhole?" Arundal groused.

Flushing, Hubert sent one of his squires to the kitchen to investigate. The boy returned to report that the meal was cooked, but the servants could not bring it yet because they had something else to do.

Hubert's face turned bright red. "Go back and give my command that food be brought at once. Tell the cooks to deliver it themselves if they cannot find servants. I will not have my guests insulted by further delay."

The boy scurried out. A long while passed with no meal arriving.

Arundal tapped his fingers on the table, and assumed an expression of haughty disapproval. Marcus propped his head on his hand and waited.

"Can we assume that you command your horse better than these servants, Hubert?" Arundal asked.

Hubert muttered curses, and excused himself to go find someone to yell at.

He had not taken more than five steps when a servant finally appeared. He did not come from the kitchen, nor did he carry any food. Rather he stepped down the stairs from the adjoining tower, toting a stool.

Another followed, carrying a plank. More came into view, forming a little procession. Some held other pieces of wood, or fat candles, or pillows. They filed through the hall, heading toward the door to the yard.

"Hell of a thing," Hubert muttered.

"Is this some Welsh feast day?" Arundal asked.

A woman carried a box as if it contained a treasure. Marcus recognized it as the one in which Nesta kept her little pots of inks.

Nesta herself appeared, surrounded by chatting women. She completely ignored the barons at the high table as she followed her retinue out of the building.

Hubert walked to the door and craned his neck. "They are going into the chapel."

"I told you, it is a feast day," Arundal said. "Probably some obscure Welsh saint that no civilized Christian has ever heard of."

Marcus knew better. They had been carrying planks and inks and candles, and he had seen their use before. Of more significance had been the moment chosen for this little procession. It amazed him that neither of the men waiting with him comprehended what had just occurred.

Nesta verch Llygad had just made it very clear that she now commanded the Welsh inside these walls.

Arundal angled toward Marcus. "The dark-haired lady with them. That was the daughter?"

"Aye."

"I will admit that she has something about her . . ." His face broke into a leering smile. "It is rumored that Edward still wants her. He may not care for this betrothal of yours."

Marcus did not need anyone to remind him of that.

"No doubt he will accept that you only sacrificed your pride for strategic reasons," Arundal mused. "Once her father's men are flushed out, he will get the archbishop to relieve you of the burden of her shame." His smile turned mocking. "Or maybe not. Perhaps he will welcome the marriage, and give you a position at court so that he has her nearby."

A pulse began throbbing furiously in Marcus's head. If he stayed at this table, he and Arundal would be wielding their swords soon.

A cook appeared, nervous and flushed, carrying a long plank on his shoulder loaded with bread. Behind him another man hauled a huge cauldron that was so heavy it made him wobble.

Hubert strode over, shouting his displeasure at the delay. For good measure, he swung to box the first cook's ear. The man saw it coming. He turned just enough for Hubert's palm to slam into the plank balanced on his shoulder.

The plank abruptly tilted. Dozens of loaves flew through the air as if a catapult had hurled them. The cook veered back in amazement at the sight they made, pushing right into his companion who was equally distracted by the impressive display.

The cauldron fell. It landed on a foot and turned. Its thick, liquid contents lapped onto the floor.

Hubert bellowed. Arundal sighed. Marcus, concluding that it would be some while before anyone ate, left the hall.

✦ ✦ ✦

Marcus entered the chapel as the last of the servants left. Hubert's shouts still rang in the distance, but none of the Welsh appeared much concerned with his anger. A few even smirked when they stepped into the yard and heard his harangue.

He found Nesta down by the altar, setting out her little pots. A table had been constructed beneath a tiny window, and rows of lit candles, stuck on yet another plank, gave her more light.

"Do you intend to make religious images now, and seek inspiration here?"

"There is no room in my chamber for it, so I decided to bring my things here."

"There is plenty of space in the hall." If she worked in the hall, he could see her.

"It is quiet and private here."

The manor priest, a short, old man with wisps of grey hair springing from his head, approached with three more candles. He gave Marcus a toothless, formal smile. With great care he lit each candle, dripped a pool of its wax on the plank, and set the candle upright into the cooling puddle for support.

"Thank you for your generosity in letting me work here, Father."

"With such labor as this do the monks pray, my child. Come anytime, when you need the counsel of our Lord." He patted her arm affectionately and headed to the yard, to wait for dinner with everyone else.

"Is that why you have brought your inks here, Nesta? To seek counsel with God?"

"If I needed a chapel for that, I would be damned by now. I bring them here so that I can avoid the hall where too many English lords dwell, and where a fool sits in my father's chair."

"Do not begrudge Hubert his little glory."

"Hubert is an ass."

"If he had been less of one, your father's men would have been put down by now. Edward's bad choice of castellan benefited you." He checked that the priest was gone, then slipped his arms around her waist. "I should curse Hubert's lack of wits. A part of me knows, however, that had he been a different sort of man, we might never have met."

She resisted his embrace for an instant, no more. It reminded him of their first one, in the garden under a moonlit sky, when her spirit had betrayed her good sense so quickly.

Resting her cheek against his chest, she pressed close so that her body lined his. "Hold me, Mark. It is cold here. I had never realized how cold. I have been chilled since we arrived, and the warmth of your embrace is delicious."

He wrapped her in his arms and held her close while the candles dripped their wax and the damp silence of the chapel secluded them from the world. The bright glow from the candles grew and spread, filling his senses with shimmering white light and gentle heat. They might have been standing on a summer hillside at dawn, so complete was the peace and beauty he experienced.

Thus it had always been at the height of their passion, but it had never been pleasure alone that brought this taste of heaven.

"Can't you get Arundal to leave?" she muttered.

The light dimmed a bit. The world intruded. He caressed her, not minding much. Until this was over, the grace would always come in fleeting moments that they stole like thieves.

"It would not matter if I could. Hubert has sent for others. Some lords from the north and east will arrive soon. I'm sure that the servants have told you that Carwyn's numbers have grown. Hubert learned of it and grew worried."

He almost heard her thoughts as she calculated the implications of what he had said. The body he held trembled slightly, as if the chill she had spoken of claimed her again.

"The manor will get so thick with English that there will be no fresh air to breathe," she said. "Perhaps I will move my bed to this chapel too, and live here. I have only one sheet of parchment left, however, so I had better devise a very detailed image in order to make it last."

He kissed her head, and tested her resolve. "Nesta, do you know how many Carwyn has with him? If it is not too many, perhaps I can see that the others do not come."

She did not respond, not even to shake her head. Her silence revealed the battle her heart raged. She would not give him the numbers, although he suspected she knew them now and could anticipate how they would grow. But neither did she lie and claim the threat was small, so that he might make the moves that would put him at a disadvantage.

He should demand the truth, but he could not. It was his fault that her heart had been split in two like this, and that speaking any words would force one side to betray the other.

She nestled closer. The way she sought comfort touched him, and he caressed her face. His hands touched moisture on her cheek, and he tightened his embrace.

"Mark, with Addis and Arundal here, and

with other lords coming . . . there is no need for you to lead this army. It does not have to be your command that sends them out, nor you riding at their head."

Her words surprised him. She had just indirectly told him what he needed to know. She expected Carwyn to raise a formidable army, large enough to put him in danger.

"Addis would never take my place, even if I wanted him to. Arundal gladly would, and may even try, and standing against Warwick when he comes will not be easy either. It is my duty, however. Would you really want me to step aside, Nesta? Would you want someone else deciding how this will unfold?"

She rubbed her face against his chest, and he knew it was tears that she wiped away with the gesture. "The weak woman in your arms wants you safe, that is all."

She gently eased away, and he regretfully let her go. She opened her box, and removed the tiny brushes, one by one.

He gestured to the table. "Make it a very detailed image, Nesta. One that takes weeks to finish. It might be wise for you to live in this chapel, and stay out of sight. If things go badly, it will not take long for others to guess the role you have played."

He left her, to do what she had to do. Her

oblique warning had subtly unbalanced the war that her heart waged. The daughter of Llygad would feel compelled to rectify that.

She watched him walk away. As long as she could see him, she could pretend that his arms still held her. She had experienced a poignant moment of utter connection in his embrace, and she held on to the memory, willing it to continue forever. With each of his steps, however, it slid away from her, leaving her finally bereft.

A wonderful embrace. It had contained the best of what they knew during their truces.

It broke her heart that it would probably be the last one.

She looked down at her last piece of parchment. If she labored without respite, would God have mercy and give her His counsel? If not, would He give her absolution later?

The brushes waited. The pots beckoned. The candles would last through the night.

The light blurred as her eyes teared. She wished Mark had been more discreet. She wished he had not ruined the memory of this last embrace by pointing her toward betrayal with his words.

Her heart tore. She experienced the horrible

shredding that she had always known would come one day. If she had been anywhere else but in this manor, if her father's memory were not so present in all of the spaces, she might have forsaken the dream right then and there.

She wanted to. She wished she could. Not for her own safety, but for the man who had reminded her what happiness could be.

A sound disturbed her. She glanced to the doorway, where Mark had recently walked. The priest stood there, barely visible.

He had been a part of this manor her whole life. He had served her father, and baptized her and Genith, and had taught them both to read and write. He was all that was left of her girlhood, and his arrival gave her untold comfort.

"Will you stay with me?" she asked. "I think that I will need your help."

He came to her. As he entered the light, it revealed his understanding and sympathy.

She sat down and smoothed the parchment with her hands. He stood by her shoulder. Sadder than she had ever been in her life, she began her final image.

CHAPTER 21

THE DELAYED DINNER heralded things to come. The servants grew lax and lazy, and the disruptions created by the visiting lords and army plunged the household into chaos. Discomfort reigned.

Worse, by evening of the next day, the Welsh population in the manor house had been depleted. Marcus suspected first. A few memorable faces disappeared. Tables appeared less cramped.

That night, when Hubert called for his personal manservant, no one arrived in his crowded chamber.

Marcus and Addis followed him down to the hall and watched him realize that the ranks had thinned. He strode outside and returned shortly, in a fury. He began an interrogation of the men who remained.

"If she keeps it up, we will be doing our own washing soon," Addis said. "I do not think Nesta's only goal is to make Hubert appear a fool."

"He does not need her help there," Marcus agreed. "They must have taken food out to the men in the camps, and simply did not return. I told Paul to be watchful, but I will not force them to stay. If the Welsh men support Carwyn, we are better with them not within the walls."

"Eventually Hubert will realize that she is behind this, Marcus."

Unfortunately, Hubert realized it at once. After bending his scowling face to Arundal's ear, he bore down on Marcus with his ally in tow.

"At least twenty have left, the strongest and most fit," he reported, his face flushed with anger. "It isn't just servants. A third of my guard have deserted too."

"You should have expected the latter, since most of your guards are Welsh," Marcus said. "It is a wonder they did not hand this manor over to Carwyn months ago."

"My men were sworn to *me*, not a thief. They held me in awe."

Marcus bit back the response his mind snapped to that.

"That woman is bewitching them to her own ends," Arundal said. "She cannot be trusted."

"She spends her days in the chapel and is hardly a threat."

"She must be stopped," Hubert hissed. "Who knows what messages she has sent to those rebels with the servants. Most likely she only had some remain here so she would have someone at hand to carry later reports."

"He is right," Arundal agreed.

Having shown some mettle, Hubert pressed on. "She has probably told them everything. I will not have a traitor eating at my board as if she is a guest. I am going to lock her away."

"*You* are going to do no such thing," Marcus said. "I will consider your complaints and decide the proper action."

Hubert disagreed vehemently. Arundal's lids lowered. Glints of suspicion sparked in both men's eyes. As they walked away, their heads bent together, Marcus had no trouble imagining their conversation.

They were questioning his judgment at best, and his loyalty at worst.

"You had better speak with her," Addis said. "I hate to admit that they are right, but if she is sending men to Carwyn, either to carry her messages or to fight at his side, she must be confined."

"I will find out what has been happening. As it is, she can do nothing more until morning."

He went to the chapel where she secluded herself, but not to speak of her little sabotage. The desire to merely see her and hold her for a brief spell drew him there.

He found her praying. She knelt on the plank floor, wearing the same garment as the day before.

She did not acknowledge his approach. She remained immobile, as if she had not heard his step.

When he saw her expression, he knew there would be no conversation or stolen embraces today. It occurred to him that there might never be any, ever again.

Perhaps it was the dim light from the candles, but he thought he had never seen her so weary, nor so sad. Her face wore both regret and resolve. He had seen that look before, on old, seasoned warriors as they left their tents to do battle.

Her eyes were closed, and she did not open them. He decided he was glad for that. He was not sure that he wanted to see what those eyes might reveal.

He wanted to touch her, so that maybe she would know that he understood. The gesture was not necessary, however. She already guessed

that he understood far too well. After all, she
might have chosen to walk down the path laid
years ago, but he had been the one to remind
her that the journey must be made now.

He did not leave immediately, despite the
way she ignored him. He stood to the side,
watching her. Loving her. Saying his own
prayers that their betrayals could be forgotten
one day.

Finally, he tore himself away. As he walked
down the nave, he noticed that no parchment
lay on the little table. Thick wax covered the
old plank that had held the candles, and only a
few low stubbed wicks rose from it now.

Paul shared a tiny chamber with four other
knights. When Marcus visited that night, they
threw the other men out so that they could
speak privately.

After the door closed, Paul reached into his
tunic. "If she sends Carwyn information, it
must be with words, Marcus. Any of the servants who have left could have brought them.
This is the only thing of hers that I have found,
and it was not going west, toward her father's
men."

He handed over a parchment. Marcus knew

what he would see even before he opened it. A tapestry design. It depicted four angels blowing horns, and a lamb in the center surrounded by rays of light.

Marcus laid it on a trunk and positioned a candle so he could study it. "Who had this?"

Paul sat on the bed and slouched against the wall. "The priest. He had been called to a dying man in the village to the east, and we caught him just as he was about to pass our sentries. He was not pleased that I took that from him. He said it was a gift from the lady, to help ease the man's passing, and told us that God would punish us for interfering with His work."

Marcus frowned down at Nesta's design. It would be her last one for a long while, since she had no more parchment. She must have worked on it all last night and most of today, and the painting showed her haste and exhaustion. Had she lost herself in it, as a form of meditation? Or had the priest mentioned the dying man, and she labored so that a holy image could be brought to him?

"Heading east, not west, you said?"

Paul nodded.

It seemed innocent enough. And, as Paul had said, if Nesta sought to communicate with Carwyn Hir, she did not need to write her words. No doubt the departing servants had re-layed the information about the lords and armies coming here.

A bit of wax had dripped on one corner of the parchment, forming a tiny, crusty blob. He reached down and scraped it off with his fin-gernail while he held the sheet down with his other hand.

The texture beneath his fingertips provoked his attention. Curious, he moved the pads of his fingers slowly and gently, and felt a series of shallow depressions and rises on the surface of the image. In his mind's eye he saw other fin-gers doing the same thing, with a different parchment. Rhys had checked one of Nesta's images this way that evening in his garden.

The parchment had been scraped, Rhys had said, and used after writing had been removed. Marcus let his fingers drift, and found evidence of scraping over the whole surface.

It was commonplace to scrape and reuse parchment, of course. Except that this was parchment that he had purchased for Nesta himself, and it had been new and clean when it reached her.

He lifted the sheet, to study it more closely. As it rose toward him, the light from the candle backlit the upper left corner.

Marcus's arm froze. Despite the inks, the

thinner areas of parchment let the light pass through. An image took form as the lines of scraping joined and flowed.

Marcus found himself looking down at a small, hidden picture of a dragon.

He moved the parchment slowly, so that the candle illuminated more of the scraping. Words revealed themselves, just as the dragon had.

He read a few at the bottom, and his chest emptied out. For an instant only air filled it, not heart and bone. In that moment he deduced the outlines of a treason so audacious that even the air disappeared.

Nay, it was too bold, too risky. Too complicated. She would not dare it. She would not even think to try.

"Go and find Addis," he ordered Paul. "Bring him here, but do not draw attention to yourself."

"He is somewhere in the camps."

"I do not care if he is in heaven or hell. Go find him. When you return, check whether Nesta is still in the chapel."

Paul hurried out. Marcus shoved the table close to a bed so he could sit. Slowly and methodically he moved the parchment in front of the light, and read the entire message scraped into it.

Every line caused his blood to run faster. It

was all there, the lords who were coming and when they might arrive. The presence of Arundal and Addis at the manor. The estimation of Carwyn's numbers.

His gaze stared at that part in amazement. According to Nesta, four hundred were already spread out in those mountains, including five prominent chieftains and their men. Addis had estimated no more than one hundred and fifty after his scouting today.

Finally, at the end, he read the exhortation to move, and move now, that he had first deciphered. In those last lines there were enough references for him to know for sure to whom Nesta appealed.

His gut twisted. He should have followed his instincts that night with David, when he had wondered if Nesta's parchments carried messages. They had, scraped into the surface and hidden beneath the obscuring inks. These designs were all that she had passed to others, but they had been enough.

And some, like this one, had not been intended for Carwyn or any Welsh leader. Nor for any marcher lord. Llygad's dream had been much more audacious than that.

And much purer. Marcus cursed himself. He should have guessed that any alliance would not be with a lord sworn to the English crown.

He read it again, forcing himself to face the dangerous implications. Despite the chill claiming his soul and blood, he muttered a prayer of gratitude that he had intercepted this message, and another one of hope that he could find a way to save the woman who had written it.

Paul returned with Addis. The two of them carried some cups and a wine bladder, and jested and laughed as they entered. Anyone watching would assume that they intended to get drunk.

"It was all I could do to keep Arundal from joining us," Paul said as he barred the door. "Hubert is bombarding his ear with the story of his life, and the evidence that someone would be getting soused warmed his interest."

"And the lady?"

"She has retired to her chamber. With the priest gone too, the chapel is deserted."

Addis looked pointedly at the parchment in Marcus's hand. Marcus explained Nesta's tapestry designs.

"I have been blind, Addis, although she was so clever that perhaps I can be excused. I wondered if she sent messages in them, but saw only images that had no special meaning. Look at what is scraped beneath the image, however."

He handed Addis the design, and lifted the candle behind it.

"Latin. What does it say?"

"Everything of importance. It also demands that her ally move." He paused, hesitating to share the truth, even with these two men whom he trusted above all others. "She writes that it is imperative for them to cross the border at once. The northern border."

Marcus had rarely seen Addis surprised before, but he did now. "Are you saying that she has an alliance with the *Scots*?"

"I am convinced of it. Nesta sold one to David de Abyndon, when he was leaving Anglesmore. She knew he headed north, not west into Wales. She spoke of a merchant in Carlisle who would buy it. I assumed at the time that if it carried a message, it would make its way back from there."

Other details came to him. Insignificant ones, that now loomed large and obvious. "She had told him of another merchant who would buy them too. One in Edinburgh. The merchants must know how to pass them on. She has probably been sending her messages on these parchments since Llygad died, negotiating the alliance even while she lived in the convent."

"Then Genith's intended husband was not a marcher lord, as you suspected, but a Scot,"

Addis said, holding the candle so that he could read the message. "Who?"

Suddenly the significance of another memory grew. "Genith spoke once of marriage to royalty."

"Well, it won't be someone of the Baillol family. Since Edward has recognized their claim to the Scottish crown, they have little argument with him," Paul said bluntly. "Most likely a man of the Bruce, then, since most Scots support their claim to the throne."

"And their lands are in western Scotland, not far north from Carlisle," Marcus said.

Addis snapped his fingers against the parchment. "You are reading in this evidence of a combined action of the Scots and Welsh?"

"One to the north, one to the west. They would make a powerful army aimed against a common foe. It has been tried before. Didn't Robert the Bruce try to negotiate such a plan less than twenty years ago, during Lancaster's uprising against the last king? Llygad ap Madoc would have known about that, and most likely was involved."

"It could work," Paul said with a note of admiration. "With Edward out of the realm, along with most of his lords . . ."

Addis's brow furrowed. The scarred side of his face suddenly looked very harsh, although the good side showed more worry than anger. He lifted the parchment meaningfully. "You cannot risk that she gets another such message through."

Marcus knew that. There was only one way to be sure it would not happen. The thought of confining her, of truly treating her as a prisoner, sickened him.

"We will say it is because she is encouraging the servants to leave, and subverting our purpose, the way Hubert accused," Addis said. "No one else but we three need to know what she has really done, yet."

Yet. A searing sensation filled Marcus's chest. He had always thought that he could protect her, but that was because he had never suspected how rash her treason would be.

She had always known the truth, however. Small wonder that she had tried to deny and fight the passion that bound them.

Addis looked at him, with eyes too perceptive and too wise. The man who had once been his warden knew him well, and that knowing passed in the gaze they exchanged.

"I will do it," Addis said.

Marcus shook his head, much as he would have liked to hand Addis this obligation. The ridge he had been walking was crumbling beneath his feet, and there was only one way not to fall.

"It is my duty. I brought her here, and she is my betrothed. It must be me, and the others must see me do it."

CHAPTER 22

THE SOUND OF BOOTS nearby did not wake Nesta.

She had been up all night, sick in spirit. Her head hurt, her stomach churned, and her chest felt so heavy there was no place for her breath. A silent moan constantly murmured below her fevered thoughts.

The men's noisy approach caused an uproar of panic among the other women in the chamber. Clutching their blankets to their necks, cowering together, they stared at the door. The acrid smell of fear permeated the tiny space.

Nesta swallowed the bile rising in her. "Be silent," she ordered the women. "They do not come for you."

Had the priest betrayed her? Fury that he might have gave her back some spine. Another reaction, however, flowed unbidden under her sudden alertness. A traitorous hope that her last act had indeed been discovered wanted to have its say. Then she would have still done her duty, but be spared the responsibility for its consequences.

It sounded as if an army came for her. She had just grabbed a blanket around her nakedness when the door swung open. It startled her to see only Arundal and Hubert and two knights standing there.

They parted, and a fifth man appeared. Marcus stepped into the chamber. The servant closest to his feet scooted back with a yelp.

Nesta's heart echoed her cry of alarm. Marcus appeared carved of stone, so hard was his expression. Even his eyes might have been made of dark crystals.

He gestured for her. "Rise and dress yourself. You will come with us now." His voice sounded cold. One would think they had never met before.

"Do I dress for a judgment, or an execution?"

"Hell's teeth, listen to that impudent tone she uses," Arundal roared. "Be glad it isn't a judgment, woman, or the execution would quickly follow if I had my way."

Marcus held up a hand for silence. "You will be kept in close confinement for now, Nesta."

She examined their faces, trying to determine how great her danger was. "For what reason?"

"So that you do not send out servants with word of every move we make," Hubert sneered.

She waited expectantly for the rest, and the accusation of the bald treason she had committed recently.

Marcus just watched her with an unfathomable expression.

That annoyed her. He could give her some sign indicating what she faced. The flaring alarm in her blood gave way to a different heat. She resented these men standing here, filling the chamber with their size and power, making the other women weep and frightening her so badly she could barely think.

She rose, pulling the blanket with her. "Then I must come as you command. One woman can hardly stand against such impressive strength."

Turning to her clothing chest, she began letting the blanket drop.

Marcus was beside her in an instant, his hands clutching the blanket's edge so it lowered no further. "Do not even consider using this old weapon, Nesta," he whispered tightly.

She shot a glance past him, to where Hubert

and Arundal watched. "Only one shoulder shows, and already these great knights have forgotten why they came. Do you fear that the King's whore will gain an ally, Marcus?" she whispered back.

"You may think to only make them into fools, but I will not stand here while they look at you."

"Then get these English pigs out of my chamber," she hissed.

Marcus did not even turn his head as he gave the order to the others. "Leave."

Hubert's face had gone slack with anticipation. "She may hide something on her person. A weapon or whatnot. I hold this manor, and it is my respons—"

"I will stay and see she does not. You may be castellan here, but by law this is my bride, and you will leave now."

Miffed, and giving Nesta a final, liquid leer, Arundal led the way out. "Aye, your woman, and your responsibility, so her acts are now yours as well. We will be sure to remind Edward of that."

"Dress now," Marcus said when the door closed.

She let the blanket drop, and knelt at the chest to choose garments. She took her time, feeling Marcus's gaze on her the whole time.

The women watched as silent witnesses. Their darting glances revealed that they were alert to what pulsed between her and the knight watching.

She dressed very slowly, making no attempt at modesty. Fury provoked her to tease him. Half of her wanted to remind him that she was not without power, small and frail though her body might be. The other half, the part barely holding down a hideous fear, desperately sought to remind this column of hard power of what they had shared, so that he might be merciful.

Admitting the fear made it branch again, shooting roots to the core of her spirit. Her hand froze in midair as she reached for the cotehardie she had chosen. She saw herself growing old in some dark chamber as these garments rotted on her body. Another image flashed in her mind, of her not old at all, being forced to kneel at a block while an ax waited.

The fear turned into unhinging terror that clouded her sight. Her stomach heaved.

A hand on her shoulder called her back, and calmed the shrieking desperation. Marcus reached for the cotehardie. He slipped it over her head and settled it on her shoulders as if she were a child.

His gentle handling broke her heart as no

coldness could. Biting her lip to hold in her emotions, she clutched at the remnants of her strength.

He waited, blocking the sight of the other women, giving her time. She dared not look at him. She feared what she would see if she did. Uncompromising resolve, that she could face. Anything else, however, any hint of regret or disappointment, would tear her to pieces.

She saw him all the same, out of the corner of her eye. He still appeared sculpted of stone, but deep fires flickered in his eyes. Little lights of pain and sympathy softened the hard face of duty. In that fleeting glimpse she perceived a sad resignation that she recognized too well. He appeared much as she had felt since she finished her last design.

She squared her shoulders and gritted her teeth. Short of one of them betraying who they were, they had both known this moment would eventually come. She would not make it harder for him, and she would be damned before she let the men outside the door see her weak.

"I am ready, Marcus."

Marcus entered the silent chapel, carrying three candles. He passed the little worktable, and approached the altar. In the glow of the single flame that burned on it, he opened the heavy, ancient tome of the Gospels that the priest used for mass.

Fanning the pages, he found what he sought. The page at the end of the Gospel of John was not filled with words. Most of it was blank.

As he reached for its top edge, he sensed a presence behind him. Not Nesta. He would know at once if she were near.

Glancing over his shoulder, he saw the old priest watching him. "So, you are back from your dying man."

"What are you doing?"

Marcus jerked his hand, and ripped out the page. The priest cried in shock, and lunged, too late, to stop him.

Marcus pushed him aside, lit one of his candles off the altar taper, and walked to Nesta's worktable where he lit the others and set them on the plank.

He opened the box of ink pots. Hopefully the images that she made carried no significance. There was no way he could duplicate angels. A few birds and animals, however . . . he might manage that. Nesta's own designs had not been especially artful of late, and perhaps the crudeness of his own would not be noticed.

He sat, pulled out his eating knife, and cut off the section of parchment that had words. The priest watched.

"Were you here when she was a girl? Did you serve her father?" Marcus asked.

The priest nodded.

"Were you going to walk to Carlisle with her design, or pass it on?"

The priest's shriveled mouth pursed. "There are horses in the village. Someone else would have carried it north."

"Do you want to save her?" He began scraping an image of a dragon into the top corner of the sheet that remained. "Or do you welcome a Welsh martyr, even if the cause is lost?"

"I saw her scraping like that for hours last night. If you know to do it too, then all is indeed lost. I see no need for a martyr, if she can be spared."

"Then come here, and help me with the Latin."

In the first light of dawn, Marcus carried his design back to the manor house. He found Paul where he had told him to wait in the hall. He shook his friend, and Paul's dark curls flew as he jolted awake.

Gesturing, he brought Paul out into the yard.

"Take four men, and extra horses, and ride to Carlisle. If you do not find David on the road, wait for him there. With that wagon and his trading, he should not have arrived yet."

"And when I find him?"

"Tell him to destroy the design that he carries, and give him this one instead. Have him bring it to the merchant Nesta spoke of."

Paul reached for the parchment. His fingers hesitated for an instant before they closed on the roll. "If I do this, I will not be here when you move."

"That is my gift to you. I know your heart is not in this, and that some of your blood would like to see Llygad's men successful."

"Not against you. I would never—"

"I have never doubted your loyalty to me, or that you would fight by my side. That is why I entrust you with this duty. It is vital that you find David, and switch the designs."

Paul gazed down at the roll in his hand. "It is not hers, is it?"

Marcus shook his head. "So you see, I give you a pain as well as a gift, old friend. If you cannot do this for me, I will understand."

A pause of vacillation beat by, then Paul smiled. "The women in my family have been Welsh, but the men have always been sworn to the crown. Still, can I trust that you plan to keep Arundal and the others from slaughtering every Welsh man in sight while I am gone?"

"That is my intention."

"Then I will find your merchant, and see that this is done. If I have to ride three horses to death on the way, I will do it."

CHAPTER 23

COLD. NUMBING COLD. It surrounded her and seeped into her skin and blood.

It was not the absence of a hearth that caused it. Nor was her tiny chamber especially damp. They had put her at the top of the tower, not in a cellar hole.

Even so, Nesta knew cold as she never had before. It permeated to her bones as she existed in the dark, silent space. The blanket left for her could not keep it away.

Knights brought her meals. They did not speak to her, or answer her questions. She lost contact with everyone and everything, and days had no beginnings or ends. She began to comprehend what eternity might be like.

She asked to speak with the priest, to confess,

but it was denied her. She wondered if Marcus had refused because the goal was to keep her from her people, or because Marcus knew just how much an ally the priest had become.

Left with her own soul for company, and her own thoughts for conversation, she could not hide from her heart. It had long ago been sliced in two, and the parts kept arguing in her head. She was helpless against it, nor would the debate ever be resolved.

She wished that she were as strong as Marcus. When it came down to a choice for him, he had not hesitated.

That was what she had wanted, wasn't it? What she had demanded. Brief, simple pleasures that could be set aside at the moment of truth. It was not his fault that her own decision had tortured her, and would continue to do so as long as she lived.

He had warned her that no matter what happened on the fields of war, she would lose if she persisted in aiding Carwyn. He had done everything possible to protect her, except lock her away before she took the steps that would damn her.

She paced as she worked it out, but actually worked out nothing at all. She wondered if her design was on its way north, and whether anyone would find out, and what that might mean when she was judged. She saw herself, again and again, kneeling in front of the block, and it sent a terrible shiver dancing down her spine each time. Marcus had been right about that too. No favor from the King would spare her.

She knew why she was so cold. The chill came from within, from her soul.

The door's movement had her awake at once.

Backing up on her pallet, she groped for her garments and began pulling them on. The vulnerability of being alone here, of being isolated in a place where no one came, pressed on her. Any man could slip up during the night, and she would be defenseless.

A tall figure slipped into the chamber. She sensed who it was, and her heart flipped with relief.

"I am sorry that I did not come sooner, Nesta."

"I did not expect you to come at all. The King's man put me here, not my lover. I understand how it must be."

"Then you are of calmer spirit than I am."

Her heart grasped hungrily at the suggestion that he had not been nearly as indifferent as he had appeared when he closed this door on her. "How long have I been here?"

"Two days."

Only two days. It had felt like two weeks. Two lifetimes.

"How goes your war, Marcus?"

"There has been no war yet. It appears there will be, however. I sent a herald to Carwyn, asking to parlay, but he refused."

"Of course he did. What can you offer him, to make negotiating worthwhile? Only a king can give him what he wants."

"I can offer you, Nesta."

"Even my father would not have accepted that bargain. When a people decide to fight for their freedom, the life of one woman, one person, becomes meaningless. Put yourself in their places, and imagine the fire burning in them, or you will never understand what is at work."

He did not reply. She sensed him over near the door, looking in her direction. His spirit filled the tiny space, submerging her in a rising pool of emotions that both soothed and frightened her.

He reached for her, as if he could see her as clearly as if a hundred candles burned. "Come with me. Do not speak or argue. Just do as I say."

A cloak billowed and fell around her shoulders. Taking her hand, he pulled her to the door.

She snatched her hand away. "You must not. I will not allow it. You will be blamed, and—"

"Will you never learn to obey? I told you not to speak." He pressed her back with his arm and moved her forward. "I am not so foolish as to help you escape. I merely want to be with you for a while, but not in this prison. Now, be silent."

He guided her through the sleeping manor. Down the stone steps, past Hubert's chamber, through the timbered hall. They stepped out into the silent yard.

The rush of crisp, fresh air made her heady. She gazed up at a beautiful sky dotted with hundreds of bright stars. Her soul stretched at the sight, and her heart filled with gratitude that he had given her this temporary reprieve and had let her taste the world again.

He waited while she absorbed it, then took her hand. "Come with me."

He led her over to the chapel. She wondered if the priest slept in his chamber at its rear, and if he would ignore them.

They did not enter the chapel, however. Horses waited in the shadows where it met the wall. "We will go away from this place, Nesta. Outside the wall, where I am not the King's man, and you are not a Welsh traitor. Put up your hood. You are wearing one of my squire's cloaks, and this is his horse, and in the night no one will think twice about the person riding beside me."

"If this is discovered, Arundal and the others will think—"

"They will think that I am a man hungry for a woman, who took advantage of a desperate lady's hope for mercy in order to ease his need. Maybe they will be right. I do not know myself anymore. If they are angry, it will only be because I would not allow one of them to try it."

They rode out the gate. The guards only noticed Marcus. The camps slept as soundly as the manor, and they trotted through them, heading to the west. Finally, Marcus led her up a low hill behind the outskirts of his army. No fires burned up here but many could be seen below, dotting the rolling land much as the stars did the sky.

"One is hard put to determine where the sky ends and the ground begins out there," she said.

He dismounted and lifted her off her horse. "The night appears endless, doesn't it? There is freedom in the sight of it."

"Perhaps I will be given a prison chamber with a little window, so that I can see stars like this some nights."

He laid his palm against her cheek. "Let us not speak of that. We came out here to be away from it."

The eyes gazing at her contained their own fires and stars, like a continuation of the lights of the night. The comfort of his touch had her spirit calming. She no longer felt chilled.

He kissed her gently but possessively, as if it was his right. As if what had occurred the last week was for the life waiting back inside the walls.

As if she had not betrayed him.

The tenderness of the kiss broke her heart. He did not know about the design. He would never be doing this if he knew. Mark would never want to steal a final taste of heaven with a woman who had so ruthlessly turned her back on their love.

The confusion of the last days returned, over-whelming her. Reaching up, she stroked her fingers into his hair and held him to her so the kiss might last longer. Love and regret poured through her. She could not contain the deluge, and it burned her throat and brimmed at her eyes.

"Mark, I need to tell you something. I—"

His fingertips silenced her mouth. He shook his head. "I said we will not speak of it. Unless you utter words of love, I do not want you to talk of anything."

Love. Words unspoken, despite their passion. Words forbidden, by her. The ache cleaving her heart said that had been foolish, and unnecessary. Keeping silent had not spared her the pain. Pretending that they only shared pleasure had not hidden the love, but only intensified its power.

He removed his cloak, and spread it on the ground. He held out his hand. "Lie with me, Nesta."

She should refuse and turn away, for both their sakes, but she could not. She had never been able to do that. Not in the name of duty and her father's dream. Certainly not in order to save herself from confusion and division and hurt.

She took his hand. He drew her down until they knelt on the cloak. Knees to knees, hips to hips, they looked in each other's eyes. His absorbed her, and the pain retreated. Anticipation of his touch and embrace, of their complete union, chased away the misgivings and regrets and left only the pure sweetness of love filling her so completely that she could not contain it.

He slipped the cloak from her shoulders. "I will see that you do not get cold."

"I am never cold when I am with you."

"Then let me love you, Nesta. Out here where there are no borders, and heaven surrounds us."

He took her face in his hands, and kissed her so sweetly that she wanted to weep. They had been parted too long, and she could sense the power of his desire despite his gentle handling. He did not hurry the kiss, however, even when she embraced him and kissed him back.

Their slow, careful connection went on and on. A whole, silent conversation passed in that kiss. They spoke of regret and gratitude and understanding. And love. Unspoken words drenched every instant.

Her confusion had been calmed, but the pain still burned. It flared and scorched her, turning the love poignant and aching. She clutched him closer and kissed him harder so that the tears that wanted to spill out might not come. She wanted to hold all of him to her, in her, so that their union would let her forget for a while that this was the last time they would know this bliss.

His response grew harder, controlling. Wrapping her in an embrace, he sat back on his heels and angled her body across his. Supporting her in his arms, his kisses moved to her neck and breasts. His fingers worked on her back, and her gown's lacing loosened. Sliding the shoulders of her cotehardie and gown down, he exposed her breasts.

He broke the kiss as he caressed them. He looked at his hand move as if the dark did not obscure his sight. With titillating touches he provoked an insistent, anxious arousal in her body. It joined the emotions pouring through her, deepening them, joining them all into one relentless ache.

Laying her down, he moved on top of her. He loosened his lower garment and lifted her skirt, and then nestled between her naked legs with his hips pressed against her thighs. She accepted his deep kiss, expecting him to take her the way her heart and soul needed.

He stopped the kiss, but did not move. He looked down at her face. She could feel him all along her body, warming her as he had promised, pressing against her vulva but not entering. It reminded her of their first night, and it incited the same crazed desire in her.

Above his head and shoulders, around them both, stretching into eternity, she could see the stars of the endless sky.

"Are you waiting for me to beg, Mark?"

"That is not what I am waiting for."

"Then what?"

"I want you so badly that I almost took you

in that chamber. However, I have decided that this time it should be slow and careful and full of pretty words."

This time. The last time.

His head dipped, and he kissed her breast. His tongue swirled, creating wonderful sensations. Not just those of desire. Not only physical arousal spiked. He did not only give her pleasure.

It was the same for him. She could tell. Could feel his heart speaking to her. She heard the sadness in their silence.

She knew which pretty words needed saying, and she could not deny them. Stroking her fingers through his hair, holding his mouth to her. "I love you, Mark. It was never just simple pleasure. That was the danger, wasn't it? Look where it has brought us now."

"It has brought us to this hillside, Nesta. It has brought us to speaking the words that our duties forbade. That you love me and that I love you, and that the pleasure has been magnificent but never simple, and that in my heart you are not Llygad's daughter or the King's woman, but my wife."

He moved, and entered her, making the claim of his words physical and complete.

She closed her eyes and savored the feel of him, the total union. He filled her perfectly.

Their bodies and hearts were so close that they truly merged into one.

"You must repudiate the betrothal," she whispered. "You know that you must."

He withdrew and entered her again. "I will not. You may have been drugged when you said the pledge, but I was not."

He was making her arousal stir slowly, build blissfully. The sensation was so beautiful. It joined with her heartache, creating an emotion that was exquisite and soulful in its combination of happiness and sorrow. "Then I have betrayed you even more than I thought. I will cause your destruction. Can you forgive me?"

"The question should be mine, Nesta, if it is spoken at all. I am the one who put you in prison."

"You know what I mean." But he didn't. Not all of it. Not the worst betrayal. He knew enough, however.

He stopped, his body half joined to hers. He laid his warm palm against her cheek. "There is nothing to forgive, my love. I did not expect you to forget who you were because of me. My desire to protect you made me demand that you do. So did my hope that I could keep you with me. I never really thought you would turn your back on it, however. I am not sure I could have loved you if you had." He kissed her. "Now, do not speak of that anymore. Tell me that you love me again, and fill the night with your cries of pleasure, and carry me to heaven as only you know how to."

She gladly told him she loved him. Again and again she said the words until they became a chant keeping rhythm to the connection of their bodies. Even when abandon obliterated her awareness of everything except his body and soul and breath and pleasure, she still said it. The cries ringing around them as they careened to the stars carried frantic declarations of her love.

"We must go, Nesta."

She had dreaded hearing the words, and her heart sank like lead. Time had slowed as they lay on the hillside, and she had never known such beauty as she experienced in his arms.

He helped her rise, and fixed her garments. He kissed her once more, wonderfully, then took her hand and led her to the horses.

After draping the cloak on her, he lifted her to her saddle. He did not let go once she was settled, but stayed there, his hands on her waist, looking up at her. He looked so long that it un-settled her.

Finally, he released her, but only to lay his

hand on her thigh. He pointed into the night. "Look to the west, Nesta. Do you see that fire in the distance, the lone one near the edge of the sky?"

"Aye."

"Ride there. Do not gallop, but make what speed you can. Addis has relieved the sentry posted there. He will let you pass."

His words stunned her. "What are you doing, Mark?"

"Once you are past our camps, ride as far away as you can." He pulled a sack from under his garment and pressed it in her hand. She recognized it as the little hide pouch that carried the dried venison. "There is coin in it too. Find a place of sanctuary, where you can hide. Do not go to Carwyn. You must flee, and make your way out of the realm."

"You said that you were not going to help me escape."

"If I had told the truth, would you have left that chamber?"

"Of course not, because if I do this, it will be suspected that you aided me."

"Let me worry about that." He tied his cloak to the back of the saddle. "Did you really think that I could let them have you? That I would allow you to be judged, and imprisoned or worse? I only put you in that chamber so that the others would not watch me too closely, so that I could get you away."

"I cannot believe that Addis approved such rashness."

"I told him that my squire would be passing before dawn, and he accepted that. He suspects the truth, but will look the other way because of our friendship."

Her heart beat hard as confused emotions began a war. Salvation waited, and her blood raced with excitement. If she escaped like this, however, she would surely destroy him.

It was a short battle. Love conquered her fear. She could not allow him to sacrifice himself.

She tried to slide off the horse. "I will not do this."

He held her in place. "You must. I command it as your husband."

"Mark, I probably would not obey on little things, let alone something like this."

"Then I command it in the name of our love."

"And I must disobey for the same reason."

"I need you gone, Nesta. I cannot do what I must if you are here. I cannot have your fate weighing on me."

She stopped struggling. She looked down at him, and in that instant his tight hold might have been a final loving caress. She cursed the darkness that kept her from seeing clearly, but her heart knew the resolve and love that his expression held.

Pain ripped in her chest, stealing her breath, rising like a fire into her throat. Tears brimmed and fell. She wiped them away with her sleeve, so that this last sight of him would not be further obscured.

"I would prefer to go back to my prison. We would not be forever parted then. Not yet."

"You must leave. You know that."

She loved him so much. Too much. The love even gave this anguish a sweetness. Its lovely light revealed her heart's deepest corners. Even her misery contained a precious beauty.

"Mark, when the battle comes, do not lead them. Please, do not. That arrow by the stream . . . it was because of the betrothal, I think. It complicates things. Carwyn does not want it to stand, and only killing you will make sure it does not."

"Do not let worry for me make your heart heavy, Nesta. I have no intention of dying."

"It does make my heart heavy. All of this does. The weight is unbearable, and the worst is knowing that if I leave now, we will never see each other again in this life."

"Then when I see you again, I will know that I am truly in heaven, forever."

He angled her down, and kissed her. Her swallowed tears refused to stay down and they streamed from her eyes. His kiss moved to each wet cheek, and then he dried her face with the edge of her cloak.

He stepped back, breaking her hold on his shoulders, leaving her bereft. The loneliness waiting for her touched her with its chill, raising a flurry of panic. Suddenly the night appeared a gaping void that light barely penetrated. If she entered it alone, she might never come out again.

"Once you pass Addis, ride like the wind, darling. Let these mountains give you sanctuary."

With a sharp swing, he slapped her mount's rump and sent her toward the tiny fires.

CHAPTER 24

SOON AFTER DAWN Nesta trotted her exhausted horse into a tiny village that clung to a
mountainside. Villagers emerged from their
huts and eyed her curiously. She did not say a
word, but only lifted her sleeve to reveal the
gold armlet and its engraved dragon.

That produced an enthusiastic welcome. A
village elder named Ifan gave her his cottage to
use. After supping on thin broth and brown
bread, she dragged her weary body to the straw
pallet, hoping oblivion would claim her.

Sleep came, but it brought little peace. Her
mind churned as if she were awake, and the
eternal debate raged on. Mark had taken a huge
risk in letting her escape, and she should obey
his last words and disappear into the mountains.

She should forsake him, and her father's dream, and save herself. The fear blazing through her wanted to, desperately.

It was weakness calling her to that path, but not the same wavering of her will that had drawn her to Mark. It had not been cowardice that sent her into his arms. That weakness had been good and beautiful and optimistic, a spiritual yearning for a taste of love that transcends worldly concerns.

The temptation to now flee both that love and the duty that thwarted it was in no way good or optimistic. The lure to run away from the battle inside her was as great as that to escape the real clash of arms about to occur.

Upon waking she saw that most of the day had passed, but she had still known little true rest. Nor had her mind reconciled the two halves of her heart.

A group of women and children and old men milled outside the cottage. Nesta peeked out the door, and saw the gifts of food that they had brought. She smelled roasting fowl, and guessed that they intended to honor her with such a feast as their poverty permitted.

She called for the owner of the cottage. Ifan entered, hunched with age and deference.

"The able-bodied men have all left?" she asked.

"They could hardly stay here with such great events occurring all but in their own fields."

She thought of the fields, and how some would lie fallow next year even if her father's plan succeeded. Men would die, on both sides. The villagers knew that, but no man had held back.

Why, then, had she? Not because of Mark. It was deeper than that. She thought of her last design, and how making it had distressed her. Betraying Mark had weighed on her, but that was not all that caused her hand to falter so often. Her message had been a call to arms, and a demand for a war that would cause untold suffering. It was one thing to sacrifice one's own life, and another to ask hundreds to do so in your name.

"We've cooked a young chicken," Ifan said. "Me and some others tried to hunt some meat, but the region has seen its game taken by others, so there is little to be found, and what is left is faster than us."

The others would be both Marcus's and Carwyn's men. Living off the land, they would have further impoverished the inhabitants. It was the way with armies, and the normal result of war, but Nesta could not help feeling guilty for it. The goal was to free the Welsh, not make them suffer.

She forced herself to remember that all great causes had their costs. That innocents would pay as well as soldiers saddened her, however.

She reminded herself that this was not about sorrow or happiness. It was bigger than her spiritual comfort, and these people, and not limited to this time and place.

But if others were to suffer, who was she to be spared? She had been an agent in creating this conflict. To leave now, to hide in the mountains and leave Wales eventually, would be the final, and most hideous, betrayal.

She did not welcome the clarity of her choice, but she could not deny the inevitable decision it forced on her. Divided heart or not, she knew what she had to do.

"I do not need meat. Let the children have the chicken. Before we feast, however, I need a scrap of parchment to write on," she said.

"We have no parchment here. Not even in the church."

"How do you record baptisms and deaths?"

"There's a linen that the priest writes on when he comes. Problem is, it fades fast, so most don't know when they were born." He chuckled and patted his chest. "Some say I am over eighty, some say only sixty. I say somewhere in between. I remember Llywelyn's war, but I was a youth then. As if it matters. When you are young, you are young. If you get old, you are old. Not the birthing that counts, nor the dying, but the living."

There was wisdom in his words. They soothed her, and reinforced the decision she had made. "Please find me some linen, just a scrap, and a means to write on it. I will also need a brave man to carry what I write."

"We can burn sticks for the writing, I suppose. But the men left are slow and feeble. If not, they would be with the banner of the dragon."

"Is there no mule in the village to carry a man?"

"There were two, but they were taken, along with half the pigs."

So Carwyn's little army had not just been living off the land, but requisitioning from the villagers. "Have more than a few animals been taken?"

His face fell, and he made a little shrug. "Some grain. And word has it there was trouble with some girls in the next valley. Such things happen."

Her back instinctively stiffened. Despite what Ifan said, there were some things that should not happen, no matter how common they might be during war, and this was one of them.

Her misgivings about her course of action

disappeared at once. Overhunting the forests was one thing, and taking the people's livestock another. This transgression could not be excused on any grounds. Her father's men needed her, for many reasons.

"There's my granddaughter," the elder said. "She knows the hills as well as any man, and is strong and quick. She will run where you want her to go with this message of yours."

A bit of linen was found, and the sticks were burnt. Nesta banished everyone from the cottage while she wrote her message.

She read her scratchy words when she was done. They would change nothing. They could not undo the past, or stop the river that now flowed. They would have such little effect on the outcome, that there was really no point in sending them off.

She would anyway. She owed it to him.

Calling the elder's granddaughter in, she handed over the message and gave instructions on its delivery. The young woman had dressed as a boy, and seemed unfazed by the danger she would face. She headed out of the village at a run as the feast got under way.

Nesta stayed in the village another night, but before dawn the next day she was back on her horse. Long before anyone else stirred, she was gone.

She rode with a new energy, and a new sense of purpose. It was time to do what she had been born to do. She did not doubt that Mark would understand.

Her horse suddenly broke its gallop and reared. She clung to its mane as the world blurred. When she regained control, she found herself facing four spears held by bearded, wild-looking men.

As she had at the village, she held up her arm so that the armlet showed. "I am Nesta verch Llygad. Take me to Carwyn Hir."

The camp was neither large nor well provisioned. A few tents had been pitched, but most of the shelter consisted of rough lean-tos constructed of saplings and boughs.

The crudeness of the scene surprised her. This was not Carwyn's stronghold, of course, where men lived for years on end. That was high in the mountains. Presumably it was more impressive.

At most three dozen men looked toward her as her escort led her out of the trees. She had not expected an army to greet her. The Welsh forces would not gather in one place until called. All through the hills, there would be other camps like this, many of them, full of men waiting for the word. Still, she had expected more than this to be encamped with the leader.

She dismounted and walked her horse toward the large fire circle, noting the weapons and equipment. Her eye caught very little armor, no more than ten swords, and a dozen longbows. An enclosure for horses contained only a few animals. The image of Marcus's camps, of the swords and helmets and well-fed men, lived in her head as she observed her father's rebels.

Carwyn sat at the fire with several other men. He did not rise until she approached very near, even though he had noticed her as soon as she stepped from the trees.

"You escaped?" he asked.

"He allowed me to leave."

"It is a generous man who permits his bride to join the enemy."

"He thinks I have left the region, and gone into hiding. The English lords with him know that I sent information to you."

"And useful information it was, Nesta. I trust that you also sent it north."

"Of course."

Carwyn gestured to the fire circle. "We are holding a council. We will finish soon, and then you and I can talk."

She sat on a log beside the one where he had

been resting. "I will join this council, in my father's name."

He did not like that. After some deliberation, he retook his place.

"Tomorrow next, then," he said to the men, continuing a conversation that she had disrupted. "We will gather during the night on the hill beyond their camps, and attack at first light."

"How many do you have?" she asked, interrupting the agreement of the others.

Carwyn barely glanced at her. "More than he does."

"How many, that you plan this attack before word comes that our allies have moved?"

"We attack now because you sent word that in a few days more will join Marcus, and then we will not outnumber them."

"Unless you have five hundred, you do not truly outnumber them now."

"Do you think that one English man is equal to three Welsh? This new husband must have impressed you greatly."

The other men snickered. She turned a furious glare on them until they flushed and looked to the ground. Rising, she gestured to Carwyn. "You and I will talk alone."

Slowly, resentfully, he followed her to the

edge of the camp. He crossed his arms over his chest. Strained forbearance turned his bright eyes dull.

"The others should not see us at odds, or hear us demeaning the other's opinion. As to my comment about needing five hundred, I was saying that one well-fed English soldier wearing armor and carrying cold steel outnumbers one Welsh man bearing a wooden pike. And ten mounted men-at-arms outmatch what I see in this camp, no matter what heart we bring to such a battle."

"Our longbows will even things."

"They too have longbows." She looked him right in the eyes. "Stop dodging my question. How many do you have?"

His mouth twitched in annoyance. "Over three hundred, but more arrive every day."

"I was told over four hundred, and that was a week ago."

"It was in our interest to have them think our numbers were greater."

A whirlwind of fury began spinning in her head. "You had a lie told to me for this purpose? You assumed that I would reveal your strength to Marcus?"

He pierced her with a knowing glare. "I have not forgotten your delay in the wainwright's shed. And I was at the stream, Nesta. I saw you save him, and also the sweet looks before and after."

She felt her face burn. "Such things do not matter, nor should you assume that you know the meanings of those looks. I have executed my duty twice over, and I am here now."

"You are here now because he allowed you to leave. I wonder why he did that. Just as I wonder why you are so curious as to our numbers."

His sarcastic tone, and the implications of his words, infuriated her. "Do not forget who I am, Carwyn, or that you can count what numbers you have only because of me. Think long and hard before you insinuate that I am a traitor."

"I know who you are. Every man in these hills knows. It is good that you have joined us. When we move, you will come, and the sight of you will be better than any banner. However, if you have come to betray us, I will see that you do not. You will not be leaving my side, or speaking with any person who can carry a message for you."

He intended to treat her as a prisoner. She leashed her outrage about that, and repeated her warning. "You must retreat, and wait for word from Scotland. Battles on the northern border will draw off the English forces that might be called here. That was always my father's plan, and you must hold to it or there is no chance for success."

"If your sister had not left, and we could be sure that alliance would unfold, your advice would make sense. If Marcus had not brought this army here, we would have waited longer until our numbers grew. But we cannot retreat now. Once gone, these men will not return, nor will they live in these hills into the winter. Events have conspired to force this, and so it will be."

"You will be slaughtered."

"Then future generations will know of our bravery, and bards will sing about us."

"No one will know or sing about you. Your blood will leach into these hills as so much other blood has, wasted. This will not be a great war, fit for songs, or even a great battle. Somewhere in London a clerk will note in his accounts that some shillings were paid to knights who punished thieves, and then he will turn the page."

He held up a hand impatiently. "Enough. I think that Marcus sent you to us so that you could argue for our submission." He took her arm, and pulled her toward one of the tents. "You will stay in here, away from the others, so you do not poison their thoughts. Do not presume to lecture me further. You might be Llygad's daughter, but you are merely a woman, and, I think, Anglesmore's whore as well as his betrothed. If so, that might prove useful."

Men slept on benches and pallets all around the chamber. Marcus was still awake, watching the flames in the hearth, facing the fact that a battle had become inevitable. Scouts had arrived in the afternoon with reports of men moving in those hills, aiming east toward Llygad's old manor.

Noise at the entry caught his attention. Addis was hauling a boy into the hall.

Addis dragged the boy forward, thrust him at Marcus, and pulled a felt hat off the fair head. The hearth's light revealed a feminine face about twenty years old.

"She was halfway through the camps before being caught," Addis said. "A good thing it was our men who found her, and not Arundal's. I don't want to think what would have happened to such a pretty spy then."

"I am no spy," she said.

"Spies always say that," Addis replied with a laugh.

"Why would anyone send a woman into a man's camp for such a purpose? No doubt there are spies there, but I am not one of them." She reached under the neck of her tunic. "He called you Marcus. If that is who you are, this is for you." She handed over a tiny linen roll.

"Where did you get this?"

"From the lady. She came to our village."

His hand tightened on the linen. "Where is your village?"

"A half-day's ride from here. A longer walk."

"I assume that you walked."

She shrugged. "I ran mostly."

"You had to pass by Carwyn's camps too."

She shrugged again. "We know how to avoid being seen."

God knew that was true. He and Addis still had not made a good count of the men in those hills. Nesta's message to Scotland had said four hundred, however.

He looked down to the little rolled fabric. His clutch was turning it into a damp wad.

A half-day's ride from here, Nesta had made this and sent it to him. He exhaled deeply, as if he had been holding this breath since sending her off. She had gotten past Carwyn's men, and was heading west as he had commanded.

Addis took the arm of the young woman. "I will bring her to the women who still use Nesta's chamber. You will remain where I put you, girl, and not tell anyone that you brought this." He began guiding her away. Glancing over his shoulder, he said, "Burn it as soon as you have read it."

Marcus already knew that he would have to do that. Nesta's escape had brought heavy suspicion on him. Only his status had prevented Hubert from making a blatant accusation, that and Hubert's conviction that the Welsh within the manor could not be trusted, and could have found the means to aid their lady. Arundal also watched him carefully now, but was equally of the opinion that Nesta might have used witchcraft to escape.

He carefully unrolled the little piece of linen. The rough, grey lines covering it had become blurred from the sweat of the girl's body and his own hand. Doubting that he would be able to decipher anything, he moved closer to the fire. The joy that she had sent this was touched by an unspeakable sorrow that her last words to him had been lost.

He stared long and hard, willing the words to emerge. Finally, sadly, he gave up and accepted they never would. Only then, as his desperation faded, did the sooty scratches and smudges form patterns and letters and become a message.

I have betrayed you far worse than you know, she had written. *You must repudiate me now, before it unfolds, or I will have condemned us both. When*

*next you see me, you must be the King's man, and I
the daughter of Llygad, although my heart will always be yours. Know that I love you, even though
we both must deny each other now. Think of me
when you gaze up at your stars, Marcus.*

He smiled, and experienced a moment of
complete peace and glowing happiness. He
closed his eyes and savored the exquisite sensation, holding it in his heart while he filled his
mind with her.

He opened his eyes, and dropped the linen
into the hearth. The flames grew to consume it.
As they rose he released the little bliss, and allowed it to burn away too. In the heat made by
her message, he faced what it had contained besides words of love.

She was not fleeing. She was joining Carwyn.
Most likely she had already.

He had prayed she would not, but he had also
known that she would.

He had counted on it.

He thought of her message, and also of the
words she had spoken their last night. She assumed that all the betrayals had been hers.
Soon, however, she would realize how he had
permitted most of what she had done, so that he
could foil her in the end.

So that he could save her.

She had never used him to achieve her ends, but he *had* used her.

Hopefully, when they were done with this, when they were no longer the King's man and Llygad's daughter, she would forgive him for that.

CHAPTER 25

THERE COULD BE MORE," Hubert said. Worry made his voice pitch higher than was seemly. "They could be on either side of us, for all we know. How the hell is someone supposed to fight in these mountains and forests."

"Now you know why the King's grandfather brought a huge army with him, and why no English king before him had managed to hold all of Wales," Marcus said.

He surveyed the far hill. The men lined up on its crest shouted insults and taunts, goading their foe below. Cheers of *ruthro Eingl,* rout the English, rang in the sky. A few ran halfway down the hill and danced little jigs before sauntering back up.

It was impossible to tell how many were behind the thick line, on the far side of the low mountain. The challenge had been made, however, and could not be ignored. The troops being sent by other barons were at least two days away, but this skirmish was not going to wait for them.

Marcus rode with Addis and Arundal and Hubert to the front of their line of knights. The newly risen sun that had revealed the waiting enemy was barely visible in the overcast sky of this bitter, damp day.

Four hundred, Nesta had written to the Scots, and probably more now. He had but two hundred and fifty. Still, if the men held to this valley and clearing, they should prevail. If they were drawn into the forests or up into the hills, however, they could indeed be routed.

Even a small victory for the Welsh could turn this skirmish into the first battle of a long and bloody war.

"What are you waiting for?" Hubert asked, pacing his steed back and forth in front of Marcus.

"For them to attack."

"I say we go up that hill," Hubert snarled.

Even Arundal rolled his eyes at that. "Oh, aye, attack men who hold high ground. That is shrewd, Hubert. How much did your father pay the King to secure your position here?"

"One hundred marks," Hubert said, missing the sarcasm.

"Do not let the Welsh know that," Marcus said. "They will fight harder to repay the insult that the King accepted such a small bribe before sending them such a great fool."

Hubert's face turned red. Marcus was glad to see it. If goaded enough, Hubert might actually fight well after his bluster fell beneath the first sword he faced.

The jeering on the hilltop suddenly ceased. An unnatural silence poured down instead of the taunts. As if attached to rods, the distant heads turned in unison to the line's center.

The line parted, and two horses rode through. A huge cry came across the valley in a wave, growing louder as the shouts from the back of Carwyn's army were joined by those of the men who had just seen their leader.

Carwyn wore armor, but he was one of the few Welsh who did. The figure beside him certainly did not. As the two horses rode back and forth in front of the men on the crest of the hill, the small figure on the second horse became very visible. Long dark hair floated behind it. Carwyn held the reins of the horse, pulling it along, displaying the rider like a banner whether she welcomed it or not.

"Damnation, the witch is with them,"

Arundal said. "Perhaps she intends to lead the attack."

Marcus moved his horse close to Addis. "I am going to send them an offer to negotiate."

"Carwyn has already refused to parlay, and won't do so now, not with our troops arrayed."

"I think that he might. I will ask for a meeting. He can bring whomever else he wants, but Nesta must accompany him."

"He will never risk coming down."

"He might if our messenger is kept up there until he returns. Especially if the hostage is an important man."

Addis flipped up his visor. His eyes reflected resignation as he absorbed just who Marcus thought that hostage should be.

"I doubt we can get Arundal to go, and Hubert is not valuable. Neither of them is clever and quick-witted enough anyway," Marcus explained.

Addis sighed deeply. He pulled off his helmet, and called for his squire to take it and his lance. Hubert and Arundal watched with surprise from twenty paces away.

"What am I to say?" Addis asked.

"Get him and Nesta to a meeting between our lines. Say that the presence of my betrothed in their ranks distresses me, and that I believe she is being held against her will. Let Carwyn think that I might agree to something disadvantageous to us."

"I do not think he will listen."

"He might not, but Nesta will. Those cheers were not only for him, but also for her. Llygad's daughter has power with that army, and Carwyn knows it."

Addis began trotting forward. Marcus called to Hubert and Arundal to stay behind, and accompanied his friend.

Addis turned to look at their astonished comrades. "Don't let them do something stupid. I don't want to be kept."

"If something goes wrong, I will ransom you."

"You seem very calm, as if things are unfolding much as you had hoped." He tightened his reins and prepared for a gallop as they approached the point where Marcus would have to turn back. "Hell, I hope that you know what you are doing."

Marcus sat in the tent that had been set up between the two armies. A table had been built out of planks and logs. Crude stools, requisitioned from the camps, surrounded it. A fire pot cast some warmth.

Addis was up with Carwyn's men, but

Arundal and Hubert had insisted on joining the parlay. Marcus would have liked to avoid that. He would not be able to speak frankly with them present.

Horses approached. All of them fixed their eyes on the flap through which their enemy would walk.

Nesta entered first. She examined the three of them with noble disdain. Even the gaze that lingered on Marcus contained little warmth.

When we meet again it will be as the King's man and Llygad's daughter, but know that you are in my heart. He held on to those words, and doubted that his own expression hid his heart as well as hers did.

Carwyn ducked his tall body through the tent flap, and two other men followed. Ale was poured and drunk.

Finally, Arundal spoke directly to Carwyn. "Surrender. We outnumber you. We have had scouts in those hills these last days, and they count no more than one hundred fifty."

"Unlike your camps, which are easy to find and count, ours are scattered and keep moving. Perhaps we have only fifty men, the ones you see on that hill. Then again, maybe we have two thousand."

"No matter what your numbers, you are at a disadvantage," Marcus said. "The men of

Barrowburgh and Anglesmore and Arundal are experienced and battle hardened and well equipped, not farmers just plucked from their fields."

Carwyn laughed. "That is the great offer that caused this delay? The offer to surrender?"

"Nay," Arundal growled. "We offer you a quick death, instead of that of a traitor."

"We offer no death at all," Marcus corrected. "I received no command from the King for re-criminations."

Arundal and Hubert were halfway through their objections when the King's command was mentioned. That stopped their words, but not their scowls.

"You do not know the half of it," Carwyn said. "However, since we indulged you in this parlay, we should hear what you offer in terms. Make it quick, however. My men have waited too long for this fight."

"I offer you what the King offered. You will disband, and I will marry the daughter of Llygad, so that amends are made for the insult done to his honor."

"If we considered such a marriage suitable amends, we could have all stayed home."

"It is the King's offer, and mine. I must add one more term, however. You, Carwyn Hir, must leave the realm."

"I'll be damned first."

"You will be condemned if you do not."

Carwyn laughed. A sneer twisted above his dark beard. "Now hear my terms. You withdraw from this valley, and from Llygad's manor, and you end this betrothal that you forced. Perhaps then you will live to fight another day."

"There will be no battle on another day. If we engage, I end this here. There will be no quarter. You have taken my betrothed prisoner, and I am not in a merciful mood."

Hubert's head snapped around. "She doesn't look like a prisoner to me."

Arundal snorted his agreement. Nesta said nothing.

Carwyn's blue eyes lit with acknowledgment, and approval. "Your responsibility to her, and for her, should be worth more than what you offer."

"That responsibility is why you hear any terms at all. Send your men down, and see where my blood is on this."

"It will be pouring into the ground out there, that is where it will be."

Marcus lifted his hand. "I have done my duty to try and avert this. If you want a battle, so be it." He reached down for a sack resting near his leg. "Here are some of your things, Nesta, so that you are not without some comforts in that camp."

Nesta reached for the sack, but another hand grabbed it first. Casting a suspicious glance at Marcus, Arundal loosened the string and rummaged through the contents.

His eyes narrowed and glinted triumphantly. Giving Hubert a knowing nudge, he withdrew a folded parchment. "Well, what do we have here, Marcus? A love poem? Or something more damning?"

Barely containing his glee, he unfolded the parchment. His face fell with disappointment. The sheet fluttered from his hand to the table.

It bore only a painted picture of a lamb and four angels.

Nesta's eyes subtly widened. Carwyn's gaze locked on the image before he darted Nesta a sharp, questioning glance.

"Reconsider, Carwyn," Marcus said quietly, looking Nesta directly in the eyes. "This will not unfold as you expect."

"Even if we lose this skirmish, we will not be defeated," Carwyn said. "Others will join us."

"Others may join you, but no one will aid you."

Carwyn began to speak, but Nesta's hand moved almost imperceptibly, silencing him. She leaned over and whispered in his ear.

A silence fell, broken only by the sounds of Arundal pawing deeper in the sack.

Nesta looked right at Marcus, and he looked straight back. He read the question in her eyes, and he let her see the answer.

She rose. "I will not be an ox sold at a market, or a prisoner who keeps trading one cell for another. Before any further discussions take place, I will speak with this marcher lord alone."

She turned and left the tent without waiting for agreement. Marcus followed, not waiting for approval either.

She mounted her horse before any squire could help, and began trotting north, toward a hill on which the flank of Marcus's army was positioned. Marcus swung up on his own horse and followed, catching up and falling into place beside her.

She did not speak or look at him until they reached the hill. "Tell them to leave," she said as she pushed her horse to climb to the top.

Marcus gave the word for the soldiers to go down the hill. There, on its top, with the English army spread out on one side and the dense forest filling the other, with the high hill in the distance banded by Welsh, she dismounted.

She would not look at Marcus. She could not. Her shock at seeing the design in the tent had not dimmed, and the war in her heart raged as it never had. Anger that he had obstructed her final move clashed with heartbreaking humiliation that he had discovered her final betrayal.

He knew about the message scraped into the parchment. He had all but said so in the tent. He had read it, no doubt, and comprehended how treasonous that betrayal had been.

He had known when he let her escape, and during their last night under the stars. . . . Her throat thickened. Half of her wanted to weep and half of her wanted to scream at him with fury.

She looked to the Welsh who waited for Llygad's daughter to return. They did not know yet that she had failed them. "I have often thought that this would have been so much easier if the King had chosen a stupid man," she said.

There was no response to that.

"How much do you know?" she asked.

"I know that you have used the designs to send plans and messages. From the look on Carwyn's face when that parchment unfolded, some went to him, but some were sent to the Scots. This last one did not arrive, however, as you can see."

She sighed. He had even surmised who their

allies were to be. She had hoped he had not. "Who else knows?"

"Addis and Paul."

Only those two. He had kept it a secret, to protect her. He had helped her escape, so she might be safe when the truth became known.

She did not like admitting that. She wanted to hate him, and to see his own deceptions as black and heartless. If she accepted defeat, she wanted to do so spitting curses at the man who had brought her to it.

"The one you sent with David also will not reach the Scots," he said.

Her heart cracked and sank. If he had only stopped the last message, it was possible the plan still stood a chance. But if he had intercepted the one before it too, where she reaffirmed the alliance despite Genith's disappearance, all could be lost.

He came closer, until she felt him near her shoulder. "There is one more thing that you should know. I replaced David's design with a new one, Nesta. It contains a very different message scraped into it. An announcement of a retreat here in Wales and a repudiation of the plan. It bears your mark of the dragon, and informs your allies that they cannot count on Wales rising."

She pivoted, finally looking at him, her mind

reeling with shock. In that instant she suddenly comprehended the fullness of what he had done.

He had not merely obstructed her. He had allowed her to proceed, so he could remain one step behind, using her betrayals to his own end.

"You think that you are very clever, don't you, Marcus?"

"Clever enough to stop you, woman."

"Is that what it was all about? Stopping me?" She all but spit the words, and cursed herself for the outburst. It revealed that more fed her fury and confusion than the death of the dream. She did not want to acknowledge the other pain scorching her.

He grabbed her to him. "Do not let hurt pride make you a fool."

She squirmed to get away as tears filmed her eyes. She gritted her teeth to hold them in. "You played with me like a puppet. You even let me escape so that I would go to them, and be present when you held this parlay."

"I prayed you would flee, but I counted on your disobeying me. It is well you are here. I do not trust Carwyn's judgment. I do trust yours. When you explain to him what I have told you here, he will accept my terms. You will see that he does."

The events of the past weeks played out in

her mind. An insidious, new suspicion about one of them made her freeze and look up at him. "Genith. Did you let her escape? Permit it somehow?"

"I saw her with Dylan. I suspected he would not take her to Carwyn. Aye, I allowed them to escape."

The revelation astonished her. "You knew about the alliance that early?"

"I did that for myself alone. She was not the daughter of Llygad whom I wanted."

She twisted violently, to break his hold. "I do not believe you. Everything that you did, *everything*, was aimed at our defeat and destruction."

"That is not true, damn it." He held her tighter yet, and took her face in his hand so she would have to look at him. "If I wanted your defeat, a battle would be raging down there right now. If I wanted you destroyed, no man fighting under your father's banner would leave the field alive."

She pushed away from him, confused and furious. She strode to where he could not reach her, and turned her back on him.

"Damn you. You let me touch the dream but not grasp it fully."

"It was not your dream, but another's. You did not choose this duty. It was given to you."

"As yours was given to *you*. Better if you had

locked me away at once, as soon as you sus-pected, so their undoing would not be my fault."

"It is not their undoing, but their salvation, that we give them today. And if I had put you away, or exposed what you were doing, you would have been lost to me."

Her breath caught in surprise. She swung around to face him.

He stood there, ten paces away, in all his youthful, strong perfection. His face showed a warrior's resolve and a lordly severity, but the deepest lights of his eyes revealed gentler emo-tions.

The implications of his last words had her wavering at once. She could not deny that he had taken a harder, riskier path to this victory than was necessary. She tried to block from her mind the evidence that he had chosen it, and because of her.

All the same, her anger began slipping from her grasp, sliding away despite the way she fran-tically clutched at it.

He held out his hand. Cold steel encased the arm, but his palm beckoned with human warmth. Her emotions still churned from an internal storm that whirled in her head and chest.

"Come and accept me, Nesta. We will say the vows with both sides as witness."

"So now you expect me to agree to be your wife? After you have done this, and used me in this way?"

"I do not only expect it, I demand it. You and I and Carwyn know that your father did not raise his banner because of you, but many of the Welsh believe it. As the King's representative, I will rectify that insult today."

"You *cannot* demand it. In this one thing, in this last, small part of all of this, what I want finally matters."

"Then accept me because you want to."

"You are so sure of what I want?"

"Aye. We want each other. That is the only thing that I have known for sure these last weeks. Wanting you was the only clearheaded truth I could hold on to."

She tried to close her ears to him. She did not want his calm, quiet words working their soothing charm. Seducing her. Luring her to weakness, as they had so often done. Confusing her, and dividing her heart.

"The King's man should not be so easily swayed by passion, Marcus."

"The King's man did his duty. If he found a way to do it and avoid a war, he is content. If he found a way to do it and also keep the woman he loves, he is satisfied. If that woman takes his hand willingly, he will consider it the greatest victory of his life."

His hand still waited for her. Down below, Carwyn and Arundal and Hubert had left the tent and watched. In the distance she could see the Welsh army's attention on her, and the speck of color that was Addis's surcotte.

"I don't really have a choice, do I?" she said.

"Your body does not. Your heart does, however. What choice does it want to make?"

Her heart. That acceptance would not be a public avowal, no matter what the watching armies would see. It was private, between the two of them alone. It was a thing apart from the words that would be said, and the bargain that would be made. It always had been.

Her heart had chosen long ago, and she was helpless against its decision. Unfettered by worries about betrayals and loss, it now shouted its affirmation. The love in it relished the freedom to grow that this marriage provided.

Mark took one step toward her. The wind blew his hair around his handsome face and the day's grey light shimmered off his armor. His wonderful eyes held understanding. "Let your heart accept me, Nesta. Let us make our love all it can be."

"Will you accept me too? In my treason I betrayed you."

"You never did during our truces. We will make a permanent one today, and we will forgive each other for what our duties required. Come and take my hand now, so they all see that you do so willingly."

She took a deep breath, and walked toward him. The whole world watched, but that did not matter.

She was shaking by the time she placed her hand in his. Trembling. Relief overwhelmed her. So did an exhaustion of the spirit. Each step took her closer to a transforming vitality, however, as an uncontrollable love filled her with its enlivening light.

Laying his palm on her face, he looked into her eyes. She saw no warrior then. No lord. No defeat or victory. All that existed was the man who made her feel alive and young and full of sparkling grace.

"This marriage will be seen by many in the wrong way," she said. "Not as England expiating a sin against Wales, but as Wales submitting to England, as a woman submits to her husband."

"Some may see it that way. Others will say England was seduced, and made weak by desire. The story of Marcus of Anglesmore and Nesta verch Llygad can be sung in many ways."

He turned his back on the watching men, so that he could kiss her privately. It was a beautiful kiss, deep and soulful. The possessive embrace in which he clutched her spoke of a triumph different from the one that others would see. His touch, his kiss, his eyes all contained a warmth and gratitude to match her own.

The bliss permeated her whole being and poured out until it united with his joy. It surrounded them like an invisible cloud from heaven.

"You risked much doing this as you did, Mark. One false step, and you would have fallen with me."

"You were well worth the risk. So was the chance for peace."

"I am grateful that you found a way to save me. To keep me," she whispered.

"You should have known that I would. I told you so that first night. I said that I would fight to have you."

He kissed her again, then turned with her under his arm and faced the plain and distant hill. "Who do you see waiting for us out there, Nesta?"

She saw English soldiers, in whose minds this day would quickly fade, since no battle had been fought. She saw Arundal, who would be well contented that a conquered people had been kept under England's heel.

On the distant hill, however, she saw Welsh men who would return to their fields and their families, and teach their sons and grandsons to be ready when the next call came. Because of Mark, the dream would not be made real this year, but, also because of him, neither would it be crushed.

"I see a Welsh army and an English army, Mark."

He lifted her hand, and kissed it. "I see only people, my love. Our people."

CHAPTER 26

Marcus gazed out the window of Joan's London house, watching the children play. They tumbled around the garden, flush–faced from the cold. The house was full of them today. Addis and his wife Moira had brought their brood over to join a little feast to welcome him and Nesta to the city.

Addis claimed to be visiting London to see to his wife's property, but Marcus knew the real reason. He had really come to give Edward his account of what had happened in Wales, should Marcus's own version be doubted.

"So, who was this Scot whom her sister was to marry?" Rhys asked, probing for the details to complete the story Marcus had just told him.

"Robert the Bruce's grandson, Robert the

Steward. He is next in line in their claim on the Scottish throne, after the Bruce's son."

Rhys whistled lowly. "It would have been a shrewd alliance. Although not so good for the girl. It is said that the Steward has sired enough bastards to fill a shire. You probably saved her from much unhappiness."

That was true. Of course, Genith would not have known much happiness with Edward's choice of husband either.

"Considering your tale, I am not sure that I should be welcoming you in my home like this," Rhys said. "Then again, you have spared me a hard choice, so perhaps I should be grateful."

"You have lived in London almost your whole life, Rhys. You even serve the King. I would not have thought the choice would have been very hard at all."

"I am Welsh. That does not change, no matter where one lives or whom one serves."

"Would you really have gone back to fight in such a war?"

"Probably, if there had been a true chance for success. I think that I would have had a lot of company on the road too." He smiled, and shrugged. "I am Welsh." The affirmation did not come in English this time, but in the ancient language of his homeland.

Marcus had a vision of men leaving castles and abbeys and universities and towns, streaming across England toward the western mountains.

He had done the King a greater service than he had thought.

That was good to know. It might prove useful soon.

"Word has it that the King is still in a sour mood," he said.

"He has been angry since his surprise return in November," Rhys said. "Slipping back into the realm like that stunned everyone. His fury took a heavy toll. Most of his councillors have been replaced, and although Stratford avoided imprisonment, the King is still very bitter there."

Stratford's sudden fall had raised a lot of curiosity. The King claimed that his chancellor had mismanaged finances and left the army on the Continent short of funds. There were whispers that Edward's anger had been stoked by other, more personal annoyances once Stratford's activities had been examined.

The crisp summons to court that had arrived at Anglesmore right after the feast of the Nativity took on new meaning with such rumors. The summons had specifically included

Nesta. Although the message had said that Edward wanted to hear about Carwyn and the rebels, Marcus suspected that the audience would not really be about that at all.

"Stratford is still the Archbishop of Canterbury. No king can undo that," Marcus said. That was a useful detail. An archbishop fighting with a king would not be annulling any marriages at that king's request. "He will survive. He always does."

Whether Marcus of Anglesmore would survive so well remained to be seen. The King could make or break a baron at will.

The women emerged from the kitchen, bearing wine cups. Joan brought her husband one, and took the opportunity to whisper in Marcus's ear. "I like her, Mark. For many reasons, but mostly because she appears to love you very much."

Marcus found himself smiling at her use of his boyhood name. He had felt none of the old bitterness when he rode into this ward and entered this house today. The events of the last months had finally put the past to rest. Choosing his own destiny had reconciled him to the years when he had been both a victim and a beneficiary of others' whims and risks.

"And I love her, Joan."

"Then my prayers have been answered. I will confide in you that there is something you must do to secure her happiness, however."

"What is that?"

"Her sister. You must find Genith, and bring her and the bard home."

Marcus noticed Nesta and Moira dawdling near the kitchen. No doubt they hung back so that Joan could raise the matter of Genith.

Nesta and these ladies had formed a friendship fast. After only a few hours together, they were all already conspiring against him.

"I suppose our household could use a bard," he said, although having a Welsh bard singing in a Lord Marcher's hall would be a hell of a thing.

His voice carried. Nesta heard, and rewarded him with a mesmerizing smile. She came to him with the wine, and he pulled her onto his lap.

Moira stood with her two cups, glancing around. All of the women had been cooking, but Moira showed the worst of it. Her green courtly garments were covered with flour, and bits of herbs clung to her dark hair. The mess only enhanced her earthy appeal. Everything about Addis's wife gave the impression of domestic contentment.

"I thought that I heard Addis return," she said.

"Not yet," Rhys said. "He must still be at Westminster, trying to smooth ruffled feathers."

Moira's blue eyes glinted with humor. She set her cups on the hall's table and settled on a bench. "He thinks some plainspokenness is in order, although I told him that smoothing feathers requires more subtlety. He does not practice the latter much, so the King is probably getting a lecture."

"I do not think there is any danger waiting for Marcus at court," Nesta said. "He did his duty as commanded. There was no need for Addis to make this journey and speak on our behalf."

She appeared fretful, as she often had since that summons had come. He knew that she worried that he would pay dearly for this marriage.

He kissed her cheek to reassure her. "Whatever happens with the King, we cannot be parted. Hundreds witnessed our marriage, darling."

"The cost might be great," she muttered.

"I do not count the cost." He meant it. If he lost Anglesmore, it was through his own acts and his own choices, not deeds done by other men. He had known the risks when he took her hand on that hilltop, and when they exchanged vows down in the valley. The months since had confirmed the truth of what he had said to her that day. She had been well worth it, and he would never regret fighting to have her.

A commotion in the garden caught his attention. The children ran to the back portal, to greet the tall man entering. Amidst the turmoil, two little hands rose up, beckoning. Addis lifted his youngest daughter into his arms and waded through the throng.

He entered through the kitchen, and the children followed. The hall suddenly filled with shouts and running feet. The boys poked and pushed and laughed, their excitement that the feast could begin provoking a noisy chaos.

Moira and Joan tried to herd the little barbarians back to the kitchen with scolds to go wash. Addis handed his daughter to Moira, and approached the window.

"No food for you two, I'm afraid. I have told the groom to saddle your horses," he said. "The King knows that you arrived today, and wants to see you both at once."

Marcus felt Nesta stiffen within his embrace. They both looked to Addis.

He understood the unspoken question. "He was very quiet at our audience. I do not know where his mind is."

Nesta slid off his lap. "I must go change my

garments. It would not do to meet the King in a gown covered with cooking smells."

Addis watched her dodge yelling boys as she crossed the hall. "There is something else, but I thought it wise to not let her hear it right now. Edward is in a black mood today because he has received unwelcome news. The Scots are on the move."

They entered the royal chambers hand in hand. Nesta had been very subdued on the ride to Westminster, and as the door closed behind them her face assumed an inscrutable expression.

Marcus hoped that his demeanor appeared just as bland, but he doubted it. This meeting would have been hard enough if it had just been him and Edward. With Nesta present, however, he would have to control thoughts and emotions hardly befitting a dutiful servant and courteous noble.

She had changed into a lovely red gown that enhanced her dark beauty and fair skin. A gold filigree headdress decorated her abundant black hair. Mysterious lights filled her eyes, and even her cool manner had a sensual appeal.

The luxury of the royal study complemented her noble presence. She looked like a queen. In a previous age, she might well have become one.

Small wonder, then, that a king had been drawn to her.

An edgy annoyance pricked at him. He did not care too much about what had happened between them years ago. He knew that Edward could never sway her now. Still, he resented like hell that he would be forced to witness this reunion.

Nesta noticed. "You are angry."

"Not with you."

"You are jealous."

"I am a man."

"And I am a woman. I am angry too. I may give him a good scolding when he comes in. There was no need for me to be here."

There had been no need, but she had been called all the same.

Had Edward surmised the role she had played in that rebellion, or had he called her for other reasons? Marcus knew the latter explanation would be less dangerous, but that hardly eased his mind.

The door opened. A page held it for the royal entry.

Nesta reached for Marcus's hand. Her soft palm was sweating, revealing how unsettled she was under the indifferent pose.

The gesture touched him. He moved closer, and laid his arm against the back of her waist. Let the King see them as one, and together in love as well as marriage.

Edward entered with a clerk, discussing some document that he carried. The page whispered, and the King's quick glance into the chamber stopped his conversation. His royal gesture had the clerk backing up while he came forward.

He was not much older than Marcus, just over thirty, but he appeared world-weary. He had grown a beard while on the Continent, and put a few pounds on his tall frame. His youthful face had acquired some lines that Marcus guessed were the result of the experiences of the last year. Edward's glorious victory at Sluys had not been followed by the quick campaign he had expected. The plans that were supposed to procure the French crown had unraveled, and the army on the Continent had been idle for months and costing the realm a fortune.

Marcus had to release Nesta to make his greeting, but he replaced his arm when it was done. Edward raised one eyebrow at that.

He gave Marcus a very direct look. "My lady, if you would leave us, please. I will speak with Marcus alone first."

Nesta had thus far bestowed one formal smile. Now she gave another. She accepted the page's escort into the chamber from which Edward had come.

The King did not even watch her leave. One would think he barely knew her.

Marcus wasn't fooled. He had noticed the glint of warmth in Edward's eyes when he looked up from the document. If Marcus had been awaiting an audience by himself, he would have cooled his heels a long while until the business at hand was completed first.

"It is good to see an old friend, Marcus, and one whom I can trust. At least someone did his duty with honor while I was gone."

"I tried my best."

"Would that everyone did. Half your best would have been better than most of what I have been cursed with. Addis came today. He told me that the trouble with Llygad's men is done with. A small problem, he said. How did he put it? *So insignificant as to not be worth a chronicler's ink.* He can be witty when he chooses, which is not often."

"An apt description, however."

Edward nodded, and appeared to drift into distraction. "The last thing I needed was a Welsh rebellion, since there is trouble up north again. Damn Scots. Rumor has it Robert the Bruce's son is returning from France where he has been in exile. Half the Scots think of him as their rightful king, despite my decision for Baillol. The French are behind this, of course. They want to draw my attention away from the true prize. They pull me in two directions. I am grateful that you kept me from being pulled in a third one as well."

"I am honored to have served you."

"It worked out well, giving you that duty. There is only one problem, as I see it." His attention sharpened as the distraction fell from his expression. "You married the wrong daughter."

Now they were down to it. "After Genith fled the realm, I married the only daughter left. The effect on your plan was the same."

"Not quite."

"Well, perhaps I should say that the effect was the same on the parts of the plan that I knew about."

For a moment Edward appeared very much the King, and one who did not like wit at his expense. His displeasure over the marriage was obvious. Marcus half expected him to start bellowing his disapproval. Once that started, one never knew where it would end.

Edward glanced to the door of the inner chamber, behind which Nesta waited. The bluster seeped out of him, as if her invisible presence restrained him. When he turned his gaze back to Marcus, the look was not king to baron, but man to man.

"You did well for me. The prize that I promised is yours. The forest lands, and the manor and estate of Llygad. I want you in my new council too, sitting once more in the chair that Anglesmore occupied years ago. It is time that your family's honor was completely restored."

"Your favor honors me," Marcus said.

"We will find a place for you at court too. I need men I can trust here, not these fools. Your wife can be lady-in-waiting to the Queen."

So, there it was. "Again, you honor me. My wife, however, prefers to stay in Wales, and I with her. She has been gone from her home over eight years now, and would like to reside there."

Edward got the message, and did not like it. "I can command your service."

"Mine. Not hers. Not the service that I think you intend."

"I am the King."

"In this you are a man, that is all. There are limits to what the crown can requisition, no matter what royal favors are bestowed."

"You risk much in displeasing me." Edward's gaze and tone turned flinty.

"I know what I risk, and I do so gladly. The

King I know is not capricious in justice. If you have changed that much, do your worst. I speak to you now as a husband, and not your sworn man. She will not have you. Nor will I let you have her. Disseize me over this, and we can always live in the mountains. There are many there who will welcome us."

A touch of caution entered Edward's eyes, along with a good deal of royal annoyance. "Are you threatening me, Marcus?"

"I am merely explaining that Nesta verch Llygad will never be homeless in Wales."

Edward folded his arms and turned thoughtful. He glanced again to the door, and then walked toward it. "You speak as a husband, as one would expect. I will talk with the lady now. The notion of living at court may appeal to her, if not to you."

She heard the door open, and was not surprised that only one man came through it.

Just as well. Sooner or later, this conversation had to be held.

The King's expression was severe upon entering, as if he had just finished an argument with Marcus. Nesta could imagine what her husband had said.

Upon seeing her, Edward's demeanor softened. He smiled. "I was hoping that time had not been kind to you. Instead, you are as beautiful as I remember."

"It was all those years in the Highlands. The cold weather is good for the complexion."

The allusion to her Scottish marriage made him uncomfortable. "The Queen—"

"If your knights had not told the world about me, if they had granted me the courtesy given your English ladies, if you had *demanded their silence,* the Queen and I would have both been spared a lot of humiliation. A high price was paid for one little mistake, and she and I paid it, not you, although the sin was yours."

He appeared quite boyish and abashed for a moment. It passed quickly.

Of course it did. He was a king.

He gestured to the other chamber. "Did you tell him?"

"The songs told him."

"That is not what I mean."

"I never told him which song was true. He asked once how it had been, and I only said that I was not forced." A vivid memory of that night beneath the window filled her head. One word from her, and everything that followed might have unfolded differently.

Just one word.

She had been unable to give it, even if the word would have been true.

"That was generous of you. Although, to my mind, it is the truth, more or less," Edward said.

"Since you did not stay long enough to learn my mind on the matter, there is no point in discussing how much more or less. I did not tell Marcus, because he could have never served you if he knew how . . . ambiguous it was."

"My lack of restraint can be excused. You bewitched me. I was in love."

"Oh, tosh. You were bored and randy and full of yourself. And I was ignorant enough to be dazzled that the young king favored me."

"Not so ignorant, it seemed to me."

"Since I was Welsh, you probably assumed I had ceased being ignorant years earlier. But I was a child. I met you in that garden expecting a kiss at most."

"I will admit that things went too far, but I did not force you."

She realized that it mattered to him. He really wanted her agreement on how it had been. He did not comprehend that the episode had become so insignificant to her that she did not care what he called it.

"Do you seek absolution, my lord? Fine, it is yours."

"Not so much absolution as an indication of affection. I have often thought of you, and that moonlit garden."

It was an unfortunate turn in the conversation, but she had been expecting it. She had plenty of experience with men looking at her the wrong way, and this one had been looking that way since he walked through the door.

"With all respect, sire, that night was a lifetime ago. It is time to forget it."

"I am not sure that I can. This marriage of yours has been eating at me since I heard of it. That old Scot was one thing, but Marcus—"

"King you may be, but listen to me now. You have no right to this ridiculous jealousy. This marriage will stand, and with your blessing. You will not hold it against Marcus. If you slight him in any way, I will see that you have so much trouble with the Welsh that the Scots will be baking their bread in York before you can spare the men to fight them."

That took him aback, but he appeared more amused than angry. "You speak too boldly. Perhaps that was your appeal. Other women dare not chastise me thus."

"Then visit us whenever you need a scolding. You can come this summer, and honor us with your presence at our child's baptism."

That surprised him even more. His gaze

swept her, as if he sought the physical proof of her claim. "You are . . . ?"

"Enough along to be sure."

He frowned. Nesta suspected it was not her sudden status as a mother that troubled him. The frown was that of a king finally comprehending political realities.

No longer interested in the foolish girl he had once wooed, he pulled open the door. "Let us rejoin your husband."

"I will tell you that Arundal spoke with me," Edward said, his tone and pose very severe. "I know that all turned out well in Wales, but his tale suggested some peculiar doings."

Marcus faced the accusation blandly. Nesta was by his side again, appearing far too smug. He looked forward to hearing what she had said in that other chamber to cause Edward the man to retreat so thoroughly, and for Edward the King to appear unsettled.

"Anything but a field covered with bodies would be peculiar to Arundal," Marcus said.

Edward's sharp gaze shifted from him to Nesta, and back again. "If both of you had not alluded today to the chance for more peculiar doings, I would be more contented. As it is, I cannot ignore that one of my barons has married the daughter of Llygad in what could be a dangerous alliance."

"There is no danger to you or England in this alliance," Marcus said.

Beside him, Nesta smiled vaguely.

The King did not miss that. "I want your oath, Marcus, that the child she carries will be educated properly. That he will be England's man, and that you will not permit this woman to divide his loyalties."

It took a few moments for Marcus to respond. He tried to appear calm as he turned to Nesta. Her smile was that of a cat who had just lapped at some milk.

"Of course," he said. He even managed to add a formal oath.

Edward pierced Nesta with a suspicious glare. "You are to obey your husband in this, as in all things. Your father's lands will be absorbed into Marcus's. Llygad's manor is not to become some shrine."

"Of course, my lord," she said demurely.

"If you have a son, he will take service with an English baron, in England, not Wales, so that he learns the proper loyalty."

"Certainly."

Her submissive agreement appeased whatever worries Edward had developed. The King's expression cleared, and he smiled. "If matters of state permit it, I will come for the baptism this summer as you requested."

Marcus glanced to his wife. "We hope it can be so."

Edward dismissed them. Marcus managed to hold his tongue until they were away from the royal chambers.

Outside in the yard, he slid his arm around her waist. "Nesta—"

"Not here. Not within these walls." She gave him a melting smile as a groom brought their horses to them. "On our way back to your sister's house, there is someplace that I would like to visit."

The house was deserted, but one guard still manned the gate. He cast Nesta an accusing look, letting her know that he had not forgiven her for the purgative that she had fed him.

All the same, he allowed them entry. They circled the house to the garden in back. Its high walls made it private and quiet and separate from the city noise.

The trees were bare now, and no roses bloomed. It held a spare beauty, however. Tendrils of ivy grew everywhere, and boxwood lined the paths. The pool had not frozen, and the sky and clouds were reflected in its stillness.

Marcus pulled Nesta to the bench by the wall, the bench where it had all started. He settled her on his lap much as he had that first night, but he did not overwhelm her with passion. Rather they nestled together in a warm embrace, enjoying the silence.

"What did you say to the King?" Marcus asked.

"I reminded him that you had served him well, and averted what might have been an inconvenient war."

"He acted as though you said more than that."

"Well, I might have suggested, in my annoyance, that he would be wise to keep you in his favor."

"You threatened our King?"

"I think he was well threatened before he spoke with me. I may have been less subtle, but the message was the same as yours."

He laughed lightly, and kissed her cheek. The eyes gazing at her filled with warmth and love, and little sparks of excitement. "What else did you tell him? He spoke of a baptism."

"Oh, that. It just blurted out, to make sure that he understood just how united we are, and how we cannot be parted, and that I am completely yours."

He looked away to the pool. "It was a ruse, then."

Laying her palm against his face, she turned his gaze back to her. Being alone with him here, in this quiet place, was so perfect and peaceful. She loved the moments when they could be like this, completely together, whether in passion or just sitting in each other's embrace.

"It was no ruse. There will be a baptism, my love. Midsummer, I think. That is what Joan and Moira say."

His hard mouth softened beautifully. His expression transformed into one of heart-stopping happiness. The arms holding her tightened gently, protectively, possessively.

"This morning I would have said it was impossible for me to love you more than I already did, Nesta. It seems that was not true."

He kissed her with the passion that they had first discovered in this garden, and which had created the child she bore.

An impossible passion, that he had demanded be given life.

A brief pleasure, that he had fought to convert to a permanent love.

It fills my heart with sparkling light. The grace of heaven could not be more powerful. They were words from a dream, and they spoke in her as she lost herself in the sublime joining of their kiss. She loved him so much that her heart could not contain it, and it poured out to fill the garden.

"I have sworn an oath to Edward that the child will be educated properly." He did not move much as he said it, and their faces still touched.

"All that we promised will be done. I would have it no other way."

He smiled. "That is generous of you. Of course, with a bard in the household, and a daughter of Llygad as a mother, I wonder if it will turn out as the King thinks."

"Are you accusing me of plotting to thwart the King's plan?"

"Heaven forbid I should suspect you of such treason."

She caressed his lips, and then touched them with her own. "If it is a son, he will turn out much like his father, I expect. A man of his people." She slid from his embrace and stood. "Now, we should return to your sister's house. A feast awaits, and I have been ravenous of late."

He appeared reluctant to go. She thought she knew why.

"Of course, we could always return here tonight," she said.

He embraced her with his arm as they

strolled to the portal. "It will be very cold in this garden tonight."

"I do not feel the cold much."

"Then we will return. I confess that the notion of having you in one of the crown's gardens has a reckless appeal."

"I thought that it might."

He stopped at the portal. Taking her face in his hands, he looked down at her. "I am not good with pretty words, Nesta. Telling you that I love you is easy, but it will never express what is in my heart. I am grateful that you came to this garden that night. I am honored that you gave all of yourself to me, after what transpired. Loving you is the best part of my life. Holding on to you became the most important thing to me after that night here."

For a man who was not good with pretty words, he could move her to tears with his simple honesty. Pressing his palm to her face, she turned her head to kiss it.

"We will hold each other forever, Marcus. There will be only one song about Marcus of Anglesmore and Nesta verch Llygad, and it will be a magnificent, long love song."

AUTHOR'S NOTE

England conquered Wales during the Middle Ages. The Normans, under William the Conqueror, took the eastern and southern regions in the twelfth century. William set up barons in these border areas, or "marches", and gave them power that exceeded that of most other barons. This bred ambitions and a sense of autonomy among the Lords Marchers that would haunt the English crown for centuries. For good or ill, these barons played pivotal roles in the rebellions and politics of the medieval period.

In the late thirteenth century, Edward I completed the conquest of Wales. For the next century there were no large-scale rebellions, although minor insurrections periodically occurred. That the Welsh were hardly pacified was proven in 1400. That year marked the beginning of the great rebellion of Owain Glyn Dwr, which would be the final revolt of the Welsh against English rule.

As Rhys predicts in this novel, Welsh streamed across England to join Owain's revolt, abandoning their positions in English manors, courts and universities to do so.

For simplicity, I have used the English terms Wales and the Welsh throughout the novel. Nesta would not have referred to her land or her people that way, however. She would have called her homeland Cymru.

ABOUT THE AUTHOR

MADELINE HUNTER has worked as a grocery clerk, office employee, art dealer, and freelance writer. She holds a Ph.D. in art history, which she currently teaches at an eastern university. She lives in Pennsylvania with her husband, her two teenage sons, a chubby, adorable mutt, and a black cat with a major attitude. She can be contacted through her web site, www.MadelineHunter.com, where readers can also find more information regarding the historical events and characters used in this novel.